ELYSIUM FIRE

Also by Alastair Reynolds from Gollancz:

Novels
Revelation Space
Redemption Ark
Absolution Gap
Chasm City
Century Rain
Pushing Ice
The Prefect
House of Suns
Terminal World
Blue Remembered Earth
On the Steel Breeze
Poseidon's Wake
The Medusa Chronicles (with Stephen Baxter)
Revenger

Short Story Collections:
Diamond Dogs, Turquoise Days
Galactic North
Zima Blue
Beyond the Aquila Rift

Slow Bullets

ELYSIUM FIRE

A Prefect Dreyfus Emergency

Alastair Reynolds

GOLLANCZ
LONDON

First published in Great Britain in 2018 by Gollancz
an imprint of the Orion Publishing Group Ltd
Carmelite House, 50 Victoria Embankment
London EC4Y 0DZ

An Hachette UK Company

1 3 5 7 9 10 8 6 4 2

A CIP catalogue record for this book is
available from the British Library.

ISBN (Cased) 978 0 575 09058 3
ISBN (Export Trade Paperback) 978 0 575 09059 0

Typeset by Input Data Services Ltd, Somerset

Printed in Great Britain by Clays Ltd, St Ives plc

MIX
Paper from
responsible sources
FSC
www.fsc.org   FSC® C104740

www.alastairreynolds.com
www.gollancz.co.uk

From a distance it almost looked natural.

A planet with a ring.

A world of ochre and mustard clouds, with nothing of the surface visible. A poisonous place, peevishly inimical to human habitation. One shrivelled moon. Ten billion such worlds clotted the galaxy: useless to all but the most desperate of species and civilisations.

The conjunction of planet and rings was not, in itself, worthy of note. It was the natural business of things, where gravity had its way with rubble and ice. Granted, it was more usual to find rings around gas giants rather than a small, rocky planet like this one. But even the tiniest of worlds might lay temporary claim to a ring system, if a moon or asteroid fell too deeply into their gravity well. Gravitational dynamics being what they were, though, such a ring system would not endure more than a few million years.

This ring system was much younger even than that.

Young because it was the work of people, not celestial mechanics.

They had come here in vast starships, crossing the gulf of light years from Earth. Down in the permanent ochre murk of Yellowstone's toxic atmosphere they had founded Chasm City, the greatest urban settlement in human history. And in a girdle around Yellowstone, an adornment to the metropolis below, they had set into orbit ten thousand artificial worlds, each an exquisite fabulation of rock and metal and glass, each with its own name and customs, each bountiful with air and water and a teeming cargo of people. They called this circling river of worlds the Glitter Band, and at the peak of its glory it was home to one hundred million living souls.

The worlds coexisted in peace, for the most part. The people were as grudgingly content as the truly free will ever be. Wealth and power were in almost limitless abundance. Matter and energy danced to human whims. Even death itself was in slow, stubborn retreat. There was no militia, no standing army. Weapons were rarely glimpsed, rarely spoken of. Crimes were exotic, Olympian achievements – crimes of passion even more so. Few social tensions arose because each world was allowed to choose its own destiny, its own political

1

and administrative path. Citizens could move between worlds as they wished, selecting the environment that best met their desires. The only binding law was the iron rule of universal suffrage. Flawless, incorruptible machinery ensured each citizen had their say, not just from year to year, but from day to day, hour to hour. Citizens were polled on every conceivable matter. The process of participation became as habitual as breathing. It was a dream of democracy. But unlike most dreams, it worked.

Or at least, most of the time.

Occasionally there was a fault in the polling systems, or a tiny loophole that some unscrupulous faction tried to exploit. This became a minor but nagging problem. And so the worlds of the Glitter Band agreed to create a monitoring taskforce, a small, independent body of trusted officials who would be free of ties to any one world, who would not themselves have the vote, but who would operate solely to keep the machinery of mass participation running smoothly, inviolably.

They were called prefects.

They were assigned a tiny, pumpkin-faced world of their own, scarcely more than a hollowed-out boulder, and it was named Panoply. So small was the scale of the problem that at first it was believed that fewer than a hundred prefects would be needed. Eventually, and after some resistance, their numbers were permitted to rise to just below a thousand. They were given vehicles, monitoring instruments, some limited forms of enforcement.

One prefect for every ten worlds. One prefect for every hundred thousand citizens. It did not seem sufficient. But it was, and for decades the prefects went about their work almost without attention. They were never liked, never welcomed, but they were very rarely required to use the powers at their disposal. When they did, it was always as a last resort.

But then the time had come when the prefects had to do something terrible. To save the Glitter Band, it had been necessary to kill part of it.

CHAPTER ONE

Late that evening, high in the Shell House, just before drowsiness snatched him to unconsciousness, he stirred from his bed and moved to the window. Fingers of orange and russet light played through the shutters, accompanied by a distant crackling and hissing that rose and fell in tide-like waves.

Cautiously, struck by some faint sense of impropriety, he opened the shutters on the glassless window and took a breath. The evening air flooded his lungs, sooty with combustion products. He coughed, a sudden human sound that seemed louder than it had any right to be, and then stifled any further coughing with his hand.

Across the grounds, far from the Shell House – but still within the family dome, on the edge of Chasm City – something was on fire.

He watched it, mesmerised and troubled. There was a glow, concentrated in a small area and hemmed in by a darker mass of trees and vegetation that obscured the heart of the fire. Above the conflagration the dome panels reflected the glow in dusky variations of the same orange tones he had seen through the shutter.

If there was a fire in the grounds . . . but, no, he thought. There was no danger of such a thing taking hold and spreading. Automatic sprinkler systems would cut in long before the flames posed any risk to the Shell House itself. And besides, his father would have programmed Lurcher to detect fire and take immediate action to extinguish it.

The only curious thing was that the robot had not already done so.

Then he caught a movement above the tree-line, silhouetted against the glow: a metallic arm sweeping into view before returning to concealment. Puzzled, certain of what he had seen, but not understanding its significance, he watched and watched – while slowly drawing the shutters, until he peered out through a single furtive slit.

Presently the glow grew less intense. The crackles and hisses ebbed to silence. The smells faded, as the air in the dome was subjected to its usual circulation and filtering process.

Still he observed, certain the evening's mystery was not over.

He did not have long to wait. Lurcher emerged from the dense cover of the inner part of the gardens. The robot strolled nonchalantly, silver legs scissoring, two of its four silver arms swinging. In the other pair it carried buckets of tools, as it often did when attending to its gardening chores. From the domed head at the top of its tall, slender body, a single eye stared ahead with unblinking focus.

His instinct was to retreat further back into his darkened room. But if the robot detected that its nocturnal activities were being witnessed, it gave no indication.

What was left of the glow guttered out. A red reflection lingered on the dome, fading until only his imagination insisted there was still a trace of it.

The fire was out. The thing – whatever it was that had been set alight, and allowed to burn – had been consumed.

He closed the shutters fully and returned to bed. Under the sheets he coughed the last traces of smoke from his lungs. It was not long before the drowsiness took its hold of him, properly this time – vengefully, almost – but in the last moments of clear consciousness a distinct certainty formed in his mind. A white tree had stood where the fire had been.

A dead white tree, hollow to the core, in which he had once liked to play.

Thalia Ng would have preferred not to have an audience while she worked. That was not the way it was happening, though. A small party of civic functionaries was in attendance, watching in a loose semicircle while she completed the routine upgrade that was her day's business in the Shiga-Mintz Spindle.

'And . . . we're done,' she said, as the core began to sink back down into its pit, status symbols confirming the upgrade had proceeded without difficulty.

'You'll be on your way now, then,' said the citizens' designated spokesperson, a functionary named Mander.

The core was nearly back where it belonged. She eyed it for a few more moments before turning to look at the thin-faced man. 'Someone might think you wanted to see the back of me, Citizen Mander.'

'It's not that,' Mander said, his Adam's apple moving hard.

The polling core sank fully into the floor. An iris whisked shut to seal it from casual tampering.

'Then what?'

'I'll say it if Mander won't,' said a tall woman standing just behind

Mander. 'We don't have to pretend you're welcome here, Prefect. Of course you can visit and do as you please while you're here.' She brushed a hand through long auburn hair, pushing it away from a shrewish face. 'But that doesn't mean we have to like it. Not after what happened. Not now that we know.'

'Know what, exactly?'

'What you're capable of,' said another man, emboldened by the woman's outburst. 'What you'll do, when it suits you.'

'You mean,' Thalia said mildly, 'the lengths we'll go to protect your interests?'

'It was butchery,' said the woman.

'It was surgery,' Thalia corrected, keeping her voice level, uninflected, unintimidated.

'It's no good arguing with them,' someone muttered. 'They've got a justification for everything. They could murder us all and still say it was in the shining name of democracy.'

It was just a spasm, but Thalia felt her fingers twitch for the handle of her whiphound, still holstered on her belt.

'If you don't like democracy,' Thalia said, 'then you're in the wrong solar system.'

'As if we have a choice,' sneered the woman.

'There's always a choice,' a red-faced man said. 'They'd just rather none of us were aware of it. But maybe it's time to consider the unthinkable. Maybe it's *been* time ever since they showed their true colours. We all know what's possible, if enough of us take a stand. Panoply won't intervene now – they're too afraid.'

'Be grateful you'll never need our intervention,' Thalia said. 'But if you did, you'd still have it. You don't have to like us to count on us.'

It was an old line, one she had picked up from Dreyfus.

Something buzzed in her ear. She pressed a finger against her earpiece, squeezing it.

'Ng.'

'It's Sparver,' she heard. 'Thalia, drop whatever you're doing. Even if the core's still exposed, leave it – we'll secure it remotely. Are there citizens with you?'

She eyed the civic functionaries, feeling the full needling pressure of their suspicion and distrust.

'Yes, and they've been most hospitable. What's the—' She was about to say 'problem' but prefects never spoke of problems, at least not in public. 'What's required of me, Prefect Bancal?'

'There's a situation inside the habitat. I'm passing coordinates to your whiphound. It'll proceed ahead of you and secure the area.'

It was probably some kind of civic disturbance, a citizen mob or some-thing the local constables were not equipped to handle.

'I'll be right behind it.'

'Not immediately. Return to your ship. There's a containment vessel in the aft stowage compartment. Retrieve it, break out a second whiphound, and follow it to the first.'

Her hand moved back to the whiphound. Nothing about this was part of the plan for visiting Shiga-Mintz. It was an in-and-out, all per-fectly routine. Nothing about second whiphounds or cases in stowage compartments.

'Prefect Bancal . . .'

'Get on it, Thal. When I say every second counts, I mean it.'

She drew the whiphound's handle from her holster. In its stowed form the whiphound – an autonomous robot whip with enforcement, detain-ment and evidence-acquisition capabilities – was a black, grip-coated rod about the size and thickness of a truncheon, inset with a battery of twist controls at one end. On sensing its removal from the holster, the whiphound extended its roving filament, pushing out a thin silver ten-tacle until it made contact with the ground. The tentacle stiffened along its length and formed a snakelike traction coil at the point where it met the floor. A single bright red eye glared from the other end of the handle.

The whiphound had gone from being an inert tool on her belt to a thing that was alive, purposeful and more than a little intimidating.

'You know what to do,' she said. 'Go.'

The whiphound nodded its handle and slinked away, picking up speed with a series of sinuous whipping motions. It made a dry whisking sound as it skated across the floor and the functionaries jerked back to allow it passage. It vanished through the doorway, already moving faster than a person could run.

'What's going on?' asked Mander, as if he had every right to an explanation.

She ignored him, still pressing a finger to her earpiece.

'Whiphound deployed, Prefect Bancal. I'm on my way back to the cutter.'

'Quick as you can, Thal.'

She took him at his word, leaving the polling core and the gawping, mystified functionaries behind, breaking into a jog and then a run. She sprinted up a ramp, through a short warren of corridors, into the bright sunlight of civic gardens, past a hissing line of ornamental fountains, up an escalator to a forested plaza, onto a high-speed tram to the dock.

She stood on the tram, one hand on the ceiling hoop, as it accelerated away from the stop. It had been three, maybe four minutes since Sparver had first contacted her. There were citizens on the tram, watching her with puzzled, worried expressions.

'It's all right,' she said, pausing to catch her breath. 'This is a local emergency, nothing to be concerned about.'

Panoply must have been pulling strings to override local traffic patterns because the tram made a non-stop sprint for the docking complex. Thalia boarded her cutter – the smallest class of Panoply spacecraft, and the only type she was authorised to operate single-handedly – while her hand kept reaching for the whiphound. It felt wrong to be back in the cutter without her weapon. But she opened the aft hatch, craned down to look inside, and found a silver object she didn't recognise.

It was a stubby cylinder, about the size of a space helmet, and there was a handle on top of it.

'The silver thing, Sparver, I'm presuming?'

'Take it. Your backup whiphound knows where to go.'

She hoisted the cylinder, then went to the foil-sealed cavity that held the second whiphound. She broke the seal, extracted the whiphound, hefted the heavy black handle for a few moments and then let it deploy.

'Want to tell me what this is all about?'

'Follow the whiphound. Your first unit is already on-site and securing the theatre.'

She left the cutter and headed back into the public spaces of Shiga-Mintz, the cylinder dangling from her left hand. It was awkward more than heavy, as if it was mostly hollow. The second whiphound slithered ahead of her, showing the way, glancing back with a puppy-like impatience. In a minute she was back on the tram, retracing at least part of her route, the whiphound slinking up and down the tram's interior, its eye sweeping menacingly.

The tram was nearly empty this time, with only a handful of passengers at the far end of the compartment.

'What do you mean, theatre?' Thalia asked, keeping her voice low.

'You'll find a citizen,' Sparver said. 'They're dying. You're going to operate on them.'

'I'm not a surgeon.'

'You don't need to be. The whiphound knows what to do.'

The tram sped on. Towns and parks flashed by outside. Thalia eyed the citizens she spotted in these rushed glimpses, strolling along paths, going in and out of white-walled buildings. Just glimpses, no chance to make out expressions or gain more than a fleeting impression of body language. But word spread quickly in a place like Shiga-Mintz, where everyone shared access to the same abstraction. The air crackled with a million invisible thoughts, flashing from skull to skull. It would not be long before everyone knew something was up.

'What's wrong with them?'

'A neural episode,' Sparver said. 'That's all we know at the moment.'

The tram came to a hard stop. The doors opened, the whiphound springing out through the widening gap, those few citizens on the platform jerking back as the slithering weapon made its presence known. Thalia had barely caught her breath from the first run, and now she was bounding after the whiphound with the extra burden of the silver cylinder. It bumped against her hip as she jogged.

A ramp led down from the tram stop into an area of manicured gardens. An agreeable enough place to spend an hour or two: winding gravel paths, flowerbeds, elegant lakes and painted bandstands. Still daytime, by the habitat's internal clock. Yet citizens were already moving out of the park, looking back with a certain unease even as Thalia barged through them, fighting against the flow.

Peacocks scattered into undergrowth, protesting at this interruption to their easy routine.

Ahead was a circular intersection of four paths. A ring of people had formed within it, and the mood was agitated. Thalia caught a flash of moving red within the ring and realised the first whiphound was establishing a widening cordon.

The second whiphound, having brought her to the first, slinked back and lowered its head in a submissive posture. She opened her right fist and it sprang into the air, retracting its tail with a crack, its handle tumbling into her grasp and allowing itself to be holstered.

'Deputy Field Prefect Thalia Ng,' she called out. 'You are under Panoply observance. Step back from the whiphound, please.'

'It's not letting us through!' shouted a man. 'Call your toy off, Prefect, before someone dies!'

The man wore a green and white outfit, and he carried a white box marked with medical symbols. A woman in an identical outfit stood next to him. Parked a little way off was a luminous green, fat-wheeled tricycle with the same markings.

'We were tasked to a medical emergency,' the woman said, anger breaking through her voice. 'It's still happening. But we can't get to the citizen with that thing of yours running around.'

Thalia pushed through the ragged circle. The first whiphound was still circling at high speed, etching a deepening line in the gravel, a plume of dust barely having time to settle before it came around again. A determined citizen could easily have crossed the cordon between the whiphound's circuits, but so far no one had summoned the nerve. Thalia did not blame them for that. It took force of will to step over the cordon herself, even knowing the whiphound would never hurt her.

'Prefect,' the female medical functionary said, with a sort of resigned calm. 'You must let us through. Whatever's happening to that citizen—'

'Is our responsibility,' Thalia said, with all the authority she could muster. 'Pull back. You've done your duty here – I'll make sure that's noted.'

'How can you . . .'

The male medic set his jaw and stepped over the cordon, glancing back at his colleague for encouragement. The whiphound sped around in its circuit, at first appearing as if it would ignore his transgression. Then with an almost effortless insouciance it flicked out its filament, tangling its end around his ankle, and between one instant and the next the man was on the ground. The whiphound released him and resumed its patrol.

The man tried to get to his feet, then collapsed back down again, yelling in surprise and pain.

'It's probably broken your ankle,' Thalia said. 'When I'm finished here you can get the medical attention you need.' She levelled her gaze at the woman. 'Don't try to help him.'

Then she directed her attention to the citizen, the man at the epicentre of all this commotion. She had only given him the most cursory of glances until this moment. He was on the ground as well, lying on his side, quivering from head to toe. He was a respectable-looking individual of no particular age, hair neatly groomed, clothes smart but unostentatious, only a dusting of gravel marring their cleanliness.

Thalia set the silver cylinder down. She knelt next to the man, digging a knee into the gravel. His eyes were rolling back into their sockets, a fine white foam spilling from his lips. She touched a hand to his forehead, and almost flinched back at the heat coming off him.

'Sparver,' she whispered. 'I'm with him now. He seems in a bad way. If there's something I ought to know . . .?'

'Give your second whiphound the command sequence "One Judith Omega". It will know what to do. Meanwhile, open the containment vessel.'

Her hands were starting to shake. She had some dark inkling what was about to happen. She fumbled the second whiphound back out of the holster.

'Containment for what?'

'Just get on with it, Thal.'

Her lips were dry. The man's palsy was intensifying. Choking sounds were coming from his mouth. 'One Judith,' she began, before pausing with a terrible heaviness in her throat. 'Omega.'

The whiphound jerked from her grasp, flinging out its filament. Its red eye swept the immediate locality then locked onto the man.

'Open the vessel,' Sparver reminded her.

There was a control under the handle. She pressed it and the lid unsealed itself. She set the lid aside, handle down on the gravel. The interior of the vessel was a sterile white, its walls perforated with tiny holes.

The injured functionary was still calling out in distress. Beyond the cordon, the mood was turning ugly. Thalia felt something sting the back of her ear, as if someone had lobbed a piece of gravel at her. She pivoted on her heel.

'I'll repeat what I said. I am Deputy Field Prefect Thalia Ng. I am here on the authority of Panoply. I am sanctioned to use lethal force in the execution of my duties. A physical assault against a prefect is considered grounds for immediate reprisal.' She swallowed hard. The words had come out well enough, but she had not found quite the effortless tone of authority that she was certain Dreyfus would have used. Dreyfus would barely have bothered raising his voice.

Dreyfus could sound disinterested even as he was issuing a final warning.

'Tell them the man's already as good as dead,' Sparver said. 'No local intervention's going to make any difference to his chances, but Panoply might be able to help.'

The whiphound had coiled the end of its filament around the man's neck. There were two edges to that filament: a blunt one, which it could use for traction – as well as twisting bones until they broke – and a cutting edge. The second edge was a busy miracle of molecular-scale machinery. It could eat its way through almost any material it encountered.

Blood swelled along a fine scarlet line as the whiphound dug deeper into the man's neck. Thalia did not want to look. She gazed around in a slow arc, addressing the horrified audience. She felt like the last actor on a stage, crouching down with some wild madness in her eyes, a bloodied dagger in her hand after some gruesome act of vengeance.

This was not what she had seen herself doing at the start of the day.

'There's nothing you could have done for him,' she said. 'None of your medicine would have helped. But we can. That's why I'm here.'

'Take the head,' Sparver said, 'and put it in the containment vessel. Seal the lid. Then get yourself back to Panoply.'

A large quantity of blood stained the gravel. It turned the stones shades of rust and pink, as if they were an expensive import. That said, there was less blood than she would have expected. The whiphound must have been doing something clever at the level of arteries and veins – a sort of surgery, rather than a quick, mindless decapitation. When the head rolled loose, she watched her own fingers scoop it up by the hair and place it neck down in the silver vessel. A head was a strange thing to hold, heavier than she had thought, and yet somehow not heavy enough.

Then she put the lid back on the container and felt a faint scuttling going on inside as some sort of process was initiated.

'Tell them to secure the body and freeze it,' Sparver said. 'A Heavy Medical Squad will be here shortly. Tell them the emergency is over and they need have no fears for their own safety. Tell them Panoply thanks them for their cooperation.'

Thalia did these things. It was her speaking, she knew it. But it might as well have been Sparver, pushing his words out through her mouth. The whiphound was cleaning itself, drawing its filament back in at a slower than usual rate.

She was about to fix it back in the holster when she had second thoughts. It was a long way back to the cutter, and she would need to get there with a man's head still in her possession.

'Forward scout mode,' she said. 'Ten-metre secure zone. Lethal force authorised. Proceed.'

She said it loudly, as much for the crowd's benefit as the whiphounds.'

The second unit scooted ahead of her. It knew the way they had come, and it would make sure there were no surprises along the way. The first whiphound broke away from its circling cordon and established a moving barricade around Thalia, daring anyone to cross it. She marched forward, the vessel clunking against her thigh, now much heavier than before.

No one stopped her.

In another habitat, elsewhere in the Glitter Band, a hooded man watched from the edge of a gathering.

He was glad of the rain misting down from the distant curved ceiling of the wheel-shaped world: it had given him licence to slip the hood over his head without appearing to seek anonymity. There were other hooded onlookers, as well as people under hats, ponchos or umbrellas. Their clothes were as drab as his own, dyed in natural shades of grey and brown.

Modest, stone-built homes dotted a gentle hillside, with smoke curling up from their chimneys. A waterwheel turned next to a mill, and off in the distance two woodcutters were at work with manual saws, lopping the branches off a fallen tree trunk. Further away, farm labourers and harnessed animals were working terraced fields.

The gathering was taking place in a gardened commons, on an area of land that jutted out into the millpond next to the waterwheel. There were footpaths and well-tended flowerbeds arranged around a collection of statues relating to significant historical events and figures from the birth of the Glitter Band. The speaker was leaning on one of these statues, standing on its plinth to gain some height over his audience. The statue was a kneeling figure, a young woman in an old-fashioned spacesuit, helmet at her feet, digging her fist into fruitless soil. Her face conveyed a mixture of desperation and determination, despair vying with strength.

The speaker leaned against her with laconic disregard, one arm resting on her head. He was tall and thin of frame, his dark purple clothes of a simple but formal cut. A collarless jacket hung from his slender shoulders. He had not bothered with an umbrella, poncho or hood, but the rain glistened off his hair, upsetting the lavish wave of his blond curls. He was nearly sixty years old, but his features were smooth and unlined, with an unsettlingly boyish quality. His eyes were a very pale blue, touched with coldness. The only distinguishing mark was a pale vertical scar under the right eye, a blemish so easily removed that it could only have been a deliberate decision to retain it.

Dreyfus studied the face with particular attentiveness. He had seen all the images of it he could ask for, but it was something else to commit it to memory with his own eyes. If it held even the tiniest clue as to the inner workings of the mind behind it, he was determined not to miss a detail.

What the man had to say was almost incidental to the recordings of similar gatherings Dreyfus had consulted, and the flow of words varied little from one performance to the next.

'Good people,' the man was saying – as he had done hundreds of times before, in hundreds of habitats. 'Good citizens, people of Stonehollow. Two years ago you were all witness to the actions of Panoply, in response to the so-called Aurora crisis. You'll have heard the official line: that an artificial intelligence exploited a subtle weakness in the security provisions of the Glitter Band, enabling it to gain control of the mass-manufacturing infrastructure, spewing out an infestation of self-replicating war machines. They'll have led you to believe that the cost of our survival – the disarming of that threat – was the surgical destruction of forty-one habitats and the loss of more than two million human lives. They'll tell you that as if it somehow excuses their actions, or even paints them in a flattering light. "Look at us, taking such momentous decisions in your interests! Look at the hard things we had to do." What they won't tell you is those actions were only needed because of the lapses they made over many years and years, after all the trust we vested in them.' He was smiling as he spoke, beaming down at his audience, the tone of his address at odds with the indictment he'd made. 'Make no mistake, though. You still haven't been trusted with the truth. What was Aurora, exactly? They won't say, despite the rumours. Nor will they offer any sort of explanation as to what became of that so-called artificial intelligence after the crisis was concluded. There's a reason for their evasiveness, just as there's a reason you won't hear about the catalogue of blunders that caused the whole tragic affair. It suits them to have you think the whole terrible business was somehow sprung upon us without warning, and not something that could have been avoided, had their eyes been on the task given to them.'

The words ought to have lost their sting by now. Panoply had been criticised before; this was nothing new. But Dreyfus knew the crisis had sprung out of a confluence of factors that could never have been anticipated. The shocking thing was not that the emergency had happened in the first place, but that it had been contained with only a modest loss of life. And – although their numbers were small, compared to the civilian deaths – Panoply's own operatives had been lost, including Dreyfus's close colleagues.

But all he could do now was listen.

'Their failing cost millions of lives,' the man was saying. 'And in their betrayal of that public trust, we see now that the entire institutional framework of the Glitter Band was never anything more than a confidence trick. The security we counted on was never there in the first place. We surrendered our sovereignty to the wisdom of Panoply and in return they left us bereft. Our shining democratic apparatus was a hall of mirrors, designed to blind us to the truth of our own powerlessness. But it needn't be that way.' He allowed himself a significant pause, beaming out at the onlookers, adjusting his leaning posture against the statue of the Amerikano pioneer. Now his voice lowered, becoming confiding, inviting the nearest onlookers to pull closer. 'Across the Glitter Band, a new consensus is dawning. Habitats don't need Panoply. Panoply wouldn't be there for them if they did! And so they choose autonomy. They are taking back control. Control to manage the affairs of their citizens in a way that suits their needs, not those of some distant, disconnected network of overseers. Nothing can stop them. Provided the citizens vote to secede, Panoply cannot deny them their wish. And so it has proven. In the last six months, eight habitats have already declared their independent status. The prefects can't touch them. They can't even step inside without an invitation! And has the sky fallen? Has the world ended? Not

13

in the slightest. These habitats continue to thrive. They continue to trade – with the Glitter Band, with Yellowstone and between themselves. Free movement of citizens and materials has not been endangered. Far from it, my friends – far from it.'

Dreyfus felt his neck hairs bristle against the fabric of the hood collar. He had heard enough. The point had not been to listen to the words, but to get a clearer impression of the man speaking them.

Devon Garlin was not the only figure associated with the breakaway movement, but he was by far the most influential and outspoken. Where Garlin went, dissent followed. His ideas took a toxic, ineradicable hold. Dreyfus had been tracking him throughout the whole breakaway crisis and he was in no doubt that Garlin's presence and prominence was critical to the momentum of the whole affair. Something about this easy-going, affable figure pushed the citizenry to act against their own interests. It was Garlin who had taken the lead in turning public opinion against Panoply; Garlin who had publicised the legal and institutional loopholes that permitted habitats to secede from the Glitter Band without penalty.

So far only eight had jumped. A manageable number, in Jane Aumonier's view. Small habitats, for the most part, with low population loads. But Garlin was still moving from world to world, disseminating his views. Panoply, meanwhile, was keeping a close eye on the mood across the entire Glitter Band. About twenty more habitats – some of them quite large – were in open debate about whether or not to secede, and almost all of the others were at least aware of the possibility. Aumonier's response was to wait and see what happened. Dreyfus was not so willing to stand back and let events take their course.

Satisfied, if not exactly reassured, he was turning to make his way back to the shuttle dock when a change in Garlin's tone snagged his attention.

'Wait, friend – I'm not done yet. You wouldn't want to miss the best bit, would you?'

Dreyfus ought to have kept walking. Others had already begun to drift away from the gathering, so it was not as if he had called attention to himself just by leaving. He should have kept walking. Not slowly turned around to face Garlin, knowing he was the subject of the statement.

Dreyfus said nothing. He looked over the heads of those before him to the man leaning on the statue.

'The rain's easing, friend. You can drop the hood.' The friendly tone of the words only brought out the steel beneath them. 'Go on. There's no need to be coy about your identity. I knew who you were from the moment you arrived.'

Dreyfus left his hood up. He had hoped not to speak, because to do so would draw exactly the scrutiny he had meant to avoid. But Garlin had rendered his efforts futile.

'I just came to hear you speak, like everyone else.'

'Are you going to introduce yourself, friend?' There was a beat, no more than that, before Garlin continued. 'I'll do it for you. Good people, good citizens! This is Tom Dreyfus. Or should I say Prefect Dreyfus? He walks among us – Senior Prefect Tom Dreyfus of Panoply. One of the very men who brought us to the brink of disaster two years ago. I wonder why he's so keen to preserve his anonymity?' Garlin let out a snigger. 'You couldn't have expected to pass unnoticed, Tom?'

'I'm here as a civilian,' Dreyfus said, doing his best not to raise his voice, not to sound in any way perturbed. 'I wanted to hear what you had to say.'

'And what did you make of it, before some other business called you away?'

'You make a very persuasive case.'

There was a murmur of conversation from the onlookers, but only Garlin and Dreyfus were speaking at a normal volume. Dreyfus prickled under the attention, feeling cast in a role he had never asked for.

'You see how it works now,' Garlin said, nodding out at his audience. 'We've got them rattled. Rattled enough that they send out people like Dreyfus to mingle with us and attempt to undermine our efforts. That's why you're here, isn't it, Tom?'

'I told you why I was here. You call yourself the voice of the people, the spokesperson for the common citizen. Why shouldn't I be interested?'

'Is that all it is, just innocent interest?'

Dreyfus looked around at his unwelcome audience. 'Don't allow yourselves to be taken in by him,' he said, addressing no one in particular but making eye contact with as many as possible. 'He's not the common man he makes out. His birth name was Julius Devon Garlin Voi – the wealthy son of Marlon and Aliya Voi. Ask him about the Shell House. He was raised in a private estate in Chasm City, not in the Glitter Band. He's been pampered from the moment he was born. And now he wants to tear apart the very society that welcomed him with open arms, like a spoilt brat breaking his playthings.'

Someone flicked down his hood and the last traces of the rain drizzled down against his scalp. Dreyfus turned again, showing no haste or anger, not even seeking eye contact with the person who had dropped his hood.

'Let him leave,' Garlin said, pushing a false magnanimity into his words. 'He's within his rights. We won't stop him doing as he chooses. We're not the ones who fall back on force and intimidation in the face of our enemies. Nor are we the ones who say that a man must be defined by his origins.'

Dreyfus began to walk away from the gathering. He had been near the back of the audience but there were still a few stragglers to push past. They moved out of his way, grudgingly. But he had only taken a few steps when something tripped him. It was sudden, and he hit the ground hard enough to knock the wind from his lungs. For a moment – probably no more than a second, although it felt longer – wet grass pushed into his face, prickling into his nose and eyes. He forced himself up. The ground here was scuffed and muddy, and his hands came away smeared with grass and soil. He had probably been tripped deliberately, but there was an outside chance it was just an accident.

Dreyfus was pushing himself to his feet when Garlin bounded over, kneeling slightly to bring their faces level.

'Let me help you up, Tom.'

'There's no need.'

'You should watch your step. No one wants to see a prefect face-down in the grass like that.' Garlin braced a hand under Dreyfus's elbow and made a theatrical show of grunting as he helped him up. 'My, you're heavy. I didn't know they let prefects carry around so much weight.'

Dreyfus wiped his hands on his knees, the fabric absorbing the stain into itself.

'You and I aren't done.'

Cold blue eyes regarded Dreyfus carefully. Finally Garlin gave a nod. 'I doubt very much that we are.'

CHAPTER TWO

Near the outer orbit of the Glitter Band, deep inside a small, pumpkin-shaped asteroid, lay a room reached through a pair of heavy bronze doors. Hung on massive hinges, each door was engraved with the symbol of a clenched, gauntleted fist. Beyond the deliberate anachronism of the doors was a windowless chamber, its curved walls clad in many spotless layers of varnished wood. The room's lighting was subdued, with most of the illumination coming from the ever-changing tactical readouts on its long, oval-shaped table, as well as the soft glow of the Solid Orrery, ticking away to itself in a corner. The Orrery was an evolving, real-time, three-dimensional representation of the entire flow of worlds in the Glitter Band, as well as the planet they orbited.

The doors hinged shut behind Thalia. She breathed in, forcing calm upon herself. The air in the room – based on the few occasions she had been inside it – always seemed to lie heavy on her lungs, as if it carried some of the varnish with it.

'Take a seat, Ng. This needn't take long.'

There were twenty seats around the table, of which a dozen were presently occupied. There was Jane Aumonier, of course, and flanking her were a mixture of Senior Prefects, Internal Prefects, Field Prefects, and a few supernumerary analysts with tactical security ratings. Thalia took the high-backed chair facing the Supreme Prefect. Aumonier's face was under-lit by the readouts on the area of table before her and they cast colours and patterns across her chin and cheekbones.

After a silence, Thalia ventured to speak.

'I haven't had time to submit a field report, ma'am.'

'There'll be no need in this instance, Ng. Your conduct was entirely satisfactory. It was an unusual development and you reacted well.'

Thalia nodded once, her hands settled before her in her lap. She wondered if the words 'unusual development' had ever been delivered with more dry understatement.

'I'm sorry about the medical orderly. He was just trying to do his work.'

17

'Don't worry about him,' said Senior Prefect Gaston Clearmountain, sitting to the right of Aumonier. 'He was lucky to get away with just a broken ankle.'

'Perhaps he'll take it as a lesson,' said Senior Prefect Lillian Baudry, who was sitting in her customary position to the left of Aumonier.

'I hope we don't have to teach too many of them,' Field Prefect Sparver Bancal said. 'Or it could get messy.'

'It's messy enough already,' Aumonier said, nodding in sympathy with Sparver, who had taken his usual position between Baudry and one of the supernumerary analysts. His seat was slightly elevated compared to the others, bringing his eye level close to the other operatives'.

'The Heavy Medicals attended him. Do we have an update on his condition?'

'No lasting complications,' said Internal Prefect Ingvar Tench, who was sitting on the extreme right of the oval table.

There was a silence.

'And the other man?' Thalia asked.

Aumonier looked puzzled by the question.

'Which other man?'

'The man whose head you had me bring back,' Thalia answered.

Aumonier's voice remained level, her posture poised and still, hardly any part of her face moving except her lips. 'The man's condition was far beyond anything the local medics were equipped to treat.'

'We didn't even let them try.'

Sparver Bancal smiled, or rather produced the nearest thing to a smile that a hyperpig could. 'It wasn't about killing or saving him. It was about evidential preservation.'

'It was just a seizure,' she said, looking from face to face for a clue. 'Something went wrong in his brain and he started having some sort of episode. Why is that any concern of ours?'

'You did well,' Aumonier said, as if they had just spooled back to the start of the conversation. 'You may continue your work with the polling cores, according to the agreed schedule.'

'Begging your pardon, ma'am,' Thalia said. 'But you were expecting it, weren't you? That's why that container was in my ship, just waiting to be used. You were *expecting* to have to cut someone's head off.'

She watched the faces of the others, measuring their reactions. None of them looked comfortable, but they were doing their best to make this seem like routine business.

'Let me be blunt with you, Ng,' Aumonier said. 'Today you brushed against the periphery of something beyond your security clearance. I won't insult your intelligence by suggesting otherwise. You are correct in your assumption that certain operational provisions had already been made.'

'Well, ma'am—' Thalia began.

'Speaking,' Aumonier said, softening the remark with the mildest hint of a smile. 'You are trusted, Ng, and expected to execute your duties with due regard to matters of security and secrecy. I am confident you will do so. But just so there is no ambiguity, there will be no mention of this matter from the moment you leave this room. You will discuss it with no one, regardless of rank; you will not allude to it in the vaguest of terms; you will conduct no queries pertaining to this business in any regard whatsoever. You are entitled to your curiosity. I would think less of you if you were not curious. For now, though, you will proceed as if nothing unusual had happened today. In time you will be privy to more informa-tion – but not now, and not for the foreseeable future.'

It's something big, then, Thalia thought. Something they haven't cleared up yet. Something they don't know when they'll clear up. Another emergency, on the order of the last one . . .

'If I could help, ma'am . . .'

'You can't, Ng,' Aumonier said. 'Or rather, you can, by putting this entire matter out of your mind. Is that clear?'

Thalia felt the pressure of the other faces staring at her own. 'It is, ma'am,' she answered, forcing herself to meet their eyes, to show confi-dence rather than cowedness.

'Then that will be all, Ng,' Aumonier said.

In the area of Panoply they still called the Sleep Lab, Doctor Demikhov's face loomed behind a distorting surface of tinted glassware. He was ad-justing some valve or temperature regulator on the side of a cryogenic vessel. Inside the vessel, looking oddly shrunken, was the severed head.

Behind Sparver Bancal, their own reflections ghosting above his own, stood Senior Prefect Gaston Clearmountain and Supreme Prefect Jane Aumonier.

'Well?' Aumonier asked, after the silence had grown interminable. 'What's the verdict, Doctor? You're the expert on heads, or so I'm told.'

Some flicker of amusement crossed Demikhov's lantern-jawed face as he straightened up from the vessel and the bench's worth of medical systems surrounding it. 'I generally prefer working with heads that have at least a fighting chance of revival.'

The head was upright, fixed into some sort of life-support collar, caged by columns of rising bubbles. It looked waxy and inert, more like a casting than something that had only recently belonged to a living individual.

'How does it compare?' Sparver asked.

'The usual mush, Prefect Bancal. Just a little less cooked than the others.'

'You have such a delicate way with words,' Clearmountain muttered.

'Nothing recoverable?' Aumonier asked.

'I haven't cracked it open yet. But the scans tell me all I need to know. Neural patterns are scrambled beyond recognition and the implants are reduced to a few micrograms of metallic slag.'

'This is our best chance to date,' Aumonier said. 'If there's anything in this head, the tiniest clue, we need it.'

'I'll go through the motions,' Demikhov said resignedly.

'One question,' Sparver said. 'Do we know anything about the melter?'

He heard Clearmountain's sniff of displeasure. Something tightened in Aumonier's already taut features before she spoke. 'The citizen was Antal Bronner. Eighty-two years old. Born and died in the Shiga-Mintz Spindle, spent less than a decade living in other habitats.'

'Priors?' Sparver asked.

'He looks clean,' Aumonier said. 'A private trader in out-system goods, specialising in exo-art. No scandals, no major insolvencies – just the ups and downs of any small-time broker.'

'Living associates?' asked Sparver.

'One wife – Ghiselin Bronner. She's been told that her husband died in a sudden medical event. She'll have questions, undoubtedly, but we won't be able to offer her all the answers.'

'We could sequester her as a warm witness,' Clearmountain said.

Aunonier gave a sharp shake of her head. 'No, tact is key for now. I'll arrange a soft interview, on her territory. Just enough to see if she's hiding anything.'

'You could always send Ng,' Sparver offered.

'After I made it clear she isn't to speak a word of this to anyone?' Aumonier asked.

'You had to for security's sake. But that's only because she hasn't been brought on board. If she understood the situation, she'd be just as keen as the rest of us to keep this under wraps. If she was given a Pangolin shot she could be up to speed by tomorrow, another pair of eyes and ears we badly need . . .'

'And another risk of a leak,' Clearmountain said.

'She's no more likely to leak than you or I, Gaston,' Sparver said. 'Unless you still believe Jason Ng wasn't totally absolved of wrongdoing?'

'I never mentioned her father,' Clearmountain said.

20

'You didn't need to – you've made it as plain as can be that you'll never let Thalia step out of his shadow.'

'Gentlemen,' Aumonier said softly. 'Let's not bicker. The fact of the matter, though, is that Gaston is correct: we've kept this watertight until now by confining it to the highest security rankings, including our good colleague Doctor Demikhov. Thalia may well be trustworthy – I don't doubt that she is – but every additional operative brings the risk of an accidental slip. Need I remind you that our enemies – opportunists like Devon Garlin – are circling like sharks, waiting for just such an opportunity?'

'I still say she could be an asset,' Sparver said.

'And in time she may well be,' Aumonier allowed. 'But for now, you must set aside your personal feelings of protectiveness towards Ng. It could have been any operational Field who had to bring back that head. Would you be so keen to bring one of the others into the investigation, if you hadn't worked closely with them under Dreyfus?'

Sparver knew better than to lie. 'Perhaps you're right.'

'She was required to execute a task in the line of duty,' Clearmountain replied. 'That's where it ends for her. She's a competent operative, but at the end of the day she's just another Field. That won't cause any difficulties will it, Prefect Bancal?'

'None at all,' Sparver said.

'You acted without my authority,' Aumonier said, without even a token attempt at pleasantries.

Dreyfus faced her across the table. He had come directly from the docking bay, not even taking the time to step through a washwall.

'Your authority wasn't required,' he answered. 'When I go to the hospice to see Valery, I do so as a free citizen. This was no different.'

'Don't split legalistic hairs with me. Devon Garlin isn't our concern. Don't force us into a position where he becomes so.'

'I think we've already passed that point.'

Aumonier studied him with a faint air of exasperation, of lofty expectations in grave danger of being undermined.

'Garlin's breakaway movement will lose steam. It'll only take a small crisis, a minor economic downturn, to have those rogue habitats scuttling back into the fold.'

'You wouldn't have said that two years ago.'

'Things change.'

Dreyfus leaned forward. 'Garlin isn't just another flash-in-the-pan blowhard. Those eight habitats aren't rushing to rejoin us. And there are at least twenty more on the verge of breaking away.'

21

'These are small numbers.'

Dreyfus offered open palms, traces of yellowish dirt still lodged under his fingernails. 'I wanted to see him for real, not just on compads and screens. To get a measure of the man.'

Aumonier sighed slowly, clearly aware she was being drawn into a conversation against her will.

'And what gems of insight did you bring back?'

'Mainly that I don't like self-professed men of the people who keep quiet about being born into one of the richest families in Chasm City.'

'It wasn't all roses. He was only sixteen when Aliya died. Tough for an only child, especially the way Marlon was fading, losing his grip on things. Yet Julius picked himself up, made his own way beyond the estate and Chasm City, and found a role for himself in life.'

'To wrack and ruin.'

Half a smile bent her lips. 'I don't have to like the man, or believe in his objectives, to see that he's made something of himself beyond the umbrella of the Voi name.'

'There's something else going on here. I'd done nothing to draw attention to myself, nothing to call out my presence. And yet he knew I was there.'

'I know. I saw it on the public feeds. "Panoply sends spy to eavesdrop on public gathering."'

'He'd been aware of me all along. And yet I'd barely shown my face. I went to Stonehollow by civilian shuttle. No one gave me a second glance at any point in my journey.'

'What are you saying?'

'He still picked up on my presence. He sensed there was someone at the gathering who didn't belong.'

'For all you know, he wasn't aware of you until the moment you turned your back on him. Then he ran an identity query on you and realised you weren't carrying implants. From there it's only a small step to guessing you were a Panoply operative.'

'And from there he guessed my name?'

'Like it or not, the Aurora affair made you something of a public figure.' Aumonier angled her head to one side, conveying at least a measure of sympathy. 'Don't make more of this than you need to. Let Garlin be my headache, not yours.'

'As if you didn't have enough to be getting on with.'

'I take it you heard about Ng's little mission?'

Dreyfus nodded, glad the matter of Garlin had been set aside for the time being. 'I saw Sparver in the docking bay. He told me what happened.

Do you think it's the break we've been hoping for?'

Aumonier looked equivocal. 'Demikhov doesn't seem very optimistic – even for Demikhov.'

'There has to be a pattern, a causal factor. We just haven't seen it yet.'

'In other words: more deaths would be helpful?'

Dreyfus leaned back, evaluating a risky idea before he put it into words. 'Might I say something?'

'You're going to anyway.'

'Assign the polling core upgrades to a DFP One, and put Thalia Ng onto a full-time investigation of the deaths. Give her a Pangolin boost, and assign a squad, if need be.'

'I can't risk it. I've already been over this with Clearmountain and Bancal. It's not that I don't trust Ng, but if so much as a word of this gets out, I'll have a mass panic on my hands.'

'You already have witnesses.'

'Civilians who aren't sure what happened, and who aren't aware of any larger pattern of incidents. That's how it'll stay, provided we maintain the present security arrangements.'

Dreyfus knew better than to argue. 'I suppose there's always a chance the dead will give us something.'

'You do have a way with them,' Aumonier said. 'Vanessa Laur just notified me, by the way. Our sequestration order came through. We have Antal Bronner's beta-level. See if you can get something useful from the poor man, will you?'

Dreyfus made to rise. 'Have you ever had to tell someone that they're dead?'

'No,' Aumonier said. 'I prefer to leave that sort of thing to the experts.'

Sparver was eating alone at one of the corner tables. He seemed hunched over his tray, as if pressed down by the low, curving ceiling. Thalia set her own tray down without begging an invitation. For a moment she let her friend get on with his meal, using the special cutlery that had been provided for hyperpigs. He ate fastidiously, taking small mouthfuls and chewing carefully. He had even tucked a napkin into his collar. His reading spectacles were set on the table before him, next to a compad.

'I hear you're doing well with the polling cores,' he said. 'Not exactly thrilling work, it's got to be said. But they wouldn't trust it to anyone but a safe pair of hands.'

'How long was that thing in my cutter?'

Sparver's cutlery clinked. 'Dreyfus will keep you on it for a little while longer. But that's only because he knows you'll do a thorough job.' He carried on eating, nodding between mouthfuls. 'This is actually not too terrible. You should try it. Or maybe it wouldn't suit a baseline palate, with your restricted range of taste receptors.' He looked at her with vague sympathetic interest. 'How do you *live* like that?'

'It was pure luck that I was near that man, wasn't it?' She pressed closer, lowering her voice. 'I've been thinking about that, and what Aumonier said.'

'I should cook for you again one of these days, show you what food's meant to taste like. Pork's off the menu, obviously, but other than that—'

'So they must have hundreds of those boxes stashed aboard our ships, just waiting for one of us to be in the right position.'

Sparver dabbed at his mouth with the napkin. 'Did you hear the news about the boss man? Took it upon himself to pay a visit to Devon Garlin.' He tapped his spectacles against the compad. 'Lady Jane's spitting nails.'

Thalia's hands were now fists to either side of her tray. 'You have seniority over me, I understand. There are things you can talk about, and things you can't. Ordinarily I'd respect that. But not after you talked me through cutting a man's head off while he was still alive.'

Sparver took another mouthful, chewing and swallowing before giving his answer.

'He wasn't still alive.'

'He was moving.' She leaned in closer still, her voice a hoarse whisper. 'He was still alive. You made me kill a man who was *still alive.*'

'Did you listen to a word Lady Jane said, about not saying anything more about this?'

'She was talking about security leaks. You don't count. Now tell me about that man.'

Sparver set down his cutlery, dabbed at his chin, then looked at Thalia with his small, sad, all-too-human eyes. 'By the time you got to him the entire medical resources of the Glitter Band and Chasm City couldn't have made a difference. What mattered was getting some fragment of evidence back to Panoply.'

She was silent for a few moments. She leaned back, getting out of his face. The food on her tray was still untouched.

'Are you just going to leave it at that?'

'I'm sure you'll get a proper briefing at some point. But I won't be the one giving it. It's not that I don't trust you—'

'Someone doesn't,' she said sharply. 'I suppose I shouldn't be too surprised. They can say they've exonerated someone, but whether they really mean it, deep down . . .'

'You think this is about your father?' He glanced down at his meal, what remained of it, then reached for his spectacles and stood to leave. 'It's about seniority, that's all. You were given a difficult duty to perform and you did it. Be content with that.'

They regarded each other for an uncomfortable moment. Deep down she knew she was being unreasonable, pressuring him into a disclosure he had no right to give. But he was not the one who had gone through that nightmare in the Shiga-Mintz Spindle.

She had done her duty, all right. Not disgraced herself. But Sparver wasn't the one who had vomited up his guts as soon as he was back on the ship, nor woken himself screaming as soon as he managed to sleep after his shift.

'He wasn't the first, was he?' she said, knowing there would be neither confirmation nor denial from her friend. 'Not by a long stretch. Not the first and I'm guessing he won't be the last. Aumonier admitted I'd brushed against something outside my clearance, something big. What is it, Sparver? What are we dealing with?'

'I can't tell you.'

'Just give me a word. A case codename. Something.'

Sparver said nothing.

Dreyfus's shoes crunched on gravel. The sound was sufficient to break the reverie of a lone man sitting on a park bench, staring into the grey distance. Irritation and confusion clouded his features, as if he had just realised that he had no recollection of arriving at the bench.

'I—' the man started.

Dreyfus raised a calming hand, softening his expression in a way that he hoped conveyed empathy and understanding.

'It's all right, Antal. You're among friends and nothing bad will happen to you.' Stopping before the man, he lowered down onto his haunches, bringing his eye line level with the seated figure.

'Who are you?'

'My name's Dreyfus. I'm a prefect. Something happened and now you're in the care of Panoply.'

'How . . .' the man began, frowning. 'What do you mean, something happened?'

Dreyfus put on a solemn look. 'You died.' He paused, letting that sink in for a second or two. 'It was violent and irrevocable, with no prospect of neural consolidation. But you had a beta-level instantiation shadowing you for many years. That beta-level has now been legally sequestered and brought to a responsive state within a simulated environment, executing inside Panoply.'

Dreyfus could have scripted the exchange that would follow.

'No, you've made an error. I'm definitely not dead. I'd know if I were dead.'

'Do you remember walking to this bench? Do you even have an idea where we are now?'

'A habitat. Somewhere.'

'You don't remember because there was no transitional experience. Under the terms of the sequestration order you were placed in immediate executive quarantine. You are the only copy of Antal Bronner presently executing. You were re-initiated a few seconds before I arrived.'

'No,' the beta-level said flatly. 'There's been a mistake.'

'I wish there had been, Antal. But look at it this way. The whole point of you was to shine now. To speak for Antal Bronner when Antal could not.'

Maybe some part of that got through. Though denial was a virtually universal reaction, the beta-levels varied starkly in the way they moved from denial to acceptance. The ease or otherwise of that shift was un-avoidably correlated with their base-personality.

'I don't feel dead,' the beta-level said, more flatly than before. He stared down at his own sleeve, as if some desolate truth lay evident in the fabric's weave.

'You didn't feel dead when you were alive, so you won't feel it now. The crucial thing is that you may be able to help us.'

'How can I possibly help?'

'We need to talk about how you died.'

'You said it was violent. Was I murdered?'

'It was a medical event, and an extreme one.' Dreyfus paused, his knees beginning to ache. He was squatting for real in the grey box of the im-mersion room, with plugs jammed into his ears and goggles chafing at his skin. 'Whether it was deliberate or not, we can't yet say.'

Antal Bronner looked around, taking in the tall hedges and the distant arc of patterned landscape rising overhead, towns and hamlets laid across it like arrangements of tiny gaming pieces.

'Will I be able to leave?'

Dreyfus smiled tightly. 'In good time.'

'I want to speak to my wife. Ghiselin does know, doesn't she?'

'Your wife's been informed of your death, and she has constables and counsellors to turn to. But I can't allow any possibility of evidential con-tamination at this stage of the investigation.'

'What evidence are we talking about?'

'You,' Dreyfus said bluntly. At last the effort of squatting had become too much. He beckoned to the seat and waited for a nod from Bronner, inviting him to sit down. Dreyfus settled his weight onto what he trusted would be a functionally equivalent surface, conjured out of quickmatter in the interview room. 'For reasons presently unknown, something went wrong with your neural machinery. Your implants sent out debilitating signals, putting you into a grand mal seizure. Then they underwent a catastrophic thermal overload.'

'What does that mean?'

'A heat pulse, which boiled the surrounding brain tissue.'

They were facing the same way now, staring out across the lawn, a silvery fog creeping its way down the distant curve of the habitat's inner surface.

'We got to you as quickly as we could,' said Dreyfus. 'Had we been there a little sooner, we might have been able to slow down the thermal event. I'm waiting for our medical examiner to see if you can teach us anything we didn't already know. In the meantime, though, I'm counting on there being something, some detail or circumstance, that might help.'

Bronner gave a hollow laugh. 'There's nothing. I'd remember if there was.'

'Has anything ever gone wrong with your implants?'

'Nothing.'

'And you've had them all your life?'

'I don't know exactly when they were put in. Allowed to grow, I should say. I was just a boy.'

'But since then – no complications?'

'None. What happened to me, Prefect?'

Dreyfus kept his tone studiedly neutral. 'Witnesses and public records place you walking through the park when you collapsed. There was no visible cause and no one else was affected. But something made it happen, and I'd like to know what. If there's anything in your past that you think might have any bearing . . .'

Bronner turned to face him. 'Like what, exactly?'

'Some borderline procedure? Black market medicine. Illicit neural modification. Contact with Ultras, or Conjoiners – you name it. Be as frank as you like, Antal. The last thing I'm going to do is prosecute you.'

'I've never gone in for anything like that. I'm not one for taking chances. I live in the Shiga-Mintz Spindle, for pity's sake.'

'I have to ask.'

'Why do you? I died. It's a tragedy for me, that's for sure. But it's not the sort of thing I'd expect Panoply to expend much energy on.

Aren't you supposed to be making sure none of us commit voting fraud?'

'There's that,' Dreyfus said, nodding slightly. 'But it's not the limit of our remit.' With a grunt of effort he pushed himself up from the bench, or rather its counterpart in the interview room. 'If I've judged you right, Antal, you've told me the truth about yourself, to the limit of your knowledge.'

'I can see I've been a disappointment.'

'Not at all – we're just getting started. This place, by the way – this simulation – we call it Necropolis.'

'And that's supposed to help me?'

Dreyfus gestured across the lawn, where the gravelled path cut through a slot in the manicured hedge. 'Follow the path. Look for an ornamental garden, a big lake, some terraces and pavilions. Sooner or later you'll bump into some other people. They all know each other by now, and they all know why they're here.'

Some dark realisation shadowed Bronner's eyes.

'The same thing happened to them, didn't it?'

The briefing was short, because Doctor Demikhov had already told them almost everything of significance. Sparver sat through it, toying with his spectacles as the neural scans and slices played across the tactical room's walls, projected over dark varnished wood.

Bronner's implants, what had been salvaged of them, resembled the mangled, blackened remains of space vehicles after a bad re-entry.

Dreyfus had not been present during the first conversation with the medical chief, but nothing Demikhov said seemed to surprise him. He just sat there, nodding sometimes, rarely bothering with a direct question. Gaston Clearmountain and Lillian Baudry listened stoically, offering the occasional clipped interjection.

Jane Aumonier said less than anyone, waiting until Demikhov was finished, out of the room and back to some other pressing business.

'If I'm going to draw a crumb of encouragement out of this whole unpleasantness, it's that the protocol worked. The whiphound performed flawlessly, as did the cryogenic vessel.'

'The only weak link,' Gaston Clearmountain said, 'was the prefect. Why did Ng take so damned long to reach him? She was already *in* the habitat.'

'She had to go back for the equipment,' Dreyfus said, mumbling out the words like a man on the edge of sleep.

'And whose bright idea was that?' Clearmountain asked.

'Yours,' said the brittle, stiff-backed Lillian Baudry, with a surprising lack of rancour. 'You didn't want routine activities hampered by prefects carrying around surplus equipment.'

Clearmountain gruffed out his disgruntlement. 'She should still have been faster.'

'Grown wings, you mean?' Dreyfus speculated.

'I was with her on the link the whole time,' Sparver put in, before his boss inflamed an already tense discussion. 'Ng was the best prefect we could have hoped to have on hand.'

'Whatever we learn from this episode,' Aumonier said, 'we're still left with essentially the same set of questions we had a couple of days ago. Tom: you've talked to the beta. Do you see any scope for progress?'

'Same story as the rest,' Dreyfus said after a moment's reflection. 'Surprised to be dead. Nothing in his declared background to explain the neural anomalies. I've already allowed him free interaction with the other betas.'

'Wise, Dreyfus?' asked Clearmountain.

'They're dead,' Dreyfus said. 'The least we can do is give them someone to talk to. Besides, we haven't time to do things by the usual routine.'

Their collective gaze had shifted to the Solid Orrery. The ten thousand habitats were ten thousand tiny points of coloured light, glinting in shades of ruby, gold, emerald or topaz, each accorded a brightness in relation to the size of structure or population load it represented.

Eight of the habitats had been enlarged and elevated above the true orbital plane of the Glitter Band, so that their true shapes were apparent. These were the eight breakaway states – technically no longer within Panoply's purview, but still a matter for consideration as far as Aumonier was concerned.

Then there were the others.

Fifty-four additional habitats, raised even further from the plane than the breakaway states. This had nothing to do with their physical locations in the Glitter Band, but everything to do with their recent significance to Panoply. There was, as yet, no overlap between the two sets of habitats. Of these, however, the fifty-fourth bore the characteristic shape of the Shiga-Mintz Spindle.

'Tom's right,' Aumonier said, her level tone drawing a line under any criticism of Dreyfus's methods. 'The betas have a vested interest in helping us explain their deaths. The more they interact, the greater the chance that some common factor will come to light. It's a slim hope, but the best we have.'

'Until the next death,' Dreyfus said. 'Case fifty-five.'

29

Aumonier gave a slow nod. 'Fortunately – or not, depending on your point of view – I doubt we'll have long to wait.'

They were walking side by side, following the trail that skirted the biggest lake in this part of Necropolis. The woman next to Dreyfus was small and wiry with an acrobat's muscle tone. Her hair was trimmed to a functional crop, emphasising the elfin structure of her facial bones. She wore a grey outfit of trousers and tunic, stitched with an interlocking design of white trees.

'It's not that I don't like your company,' she was saying. 'But I'm starting to feel as if we've already been over this a hundred times.'

'We probably have,' Dreyfus said, walking with his head down and his hands behind his back.

'Then the point of these little chats is . . .?'

'Maybe all it will take is the hundred and first interview. You'll let something slip, and that will give me the breakthrough.'

'Let something slip,' she repeated, mimicking his tone. 'As if I'm deliberately withholding something.'

'I didn't mean it that way.'

'Let me get something straight in my mind. I'm a digital artefact: a pattern of algorithms, designed to emulate the responses of the living instantiation of me.'

'They don't usually put it so bluntly, but yes – that's about it.'

'And you've got me sequestered. You've moved a copy of my digital code into your machines inside Panoply.'

'Not just moved, but put a legal and binding embargo on the continued execution of any remaining copies of you beyond Panoply. We only want to deal with one copy of you, and it's simpler for you if there are no conflicts when we release you back into the world.'

'Whatever works for you. But one thing's clear enough to me. You already have the means to pick me apart, to examine my coding structure – my decision-branch algorithms, my life-logs. You can see through my soul like it's made of glass. So why the time-consuming charade of these interviews? Can't you just *know* everything there is to know about me?'

'Let me explain how that would work,' Dreyfus said. 'Only another artificial intelligence would be able to pick through your digital structure and hold all the details of your life-log in its memory. We have machines that can do that, it's true. But any machine would still have to break everything down into a form that I could assimilate, and I'd still have to phrase my queries as natural language expressions. In which case I'd end up having a conversation much like this one, only with a whole unnecessary layer of mediation between me and you.'

'Mm.' She made a face that told him she accepted his answer but still found something unsatisfactory in it. 'And do my thoughts come into it?'

'You're continuing to exist and can interact with other beta-levels. Isn't that better than being frozen in limbo?'

'This isn't living, Prefect Dreyfus – no matter what you might like to think.'

'You'll feel differently when we release you.'

'Why should I? It'll still be just another pale imitation of life.'

'Only if you want it to be. Beta-levels can still serve a social function.'

'Serve a social function?' she echoed. 'How thrilling you make it seem. The afterlife as public servitude. I could water some flowers, tend some grass, is that what you mean?'

'I wish there was something I could say to make it seem better.'

She had been the first of the dead to come to Panoply's attention, and her beta-level the first to be sequestered. Dozens more had followed in the ensuing months, but she would always be the first victim, emblematic of those to come. He still remembered the false optimism of the early days, the slowly waning hope that some common link would be found among the cases. Whatever it was, though, it had not come to light through routine interviewing. Even the Search Turbines, programmed to probe into the fine-grained details of a life, had found nothing of significance.

So why did he keep coming back to Cassandra Leng?

Because he liked her, he supposed. Her bluntness, her unsentimental acceptance of death. Some of the other betas wanted things from him: information, promises, changes to their terms of sequestration. Cassandra Leng seemed not to care about any of that. And in her directness he believed he was getting as close to a truthful account of her beliefs and opinions as with any of the other dead.

Something else, too – and with it a prickle of distant guilt. Her directness reminded him of his wife.

'I'm not really buying this cynicism, Cassandra,' Dreyfus said. 'Your living instantiation must have believed there was some worth to a beta-level or you wouldn't have gone to the trouble of having the emulation created.'

'I did it for the living, not for myself – the way you make out a will so that people around you will be happier. To make *them* feel better, not for your own benefit.'

'Is that really all there was to it?'

From the lake side they had a good view of the terrain as it swooped up beyond the gardens, rolling up into a tube. Lakes and hamlets glimmered in a haze of silvery distance. A small island rose from the lake, with a skeletal tower jutting into the fog.

'We may as well face it, Dreyfus,' she said, letting out a quiet sigh. 'I'm dead and gone. I died after taking a reckless gamble with my own life.'

'It wasn't the risk-taking that killed you, it was just where you happened to be when the neural overload took place.' The hundred-and-twelve-year-old Leng had perished during a high-risk sport, an elaborate and dangerous cross between firewalking and tag, played out in the bowels of the Colfax Orb, a habitat that made a living for itself by courting hedonists, thrill-seekers and the borderline suicidal. 'But what were you hoping to get out of that place to begin with?'

'Shall I let you in on a dirty little secret, Dreyfus?'

'If you like.'

'Utopia is stifling. What's the point in longevity if every day is a grey duplicate of the one before?'

'Life is still precious,' Dreyfus said. 'Still worth cherishing. No matter how it looks most of the time.'

'I don't disagree. But you either live on the limits, or you're not living. I knew that, and I accept the consequences.'

'You'd see yourself as a risk-taker, then.'

She glanced at him, rolling her eyes. 'Oh, this old hobbyhorse of yours. We've been over this, remember?'

'I still think there's something to it.'

'You're entitled to your theories, Prefect – and I'll humour them, while I'm here. Ask around, share stories, trade memories – as I've been doing for months and months already.'

They walked a little further. By some degrees the mist had lifted from the lake, and now the central island was more visible than it had been only a few moments earlier. The skeletal tower was actually a pylon, supporting the thin thread of a monorail line, swooping overhead and out across the lake.

'There's a new man, Antal Bronner. Have you spoken to him?'

'He's only just arrived, the poor confused soul. It would be a little cruel of me to inflict myself on him so soon after he came here, wouldn't it?'

'Not everyone shares your view of death.'

'I'll talk to him, for what it's worth. But I wouldn't get your hopes up. He looks boring to me. Not a risk-taker at all.' She looked at him with something close to amusement. 'I think it may be time to find a new theory, Dreyfus, if that's the best you've got.'

'It is,' he said. 'For now.'

Sparver knocked on the door, waited, knocked a second time. Half a minute passed, then Thalia opened the door just enough to show her face. She was wearing off-duty clothes, her hair wet and glistening as if she had just stepped through a washwall.

'What?' she asked, caught between irritation and interest. 'Come to give me a second dressing-down for overstepping the mark?'

'Not exactly.'

He didn't have to ask to be invited; they understood each other at least that well. Sparver waited until she had closed the door behind them, then moved to the low table in the middle of the room. He was about to conjure himself a chair when Thalia saved him the effort and produced one to his usual specifications, which she knew by heart.

'You want tea, I suppose?'

'No, I'm not sure I have the stomach for it.'

Sparver took the chair and bid Thalia sit opposite him. She wore a black gown cinched at the waist, patterned with green-gold dragons.

'Something on your conscience?'

'Yes, as a matter of fact. I've been thinking everything over, especially in the light of our last conversation.' The chair she had made for him was low, almost like something fashioned for a child, but there was no slight in that. She knew his tastes perfectly well and he much preferred a chair that let him keep his feet on the floor, instead of having them swing in mid-air. 'You were right, and I was wrong. You are involved in this, and you do deserve to know the fuller picture. But it's difficult, and this won't end well for me.'

'Then you'd better say nothing.' There wasn't much charity in her tone.

'No, I've made up my mind.' He looked her in the face. 'Something bad is happening, Thal, and you've only seen a tiny part of it. We don't know what it is, or where it's leading. Actually, that's not quite true. We know it's getting worse.'

'All right,' she said, cradling the tea she must have prepared for herself before he arrived. Sparver picked up the smell of ginger, Thalia taking her tea the way Dreyfus liked it. He wondered if she had adopted the habit out of preference, or because she wished to emulate or endear herself to Dreyfus. Whatever the explanation, he had no use for tea made that way. Ginger made him sneeze. 'What is it?'

'You asked about the case codename. It's Wildfire. People are dying, and we don't know why. That man you attended to, Antal Bronner. He's just the latest Wildfire case and there's no pattern that we can see. They're going through their lives, and then suddenly something goes wrong with their heads. A malfunction of their neural implants, leading to a thermal overload and massive destruction to surrounding brain tissue. That's why Demikhov wanted that head frozen as quickly as possible – so he had some chance of working out what's going on, before the evidence cooked itself. But we weren't quick enough.'

'You mean I wasn't.'

'You did all you could. I've vouched for you in that regard.'

'Oh. I need vouching for, do I?'

'They're on edge, the senior prefects. You can't blame them. This doesn't fit any patterns. It's not confined to one habitat. It's dispersed, emerging unpredictably. An asymmetric threat.'

Thalia sipped at her ginger-scented tea. 'I guessed that man wasn't the first. You wouldn't go to the trouble of preparing for something like that unless you'd already seen it before and were expecting new cases.' She looked up from the tea, as if half fearful of the answer he was about to give.

'Antal Bronner was the fifty-fourth that we're aware of. There's no clear link between them, or where they happen.'

'How long has this been going on?'

Sparver got up from the conjured chair. 'It's around four hundred days since the first case. But that's as much as you need to hear from my lips. The rest, you'd better hear from Lady Jane.'

'Why should she tell me any of it?'

'The damage has been done,' Sparver said. 'You know too much to go back to checking cores now. She'll have two options: either wipe your memory, or put you to work doing something useful. I know which I'd choose.'

'I hope you're right,' Thalia said. 'For both our sakes.'

CHAPTER THREE

The atmosphere in the tactical room was exactly as frosty as Thalia had expected. Dreyfus had taken his customary seat to the right of Gaston Clearmountain's chair, between Clearmountain and a supernumerary analyst. Thalia and Sparver were sitting opposite Aumonier; Sparver's usual position on the other side of the table was vacant.

'We had higher hopes for you than this, Ng,' said Lillian Baudry, raising her voice over the soft whispering of one of the analysts who was briefing an Internal Prefect on the extreme left of the table. 'It's a shame to see them dashed.'

'Ng committed no actual breach of rules,' Aumonier said. 'She may have violated commonplace professional etiquette, but that's an entirely separate matter.'

'Security was breached,' said Ingvar Tench.

'The fault for which lies with Sparver Bancal,' Aumonier said, directing her gaze slightly to Thalia's left. 'You knowingly violated a high-level directive. You were under express orders not to disclose the nature of this emergency to any operative below full field status.'

'With respect—' Sparver began.

'I'm not done,' Aumonier said, with fierce calm. 'Grave damage has been done, Bancal. There's never been a higher need for secrecy. Panoply is already under pressure with the breakaway problem, our hands are tied, and now we have this developing crisis to contend with. So far we've been lucky – extraordinarily so. How many is it now, Tang?'

Robert Tang, the other Internal Prefect present beyond Ingvar Tench, glanced at his readouts. Tang was a small, fastidious man known for his close attention to detail. 'Fifty-four known deaths at present, Supreme Prefect.'

'Fifty-four,' she said. 'Fifty-four dead and no one – beyond us – has yet drawn a line between them. The instant this becomes public knowledge, we'll have a panic on our hands like nothing we've seen. And yet here you are, treating secrets with the utmost disregard—'

'Why would we have a panic, ma'am?' Thalia cut in, doing her best to take some of the heat off her friend.

'Speaking.'

'I'm sorry, Supreme Prefect.' Thalia steeled herself before forging on. 'But yesterday I was sawing a man's head off in a public place. Doesn't that entitle me to know a little about what's going on?'

'It entitles you to nothing,' Aumonier said.

'She shouldn't even be in this briefing,' Baudry muttered. 'It's already above her clearance.'

'That horse has bolted,' Dreyfus said, in a barely awake drawl. 'Ten to one she already knows the case codename. You may as well show her the Wildfire curve.'

'I don't think—' Aumonier began.

'She can be an asset to us,' Dreyfus said, rousing himself a little. 'But if she's to play her part, she needs to know all of it.'

'I don't agree with this,' Baudry said.

'You don't have to,' Dreyfus said.

With a sigh Aumonier nodded at one of the analysts. 'The most recent projections – folding in the fifty-fourth death.'

The analyst made a quick, deft conjuring gesture. A graph lit up on the wall, projected directly over the dark, varnished wood. A scattering of fifty-four dots were clustered around a bunch of curving lines, steepening from left to right. The lines were annotated with thickets of blurred symbols, but the more Thalia squinted the less they came into focus.

'Prefect Dreyfus says you have the mettle,' Aumonier said. 'Let's see it.'

Thalia looked at the graph a little longer. 'I can't read the annotation,' she said. 'I presume that's something to do with security dyslexia. But I know an exponential curve when I see one. How far along the time axis are we?'

'Four hundred days, near enough,' Dreyfus said.

'Are both axes linear?'

'Yes,' Robert Tang said.

Thalia nodded. 'Then your curve looks to be reasonably well approximated by e to the power of x, where x is the number of days divided by a hundred. Let's see. You'll hit one hundred cases around day four hundred and sixty, or barely two months from now, which sounds manageable. But you're on a doubling time of about seventy days, which means a thousand cases about two hundred and ninety days from now, and two thousand only seventy days after that. I'm sure I'm over-simplifying it, but . . .'

'You've grasped the essentials,' Aumonier said. 'Based on the present pattern, we lose the entire population of the Glitter Band in less than four years. Half the population would have succumbed only seventy days prior to that point. There'd be nothing resembling civilisation left by then. Critical services, from security to life-support management, would have long since collapsed. By some projections the end-point would be crossed when we lose one tenth of the population, in less than three years. Personally I think that's optimistic. Panic would have set in long before that, and far beyond our means to control. We're a tiny dose of order in a body politic on the constant edge of chaos.'

'But it won't come to that, will it?' Thalia asked, looking around those present. 'There are only fifty-four cases at the moment. There'll turn out to be something special about these people, something that predisposes them to . . . whatever this is.'

'If there is,' Baudry said, 'we haven't found it yet.'

'Close the graph,' Aumonier told the analyst, before returning her gaze to Thalia. 'Prefect Dreyfus says you could be valuable to us, Ng. Fast, resourceful and able to make connections.'

'I'd like to help, ma'am, if I'm able.'

'I'm minded to make the best of this regrettable situation.' She continued giving Thalia her long, level look. 'From this moment on, you'll be given probationary upgrade to Field One, along with Pangolin clearance and full access to all materials relating to Wildfire.'

'This is highly unorthodox,' said Baudry.

Aumonier smiled at the woman sitting to her right. 'Orthodox or not, Lillian, it's my decision.'

Tang and the analysts looked down at their work.

Thalia's mouth was dry. She felt obliged to say something. 'Thank you, ma'am.'

'Don't thank me,' Aumonier said curtly. 'I'm about to make your life significantly less pleasant.'

'She'll need a team,' Dreyfus said.

Aumonier nodded. 'And normally I'd assign two deputies to any Field working on a similarly difficult case, but in this instance security considerations remain paramount. She'll have to make do with a single subordinate.'

'Did you have anyone in mind?' Thalia was thinking of the up-and-coming deputies she had scouted in the refectory and training rooms.

'You'll be working with Bancal. I'm demoting him from Field Prefect One to Deputy Field Three, with immediate effect.'

Thalia glanced at Sparver, unsure what to say. Even a mouthed apology seemed insufficient.

37

'Consider it a temporary reduction in rank, Bancal,' Aumonier went on, 'as a disciplinary action. You'll report to Ng and assist her in the investigation. You may retain Pangolin clearance.'

'That's very generous of you,' Sparver said.

'Don't be flippant, Bancal. I expect your full and unswerving cooperation in this investigation. Is that understood?'

Sparver lowered his head, the severity of her reprimand evidently getting through.

'It's understood, ma'am. I apologise for my error.'

'Good – please don't make a second one. I need you ready and able to move on the next death, whenever it happens. In the meantime you can accompany Ng back to the Shiga-Mintz Spindle.'

'To interview the wife?' Thalia asked, giddy at the sudden shift in her rank and responsibilities.

'A little more than that. A short while ago Ghiselin Bronner issued a formal request for protection, over and above the security arrangements of the local constables.'

'Then she knows something,' Dreyfus said, a glimmer of hope cracking through his voice.

Aumonier sounded less hopeful. 'Whatever the case, it's not a request we can afford to ignore. But it has to be handled delicately. We don't want the constables sensing there's anything out of the ordinary, or feeling that their capabilities are in question. We're going to need them on our side in days to come, across the whole Glitter Band, and they mustn't feel undermined.'

'I think I can handle it, ma'am,' Thalia said. 'With Sparver's assistance, of course.'

'You'd better,' Aumonier said. Then she turned to the small, neat Tang. 'Prepare a Pangolin shot for Ng. She can take it immediately so the structures embed as she sleeps. Enjoy your last good night's rest, Ng. When you open your eyes, you'll wake up to our world.'

Thalia remembered how it had felt to hold a man's head. 'I'm already in it, ma'am, and I don't think I like it very much.'

Julius and Caleb were called back to the Shell House in the middle of the morning.

'I know why,' Julius said. 'It's Doctor Stasov.'

'It could be anything,' Caleb said.

'No,' Julius said, asserting himself before his larger, more confident twin. 'I know it's him. After you'd gone off to the white tree I hung around in the house. The door to the private corridor was open and I went down it.'

'And?' Caleb asked.

'I saw Doctor Stasov. He was already here.'

'If this is another one of your stupid stories, like the Ursas . . .'

'I saw him. I walked past a door and there he was, lying on a bed. He was asleep, on his back, with his clothes on and that bag by the side of the bed.'

'Asleep?'

'I wasn't going to wake him up, was I? I could hear Lurcher coming and I didn't want to get caught. But I'm telling you, Spider-fingers is here. How could he be sleeping on a bed if he wasn't here?'

'You just saw some black clothes crumpled up.'

'You'll believe me in a minute,' Julius said. 'Something's going to happen to us today, you'll see. Something to do with the machines he put in us last time.'

The boys crossed the lawn and stood in front of the raised stone terrace which fronted the curved, organic lines of the Shell House. Their mother and father were already standing on the terrace, Father impassive, Mother with that slightly anxious, doubtful look they had been seeing more of lately. Behind them waited Lurcher, a slender tapering silver statue with its four hose-like arms drooping at its side.

Beyond the house, through the green-tinted facets of the dome that enclosed their property, the spires and towers of Chasm City shone like a distant dream.

'The Doctor isn't here,' Caleb whispered.

'There he is,' Julius said.

Doctor Stasov came through the double doors that opened onto the terrace. He had his bag in one hand. It sagged so heavily it almost skirted the ground as he walked, throwing him off-balance.

Caleb gave Julius a look of grudging acknowledgement.

'Stand up straight, both of you,' said Father. 'Show Doctor Stasov how well you've been coming along.'

Stasov brushed a swoop of white hair from his dark eyes. They were pink-rimmed, lacking focus.

'I used to have trouble telling them apart,' Doctor Stasov said, his voice faltering. 'But not so much now. They're growing into distinct young men.'

Even Julius had been aware of the growing differences between them. They had never been identical twins, but when they were smaller they had been easily mistaken for each other. Julius was lagging now, though, Caleb was taller and bulkier and broader across the shoulders and chest. Both had grey-blue eyes, but Caleb's were steelier, and there was something in the set of them that was already more challenging, echoed in the defiant, cocksure set of his jaw.

They wore only shorts. Their knees were smudged, their loose blond hair was dishevelled. Until they were called back to the house by Lurcher they had been scrambling up and down the huge hollow trunk of the white tree, playing games among the mazy warren of its roots and branches.

'Growing too quickly,' Father said. 'A little less time horsing around in the garden, a bit more time in the classroom, wouldn't hurt either of them.'

'They're boys,' said Mother.

'You have struck a healthy balance between education and development,' Doctor Stasov said, giving a diplomatic nod to both parents. Where Doctor Stasov wore black – offset only by a puffed white collar – Mother and Father were dressed in the stiff finery of Chasm City's social elite.

'Do you think they're ready for it?' Father asked.

'I have no doubt, Mister Voi.'

'What about you, Julius and Caleb?' asked Father. 'Do you think you're ready to learn something new?'

The boys answered in a trebly near-unison.

'Yes, Father.'

'Before we begin,' Father said, 'show Doctor Stasov how well you have adapted to the first integration. Clad yourselves. Make plumage.'

Julius and Caleb glanced at each other, neither quite able to supress a smile at the trivial nature of this challenge. They closed their eyes for a moment, more out of habit than necessity, signalling concentration. Then each lowered a hand down the length of their own body. Where their hands passed, patterns of colour and texture condensed out of the air, threads and cross-threads thickening into a widening band of fabric which enclosed each boy in a kind of gown. When the gowns had reached just above their knees the boys lifted their hands away and settled them by their sides, as if waiting inspection.

Their gowns glittered in metallic shades: silver for the bigger boy, gold for the slightly smaller. A gentle breeze moved through the surroundings of the Shell House and the gowns rippled as if they were real.

'Impressive,' Doctor Stasov said, his lips hardly moving as he spoke. Like the clothes he wore he was made up of monochrome contrasts. His skin was an ashen white, his mouth a grey-rimmed hole, his eyes black tunnels. His hair was silver, combed low over his eyes. His fingers were long, bony, pale and seemed to have one or two joints too many.

'Their control's becoming more fluid, both of them,' Father said. 'It's

40

rudimentary as plumage goes, but that will improve with practice.'

'It had better,' Mother said, nodding to the dome wall, the glittering promise of the spires beyond. 'There's a city and a world out there that will expect more of you than parlour tricks. You're Vois now. With that name comes a burden of responsibility.'

'They have time to learn,' Father said, reaching into his pocket – a deep physical pocket, in a physical garment – to draw out a thick, dark rod about as long as his forearm. He held it out before him with just the one hand, the tendons in his wrist taut as bridge cables.

'What is it?' Julius asked.

'Take it and I'll explain.'

Still wearing his plumage, Julius stepped onto the edge of the terrace and took it in both hands. It was heavier than it looked.

Caleb watched.

'It's a malleable staff,' Father said. 'A training device, made from solid quickmatter.'

'What am I supposed to do with it?' Julius asked, conscious of Doctor Stasov peering at him through that curtain of hair like a watcher behind a waterfall.

'Quickmatter will respond to gestural commands,' Father said. 'But that's a coarse, unsophisticated way of controlling it. Fine if you want to make a chair, or open a passwall – but you can do better than that. Your will alone is sufficient.'

'I don't see how,' Julius said.

Father smiled with strained patience. 'Concentrate your attention on the malleable staff. Press your thoughts around it, enclose it within them, and imagine the way it might stretch or bend under the pressure of those thoughts.' He made an encouraging gesture. 'Go on. See if you can make it flex a little.'

Julius stared at the staff, a frown notching its way into his forehead. He let go with his left hand, holding it near the end with the right, as his father had done, and tried to make it bend. But the staff felt dead and inert in his hand. His thoughts dashed off it like waves against a cliff.

'Think only of the staff, and only of bending it,' Father said, lowering his voice encouragingly. 'Doctor Stasov has unlocked the capability in your neural machinery, but you must learn how to direct it.'

Julius stared and stared, but the staff remained obstinately unwilling to change itself.

'Why is it so hard?' he pleaded.

'It won't be, when you've learned,' Father said. 'But quickmatter won't respond to an ill-formed instruction, or a passing whim. It would be far too dangerous if it did.'

'You could do a horrible thing to someone,' Caleb said wonderingly. 'Chop them up or something. Squash them. You wouldn't want that to happen, would you, Julius?'

'Shut up, Caleb,' Julius said. 'You're so clever, you make it bend.' He handed – jabbed, rather – the malleable staff into his brother's hand.

'I told you they weren't ready,' their mother confided. 'We should ask Doctor Stasov to undo the permission, give them more time.'

'You know how awkward it is for the doctor to schedule these appointments,' Father said.

'Julius might need more time,' Caleb said. 'I don't.'

Holding the staff with more confidence than his brother, he stared at it for a few moments, narrowing his eyes but not closing them. The staff stayed as straight as when Father had given it to Julius.

'Could I really hurt someone?' Julius asked, watching his brother's efforts. 'Or get hurt?'

'Not easily,' Father said. 'Quickmatter knows not to do us harm. That's built into it at a very deep level – a kind of morality, like Lurcher's programming. That's why it won't change unless the intention is precisely directed – a skill both of you will have to learn the hard way.'

'Progress, I believe,' Doctor Stasov said.

The change was slight, to begin with, but it was real and could only be the product of Caleb's shaping will. The staff was assuming a gradual curve, and the angle of the deflection was increasing. Caleb's hand shook with the effort of maintaining the neural focus, his eyes nearly crossing as he forced his desire onto the quickmatter.

'Good . . . very good,' Father said. 'Better than I expected, for a first try.'

'It's hard, Father,' Caleb said, the strain making him look older, finding the invisible weaknesses in his face that would eventually turn into folds and wrinkles.

'You've done very well. Give the staff back to your brother. Julius – see if you can straighten the staff. It's sometimes easier to restore something to an earlier state, if you have a clear idea of the desired end.'

Julius took the bent staff and tried to undo Caleb's work. But the staff was as unresponsive as it had been before.

'I can't,' he said, offering the staff back.

'You tried, and that's all we expected for today,' Father said. 'I remember my first time – your mother hers. Don't you, dear?'

Her answer was terse.

'Of course.'

'Days of frustration before the quickmatter moved to our will,' Father went on. 'After that, though, I knew all the doors stood open, and the world was mine for the shaping. Here.' He reached out for the staff. 'I'm a little out of practice – that's the price I pay for living here – but I still have the knack, I think.'

He made the staff straighten out. Then the end pinched itself into a knob, and the knob shaped itself into a tiny human head, with eyes and nose and mouth. For a few seconds Father looked as if he was satisfied with that, before holding the staff up so the head was level with his view of their mother, and he began to shape the head's proportions and features to correspond to hers.

Julius and Caleb looked on, their father's face set with quiet concentration.

The quickmatter moved like clay under an invisible hand, bulging, clefting, gaining lines and texture here, smoothing over there. Whether or not the end result was a close likeness to their mother was almost beside the point; it was certainly recognisable as a woman and aspects of her strong nose and jaw were undeniably captured.

Father twisted the staff around to show her the result.

'You haven't lost your touch,' she said, showing a cool indifference to the performance.

Father pinched his lips, perhaps about to say something before thinking better of it, especially in the presence of Doctor Stasov. He passed the staff back to Caleb. 'See if you can undo my crude efforts,' he said. 'And both of you take an hour a day to learn to shape the staff.'

'We'll try,' Julius said.

Caleb nodded. 'Yes, we'll do our best.' Then he patted Julius on the shoulder, his hand ghosting through the plumage. 'Let's go back to the tree. We can take the staff out into the gardens, can't we?'

Doctor Stasov gave a nod, his hair curtaining down to his nose. 'No harm will come of it. But return to the house before mid-afternoon. I'd like to run some minor tests before I leave.'

The boys started walking away, Caleb swinging the staff low, so that his mother's head swished through the grass. It cost a slight but constant mental effort to maintain the plumage, so the boys gladly discarded their gowns when they were beyond the immediate sight of the house.

'Give me the staff,' Julius said. 'I want to get better at it.'

'You couldn't do it at all. How can you get better at something you can't do?'

'You're not so good. You were straining so hard I thought your eyes were going to pop out.'

Caleb snorted. 'I just put that on for the grown-ups. I sensed the presence of that quickmatter staff long before they brought it out to show us.'

'It's easy to say that now. I don't remember you going on about quickmatter until you saw Spider-fingers was here.'

'I knew it was in the house somewhere. I just didn't think it was worth mentioning. You *could* tell it was here, couldn't you?'

'Yes,' Julius said doubtfully, wondering how far he could push a lie. 'I knew it was in the house somewhere. But you still found it hard.'

'Not as hard as I made it seem. Look.'

With an easy-going nonchalance, Caleb passed the staff back to Julius. Julius held the staff up before him, looking at the little human head and trying to persuade it to undo itself, to collapse back into the smooth form of the original staff. Then he realised the face had changed. It was an ugly, distortion of their mother's head, with demonic eyes and a wide, grinning mouth jammed full of sharp teeth.

Julius started, the shock of it nearly making him drop the staff.

'Don't worry, little brother,' Caleb said. 'You'll get the hang of it eventually.'

By the time Thalia woke, the Pangolin shot had worked its alchemy, modifying neural processing structures that allowed her to read and comprehend material that would normally have been above her classification grade. Pangolin – and the related security protocols – were the closest thing prefects had to neural hardware. But the structures were deliberately self-dissipating, requiring continual booster shots to maintain their functionality. Left to their own devices, the structures would break down under the action of normal body chemistry, their waste products harmlessly absorbed and excreted.

She still woke feeling as if her brain had been through a mangle. The geometry of her apartment felt subtly askew, not quite a mirror of itself, but shifted, and each adjustment was pregnant with vast and ominous meaning. She had been warned about this: one of the side-effects of Pangolin was that ordinary visual structures acquired a heightened semantic weight. Prefects adjusted to it eventually, but the transitional phase could be akin to a religious mania, finding false significance in every wrinkle, every smear of foam in a mug of coffee.

It was the price that had to be paid, though, and at least the security briefings on her compad were now fully legible. She skimmed the executive summaries over coffee and warm buttered bread, then stepped through a clotheswall, the wall forming her uniform around her to her customary preferences, then buckled on her belt and whiphound and set

44

off for the docking bay, where she had been promised her own Medium Enforcement Vehicle.

For a moment she stood at the observation window overlooking the dock. Her hands were tight and sweaty on the handrail below the window. She had been given the promotion she had always counted on, but she had never imagined it happening under these circumstances. And if Sparver's demotion was a temporary thing, so too – she was certain – was her elevation.

'Do not mess this up,' Thalia said under her breath, calling her father's image to mind. 'For both our sakes.'

Panoply's main docking and berthing facility was situated in what was nominally the nose of the pumpkin-faced asteroid. The freefall space was a three-dimensional jigsaw of launch racks, berthing cradles and access tubes, with a frequent coming and going of vehicles, passing through a huge double-doored spacelock. The chamber was not normally pressurised, though, so the spacelock doors were both open, with her assigned MEV already slid out onto its launch rack, aimed at the door like a chambered bullet.

Thalia dried her palms, walked into the pre-boarding area and reported to the dock attendant, a man named Thyssen.

'Field Prefect Ng,' she said crisply, without a smile. 'Requisitioning Medium Enforcement Vehicle Seventeen for immediate deployment. I take it my ship's fuelled and armed?'

'Gone up in the world, I see,' Thyssen said, his world-weary features conveying neither surprise nor interest in her recent promotion. 'Your proficiency level just about clears you for the MEV. Don't mistake that for an expert rating.'

'I wasn't about to.'

'Your ride is ready for departure, Ng. See if you can bring it back without a dent.'

'Deputy Field Prefect Bancal should be here shortly,' she said. 'Send him aboard when he arrives.'

'No need, Ng. Bancal's already aboard.'

Thalia maintained her composure as she made her way along the pressurised docking tube into the waiting ship and forward to the flight deck. Sparver, as she had been forewarned, was already seated in the right-hand pilot's position, an arc of controls sweeping before him, displays and inputs already active.

She regarded him for a few moments, hoping not to sour their new working relationship before it had started.

'You're keen,' she said neutrally.

'I felt I could use some familiarisation time. I'm rated for MEVs, but it's at least a year since I've been in one.'

'I also have the necessary rating.'

Sparver twisted around to meet her eyes. 'Yes, and who's your deputy now?'

'You are,' she answered, with the nagging sense that she was being led into a verbal trap.

'That's correct. And when Dreyfus had his hands on one of these, who did he generally ask to do the actual flying?'

'His deputy.'

'Which tended to be me. I assumed you'd accept the same arrangement, Thal. Operating one of these is mostly automatic, but you do have to keep an eye on things.'

'And I couldn't?' She was trying not to be baited, certain Sparver meant no ill by it, that he had genuinely been thinking of the arrangement that made the best use of her talents. But she had to draw a line now or accept a slow, benign erosion of her status. 'I'm flying, Sparver.'

Sparver gave a very humanlike shrug. 'Of course. Absolutely not an issue. I just thought—'

'We'd do things Dreyfus's way, yes. And that's fine, most of the time.' She eased into the left-hand pilot's position, reaching out to assign the controls to her side, watching as some of the tactile interfaces reshaped themselves from hyperpig to human configuration. 'But at the moment, until I say otherwise, we're doing things the Ng way.'

'That's good,' Sparver said. 'I like the Ng way.'

Vanessa Laur looked up from her work as Dreyfus approached.

'If you've come to complain,' she said, barely bothering to meet his eyes, 'your words will fall on exactly the same deaf ears as last time. And the time before. We operate these Search Turbines for the greater benefit of Panoply, not for your personal convenience. Your queries are scheduled into the task queue just like everyone else's . . .'

'I haven't come to complain, Vanessa.'

Dreyfus eased into the vacant chair next to Laur. She sat at a hooded console, next to a slanted floor-to-ceiling window looking out over the Turbine Hall where the towering data-retrieval machines spun in their glass tubes. A handful of technicians were down in the hall, carrying compads and moving between the tree-sized tubes with expressions of almost monkish servitude. It was as if the tending of the fearsome Turbines was the last and most sacred calling of their lives.

'That's a development. Are you feeling well, Dreyfus?' She reached out and placed a hand on his brow. 'Not feverish, not been working too hard lately?'

He pushed her hand away gently. Internal Prefect Laur had assumed her position as head of Archives shortly after the death of her predecessor, Nestor Trajanova. As far as Dreyfus was aware Laur had never had any contact with Trajanova prior to this assignment, since she had been working in an entirely different section of Panoply, under a separate chain of command. But by some curious osmosis Laur appeared to have gained all of Trajanova's working habits, including a general disdain for anyone who demanded her services without ample justification, and a personal animus reserved specifically for Dreyfus himself, perhaps because he was often in the habit of making vague or poorly constrained information retrieval requests. Dreyfus was forced to tolerate these quirks because Laur had also inherited Trajanova's supreme attention to detail, as well as a deep understanding of the Search Turbine architecture.

'I want you to run the query again,' he said patiently. 'I could push it through myself, but we both know that you're much better at formulating this sort of thing than I am.'

'I've had a lot of practice, with the demands you make on us.'

'Each of us has our part to play, Vanessa,' he said soothingly. 'You're right that the Turbines need to be used fairly and efficiently. That's why I'd rather not clog them up with poorly formed search parameters.'

Something pinched in her face. 'And in what way is running this query going to benefit any of us, when it's come up blank on every previous occasion?'

'There are more dead now. Somewhere in that mass of new information may be the common factor we missed before.'

'There isn't one. We've been over it.'

'It's not a cut-and-dried link I'm after, just a common predisposition. A propensity, you might call it.'

'The one that Ng brought back – case fifty-four – he didn't fit your theory very well, did he?'

'There'll always be outliers, or types of risk we don't recognise at face value. That's why I'd like you to expand the terms of reference this time. I know it'll be costly in terms of search time, which is why I'm not asking lightly.'

'Demanding lightly, you mean.'

His smile grew strained. It was an old, slightly tedious game but they both understood the rules by now. 'Go beyond the obvious this time, Vanessa. I'm interested in an addiction to risk in all its facets, from dangerous sports to serial infidelity to reckless speculation on the stock markets. Can you do that for me?'

She sneered away his question. 'Just for once you might bring me an actual challenge.'

Dreyfus allowed himself a smile. 'You know, there are days when I almost miss Nestor Trajanova. Almost. Do they put something in your coffee, down in Archives?'

Laur grunted something in reply. Blanking him, she turned her full attention to the console. Her nails hammered on keys, shaping the symbolic chains that would direct the Turbines. Dreyfus turned his eyes to the hall, where the technicians still moved. Beneath his feet, the floor thrummed with the powerful threshing of machines.

Aumonier was in the tactical room when the next death happened. It was mid-morning by Panoply time, and they were working through the normal caseload, things unconnected with Wildfire or Devon Garlin. Small-scale polling irregularities, scheduled core upgrades, lockdown reviews, matters of internal discipline and promotion, training and recruitment, material procurement. This was the common grind of Aumonier's work, and she found none of it boring. Eleven years under the scarab had seen to that. She had crushed the very concept of boredom, eradicated it from the range of mental states she was capable of experiencing.

It was the Clockmaker's one gift to her.

A young female analyst was just going over the numbers for new whiphound orders when a chime sounded from the table before her.

'Incoming call request from Chasm City,' the analyst said. 'It's Hestia Del Mar, Supreme Prefect.'

'I thought I told her to call back next week.'

'You did, ma'am,' the analyst said, hesitating. 'And it's next week.'

Aumonier sighed. 'Put her on.'

The analyst closed any tactically sensitive displays on the walls and table, while the Solid Orrery defaulted to its baseline configuration. Hestia Del Mar's face appeared on the wall opposite Aumonier, requiring the prefects and analysts on the other side of the table to swivel around in their high-backed chairs.

'Detective-Marshal Del Mar,' Aumonier said, politely enough but without much warmth. 'How good of you to remember our arrangement.'

'I'm just glad I caught you, Supreme Prefect. For some reason I've been unlucky in the past, always managing to call when you're otherwise engaged.'

48

Aumonier smiled with excessive sweetness. 'Work presses on us both, I'm sure. How may I finally be of help?'

'I thought the terms of my request were already clear, Supreme Prefect. I wish to discuss intelligence-sharing between our two agencies.'

Hestia Del Mar was a curly-haired, broad-faced woman with a humourless demeanour and a severe attachment to her work. It had taken Aumonier a little while to pin down why she found her so intensely irritating.

They were alike.

'We have perfectly workable arrangements already in place, Detective-Marshal. The formal channels have served us well enough in the past, haven't they?'

'As I don't need to remind you, Supreme Prefect, these are different times. Nervous times, I don't mind saying.'

'Oh dear. Is there trouble in Chasm City?'

'There's trouble everywhere, as I don't doubt you're aware. The breakaway movement. Citizen unrest. Heightened tension between the orbital communities and the Ultras. Doubts over the efficacy of Panoply's security provision.'

'Our worries, not yours, I'd say?'

'Instability in the Glitter Band affects all of us, Supreme Prefect. Our trading arrangements go back a century and a half. Can you imagine how concerned we are, with the orbital community threatening to tear itself apart? Yellowstone's economy may be robust, but we're not immune to jitters.'

'If it's just jitters, I'd say we have nothing to fear.'

'Perhaps not now, but who can say what lies ahead? The formal channels are too slow, Supreme Prefect. Our agencies must be able to share intelligence just as speedily as the physical movement of individuals – if not faster.'

Aumonier's face tightened. 'If and when we have need of that sort of intelligence-sharing, Detective-Marshal, I'm sure our respective organisations will rise to the challenge. Unless there's some particular difficulty that I can help you with immediately?'

'I'd hate to put you to any trouble, Supreme Prefect, knowing how busy you are.'

'No trouble at all, Detective-Marshal. How may I be of assistance? Is it about the tax irregularity business you wanted me to look into, the orbital holdings you were concerned about?'

'No, I've given up on that. Perhaps in a year or five, when you aren't so preoccupied, you might be able to spare someone to check on the status of those rocks. But that isn't my highest priority right now.'

Aumonier pushed aside the twinge of guilt that she was undoubtedly meant to feel.

'So what would be, Detective-Marshal?'

'We've lost track of three persons of interest. Three fugitives, connected to a known criminal syndicate. Insurance fraud, insider trading – that sort of thing. They may have used false identities to leave Chasm City.'

Aumonier deployed a sympathetic look. 'How unfortunate for you.'

'It would be useful to us if we could pinpoint their movements and activities while they were off-world. It might give us a lead on their present whereabouts.'

'I must remind you that we don't retain exhaustive records of all citizen movements, Detective-Marshal,' Aumonier said regretfully. 'Under the Common Articles, such information must be discarded after ten years, unless a citizen quorum deems it pertinent to an ongoing enquiry.'

'You're a police officer, Supreme Prefect. We might wear different uniforms and operate under different codes, but at heart we're both upholders of the law.'

'Your point being?'

'You and I both know you wouldn't discard that information without a fight. Panoply has its private archives, doesn't it? Those Search Turbines of yours. Don't tell me you don't keep a backup record of citizen movements, just in case it relates to a breaking case.'

'I am obligated to the Common Articles, Detective-Marshal. Please don't suggest I'd take those obligations lightly. We are the servants of democracy, not its masters.'

'Eloquent words, Supreme Prefect. But you can do me this one favour. See what you have on my fugitives. Any movements, any priors. Their names are as follows—'

There was another chime from the table. The tone was distinctly different this time, though. Aumonier held her composure, even as the atmosphere in the room shifted. As Lillian Baudry looked down at the status update, her face clouded at the arrival of sudden and unwelcome news. Aumonier wondered if Hestia Del Mar noticed the change.

'You must forgive me, Detective-Marshal. A matter of some urgency has just come up.'

'I've waited a whole week, Supreme Prefect. Can you not spare me even a couple of minutes of your precious time?'

'Not personally, Detective-Marshal. I'm sure you understand. Perhaps if you submitted your query through the usual channels?'

'The usual channels have got me precisely nowhere, Supreme Prefect.

My requests are very politely logged, and then very politely ignored. That's why I've tried to go all the way to the top. For all the good it's done me.'

Baudry grimaced, her eyes conveying various shades of bad news.

'You have my apologies, Detective-Marshal. It's just—'

'I know, there's always an "it's just . . ." with you people. One day the tables will turn, you realise, and you'll be the one banging your head against bureaucratic walls.'

Aumonier turned to the young female analyst. 'Jirmal. I'm going to hand this call over to you now. Speak to Detective-Marshal Del Mar and make a note of her requests. Use your discretionary authority to assign resources as appropriate, with a note that you have my backing.' She returned her attention to her opposite number in Chasm City, offering a smile and hoping it might be reciprocated. 'Jirmal will do all she can, within reason, Detective-Marshal. You can't ask for more than that.'

'I still have the feeling I'm being fobbed off, Supreme Prefect,' Hestia Del Mar said, resolutely maintaining her stony expression. 'Still, it's marginally better than the blank indifference I've received so far. I suppose I should count my blessings.'

'We are all trying to do our best,' Aumonier said.

'We are. It's just that some of us are doing a better job of it than others.' The face on the wall vanished as Jirmal continued the conversation on her compad, using earphones to keep the conversation low. Glass privacy baffles rose out of the table, framing Jirmal from either side so there was no chance of the Detective-Marshal picking up any part of the ordinary discussion going on in the tactical room.

After a moment Aumonier swivelled her seat, facing the Solid Orrery at the end of the room, and gave a nod to Lillian Baudry.

'Let me guess.'

'Threshold triggers picked up another Wildfire event,' Baudry said. 'Picture's still firming up, but it looks clear-cut to me.'

The Solid Orrery returned to its prior condition, showing both the breakaway habitats and the fifty-four locations where the Wildfire had struck, the relevant habitats elevated above the Glitter Band on fine glowing threads.

But now a fifty-fifth habitat was rising, oozing upwards, swelling from a pinprick as quickmatter organised itself into a physical representation of the structure. It was a wheel, a cog-shaped world with a hub, spokes and a torus of habitable space wrapped around its rim. Aumonier did not immediately recognise it. Her knowledge of the habitats was exemplary, but there were several hundred that fitted this basic configuration, and dozens in approximately the right orbit.

'What is that place?' she asked.

'Carousel Addison-Lovelace,' said Baudry, heavy-lidded eyes scanning a readout. 'Current status . . . unoccupied.'

'Someone's died there,' Aumonier said. 'That doesn't fit my definition of unoccupied.'

'Just a moment.' Baudry was speed-reading. 'Addison-Lovelace was mothballed twenty years ago, just after the recession of oh-nine. Seems an eco-collapse took hold and they didn't have the capital reserves to fix the problems. The habitat was declared bankrupt, then sold off to asset-strippers. All citizens relocated – only a few thousand – and then the whole place depressurised and cleared for redevelopment.'

'A few thousand isn't many for a place that large,' Aumonier mused, feeling she must be missing something. 'All right – what do we know about the death?'

'It started about twenty-three minutes ago,' Baudry said. 'Triggers flagged a spike in medical queries from the vicinity of Addison-Lovelace.'

Aumonier frowned slightly. 'The vicinity, not the place itself?'

'Construction and reclamation workers, Jane – floating in free space near the wheel, or working on its outside. Something happening to one of the workers – some kind of fit or seizure.'

'Why am I only hearing about it now?'

'It was still ambiguous. It took the other workers some time to get their colleague back into a pressurised shack, which is when the character of the queries shifted and began to strongly correlate with a Wildfire event. Three minutes ago the triggers exceeded the detection threshold.' Baudry drew breath. 'The deceased citizen appears to be one Terzet Friller, no known priors . . .'

As the Senior Prefect spoke, a biographical snapshot began to assemble on the wall. A face, a name, the bare bones of a life. Just another citizen of the Glitter Band, one among a hundred million, some poor soul who until this moment had never been of the slightest interest to either Panoply or Jane Aumonier.

'Run the projections again.'

Next to the face appeared the familiar graph of deaths against time, plotted through with the rising curves of the best-guess mathematical models. Now there were fifty-five data points instead of fifty-four. Aumonier knew the projections off by heart by now, and she was relieved to see the addition of Terzet Friller to the toll of dead did not lead to any significant change in the long-term predictions. Not exactly good news, she thought, but not bad news either.

'I assume the brain will be too cooked to give us much,' she said. 'But

Demikhov ought to get a look at it anyway. Do we have any assets close enough to be useful?'

'Nothing within an hour,' Baudry said, studying a complex, scribble-like plot of operatives, ships, orbits and possible inter-habitat trajectories. 'We can have a Heavy Medical Squad on site within three, if they're tasked and dispatched immediately.'

'Ng's already out there, isn't she?'

Baudry nodded. 'Confirmed on-site at the Shiga-Mintz Spindle as of thirty minutes ago, contact established with local constables, and now making her way to the Bronner residence.'

Aumonier turned to the Solid Orrery. The Shiga-Mintz Spindle and Carousel Addison-Lovelace were in different orbits of the Glitter Band, but by chance both were presently within the same quadrant, on the far side of Yellowstone from Panoply.

'Bancal and Ng already have Pangolin clearance – no sense in involving non-cleared prefects when we already have two cleared assets in the field.'

'We could re-task Ng?' Baudry suggested.

'No,' Aumonier said carefully, balancing priorities. 'Let her collect the widow first, then the victim.' Then she turned back to the analyst, who was just concluding her call with the Detective-Marshal. 'Follow up her request, Jirmal. But when I say use your discretion . . .'

'You want me to assist her, but not at the expense of diverting resources from Wildfire, ma'am.'

'You understand me perfectly,' Aumonier said.

Thalia rubbed her hand along the parapet's pleasingly rough texture, shooing away a dull-eyed pigeon that was in no hurry to leave. They were walking along a balcony that fronted a long row of sleepy, whitewashed residences, built back into the rising slope of an artificial hillside. On the other side of the parapet the land fell away along the curving geometry of the cylinder-shaped habitat, with towns, lakes and woodland dwindling into blue-green haze.

'This is the sort of place my father said he'd like to retire to,' Thalia said to Sparver. 'He said he wanted somewhere where he could practise his watercolours, and it was no use if the view changed every time someone sneezed. I never really understood what he meant back then.'

'And now?'

'I'm starting to get it. Although maybe I'm just getting older.'

'Word to the wise,' Sparver said in a confiding tone. 'Never tell a pig you're feeling old. You won't get much in the way of sympathy, given our average life expectancy.'

'You understand it, though, don't you? I think we're all the same, deep down – all of us in Panoply. We like quiet, stillness, stasis over change. The rest of society's on some sort of headlong rush to explore every possible way of living, and we're the brakes, the anchors, stopping it from whirling out of control. That's what my father understood all those years ago.' She kept sliding her hand along the parapet as they walked, feeling its cool integrity under her skin, not even minding the occasional smear of sun-baked pigeon shit. 'He'd have liked it here – if he'd ever got the chance to retire.'

'Maybe it would have suited him,' Sparver said. 'But I'll say this. It's not the kind of place Dreyfus was hoping to associate with victim fifty-four.'

'It isn't?'

'Look at it, Thal. Nice stone houses, nice stone walls, nice parks and lakes, pleasant weather, everything tidy and respectable and a bit tedious and safe for most tastes.'

'Why would that make a difference?'

'Dreyfus reckons there's a strain of risk-taking among the dead. A propensity, he calls it.'

'And what do you think?'

Sparver walked on thoughtfully. 'I might have believed there was something in it, at least for a while.'

Instinct had Thalia lowering her voice while they spoke of such a sensitive matter. But they were safe enough in the Shiga-Mintz Spindle, where a stone was just a stone and the walls very definitely did not have ears. It was one of the least surveilled habitats in the Glitter Band.

'Might have?' she asked.

'The first case, Cassandra Leng, died while she was playing lava hopscotch in the Colfax Orb. She was a professional gamer; regularly gambled with her own life. Some of the others fit the pattern, too. Not just risk-takers in that sense, but across the field, from con-artists to rash investors, to serial philanderers. The trouble is, where do you draw the line? Breathing's a risk. And some of the dead don't fit the pattern at all.'

'But you think – or thought – that there might have been something in it?'

'Fifty-four was the nail in the coffin, though. We've both seen the background documents, Thal. There's nothing about Antal Bronner that fits Dreyfus's theory. And the fact that he chose to live here, of all places . . .'

'Not the sort of place to suit a risk-taker, is what you're saying?'

'Not unless you have a deep phobia of pigeons.'

They were nearly at the Bronner dwelling. Thalia was surprised not to see a presence outside the home. Upon docking they had liaised with the local constables at the hub, politely declining the offer of an escort to the housing development. They had been told that constables would meet them at the household, where they were providing Ghiselin Bronner with the additional security she had seemed to think necessary.

'We've got the right address, haven't we?' she started saying, just as her bracelet chimed. She touched her throat microphone, said 'Ng,' and listened through her earpiece to the supernumerary analyst on the other end who was relaying orders directly from the tactical room. She acknowledged the call, then closed the link.

'Going to let me in on the secret?' Sparver asked.

'There's been another death. When we've collected Ghiselin Bronner, we're to make a detour on our way back to Panoply and recover the body.'

'Body, not just the head?'

'That's what they told me.'

They stopped at the entrance. The front door was set back into a cool-shaded porch, and the door itself was slightly ajar. Thalia straightened the hem of her tunic, ran a hand across her brow to fuss her hair into shape, then knocked on the door. When no one answered after half a minute she knocked again, then waited the same length of time before glancing at Sparver.

Sparver reached in and pushed at the door. It creaked as it swung wider. When it was halfway open Thalia called into the gloom beyond.

'Constables? Madame Bronner? This is Prefect Ng. The constables at the hub said we'd be expected.'

There was still no answer, so Thalia stepped into the dwelling. A vague unease had her hand moving for her whiphound, but she resisted the impulse to unclip the weapon, not wishing to seem jittery in front of Sparver.

'Ghiselin?' she called out, louder this time, her voice booming back at her from the rounded masonry of the interior. Her eyes were adjusting to the light inside the dwelling, and it was airier than it had seemed only a few minutes earlier. Beyond the reception area where she now stood, arched passageways led off into a series of rounded chambers, cutting back into the hillside.

The reception area was austere in its furnishings and decoration. The walls were a textured white, set with alcoves and projecting ledges, but there were no pictures and only a few minimalist ornaments. Natural daylight came down through ceiling ducts.

She touched her microphone. 'This is Ng. Prefect Bancal and I have entered the Bronner residence, but there's no one to welcome us. Proceeding further.'

They moved from the reception room into an adjoining chamber. It was a sort of lounge or dining room, with stone chairs around a low stone table. Again there were alcoves, containing skeletal white candelabra. A fluted glass vase had toppled onto the table, flowers hanging limply over the table's edge, a puddle of water contained from spreading by its own surface tension. Something was off. The rooms were devoid of clutter or careless ornamentation. The person who lived here would not have allowed that untidy mishap to sit unattended for long.

Thalia directed a wary look at Sparver. Sparver gave a nod, then unclipped his whiphound. He flicked out the filament and spoke softly. 'Rapid search mode. Observe and report only.'

The whiphound nodded its red-eyed head, then slinked through an archway into the next chamber.

They walked on into the next room, while the whiphound moved further into the residence.

'Ghiselin?' Thalia called again, the timbre of her own voice shifting now they were deeper into the property. 'It's Panoply. We've come to talk to you about Antal.'

They moved through a parlour, then a bare room with bedrooms and bathrooms branching off it. The whiphound was just coming out of one of these rooms. It raced further into the property, with nothing yet to report. There were no windows, not once they had moved away from the front of the dwelling, but the ceiling ducts maintained the airy ambience of the earlier rooms.

'There's been a communications screw-up,' Thalia said. 'She must have gone out, and the constables went with her.'

'She left her front door half-open. Who does that, when they've already asked for additional protection?'

The whiphound came back. It halted, keeping its head level, its red eye sweeping back and forth between them.

'It wants us to follow,' Sparver said.

CHAPTER FOUR

It was a public transmission, distributed by expensive if entirely legal means, broadcast across a thousand media fronts. Within a few seconds – the maximum light-travel time for even the most knotted signal routing within the Glitter Band – it would have been seen and heard in a thousand habitats, maybe more.

The face loomed large – in interior mental visualisations, on private screens and private walls, in the gene-tweaked flesh of hands, on the backs of lovers, on the soaring display surfaces of civic plazas and recreation spaces, in the curtaining spray of fountains and waterfalls, lasered onto individual droplets of water. Every channel that was available, and not blocked from displaying this paid transmission, now showed the face.

From the head of curls to the unlined, cherubic features, to the neat vertical nick of a scar under the right eye, it was the face Dreyfus had seen first hand.

'Good people, good citizens,' the face said. 'I won't take your time – we all have lives to be getting on with. Most of us do, at any rate. You know me by now, and if you *don't* yet know me, then I trust we'll consider ourselves friends before very long. I'm Devon Garlin, and there are things they would rather I didn't tell you.' The face flashed a smile, vertical lines bracketing either side of Garlin's mouth. 'They don't trust us, you see. They don't trust us to trust *them* and after the mess they made of things two years ago it's not hard to see why. They've been praying they won't be tested again, knowing full well how lucky they were the first time. But something's in the air, friends.' He lowered his voice confidingly. 'Nothing official yet – and nothing you'll have seen or heard on any of the public nets. But rumours slip through the mesh. Have you heard anything, lately? That there's something building, something they can't stop?'

Dreyfus watched the transmission as it played across one of the walls near the refectory, displayed as a matter of routine simply because it had been identified as a high-reach broadcast, of natural interest to Panoply.

He bristled, sweat prickling under his collar. It was hard not to read a mocking glint in the arctic blue of Garlin's eyes, as if he knew Dreyfus would be listening.

'People are dying,' Garlin said. 'A few dozen so far – a few drops in the ocean. But the numbers are going up and they don't know what's causing it. They're trying very hard not to let this become public knowledge. But word is spreading. Concerned citizens, witnesses, medical personnel; these people won't be silenced just to suit Panoply. And nor should you. As I said, it's all just rumour – for now. Perhaps there's nothing in it, and we can all sleep safely in our beds. But if you hear of a death that happened suddenly, or if you see prefects behaving oddly – going about their business more furtively than usual, if such a thing is possible – then take a moment to ask yourselves this: what's the point of a security organisation that cannot give us protection when we most have need of it?'

Dreyfus became aware of a presence at his side. He glanced away from the transmission. It was Jane Aumonier, hands behind her back, chin lifted, absorbing the words with a look of stoic acceptance. The light from Garlin's face brushed a delicate edge onto her profile. Dreyfus watched her for a few seconds then turned back to the wall. Neither of them spoke as the statement continued.

'Whatever becomes of this worry they'd rather we didn't know about, there is another way. Spurn the false assurances of the prefects, shun the promises they can't keep, the trust they can't uphold, and find a common security outside the hidebound framework of Panoply. Eight habitats have already thrown aside their shackles and discovered that there is life – and security – beyond the old, moribund institutions. More are poised to follow. Soon it will be a flood. The prefects will tell you we're damaging the glorious integrity of the Glitter Band, but that isn't true at all. What the Glitter Band is, and what it could be, are two different things – but to make a better world we first have to take back control of what was always ours.' Garlin extended an open, beckoning hand, and that smile creased his face again. 'Good people, good citizens – join us, and turn your faces to the light.'

The transmission finished, the wall darkening. But Dreyfus could still feel the lingering presence of that face, as if it had imprinted itself on Panoply's very fabric.

'Good people, good citizens,' he said, sneering out the words. 'I'd like to ram those sentiments down—'

'It's an act of provocation,' Aumonier said levelly. 'And we won't allow ourselves to be provoked, will we? We might not like it, but he's broken no rules by issuing this statement.'

'What about inciting public unrest?'

'By saying there are rumours? I'm afraid that's not presently a crime.'

Dreyfus pointed a finger at the now-blank wall. 'How does *he* know? How did Devon Garlin get to be so well informed?'

'I can see where that thought's leading. You are *not* going to put him in the frame as the cause of these incidents.'

Dreyfus waited a moment before answering. 'You can't deny they're working well for him.'

'Making him a lucky opportunist, a man who knows when fate's handed him an advantage. That's all.'

'If you say so.'

'You have a grudge against him – a personal one, after what happened in Stonehollow. Maybe you don't like the thought of the wealth and privilege that spawned him, either. But it's no crime to be born into an influential family. Letting him get under your skin is exactly what he wants, exactly what he's hoping for – prodding us into an over-reaction, making it seem as if he's got us rattled.'

Dreyfus forced himself to nod, seeing the truth in her argument even as his blood boiled against her reasoned, sensible tone. 'I don't like demagogues,' he said.

'So I've heard,' Aumonier said.

Thalia took a careful look at the body. The whiphound had brought them to a fallen constable, slumped on the floor with a stun-truncheon just out of reach of one outstretched hand. The constable was a red-headed woman, wearing mustard-coloured tunic and trousers, only her burgundy armband and equipment belt marking her active assignment to the citizen constabulary.

'She's breathing,' Thalia said. Kneeling now, she shifted the woman's posture into the recovery position, making sure her airway was unobstructed.

Sparver called from the room next door. 'There's another one here, also out cold.'

Thalia brushed the woman's hair from her eyes.

'Signs of injury?'

'No bruising, no sign of a struggle.'

Thalia unclipped her whiphound and deployed its filament. 'Maximum alert,' she said, before touching her throat microphone. 'Ng again. We've found two constables, unconscious but breathing. Looks as if they've been knocked out by something, possibly some sort of anaesthetic weapon. Request immediate assistance, including a Light Medical Squad.'

She listened to the response with a sinking heart. Even with an emergency intervention, no other Panoply unit could be with them for at least two hours, and that was an optimistic estimate.

'They can't wait that long,' she replied. 'See if you can get through to the constables at the hub, and tell them to mobilise local medical services.'

'Thal,' Sparver called. 'You need to see this.'

Knowing she had done all she could for the fallen constable, she pushed up from the ground. 'What?'

'You'd better come. You know how I am with faces.'

Thalia moved towards his voice with trepidation, her whiphound slinking after her. She stepped around the second fallen constable, a shaven-headed neutrois citizen dressed in a yellow gown, with the same belt and burgundy armband as their colleague.

Sparver had already gone through into the next room, where he was standing with his back to her, arms folded while he inspected the scene before him.

'It's Ghiselin Bronner,' Thalia said.

'What I thought. I wouldn't get too close, though, until we know she isn't booby-trapped.'

Ghiselin Bronner was sitting upright in one of her own chairs, facing Sparver and Thalia. She had been tied to the chair by her waist and arms, and her legs had been bound together just above the ankles. She was clothed, wearing a high-collared red dress, but the fabric of the right sleeve had been hacked or torn away to expose her forearm. Fixed to it was an apparatus like an overly ornate wristwatch. She was gagged, her face slumped down into her chest, her eyes closed.

Thalia stepped closer, warily. The woman looked dead, but it was the device attached to her arm that most concerned her. The watch face was a battery of glass vials, arranged in a radial fashion. Little alloy plungers had already pushed out the contents of a couple of them.

'You seen anything like that before, Sparver?' Thalia asked, wondering if it might be a bomb or an anti-tamper device.

Sparver seemed oddly reticent.

'The evidence archive, once or twice.'

'You going to enlighten me?'

'It's a Painflower, an interrogation machine. There's a little clockwork timer in the base, and it delivers escalating doses in sequence.'

'What the hell is such a nasty thing doing here?'

'I almost hate to speculate. It's black market technology, imported from Sky's Edge: home-made torture tech from the murkier fringes of the war. When the Ultras have a score to settle, this is one of their preferred methods.'

There was a little click, and a mechanical buzzing. The third plunger in sequence had begun to depress into its vial. Thalia and Sparver watched, both of them taken aback that the device was still operating.

Ghiselin Bronner jolted awake, her head snapping back as if it had been yanked by a cord. Her arms flexed and tensed and her back arched against the chair. Her eyes bulged. A sound came from her mouth, muffled by the gag. Her head twisted, eyes fixing on Thalia – some wild, terrified acknowledgement flashing between them.

'It's all right,' Thalia said. 'We'll get it off you.' Putting aside any concerns that there might still be a booby-trap, she moved to Bronner's side and loosened the gag. Bronner drew breath, her eyes still meeting Thalia's, and then she gave out a terrible rising moan. Thalia squeezed her hand. 'Sparver. Can we get the Painflower off without making things worse?'

'Depends,' Sparver said. He looked at Thalia, then at the woman, as if unsure how candid he could be. 'Sometimes there's an anti-tamper trigger. A terminal dose.'

Ghiselin Bronner stopped moaning. She breathed in and out, each breath heavier than the last. Then, her jaw clenched tight, she said: 'Get it off me. I don't care.'

Sparver put out a hand and summoned his whiphound. It jumped into his grip, retracting its filament with a clean snap.

'Sword mode,' Sparver said. 'Five-centimetre blade, anaesthetic edge.'

His whiphound pushed out a bright stiff line. He leaned over Bronner. 'I'm going to cut it off. I'll be as careful as I can, but it would still be best if you didn't flinch.'

'Do it,' she said, before biting down on the pain.

Something clattered in the adjoining room. Thalia twisted around. The neutrois citizen in the yellow gown was still exactly where Thalia had stepped over them. She looked back at Sparver, then Bronner.

'He's still here,' Bronner said.

Thalia summoned her whiphound, retracting the filament but holding it in her hand rather than clipping it to her belt. 'Stay with her,' she told Sparver.

'Thal—' Sparver began.

She was already turning, already on her way out of the room, in the direction of the noise. They had already swept this part of the property, she told herself. If there had been someone present besides the constables and Ghiselin Bronner, the whiphounds would have picked up on it.

But something was leaving the room. She saw the ornament they had stumbled against, a larger version of the white candelabra, now lying on the floor. It was skeletal, with a narrow trunk and bony arms supporting spherical candle-holders. The fleeing figure was a human form, but sketched out of mismatched edges and shadows, very nearly invisible except when it moved.

'Stop,' Thalia called out. 'You are under Panoply observance. I have authorisation to use lethal force.'

The figure hesitated, looking back at her – a man-shaped collage of mirrors and prisms. 'Not your problem, Prefect.'

She deployed the whiphound's filament, allowed it to form a traction spool, and then let go. 'Mark and acquire,' she ordered. But the whiphound kept sweeping its head in a scan pattern, trying and failing to lock onto the subject.

Chameleoflage, Thalia realised.

The man must have realised that this was his chance. He moved more quickly now, striding over a low table, ducking under an archway and bounding towards the front door.

'Here,' she said angrily, snatching the whiphound, retracting its filament and snapping it to her belt. Perhaps it would have a better chance at subject acquisition in daylight.

The front door creaked open. Thalia sprinted back through the rooms after the man, skipping over the first fallen constable. By the time she reached the reception area the door was wide open. She bounded out onto the balcony, momentarily dazzled by the brightness of day.

She looked left and right, certain the fleeing man would not have had time to reach either end of the balcony.

But there was something, she realised – a sort of clotted smokiness against the air above the parapet to her left, where there ought only to have been a view of distant rising terrain. She squinted, forcing her eyes to make some sense of the confusing impression. The fleeing man was on the parapet, crouching as he tried to lower himself over the wall, down to the level below.

He was only twenty paces away.

'Stop!' she called again. 'No further warnings! I will use lethal force!'

'Use it, Prefect,' the man called back, lowering further so only his head and upper torso were visible over the parapet.

Thalia jogged after him, re-deploying the whiphound once again. 'Mark and acquire,' she said, but this time holding the handle to concentrate its scan. She felt it twist in her grip, signalling acquisition. But the man was stretching lower, barely any part of him now visible. She hurled the whiphound, shouting 'detain!' as she did, and prayed she had not made matters worse.

The man slipped out of view. The whiphound landed next to the parapet, flicking out its traction spool at the last moment to cushion and orientate itself, and in another instant it was slithering over the wall. Thalia bounded after it.

The man was below, sprawled on the ground, the whiphound wrapping its filament around his legs, taking care to keep the sharpened edge away from any physical contact with its subject. The man was struggling, trying to claw himself along, but his efforts were futile. His chameleoflage outfit was starting to malfunction, blocky areas of it showing the wrong colour and background, so that it looked like a restlessly changing harlequin pattern. He had been wearing a full-length gown, with a narrow-slitted hood drawn tight over a pair of goggles.

'Don't fight it,' she advised. 'I'm coming down to you.'

'Take your time,' a hoarse voice said, a hand touching her wrist gently. 'You can have him later – I understand that he's your concern, not mine. But we do have some unfinished business.'

It was the female constable, the one Thalia had assumed was out cold. Thalia appraised the red-haired woman, looking at her eyes for signs of concussion or a brain bleed and seeing only stubborn focus and an eagerness to be getting on with her duties.

'Do you remember what happened?'

'A man came to the house, forced his way in. After that, nothing.'

'He got to Ghiselin Bronner. She's alive, but in a pretty bad way. I've asked Panoply to alert your people and let them know medical help is needed, but if there's anything you can do to speed things up . . .?'

The woman's hand tightened on the haft of her stun-truncheon. 'What did the bastard do to her?'

'Fixed some interrogation device to her. My deputy's in there trying to get it off.' Thalia nodded over the wall, to the level below. 'But he's our concern now.'

'How is Dane?'

Thalia realised she must mean the other constable. 'Out cold, like you were. But I think he'll be all right.'

The woman gave Thalia a look that was just as long and appraising as the one she had received from Thalia. She nodded slowly. 'All right, Prefect – since you asked nicely. The fucker's yours. I'll make sure the medics are alerted.'

'Thank you . . . what's your name, by the way?'

'Trelon. Take this, Prefect.' Trelon offered Thalia the stun-truncheon, armed now – its blunt end giving off a dancing blue spark and a sharp ozone tang.

Thalia nodded her thanks, took the stun-truncheon, went to the end of the balcony, down the connecting stairs to the lower level, and then backtracked until she reached the man. The whiphound was still holding him.

A handful of citizens had begun to drift out of their homes, gathering along the balcony to see what was happening. They were all keeping a sensible distance from the detained man, and all of them edged briskly aside as Thalia passed, the truncheon crackling in her hand.

'Nothing to see here, citizens,' she said, knowing how little good it would do.

She knelt next to the man, extended her free hand and tugged his cloak looser so she could see more of what was under it. He wore a tight black outfit sewn with many pockets and loops. He was very skinny, young-looking, hairless, and the goggles were jammed so tightly over his eyes they seemed to be part of him.

'Who are you?' she asked, softly at first.

'None of your concern, Prefect.'

'Ultras sent you. What was your interest in Ghiselin Bronner?'

The man bared his teeth, grinning at her. 'What's your interest?'

Thalia considered the stun-truncheon. It felt heavy and dependable in her hand, and she had no doubt it would be an unpleasant thing, to be touched by that dancing, crackling spark.

She set the truncheon aside, then spoke into her collar. 'Ng. I have detained a subject near the Bronner residence. Medical assistance has been requested from local authorities. I'll remain with the subject until Prefect Bancal is available to assist me with moving the subject to our vehicle.' She paused, swallowed, and added: 'Unless there are further instructions, I will continue with my agreed duties when we leave the Shiga-Mintz Spindle.'

She closed the link. The subject wriggled under the whiphound's embrace and the whiphound tightened its hold, its single red eye fixed on him with malevolent intensity.

'You could hurt me, Prefect. Why don't you?'

'Because you want it,' Thalia said.

Aumonier closed the doors to the tactical room and turned to face the gathered prefects and analysts. Almost without thinking she studied their faces and postures for signs of fatigue, looking for anyone who might be pushing themselves past the point of effectiveness. They had all been working harder than usual these recent weeks, as the crisis bit deeper. Red eyes, poor complexions, slack muscle tone and flashes of irritability were almost a given now. What concerned her was the traces of more extreme tiredness, such as forgetfulness, bursts of micro-sleep (however artfully concealed) and a general fading of operational focus, leading to the risk of sub-optimal or even dangerously incorrect decision processes. The older hands, such as Clearmountain and Baudry, were rarely the subject of her interest. They knew their own limits by now, and they also knew it was worse than futile to attempt to match Jane Aumonier's own working patterns. They were not like her. They would never be like her, because they were fortunate enough not to have been through the experience she had.

But it was sometimes necessary to remind others, especially the newer entrants. Some of the truly foolish even tried to put in more hours than Aumonier, always trying to be first in the tactical room when she arrived, and still there when she left. They volunteered for extra duties, put in double shifts, covered for others with a too-eager enthusiasm. They meant well, but it was a short-cut to burn-out and operational ineffectiveness.

Sometimes it only took a quiet word to put them right. 'You're not me,' she would explain to them. 'Be grateful for that, and enjoy your dependence on sleep. It's your brain's chance to break out of linear thought patterns. Even asleep, you're doing useful work for Panoply.'

When that failed to do the trick, when the bags remained under the eyes, she had one other option open to her. She would take them to the 'office', the room she only rarely visited these days, the spherical chamber in an area of Panoply where there was no artificial gravity, and where she had spent every second of those eleven years. She would point to the spot in the middle of the room where she had been obliged to float in weightlessness, safely distant from the walls or any visitors. When people had come to her in the office, they had been required to tie safe-distance tethers to themselves, to prevent them drifting too close.

'I'm the way I am because of what happened in this room,' she would tell them. 'Not because I'm strong, or better than you, or more dedicated to Panoply. Not because I care about the Glitter Band more than you. It's because I'm damaged. Because the thing that happened to me in this room broke my mind, and all the king's horses couldn't put me back together again.'

If they got to that point, then some of them were foolish to think the lesson was over.

It was not.

'I'm going to leave you in here now,' Aumonier would say. 'For twenty-six hours. The room will be dark. You can't touch anything or speak to anyone. No one will visit you. You'll just float here in the middle, alone. I have a feed from your biometric bracelet, though. It will tell me if you are awake or unconscious. If you fall asleep at any point in these twenty-six hours, even for an instant – a bout of micro-sleep, just the barest closing of your eyes – you will be dismissed. There will be no appeal, no disciplinary review. You will leave Panoply.'

If there was a lie in that promise, it was a small one. She never let any of them spend more than thirteen hours in the room. That was enough; more than sufficient to make her point. When she pulled them out, they would always swear that the time had been much longer than a day.

'It wasn't. It was thirteen hours, and you didn't manage to get through that without several episodes of micro-sleep. You're forgiven, though, because you're only human and now you have some idea of what I went through. Only a small idea, though. You endured thirteen hours and if the scarab had been on you you'd have died. I was in there for eight thousand times as long.'

She rarely had trouble with them after that.

'How are we feeling?' she asked the room. 'I want total honesty. Everyone wants to play their part, and that's to be respected. But I'd sooner one of you took a day away from Wildfire now and returned fresh, than end up in a state of nervous collapse where you're no use to me for weeks. Believe me, I respect hard work. But nothing impresses me more than admitting to our own limits, and not being ashamed of them.' She was standing, arms folded across her chest, facing her own empty chair across the table, Dreyfus to the right of it. 'Well, a deafening silence. And yet you all look like death warmed over, except for Tom, who looks like death warmed over twice. In which case I have some news for you all, just in case anyone was starting to think things couldn't get any more complicated. Have you all been briefed on what Ng and Bancal found in Shiga-Mintz?'

The analyst next to Dreyfus glanced up. 'Feeding through on all Pangolin surfaces now, ma'am.'

'I'll spare you the bother of reading.' Aumonier walked around to the left of the table, skirting past the Solid Orrery. 'Ng and Bancal have the Bronner widow, and she's out of immediate danger. But that's only because luck threw us a bone. Ghiselin Bronner was in the middle of being interrogated by an Ultra spy, using a chemical torture device. If Ng and Bancal had got there twenty minutes later, she'd have been dead.'

'A Painflower?' Dreyfus asked, pinching absently at the corner of an eye.

'The interrogation instrument of choice. And it's not supposition that there's Ultra involvement. We have detained the agent.'

'Could we be dealing with a false-flag operative?' asked Senior Prefect Miles Jaffna, squinting through narrow, rectangular glasses at the summary feed appearing before him on the table.

'To stir things up with the Ultras?' Aumonier shook her head crisply as she took her place at the table. 'I'd almost welcome such a transparent gambit, Miles. At least it would fit our previous case history of zero involvement with Ultra elements. But it's no false flag. We've a known profile on the assailant. Theobald Grobno. A small-time dogsbody for the Ultras, a button boy sent in to settle scores and eliminate unwanted competition. Grobno's the real deal and we can backtrack his movements all the way to the Parking Swarm.'

Aumonier thought about the swarm, that ever-shifting cloud of Ultra starships, laying over in the Yellowstone system for trade, repairs or merely the settling of ancient scores. Ultras were human, technically, but their motives were often deeply alien and she never relished any overlap between her business and theirs. Life was complicated enough.

'How the hell did an Ultra assassin get inside Shiga-Mintz?' Dreyfus asked.

'The usual chain of follies. Weak security screening at the hub, a plausible fake biography, some moderately clever implant tampering to help him slip past routine scrutiny. We don't think the equipment came in with him. More than likely a previous operative had stashed the Painflower, the assassin goggles and the chameleoflage cloak at a safe location inside Shiga-Mintz Spindle.'

'Then by association,' said Senior Prefect Mildred Dosso, pushing a loose lock of hair back under a clasp as she spoke, 'we can figure the Ultras for the death of Antal Bronner as well? And by implication the remaining Wildfire cases?'

'Wouldn't that be lovely?' Aumonier said. 'Then all we'd have to concern ourselves with is an implicit declaration of war against one hundred million citizens.'

They all turned to look at the Solid Orrery, with its representation of the Glitter Band and off to one side the tight pollen cloud of the Parking Swarm, lying in a high but not too distant orbit. None of them needed to be reminded of the potential destructive power of the Ultra ships gathered in that swarm, or the tensions that had come to the boil in the past.

'It doesn't fit,' Dreyfus mused aloud. 'Doesn't mesh. Ultras haven't figured in the other deaths. Why now?'

'Perhaps they've only just slipped up,' said Internal Prefect Claudette Saint-Croix.

'If there was a common factor linking these people, some reason for a systematic vendetta, we'd have picked up on it by now,' Dreyfus said. 'Besides, there was never a Painflower associated with the other deaths. Why would they switch from one method to another, just for the sake of the widow?'

'We can't dismiss the connection just because it makes us uncomfortable,' said Miles Jaffna.

'I don't suggest that we do,' Aumonier said. 'But we won't assign undue significance to this incident until we know more about the Bronners. Maybe the widow will tell us something, now she knows how close she came to dying.'

'And the Ultra?' Dreyfus asked.

'Ng and Bancal are still best placed to investigate the Terzet Friller death at Addison-Lovelace. They'll proceed there now, and leave Grobno under whiphound detention at the Shiga-Mintz Spindle. When the Heavy Medical Squad arrive for the widow they can collect Grobno at the same time.'

'I'd like some time with him,' Dreyfus said.

'You'll get it,' Aumonier replied. 'But we'll tread carefully with this one, Tom. I've managed to keep the Ultras on our side for the last two years. I'd rather like to keep things that way.'

Sparver had done well with the whiphound, managing to get the Painflower off Ghiselin Bronner with only a few superficial cuts to show for the process. The local medics were with her now, assessing her condition and dressing the minor wounds and puncture points already inflicted on her by the Ultra device. She was still in a state of shock, eased into a chair in one of the adjoining rooms while the medics fussed around her, clearly excited that they had been caught up in such an unusual incident.

'You've got the man?' the widow asked.

'Yes, he's in our custody now. And under that chameleoflage cloak he's just a weedy boy with a few neural tweaks.' Thalia had been over this once already, but Ghiselin Bronner evidently needed extra reassurance. 'We have the weapon he used on the constables. It was a stun-pistol, very short range and not capable of killing anyone.'

'Are they going to be all right?'

'Dane and Trelon? Yes – they'll get over it. He only wanted to put them to sleep while he dealt with you.' Thalia touched the woman's hand, where it rested on the chair. 'That's where I end up with some awkward questions. According to my deputy—'

'The pig.'

'Yes.' Thalia licked her lips, not really liking what she had heard in the woman's tone. 'According to my deputy, this has all the hallmarks of the Ultras settling a grievance. They couldn't get to you without getting past the constables, but the agent was obviously under orders to use minimum force in the process. You were the only target, in other words. And in light of what happened to your husband—'

'Which I still haven't been told about.'

'There are some aspects of his death which are sensitive.' Thalia was trying to offer sympathy, but the widow's manner was making it hard. 'Let me turn it around, though, if you don't mind. You were the one who requested additional security measures.'

'And look how well that worked.'

'Something must have concerned you, Madame Bronner. You were told that your husband's death was a medical event, yet you immediately reacted as if he'd been killed and you were likely to be next.'

'They got to him, clearly. Why is that a mystery?'

Thalia would have dearly liked to consult with Dreyfus and Aumonier and all the others in the tactical room about how much she could and could not say. But it was on her now, and she supposed making such a call was exactly what it meant to be a Field Prefect. 'We don't think there was any Ultra involvement in your husband's death.'

'An Ultra was just trying to kill me!'

'I need you to be frank with me, Madame Bronner. Ultras don't pick on random citizens for interrogation. Was there some reason that you and your husband might have got on the wrong side of them?'

Ghiselin Bronner raised a hand. 'Please – she's tiring me with these questions.'

A medic and a constable came over to her side, intent on steering her away from the widow. Thalia was about to assert her authority when Sparver intervened, saying in a low voice: 'We'll get our chance with her when the Heavy Medicals arrive. Some new orders just came in from Panoply. We're to head straight to Addison-Lovelace.'

Thalia edged away from the others.

'With the Ultra?'

'No – Lady Jane wants the Heavy Medical Squad to bring him in. Quicker than waiting for us to detour to Addison-Lovelace, knowing we could be there for a good few hours.'

'Typical,' she muttered.

'Is it?'

'Of course. The first time the case opens up into something larger, I'm sidelined.'

'It's just expediency. We could run the prisoner back directly, but then there'd be a delay getting someone to Terzet Friller, and that's just as critical.'

'You think the Ultras will send anyone else, either to silence the first one or have another go at Madame Bronner?'

'Good luck to them if they do, between your whiphound and all the constables that have just showed up. No, they've had their one try and maybe it was enough. For all we know the kid was already relaying information to his superiors when we arrived.'

Thalia did her bit for Panoply-Constable relations by saying thank you and goodbye to all present, taking special pains with Dane and Trelon, assuring them they would be kept fully informed of developments relating to the Ultra. This was only true up to a point, she knew. If the present incident intersected strongly with the Wildfire investigation, then there would be a limit to what could be shared, at least while the emergency was being kept under wraps. But it was good to let the constables know they had been appreciated.

Hindsight was a wonderful thing. A few months ago a general directive had gone out to all prefects to do their best to bolster relations between Panoply and the local constabularies. Thalia had made nothing of it at the time, but knowing what she did now the implications were stark. Panoply was looking ahead to the inevitable point when the number of Wildfire cases became impossible to manage. At best there were a thousand prefects – actually rather fewer who were available for field duty. But the constabularies added up to a potential voluntary citizen militia numbering close to five million, if all were activated and mobilised across all habitats. Still only one in twenty of the entire populace, and that was an optimistic upper estimate, but perhaps enough to make a difference, or at least delay the collapse of all order.

They reached the corvette, at last able to talk as freely as they wished. Inside the ship there was an update from Panoply, a biographical summary of the Ultra, cross-matched from biometric and genetic data sampled by her whiphound and then fed through to the Search Turbines.

'He's only known to us because he screwed up already,' Sparver said. 'Dreyfus is saying it doesn't fit in with what we already know about Wildfire, and I'm inclined to agree.' He was unbuckling his belt and whiphound, stowing them for the duration. 'I'll tell you something else.'

Thalia had half her attention on the flight controls, locking in a rapid crossing to Addison-Lovelace. 'Go on.'

'Far from being an outlier, Antal Bronner has started looking like a clear fit to Dreyfus's theory. What's more risky than getting on the wrong side of the Ultras?'

'Supposition, until we know more.'

Sparver touched his snout. 'Trust your deputy's instincts.'

They undocked, pushed back, cleared the immediate airspace around Shiga-Mintz and then fell onto their course. To save time rounding up her subjects, Thalia called ahead and requested a general gathering of Terzet Friller's colleagues at some location close to the docking hub, regardless of present shift patterns or those applicable at the time of death. She was careful to stress the routine, procedural nature of the interviews, making it clear she was not looking for a culpable party.

'Dreyfus wouldn't have done it that way,' Sparver said, when she had closed the link. 'He'd have kept them stewing. No point letting people know they're off the hook before you've grilled them.'

'When I want your opinion about Dreyfus's way of doing things,' Thalia said, stung, 'I'll be sure to ask for it.'

She checked the console. They were still more than thirty minutes from docking, and she felt she had said all she needed to for the time being. If she said more, something very unwise was likely to slip out of her mouth.

It was going to be an exceedingly long half-hour.

CHAPTER FIVE

Julius could have found his brother the easy way, by querying his location in the consensual information field, but that would have gone against the spirit of their games. Not that they were much given to hide and seek lately. They had grown in the last year, and there were narrow places inside the white tree that it was difficult for Julius to squeeze through, and all but impossible for the larger, beefier Caleb. Beyond that, both boys now accepted that they had much more challenging pursuits available. Nonetheless the tree still formed the focal point of their day's play and education. Julius knew if he could not find his brother in the winding white chambers of the Shell House, the tree was as good a starting place as any.

There was a hollow, sheltered space near the top, reached most easily by shinning up inside the trunk, with room enough for Caleb and Julius to sit in relative comfort and still have a commanding view of their surroundings. Julius saw Caleb's feet and legs dangling down into the trunk before he saw the rest of him.

'Do you ever think of the other place?' Julius asked, heaving himself up by his elbows and squeezing onto the natural shelf that formed a kind of seat. 'I had a dream about it last night.'

'I keep telling you, no one's interested in your stupid dreams.'

'I was looking out of a window, and it was all stormy and yellow outside. Another boy was trying to tell me something important. It was something to do with the Ursas and why they were there. I didn't really understand what he meant, but I knew I had to tell you as well.'

'I've come up with a new game for us,' Caleb said, affecting bored indifference.

'Don't you ever have dreams like that?'

'Shut up and listen. I've made some animals for us to hunt.'

'I don't want to hunt animals.'

'They aren't real.' Caleb pinched Julius's arm, a little too hard for it to be brotherly teasing. 'They're just illusions, like plumage. I can see them wandering around, moving through the trees and gardens. Lions, tigers, some deer and rhino. Maybe an elephant if I can be bothered.'

Julius sniffed uninterestedly. 'I can't see them, and I've just walked through the gardens.' He had a certain intuition about where Caleb's ideas and games tended to lead, and it was usually some form of unpleasantness.

'You can't see them yet because you haven't given me permission. It's more serious than plumage. Everyone knows what plumage is, and where you expect to find it. These are different. Now, do you remember Father talking to us about symbolic consent?' Caleb nodded encouragingly. 'Yes?'

'I suppose,' Julius said again. Idly he traced his fingers over the area of the tree's dead interior where they had taken turns to assert their names, over and over again, using knives stolen from the household.

I AM JULIUS
I AM CALEB
I AM JULIUS
I AM CALEB

'It works like this,' Caleb said. 'I shape an image with my plumage, something simple but definite. Look at my hand, brother, not those stupid scratches.'

Julius looked. Caleb had his hand open, his palm to the sky – to the dome, rather – above the tree. Floating just over his palm was a yellow star, one of the jester-faced ones that Caleb liked to make when he juggled.

'Now what?' Julius asked.

'You reach out and take the symbol. I'll permit it. The act itself gives me authority to modify your perceptual field, within agreed constraints. In simple terms, it just means you'll see and hear the same animals I do. Smell them too, if they're close enough.'

'Can't we just look at the animals, instead of hunting them?'

'If that's what you want, of course. But you have to see them first, don't you?'

Tentatively Julius reached out for the yellow star. His fist closed around its insubstantiality. But his skin prickled at something, almost as if he had squeezed an electrically charged soap bubble, and when he moved the star from Caleb's open palm to his own, it was hard to shake the sense that a physical transaction had taken place.

Symbols appeared in Julius's vision. The exact pattern of them was unfamiliar, but he had already learned how to navigate and select options. Now he was being given a range of time variables, which determined how long the symbolic consent would remain in play. One hour, thirteen hours, twenty-six hours, a week, and so on – with the option to specify his own time limit or set it according to flexible conditions.

Julius knew that Caleb would expect him to be timid at this point, to choose the weakest setting.

'Twenty-six hours,' he said.

'Very good,' Caleb said, sounding more impressed than Julius had expected. 'I didn't think—'

'Just show me the animals, all right? Because I bet I can shape better ones than you.'

Caleb grinned. 'I'd be happy to see you try. But it'll take you longer than you think.'

'I don't know. I think I'm getting better at visual shaping than you. You're better with quickmatter, but then you never let me get enough practise with the malleable staff. Is it because you're worried I might turn out to be better with that as well?'

'Let's go hunt,' Caleb said.

Even Julius had to admit the animals were something of a triumph on Caleb's part. Whatever crudities he had been expecting, the actuality was much more lifelike and detailed than he would have been prepared to give his brother credit for.

Caleb stayed coy about exactly how many animals he had set loose in the grounds of the Shell House, but it had to be twenty or more. Each animal was a ghost, imprinted on their vision by neural interfaces tapping into the visual processing system of their brains. But the ghosts all had goals and routines of their own, carefully matched to the likely characteristics of the real animals, and as far as Julius could tell the hunter-prey relationships were convincingly replicated. The tigers stalked alone; the indolent lions hunted in packs; the deer moved in ever-nervous herds, responsive to the tiniest gesture or shift in their environment. What the animals did not do was predate on each other, but their mock interactions were sufficient to create a complex, dynamic system of movements, an emergent whole that was undoubtedly richer than any of Caleb's base-level algorithms.

It helped that the Shell House grounds were easily large enough for such games. The enclosing dome – the limit of Julius and Caleb's world – was three kilometres across, with a circumference of more than nine kilometres. The Shell House only took up a small area under the middle of the dome, with the rest of the space given over to the gardens and woods. Paths radiated out from the forecourt of the house, connected by circular crosswalks, but the formality of the grounds only extended a kilometre out from the house, with the remaining parts becoming increasingly wild and rambling, including pockets of dense woodland. Twenty or more ghost animals were easily lost in that expanse, so there was no danger of Caleb's game being over too soon.

'They won't go near the house, that's all I know,' Caleb said. 'And even if they did, Mother and Father wouldn't be able to see them, nor would Doctor Stasov, if he was dropping by.'

'You haven't given them permission, but how do you know they can't see them anyway?'

'I set the rules, not them,' Caleb said.

They came across a tiger first of all, creeping its way through foliage with complete obliviousness to their presence. Julius pointed and whispered, mesmerised by the huge and beautiful form. Caleb said there was no need for stealth: he had set up the animals' algorithms so they had no awareness of their human watchers. 'I could make them respond to us,' he mused aloud, as if the idea was new. 'Hunt us, even, or flee from us. It wouldn't need much of a change in their routines.'

Julius's heart sank. Caleb already had something laid out in his head, some grand plan stretching weeks or months into the future, for which Julius would be no more than a component, willing or otherwise.

'Isn't it just enough to make the animals?' he asked, knowing the reaction his question was likely to provoke.

'That's your problem – always satisfied with what you've got. Here. See if you can shoot the tiger.'

Caleb had passed Julius the malleable staff. He had shaped it into the form of a hunting rifle, with a stock, a pair of long barrels and a stub of a trigger. Julius took it dubiously, knowing it would be forced on him one way or another. Deciding it was better to go along with his brother than argue about it, he settled the stock against his shoulder and sighted along the barrel. The tiger was still passing behind the foliage, its form broken into a near-abstract pattern of moving stripes, hard to correlate into a single creature. Julius aimed the rifle at what he thought was the tiger's middle, and squeezed the trigger stub.

The rifle made a loud bang and a line of fire struck out from the barrel. The tiger roared and slumped into the foliage, taken down with a single shot.

Julius passed the rifle back to his brother. 'If you expect me to be impressed that you put the bang and the flash into my head . . .' he started, but the words dried up on his lips. The fact was that Caleb had impressed him. Julius felt as if he had killed the tiger; as if there had been more than just a symbolic function to the quickmatter rifle.

'Let's see what else we can kill,' Caleb said.

Dreyfus waited until he had confirmation that the Heavy Medical Squad had departed the Shiga-Mintz Spindle with both the Bronner widow and the Ultra agent. He slept for three hours, waking ten minutes before the ship was due in, splashed cold tea down his throat, then washed and clothed himself before making his way down to the docking bay.

Ghiselin Bronner had been kept in a separate part of the ship, unaware of the other passenger, and the squad had the good sense to off-load her first. Dreyfus made a point of meeting her as soon as she was through the airlock. She looked older and thinner than the biographical images he had already seen, more than could be accounted for by the strain of the last couple of days.

'Thank you for your cooperation in coming here,' he said, adopting a suitably deferential tone. 'It's appreciated, especially after your ordeal, and coming so soon after the loss of your husband. You had every right to expect better protection.'

'Your operative seemed to imply I was lucky to have been helped at all.'

'My operative?' Dreyfus asked mildly, determined to keep things civil.

'The girl.'

Dreyfus smiled tightly. 'I'm sure she meant well by it. We were certainly fortunate to reach you when we did. I'm glad we did, and glad we got that device off you before it inflicted any more discomfort.'

'Discomfort? That's what you call it?'

'It was an Ultra device, and an Ultra agent was sent to deploy it. That's unusual, Madame Bronner – wouldn't you agree?'

'Is it? You tell me.'

'As a rule, they restrict their vendettas to other Ultras, or those among us who have business dealings that intersect with their own. Yet you attracted their attention. Can you think of a reason why?'

'Have you considered mistaken identity?'

'I'd be rash not to, and it's always a possibility. But after your husband died, you seemed to fear for your own safety.'

'My husband was murdered.'

'Antal died, but we don't know that it was murder. I can also say it's highly unlikely there was Ultra involvement.'

'You can stand there and say that, after what happened to me?'

'Things aren't always as they seem, Madame Bronner.'

She gave him a long, appraising look. 'It's true what they're saying.

Panoply isn't serving us any more. It's been failing us for years. Perhaps we'd all be better off without you after all.'

'The beauty of a free and open society,' Dreyfus said, 'is that we're allowed to hold differing views.'

'I want to speak to Antal.'

'I can't permit it for the moment, I'm afraid – not until I'm certain there's no risk of evidential cross-contamination. Rest assured that you'll be looked after.'

He nodded at the prefects who were already waiting to escort Madame Bronner away from the dock. He was happy to let them handle the questioning. He had formed his opinion of her and did not expect to be proved wrong. She would trip herself up sooner or later, probably sooner, and it would not take his expertise to provoke her into a mistake.

It was the other guest that interested Dreyfus.

He waited until Madame Bronner had cleared the area, then had the Ultra brought to a windowless cell close to the docking area. They sat opposite each other, the Ultra under restraint, Dreyfus with his hands on the table, measuring up the shifty, guileless individual opposite him.

'Let's cut to the chase, Theobald. We know your employment history. You're a low-status button boy, operating out of the Parking Swarm. You're not reliable enough to be trusted with the big fish, but someone like Madame Bronner, she's right up your street. Do you have anything to say?'

Grobno lifted his chin in cocksure defiance. 'What would you like me to say?'

'Tell me why you killed Antal Bronner.'

'That wasn't me.'

'Really? The husband dies, and a little while later we find you with a fatal interrogation device strapped to his widow?' Dreyfus made a pained expression. 'You expect me not to draw the obvious conclusion?'

'I didn't do it.'

Dreyfus took out his whiphound and placed it on the table before him, rolling the handle back and forth so that it made a heavy rumbling sound. 'I'll be honest with you. I've got better things to be dealing with than this. I know you'd rather face justice in the Parking Swarm, where you have friends and handlers who'll look out for you—'

'No,' Grobno said. 'Not there.'

Dreyfus feigned surprise. 'You'd rather submit to our justice? I can't promise there'd be any grounds for leniency, Theobald. Even if you could persuade me that you had nothing to do with Antal Bronner's death, you *were* trying to kill his widow . . . although I suppose one could make the case that you'd have removed the Painflower if Prefect Ng hadn't disturbed you.'

Grobno leaned as far forward as his restraints would permit. 'I didn't kill the husband. I don't know what happened to him, just that it wasn't our doing. But given what the two of them were involved with—'

Dreyfus cut across him. 'Which was?'

'You haven't found out for yourselves?'

'Assume there are still some unanswered questions.' Dreyfus kept rolling the whiphound. 'It'll help your case, Theobald. I'll stress that you were cooperative, and state my belief that you had no intention of murdering Ghiselin Bronner.'

'Is that a promise?'

Dreyfus nodded. 'You have my word.'

'They were swindlers, both of them. The Bronners set themselves up as private brokers. They dealt with Ultras, acted as intermediaries for richer clients. Did it all at second- or third-hand, never needed to go near the Parking Swarm. Specialising in rare art goods from out-system. That worked for a while, only then the Bronners got greedy. Realised they could just as easily buy and sell to the Ultras alone.'

'How would that work?'

'By lying. Making up fake histories, fake provenances. Buy from one crew, inflate the value of an artefact, and then sell it back to another crew. Keep the margins small, not draw too much attention to what they were up to. Never deal with the same crews twice.'

'But eventually . . .?'

'They got found out. By then they had a lot of crews lined up to get back their losses. When Antal Bronner died, it looked like a hit – another crew making a move. Everyone assumed the widow would be next. So I was sent in to get to her first. Nail her down, squeeze her for information on hidden assets, lists of clients . . .'

Dreyfus put the whiphound away. 'That's helpful to me, thank you. We'll dig into the widow's finances – run a deep audit. I don't suppose there's any point in asking who sent you?'

Grobno slumped, as if some vital energy had just drained out of him.

'I've told you everything I know.'

'I suspect you have, Theobald.' Dreyfus stood from the table. 'It's unfortunate for you that you got snagged up in something much bigger than a simple grudge over a pair of small-time brokers.'

'What will happen to me now?'

'You'll remain here for the time being. Once I've debriefed the other prefects, there'll be a decision about how to proceed with you. Generally

78

in these matters – matters to do with Ultras, I mean – they tend to follow my recommendations.'

'Then you'll say that I shouldn't go back, won't you? You were right, Prefect Dreyfus. I'm nothing to them – just a button boy. And now I've let them down . . .'

'You don't fancy submitting yourself to their mercy.' Dreyfus put on a sympathetic look. 'Well, I don't blame you for that. Ultra justice can be a bit of a lottery.'

'Then you'll keep to your word, won't you? You won't send me back.'

'I said I'd stress that you were cooperative,' Dreyfus answered. 'I never said who I'd be stressing it to.'

He left the room.

As they completed their approach, Thalia got her first good view of Carousel Addison-Lovelace. It was an eight-spoked cogwheel, two kilometres in diameter, the rim of the wheel only a few hundred metres in cross-section, the outer surface pebbledashed in a continuous dark strip of compacted asteroidal rubble. The walls of the wheel were windowless, blank except for the occasional radiator or service port. Whatever went on in there was safe from prying eyes.

The spokes met at a circular hub, the main docking and utility core for the wheel. There were lights on, windows lit and ample evidence of ongoing activity. A dozen or so ships were already docked, clustered tight like a huddle of skyscrapers. They were construction and cargo haulers: ugly, utilitarian affairs, their skeletal frames wrapped around a gristle of engines, fuel tanks and freight modules.

A vacant port lay near the middle of the concentration.

'This will be tight,' Thalia said, using manual thruster control to synchronise the corvette's axial spin with the habitat.

'You want some help?'

'No, thank you.'

Outside, the hulls of the cargo transports began to slide by, seemingly close enough to touch. An anti-collision caution alarm sounded. Thalia silenced it contemptuously, thinking it was just being over-cautious, then had to apply a pulse of corrective thrust as one of the hulls loomed in without warning.

'Rotation's off-centre,' Sparver said.

'I noticed.'

She had it down now, anticipating the fore-and-aft movement of the surrounding hulls caused by the oddly lopsided spin. A few moments later the corvette clamped on with its nose lock, then extended safety bracing to the surrounding ships. Thalia sent a routine message back to Panoply, confirming their arrival, then floated to the stores locker to buckle on her whiphound.

Sparver was at the suitwall, waiting to go through.

'No need,' Thalia said. 'Suits will only slow us down, and we can't very well conduct interviews while wearing them. The hub's pressurised and we shouldn't need to go any deeper into the habitat. Unless you have other ideas?'

'I'm at your disposal,' Sparver said, moving to the normal lock.

Thalia eyed him, picking up a note of insubordination in his answer, then pushed on ahead, cycling through to the reception area on the other side.

It was a grubby, cluttered place, stuffed with boxes and half-abandoned equipment. About three dozen workers were waiting for them in the near-weightless area, stationed at odd angles and wearing a colourful motley of space suit components. Many of their suits had been decorated with customised paint jobs and welded-on refinements.

The workers had their helmets off, and some of them had undone their gloves, stretching their fingers and rubbing ointment into tired joints. Male, female, neutrois, a range of ages and ethnicities, but all with the same hardness in the eyes, all with the same look of lean, leathery toughness. Scars, grafts, prosthetics – a toll of damage earned, accepted, shrugged off as a necessary precondition of the work.

The place smelled of oil and old sweat.

'I am Prefect Ng,' she said. 'This is Prefect Bancal. Thank you for gathering here ahead of our arrival. Is everyone now present?'

'This is the lot of us,' said a lean man with a taut, angular face, lavishly cobwebbed in tattoos. 'You think one of us had it in for Terzet?'

'What is your name, sir?' she asked.

'Virac. Slater Virac.'

'Well, Mister Virac, I don't think any of you were responsible for Terzet Friller's death. But it happened under unusual circumstances, and the nature of that death is of interest to Panoply.'

Slater Virac gave a sceptical look to one of his colleagues. 'Someone caring about us? That's a first.'

'I'd like to know as much as you can tell me about Terzet Friller. Were they a good worker?'

Virac shrugged inside his suit. 'Enough to depend on. But it's not as if they'd been working on the team for years and years.'

Thalia nodded. 'How long, exactly?'

'About a year, I'd say,' answered a woman sitting behind Virac. 'A little longer.' She had a lazy drawl and a glittering green multifaceted artificial eye, jammed into her socket like a fat jewel. Her helmet, cradled in her hands, had a beaked protuberance which made it look like a turtle's head. 'Terzet and I worked together quite a lot. They cut a few corners now and then, but they were still someone you could trust.'

'And you are?' Thalia asked.

'Brig. Been on the squad about two years. I was a Skyjack before, but the pay's better here.'

'Maybe not the working conditions, or the life expectancy,' said a deep, raw-throated voice from the back of the room. 'But if I wanted a quiet life, guess I'd have signed up as a prefect.'

'Yes, it's a bed of roses, being a prefect,' Thalia said. 'Where is the body now?'

'Next door,' Brig said. She was doing something to her helmet, touching up an area of the artwork with a fine stylus. 'Nothing we could do. That suit looked old to me, just waiting to go wrong. I kept telling Terzet to get it overhauled. You take enough chances out here as it is, no sense in not being able to depend on your suit.'

'What do you think went wrong?' Thalia asked.

'What it looked like, Prefect. Thermal control stopped working. Cooked Terzet like meat in an oven. Nothing pretty about it, either. Hope you've got strong stomachs . . .'

'We'll worry about our stomachs.' Her tone turned colder, more formal. 'Show us to the body, please.'

'Anyone want to draw the short one?' asked Virac.

'I'll do it,' Brig said, snapping her stylus away into a sort of paintbox.

Thalia and Sparver followed Brig into an adjoining room that was sealed off by a pressure bulkhead. A long, rectangular equipment container had been converted into a makeshift mortuary slab. Terzet Friller's spacesuited form was resting on the container, strapped down to prevent it drifting loose.

The bulkhead door had closed behind them. Thalia moved around the body, taking it in without comment. The suit was just as motley and colourful as the ones the others had been wearing, but Thalia did not think it looked significantly older or in less good repair. Maybe a few more dents, a few indications of parts being swapped or crudely repaired, but nothing that marked it out for imminent failure.

'Was there any warning, Brig? Did they feel unwell, strange, anything like that?'

'We never heard any warning. That was part of the problem, though. The comms were always dropping out.'

'Generally, or with this suit?'

'Both, but especially with Terzet's equipment. Some loose circuit somewhere in that helmet, got worse and worse over time. Not that it mattered, mostly. We had our work assignments, and a lot of it didn't depend on communication.'

Thalia thought of Terzet Friller experiencing the first warning signs of Wildfire, and being unable to call for help. What had happened to Antal Bronner was bad enough, but at least he had been surrounded by other people, able to communicate his distress even if no one could help him. But to be stuck in the iron bottle of a spacesuit, denied even the solace of one's cries being heard . . .

'Did they have enemies, that you knew about?' Thalia asked.

'Look, I'll be honest with you. We were on friendly terms, but no more than that. Even when Terzet was on the slab, getting worked on, I was the one who had to keep the conversation going.'

'The slab?' Sparver asked.

'I get it,' Thalia said. 'You were the one who painted all these spacesuits.'

'You don't have to be too good to get this gig. Chirchik was the artist everyone used, until she got caught in the transfer wheel when it started moving. Because I cleaned up after her I got to inherit her paints and brushes.'

'You're not so bad,' Thalia said, thinking of her father's watercolours.

'Nothing too hard about it. They tell you what they want, you paint it for them. Chirchik left a book of designs. Most of the time they pick something from the book and you stencil it on.'

Thalia surveyed the artwork decorating Terzet Friller's spacesuit, trying to find some common theme or sudden insight into their character. But there were too many disparate images for her to make easy sense of them. Burning skulls, flaming ships, clusters of stars and comets, other spacesuited figures, sketchy representations of artificial worlds and their interiors. An island with a single bony white tree, its angular branches holding white fruit.

She supposed the art commemorated earlier assignments, hard-won jobs and fallen comrades.

'We'll need to remove the helmet,' Sparver said.

'Go ahead,' Brig said, sounding unsurprised.

The neck seal had been only loosely reconnected. Thalia snapped it wide, then tugged the helmet slowly back from the neck ring.

Although she had been preparing herself, the shock was still consider-able. It was an acrid melange of spoilt meat, waste food, urine and sweat, left to mingle and amplify in the equivalent of a pressure cooker, for what smelled like weeks rather than hours.

She tightened her lips, hoping her natural revulsion did not show too strongly. 'Did you ever hear of this sort of thermal overload before, Brig?'

'Once or twice, maybe.'

Thalia set the helmet aside on a friction surface. They could all see Terzet Friller's head now. It was pale and puffed out, like a piece of bread crudely shaped to look like a person. Blood had burst from the nose, eyes, mouth and ears, and crusted dry. The mouth was open, the swollen features lending the corpse a sordid, cherubic appearance.

Thalia turned to Brig. 'Would you mind leaving us for a short while?'

'No, I don't mind – not that I understand why the death of one of us is such a big deal.'

'I appreciate your cooperation. We'll only need a few moments alone.'

She waited until Brig had left the room and closed the door behind her.

'Friller's too far gone to be of any immediate use to Doctor Demikhov,' Thalia said.

'But he'll still want to open the head up,' Sparver said.

'What's he hoping to learn? There's nothing in there but boiled meat.'

'You can be the one to tell Demikhov he isn't going to get some evidence to poke at. Even if there's nothing he can get from the implants, he'll want to verify that it fits the pattern of the other deaths.'

'Just as long as we don't have to sit with that body next to us, all the way back to Panoply.'

Thalia put the helmet back on the body, then followed Sparver through into the reception area. The workers were already looking restless and impatient. Brig was in the middle of a heated discussion with three others, voices rising to the point where it seemed a fight might break out at any instant.

'I know this may seem like an over-reaction, but Prefect Bancal and I will need to take Terzet Friller back with us to Panoply. You have my word that the body will be treated with respect and returned to you in good time.'

'You can take the body,' Virac said dismissively. 'But the suit stays with us. Tell them, Brig.'

'How it works around here,' she said. 'Your suit is your credit. It's how you pay your way onto the squad, move shifts around, trade up to better equipment. Friller was in deep with the collective. We all own a piece of that suit.'

'You said it was in bad repair,' Thalia told her.

'It was – is. But we'll cut it up, divide our share of it.' Brig knuckled the alloy shin of her own suit. 'Can always use replacement parts. Cut 'em out, weld 'em in. The tradition is you keep the artwork as it is. That way you're always carrying a piece of someone else's life.'

Thalia nodded. 'I understand, and I've no wish to disrespect your traditions. Can you assist me in removing the body from the suit? Prefect Bancal will go back to the ship for a forensic body bag.'

'If you don't need the suit, why does the body interest you?' Virac asked, narrowing his eyes suspiciously.

But Brig said: 'She's just trying to do her job.'

While Sparver went back for the body bag, Thalia, Brig, Virac and two other workers helped her remove the suit. It came apart at a number of seams but the process was still exactly as unpleasant as Thalia had expected. The hardest part, though, was fielding the continuing series of questions from Virac and his colleagues.

'We've heard about those rumours,' one of them said. 'That there's something building, something you can't stamp out. This wouldn't be about that, would it?'

'I wouldn't put too much stock in rumours, if I were you,' Thalia said, with crisp politeness.

'Then there's nothing in what that man says?' Brig asked.

'Which man?' Thalia replied, trying to sound only mildly interested in the answer.

'Nice try,' Virac said.

Sparver came back just as they divested Friller of the final parts of the spacesuit, now laid out like painted trophies on the gripping surface of an adjoining pallet. Thalia and Sparver slid the body into the bag, sealed it, made their farewells, and went back to the ship. They stowed the body in one of the evidence compartments, then signalled Panoply and announced their imminent return.

Thalia took the corvette's controls, detached from the dock and backed slowly out of the way of the other parked ships. As soon as the nose was clear of any obstructions she tapped the steering jets and applied cruise power, thinking she would be very glad when that bagged-up body was no longer her immediate responsibility.

'You handled that well,' Sparver said. 'I'd have come down with the weight of the law, insisted we take what we asked for. But sometimes the gentle touch works wonders.'

'It's called diplomacy. You never know when we might want those people on our side again.'

'Demikhov won't complain, anyway. He wouldn't have given a second glance at the suit in his hurry to cut open some bone. At least they all get to keep a part of Friller now.'

Thalia applied emergency reverse thrust, both of them straining forward in their couches.

'Did I miss something?' Sparver asked.

'No.' She turned the corvette around, and aimed it back at the eight-spoked wheel. 'But I think I might have.'

Vanessa Laur raised an indifferent eyebrow as Dreyfus approached, soft-shuffling along the humming floor.

'Come to quibble over my analysis?'

'No,' Dreyfus said. 'I was coming to thank you for expediting that search as quickly as you did. Unfortunately the numbers still aren't large enough to produce a convincing correlation. I'm going to ask something more of you.'

'And there was me thinking you'd come all the way down here just to thank me.'

Niceties over with, Dreyfus settled his features into a businesslike mask. It was a relief to be back on familiar terms: at least they both knew where they stood.

'You have access to all new case files as they come in. Friller is the latest, but we can expect a new one within the next twenty-six hours or so. Continue looking for risk factors, and keep updating that likelihood parameter. That's the easy part.'

'Oh, good.'

'In parallel with that, assuming the risk propensity is a common factor, I want you to give me an estimate of how many more cases might be out there. Healthy, happy citizens, just walking around unawares, completely oblivious to the fact that their heads may be about to explode.'

'You've got to be kidding, Dreyfus. This is a castle built on sand, and now you want to build another one on top of it?'

'Whatever metaphor suits you, Vanessa. All I want is your best guess for how many non-affected citizens might fit the same profile. If there are a thousand potential victims out there, I need to know. Ten thousand, one hundred thousand, however many it is. That way we can begin to draw up appropriate plans.'

'And if it's more than that?'

'Then forget making plans. We'll be busy enough digging graves.'

When he was done with Laur he went to the refectory, grabbed an apple, and made his way to the tactical room, polishing the apple on his thigh as he walked. He pushed through the doors to find Aumonier and the usual retinue of seniors and analysts present. One of the analysts was reading solemnly from a list of technical procurement delays and cost overruns, his voice taking on a chantlike drone as he recounted each item.

Aumonier seemed glad of the interruption. 'Tom, good. Come in. It's about time we discussed the Grobno problem.'

Dreyfus eased into his customary seat, to the right of Aumonier and between Clearmountain and the dour-faced analyst who had just been interrupted.

'Actually,' he said, 'I don't regard it as a problem – more of an opportunity.' He crunched on the apple, ignoring the frowns from some of the less experienced operatives. 'Antal Bronner was a genuine instance of death by Wildfire, but to Grobno's employers it looked like a hit by a rival squad of Ultras, trying to get their own back on the Bronners. They assumed Ghiselin Bronner was next, so they sent Grobno in to squeeze her for secrets before the others got to her.'

'That hardly exonerates Grobno,' said Clearmountain.

'I'm not saying it does – just that pushing him through our judicial apparatus would be a waste of time and resources we'd be better off directing at Wildfire.'

'So we just let him go?' Clearmountain asked.

'He'll get his day in court,' Dreyfus said. 'Do you remember Seraphim, my friend in the swarm? All right, friend might be stretching it. But the Harbourmaster and I have depended on each other before and I feel I can trust him. 'He's given me his categoric assurance that Grobno will receive a fair and open hearing once he's returned to the Ultras.'

'A fair and open hearing where Ultras are concerned?' Clearmountain asked, looking around with a cynical smile.

Dreyfus took a final crunch from his apple and allowed the browning core to drop to his feet, where it was detected and quickly absorbed into the floor. 'Two years ago we depended on the Ultras for help. Nothing's changed since then.'

'No,' Ingvar Tench said, 'other than a complete shift in the public mood, the undermining of confidence in our authority and a growing mistrust of foreign elements like the Ultras.'

'Fortunately the public don't make our day-to-day decisions for us,' Dreyfus said drily. 'The Ultras are here to trade – everything else is incidental. If they harmed the Glitter Band, they'd be cutting off one of their main avenues to profit.' He paused, directing his address at Aumonier, sensing this was his one chance to make a persuasive case. 'I think we all agree that hard times may lie ahead, be it Wildfire or the breakaway crisis. Under these circumstances we may well end up depending on the Ultras again – perhaps more so than last time. Even the smallest gesture of trust that we can offer them now may be vital. Seraphim agrees.'

'He's hardly a disinterested witness,' Aumonier said.

Dreyfus conceded her point with a slow, dutiful nod. 'All the same, he and I have kept open channels of communication since the Aurora affair. I wouldn't want to spoil that good work.'

'Then your proposal is . . .?' she asked.

'I'll take Grobno back to the Parking Swarm – hand him over personally. It won't take me long, and I'm due a visit to Hospice Idlewild anyway.'

There was a silence from the gathered prefects and analysts. Even Dreyfus's bluntest critics knew better than to comment on his business at the Hospice.

'I would be glad to wash my hands of Grobno,' Aumonier said. 'And you're right about relations with the Ultras. I don't like their ideas of justice, but I'd sooner have them on my side than against it. And if you were going to visit the Hospice – as of course you must – then the proximity of the Parking Swarm would save a second round-trip. From a perspective of self-interest, I'd like to minimise the time you're away from Panoply.'

'I'm glad I can be of use,' Dreyfus said, already rising from the table.

CHAPTER SIX

Most of the workers had dispersed back to their work assignments by the time Thalia and Sparver returned to Carousel Addison-Lovelace. Less than a dozen were still in the meeting area, loafing around in their motley spacesuits, making idle conversation as they carried out minor repairs or finished some desultory game of cards or dice.

'I thought we'd seen the last of you,' said a deep-voiced man. He had a prominent, motile brow ridge, as if there were a tube of well-exercised muscle above his eyes. Two plastic lines curved up from under his chin and went into his nostrils. 'You got what you came for, didn't you?'

'Who are you?' she asked.

'I'm Mallion Ross.'

'Very good, Mister Ross. Do me a favour and call Brig back.'

Ross scooped up his helmet, jammed it on loosely and spoke in a low voice, evidently using the workers' private communications channel. Thalia crossed her arms and waited patiently. A few more workers packed in their games and went back to their duties.

'Any time you feel like telling me . . .' Sparver whispered.

Ten minutes passed and Brig returned, looking flustered and prickly about being summoned back so soon. She set her beak-faced helmet aside and fixed Thalia with a wordless, quizzical stare, green light flaring off her jewelled eye.

'I'd like to see the suit again,' Thalia said.

'We explained. You don't get to keep the suit. It's our property now, not yours.'

'Let me clarify something,' Sparver said. 'My colleague was being very reasonable with you earlier. She could have taken the suit there and then. But she decided to be nice about it, and now she's asking nicely again.'

'I don't care how nice she's being. The suit stays here.'

Sparver's hand moved to his whiphound, releasing it from its holster. 'Maybe you don't know what a Panoply enforcement action looks like.'

Thalia touched his wrist. 'I said I'd like to see the suit again, Brig. That's exactly what I meant. I want to look at it, not take it away.'

'Why would you want—'

'I'd go along with her,' Sparver said, making an ill-tempered show of snapping his whiphound back into place.

They went back into the adjoining room, Thalia nodding at Brig to seal the door behind them. As far as she could tell nothing had changed since they were last here, with the suit parts still laid out on the tractive surface, arranged in the rough anatomical order of the original suit.

Thalia picked up one of the larger pieces of detachable plating. It was a curved piece which fitted across the abdomen, tucked under the contoured breastplate of the life-support system.

'Did you paint these scenes?'

'I painted whatever was asked of me. Does that make me a suspect, now?'

'Ease off. I'm just trying to get a better insight into Terzet Friller's state of mind, their identity and preoccupations. From what I can gather you wear your achievements on these suits.'

'It's no crime.'

Thalia sketched a finger across a scene from the middle of the plate. 'This landscape, this island with this strange white tree rising from the middle of it. Was that yours?'

'What if it was?'

Thalia was starting to think that perhaps the whiphound was not such a bad idea after all. But she forced composure upon herself. 'Did Friller explain the significance of this image? Was it related to something they'd been involved with in the past?'

'Why would you latch onto that?'

'Brig,' Sparver said, a warning rumble in his voice. 'The general idea is that we ask the questions, you answer them.'

Brig drew breath and sighed. After some considerable internal struggle something eased in her face. Perhaps she was beginning to realise the futility of putting up this non-cooperative front.

'When you came back and said you wanted to get at the suit, I thought you were figuring one of us for sabotage.'

'No,' Thalia said. 'But there's something in this artwork that bothers me. The white tree . . . whatever it is.'

'It's not a tree,' Brig said.

'Are you going to enlighten us?' Sparver asked.

Again Brig seemed to wage a private war with herself before answering. 'Terzet got onto this job for a reason. It was plain to all of us. We were here because the reclamation contract pays well, not because we were in any hurry to spend time in this place.'

'And Friller?' Thalia asked.

'Money drew the rest of us here,' Brig said. 'But that wasn't why Terzet came – least, I don't think so. I don't think money was the problem. They never said much about their past, but you can tell when someone's slumming it, living below their means. Every now and then the mask slips.'

'And what was behind the mask?' Sparver asked.

'Someone wealthy – or someone who'd had wealth, not so long ago. The way they spoke, the places they'd been – you could tell. Also, Terzet had some sort of unfinished business to do with this place.'

'They'd been here before?' Sparver asked.

'I don't know. Maybe. Whatever it was, it didn't sit well with the rest of us. People like Virac, or Ross – I know what makes them tick. Same with me. Risking our necks here is the means to an end – not the end itself. But none of us were sure about Terzet.'

'You said it isn't a tree,' Thalia said.

'It's a place. A building. Here, in one of the chambers we've been clearing out.'

'I'd like you to take us to it,' Thalia said.

'It's just a building. Why has that caught your eye?'

'Because I thought I'd seen it before,' Thalia said. 'I wasn't sure, and I needed a second look. But now I'm certain.'

Sparver looked on, his expression giving nothing away.

Dreyfus signed for a cutter, secured his prisoner in the only other seat, then locked in his destination as the Parking Swarm. The ship turned away from Panoply's pumpkin face, acceleration building smoothly as Dreyfus applied power.

'You're a lying smear of shit, Prefect.'

Dreyfus rewarded his passenger with an easy-going smile. 'I didn't lie, Grobno. I said I'd speak up for you.'

'You say you care about justice. You have no idea what—'

'I have every idea,' Dreyfus said, cutting him off gently. 'I've seen Ultra justice at first hand, and I know how cruel it can be.'

'Then you're a monster, if you know—'

'I don't know,' Dreyfus mused. 'I'd rather go with pragmatist. Why are you so concerned about Ultra justice, anyway, Grobno? Aren't they your people?'

'You don't understand them. Don't understand *us*. It won't be a fair trial.'

Dreyfus made a sympathetic face. 'That's too bad. Fairness is all you deserve, especially after the fair way you treated Ghiselin Bronner.'

'I didn't kill her.'

'You were giving it a good go when my operatives interrupted you.'

'I had a job to do. She wasn't going to die. I was going to take the Painflower off her before—'

'There. You've got your defence all lined up. What are you worried about? You'll sail through.'

'Bastard. I got caught, all right? That's what you don't do. You never get caught. They'll get to me, punish me for making them look bad. You don't realise . . .'

Dreyfus tuned him out, letting Grobno ramble on. He was still at it when the Swarm came within visual range. '. . . and I'll make you regret promising me what you did, lying to my face. You think you can get away with that sort of thing, but you're wrong. I've got friends as well. They'll—'

'Cheer up, Grobno – you're missing the view.'

Through the cutter's forward windows, the Parking Swarm was a tight-packed ball of ships about a hundred kilometres across. Compared to the stately, regimented orbits of the Glitter Band, it appeared chaotic – but there was order here as well, just not as obvious to the eye. Near the middle, where the ships were packed the most densely, was the dark kernel of the central servicing facility, a habitat-sized space station in its own right. Shuttles and taxis buzzed about, flitting between the facility, the parked ships, and the wider environment beyond the Swarm. Movement of the larger interstellar vehicles was much rarer: whole days or weeks might go by without a departure or arrival. When Ultras came to trade with Yellowstone, they often measured their stopovers in months or even years, using the time to perform long-delayed repairs or upgrades to their battered, time-worn vessels.

The Swarm was not quite lawless, but it was certainly a law unto itself. Panoply's technical reach encompassed even this volume of space, but the effectiveness of its authority here was at best debatable. In the past, prefects had paid the ultimate price for presuming they had immunity from harm within the Swarm.

Dreyfus had almost made that mistake himself. But now he took manual control and brought the cutter to a polite standstill, a few kilometres from the outer margin. He kept the cutter's weapons sheathed and waited for the sweep of a traffic radar to confirm he had been noticed.

He flicked a control on the console. 'Harbourmaster Seraphim? It's Dreyfus. I came as agreed. Might I have approach permission?'

A few more minutes passed before he had the luxury of a response.

'Dreyfus,' said the voice buzzing from his console. 'As good as your word, as ever.'

'I find it helps.'

'You've brought the package?'

Dreyfus shot Grobno a glance. 'Yes. The package is sitting right next to me. We've had a merry old time.'

There was a silence. The cutter's life-support system gave out a faint hush of white noise, broken only by the occasional chirp from the proximity sensors on the console.

'Bring him in,' Seraphim said.

They had met before, and communicated on many occasions, but that did not make the Harbourmaster any less strange in Dreyfus's eyes. It was a strangeness tempered only by the knowledge that there were much odder varieties of human form among the Ultras, some of which stretched the definition of human to breaking point.

'Not quite the goodwill ambassador we might have chosen, in these strained times,' Seraphim observed, nodding at Grobno. 'I trust you'll accept that our mutual friend was conducting his business in an entirely unofficial capacity?'

'If it's that or war, I know which I'd rather,' Dreyfus said.

They were facing each other in a plush-lined reception room, deep inside the central servicing facility. Displays set into the walls showed cycling views of a dense, needle-like thicket of ships. Grobno was secured and scowling in a corner, an improvised gag providing a welcome end to his interjections.

'War?' asked Seraphim, addressing Dreyfus from a huge, surgical-support chair, currently performing some sort of blood transfusion on its occupant.

'You allow your people to go around murdering innocent civilians in the Glitter Band, don't be too surprised when it gets interpreted as an official policy. Things are tense enough as it is.'

'Yes, I'm aware of your recent difficulties,' Serephim said, voice buzzing from the metal grille which replaced his mouth. His head was small, the skin stretched tight over bony angles and contours. A tail of hair, carefully braided, hung down over his left shoulder. 'Breakaway movements, dark rumours of a developing emergency. Quite a bit on your plate. How's the tea?'

'I'll take it over whatever you're pumping into yourself.' Dreyfus sipped at the concoction that had been provided, doing his best not to pinch his features in distaste. 'And I won't take up any more of your time than

I need to. Grobno's dirt. But having gone to the trouble of bringing him here, I expect him to receive a fair trial.'

'They won't look kindly on him, Dreyfus. It's bad enough to go meddling in Glitter Band business. But to go meddling and *fail . . .*'

'Yes, a double black mark. But what I said stands. He didn't kill Antal Bronner, and I'm minded to think he meant to leave Ghiselin alive. The constables were stunned, when he could have killed them.' Dreyfus directed a telling glance at the gagged Grobno. 'He showed restraint. I expect there to be restraint in his trial. You'll see to that for me, won't you, Seraphim? I'm serious.'

'If I didn't think you were serious,' Seraphim said, 'you would not be enjoying our hospitality.' He paused to adjust a surgical line running into his arm. 'Rest assured that your generous opinion of him will be . . . noted.'

'Good – I'll be watching developments. While I'm here, too, you can set my mind at ease over a related matter.'

'By all means.'

'You knew about Ghiselin and Antal Bronner. I'm going to give you five other names.'

'Continue.'

'Cassandra Leng. Edouard Gresnick. Della de Marinus. Simon Morago. Terzet Friller.' Dreyfus paused and took a slip of paper from his uniform, passing it to Seraphim.

Seraphim looked doubtfully at the list.

'They're just names, Dreyfus.'

'All I want from you is categoric assurance that none of these people are or were the subjects of any particular vendettas or grudges known to you or your Ultra associates.'

'Then these people . . . one may presume . . . are now dead?'

'Very,' Dreyfus said.

'I guarantee the safety of the ships and crews inside the Parking Swarm,' Seraphim answered. 'I am not responsible for the individual actions of those crews.' Beneath him the chair hummed and gurgled as hidden pumps pushed fluid around. 'But I will make enquiries. *If* actions have happened . . . actions that violate our own system of ethics . . .'

'You have ethics now?'

'I wouldn't take such a combative tone – not when you come begging favours.' Seraphim cocked his head, studying him from a slightly different angle. 'You seem a very troubled man – more than usual, if that was possible.'

'It comes with the times,' Dreyfus said.

*

While Sparver prepared the suits, Thalia used the corvette's communications suite to call back to the Shiga-Mintz Spindle. The Heavy Medical Squad had left the Bronner residence when they brought Grobno and the widow back to Panoply, but a small forensic team was still on-site, completing a thorough sweep of the house.

'Prefect Boniface?' she said, recognising the face on the display. 'This is Ng. I was at the Bronner residence before the medicals came in. I have a slightly unusual request.'

Boniface was indoors, gowned technicians working behind her. 'How may I help, Prefect Ng?'

'Slip your goggles on, then send the feed through to me. I'd like you to go through to the first or second room from the front of the dwelling. Assuming nothing's been disturbed since I was inside, there's something I'd like to show my deputy.'

'Just a moment.' Boniface took out her goggles, fiddled with a setting, then pushed them over her eyes. After a second the scene switched to Boniface's point of view. 'Are you getting this, Prefect Ng?'

'Very clearly.' Thalia looked over her shoulder, suddenly aware Sparver was watching. 'Go through, please, and pan around to the shelves or alcoves or whatever you find in those rooms.'

'What am I looking for?'

'Keep going. I'll know when I see it.'

Sparver murmured: 'And with luck, so will I.'

She twisted round to meet his eyes. 'I saw what I thought was a white tree, on Friller's suit. Brig says it's a building, and I believe her. But I knew I'd seen that form somewhere else, and recently. It was in the Bronner residence.'

'A white tree?' Sparver asked.

'No.' Thalia leaned closer to the console. 'Hold that angle, please, Prefect Boniface.'

'It's a candle-holder,' Boniface said. 'There are others like it, now you mention it. I didn't pay much attention to them before.'

'Nor did I,' Thalia said. 'I just put it down to the Bronners' taste in minimalist decor.'

'And now?' Boniface asked.

Thalia glanced back at Sparver. 'Well? Do you agree that there's a similarity?'

'It *could* be coincidence.'

'It's more than that. You saw what was on Friller's suit. A skeletal white tree, with a narrow trunk and branches holding some sort of weird white fruit. And now this. A skeletal white candelabra, with the candle-holders

94

like white spheres. It's a symbolic connection between two of the Wildfire cases – the first we've seen.'

'Maybe there's something in it,' Sparver allowed.

Thalia turned back to the console. 'Thank you, Prefect Boniface. Can you bag and tag those candelabra, please, and have them brought back to Panoply under an evidential docket?'

'You really think there's a connection,' Sparver said, when she had closed the call.

'Maybe it's nothing. But now I'm more determined than ever to have a look at the building inside the rim.'

Suited up, they returned inside and met Brig in the reception area, her beak-nosed helmet now clamped down over her neck ring. She waved them through a short warren of rooms and corridors until they reached one of the functioning spoke elevators. Brig made sure they were properly orientated, feet hooked into stirrups on what would become the floor as they travelled out to the rim from the weightless hub.

It only took a minute. The elevator shot up the spoke, then broke through into the enclosed volume of the rim, descending – or so it then felt – through a vertical glass tube that stretched from the rim's ceiling to its floor level. Thalia couldn't see much beyond the glass, only the vague, dreamlike impression of a darkened landscape, stretching and curving away.

'Tell me what you know about the building,' Thalia said on the suit-to-suit channel.

'Just that it's there,' Brig said. 'There are eight partitions around the rim, and we were all assigned different jobs. I didn't ever work in chamber two, and that suited me fine. I don't believe in ghosts, or bad spirits. But they still couldn't have paid me enough to spend long in that place. '

'What was so bad about it?' Sparver asked.

'I don't suppose either of you remember what it was like before the Eighty. There wasn't much you couldn't do in the Glitter Band, or down on Yellowstone. But then things changed. They tightened the laws, made lots of things illegal. Most places buckled under and accepted the new restrictions. But not all of them.'

'Like this one?' Thalia asked.

'Trick was to stay just the right side of the new regulations, while bending every rule as far as it would go. All those things you couldn't do elsewhere, those services you couldn't buy, those experiments no one could run – they could still do them here, if they paid well enough. It was all still legal – just. What went on here – you can't call them crimes, exactly. But they were against *something*, and things like that leave a stain on a place. A sort of spiritual blemish – like a bad atmosphere. Are you superstitious, Prefect?'

'Not at all,' Thalia said.

'Then you haven't been around long enough,' Brig said.

The elevator arrived. They stepped out, climbed a short pedestrian ramp, then stood in the barely lit silence of the chamber. A few service lights glimmered from the ceiling, just enough to throw a dismal, twilight pall over the surroundings. Thalia allowed her eyes to adjust to what light was available through her visor, slowly taking in the size and shape of the interior space. Bulkhead walls blocked her view in either direction around the rim's curvature, each about half a kilometre away.

'Wasn't it wasteful to dump all the air that was in this place?' she asked, noting the hard vacuum reading on her visor display.

'We didn't,' Brig said. 'This is chamber one. Behind us – that way – is chamber eight. That's the one we're using as a reservoir, holding all the air and water we pumped out of the other seven. Easier to work in vacuum, especially if you have to replace parts of the outer skin.'

'Does anyone still live here, apart from the reclamation crew?' Thalia asked.

'No; this place was abandoned thirty years ago – left to rot, more or less. Biome collapse, trophic cascades, oxygen balance gone haywire, the whole works. No one had deep enough pockets to fix it after the main sponsors cleared out.' Brig was going ahead, leading them along a raised path heading in the direction of the end wall separating chambers one and two. 'Economy's different now. Makes more sense to clean out and re-invest in a place like this, rather than build a new habitat from scratch. Not complaining – works for me. And there's no one left here, apart from us and a handful of robots we haven't flushed out yet.'

Thalia bristled, but kept her voice level. 'Robots?'

'Oh, just some old monitoring servitors, still convinced they've got a job to do. Get under our feet now and then, but they're harmless enough. You don't have a problem with robots, do you?'

'Why would I?'

'Just asking,' Brig said.

The path was raised on stilts, meandering across a kind of glassy, solidified mudflat that was cracked like old varnish. The ground level was about three metres under the close-fitting planks of the path. Spiking out of the mudflat were the brittle remains of old vegetation, shock-frozen reeds and bulrushes. The mudflat had very clearly been a lake bed, with buildings dotted around it on their own islands.

'What happened to the people who lived here?' Thalia asked.

'There weren't as many as you'd think,' Brig said. 'Just a few thousand, across the whole habitat.'

'That's hardly anything, for a place this large,' Sparver said. 'I'd have expected a few hundred thousand, half a million, easily.'

'This wasn't ever a place where people came to live. Ordinary folk – if you can call them that – visited, made use of the services, and left.' Brig pointed ahead, to where a spider-legged thing had scuttled up onto the walkway. 'That's one of the robots. It's detected us and noted our presence. That's all they do. If I had a gun I'd shoot it.'

Thalia regarded the robot. Previous encounters had given her a profound mistrust of such machines, but the spider-legged thing presented no obvious threat. It really was just an eye on a set of spindly, many-jointed legs, its unblinking lens staring back at her with a dumb reptile vigilance.

'Tell me more about these services,' she said.

'People think everything's possible somewhere in the Glitter Band,' Brig said. 'Really, though, that's never been the case. There've always been limits, safeguards – usually for good reason.'

'You're preaching to the choir,' Sparver said.

'Then you know what I mean. People don't like being told what they can and can't do.'

'Do you think Terzet Friller might have been one of those ordinary folk?' Thalia asked. 'Someone who came here, made use of whatever it is they do here . . . and then came back because of unfinished business?'

'Like I said, Terzet wasn't all that keen to talk about themself. I'll ask again, Prefect – the same thing the others wanted to know. Why are you so damned interested in a single death on a reclamation project?'

'Would you rather we didn't care?' Sparver asked.

'It's not that. But we all know there aren't many of you to go around. So when you do take an interest there's a good reason for it. Usually to do with something bigger than a single death.'

'One unexplained death on our watch is one too many,' Sparver said.

'I wish I believed that, Prefect,' Brig said. 'And I wish you believed it, too.'

Ahead of them was another of the spindle, single-eyed robots. It watched for a few seconds than scuttled into darkness. Thalia felt a shiver of unease run down her spine, and told herself to snap out of it.

'Unidentified vehicle,' said a female Mendicant's voice – calm but with an undercurrent of authority. 'You are on a fast vector for our docking pole. You are of course welcome to visit our facility, but we would strongly encourage you to decelerate, disclose your identity, and clarify the purpose of your approach.'

'Sister,' he answered. 'It's Tom Dreyfus. Normally I come by civilian shuttle, but I happened to have Panoply business nearby. I apologise for the fast approach and the lack of a transponder signal – but I imagine you know why I'm here. Would you happen to have a docking slot available for me?'

The answer was a little while coming, as if the Mendicant on traffic duty needed to speak to someone in a senior position before giving her assent. 'Yes, of course, Prefect Dreyfus. You should find a number of open docking slots. Make use of whichever one suits, and there'll be a welcoming party waiting for you on the other side of the lock.'

'Thank you, Sister.'

Hospice Idlewild was a makeshift sort of place, but scrupulously well tended. It went back quite a way. The Mendicants had made it by joining together a pair of diamond hulls discarded by Ultras, fusing the cone-shaped forms at their wide end and lining the interior with rubble mined from Marco's Eye. The habitat's nearest pointed end, bristling with docking ports and servicing structures, loomed large. There were many ships parked there, some much larger than the cutter, but Dreyfus had no trouble finding somewhere to dock.

He released himself from the seat, but for a moment he did not leave the little ship. Dread and hope battled within him. It was still possible to go back. He could feign some emergency call from Panoply, and no one would be any the wiser.

Except, of course, Dreyfus himself.

Dreyfus left the ship. He pulled himself through the docking connector using the built-in rungs. Two Mendicants, a young man and an older woman, were waiting for him. Both wore the long-hemmed black vestments of their order, with wimples over their heads and metal snowflakes chained around their necks. The young man had an earnest, eager look. Dreyfus had never seen him before, but he nodded his recognition at the woman.

'Sister Catherine – it's good to see you. I'm sorry it's been a little while since my last visit, but these last three months . . .'

Catherine had a long, grave face and a down-curved mouth which did not lend itself to jocularity. 'More like nine months, Tom – unless my recollection is flawed.'

'It can't be that long,' he said, before trailing off, certain as he could be that Sister Catherine had no reason to exaggerate.

'You've been busy. These are difficult times.' If there was forgiveness in that answer, it was sparing of warmth. 'You won't have met Brother Sebastien – he only joined us half a year ago. And the Mendicant you spoke to from your ship was also unacquainted with you.' Sister Catherine beckoned him forward. 'Come. We'll say no more of it. I know these visits weigh heavily on you.'

The Mendicants led him along a series of laddered shafts, gradually moving further away from the habitat's central axis. Eventually there was enough gravity to make walking practical. Sister Catherine threw open a door and daylight blasted through. They stepped into the green-carpeted core of the world, a line of artificial sunlight spearing it from end to end. Paths ambled away in various directions, some of them sloping quite steeply. 'Watch your footing,' Sister Catherine warned. 'There was a mud washout here a few weeks ago and we still haven't shored up all the paths. The stones tend to end up further down the valley, and it's back-breaking work bringing them up again.'

'There are never enough of you,' Dreyfus said.

'We're always open to volunteers,' Sister Catherine said. She had a walking stick, jabbing it into the descending ground as if impaling a snake.

'One line of work's enough for me, Sister.'

'We're busier than usual,' Brother Sebastien said, speaking for the first time. 'A ship came in – a high number of sleepers needing our care. They'd had some sort of problem with their shields. We'll help those we're able to, of course. Many will be able to go on to a normal life in the Glitter Band. But not all who remain with us in Hospice Idlewild are able to offer much practical support for the community.'

'Valery has always been a blessing to us,' Sister Catherine said, as if Brother Sebastien's words might have been misconstrued. 'She tends the flowers with great care and affection.'

'It takes more than flowerbeds to keep a world running,' Dreyfus said.

'We know, Tom,' Sister Catherine said. 'But we do what we can.'

There were no trams or monorails in Hospice Idlewild, merely the paths, few of which were large enough to qualify as roads. They spidered off in all directions, up and over the ceiling of the world, meandering through swathes of forest, linking the clearings where the Mendicants had established white-walled hamlets, clinics, convalescent lodges and schools for those in their care. Occasionally here were rockfaces and waterfalls, some of them upside down, but none so large or impressive enough to stir any sense of the sublime. The overall effect was more one of a world-enclosing miniature garden, with every aspect selected for the maximum impression of harmony and tranquillity.

Nothing about the habitat had any sort of soothing influence on Dreyfus. The personal ties were too raw for that.

The path levelled out and they walked past an open-air clinic where black-clad Mendicants were working with a dozen or so white-gowned patients, helping them with walking exercises and simple games to improve hand-to-eye coordination.

'The recent arrivals?' Dreyfus asked.

'No, far too soon for them,' Brother Sebastien said, lowering his voice as they moved into earshot. 'These came into our care just before I joined. Mild to severe revival amnesia, with some locomotor deficits. But they are responding well to the therapies, and I expect most will leave us within the month.'

'Incomers, or economic frozen?'

'Another ship,' Sister Catherine said. 'In from Fand. Nothing wrong with it, this time – just the usual statistical sample of bad-luck cases. Put twenty thousand sleepers on a starship, and a few dozen will come out of the holds with their memories gone, or worse.'

Dreyfus watched a female Mendicant offer some spoken encouragement to a young woman with a heart-shaped face and dark eyes. They were tossing a black ball to and fro. The young woman smiled something back, perhaps no more than a single word of acknowledgement, but enough to put a twist in his guts.

'It's kind of you to do what you can for them.'

'They would find a similar quality of care elsewhere in the system,' Sister Catherine said. 'Perhaps a little better than what we can offer. But what we do, we do without expectation of payment. No one is in debt to us, or indentured into our service. That is not always the case beyond the Hospice.'

'I don't doubt you.'

'Besides, there is a sort of insurance in what we do. Our methods may be simple, but they are robust. If some terrible thing were to happen to the rest of the Glitter Band, the ships would not stop coming. That would take decades.' Sister Catherine paused to open a small white picket gate that led from one part of the clinic to another. 'Who would care for the sick and needy then?'

'Do you think terrible times are coming?' Dreyfus asked.

She stepped through the gate and jabbed down her walking stick. 'I think it is best to be prepared, wouldn't you agree?'

Beyond the picket fence was a short path bordered by stunted trees, and beyond that was a U-shaped enclosure of low, white buildings with thick walls and rough-edged windows and doors. The buildings were arranged around a patch of dry, sun-dappled ground set with chairs and tables. A number of Mendicants were sitting at these tables, working with gowned patients. Sister Catherine turned back to Dreyfus, nodding once. He knew then that Valery had to be among these patients.

'Over there, Tom – at the table in the corner.' Sister Catherine moved her stick from one hand to the other and settled a forgiving touch onto Dreyfus's shoulder. 'I have some work to attend to. Sebastien will take you to your wife.'

Slowly Thalia's eyes had adjusted to the ambient light, picking out the sheer face of the wall as it loomed over them. The cliff-sized bulkhead was semicircular: flat across the base, and rounded at the top where it met the inner ceiling of the wheel. There were iris-like pressure doors in the wall at various heights, but Brig had informed them that there was a service lock at floor level, giving access to the next chamber via a short tunnel.

'You'll see what you're looking for easily enough. I'll be just fine waiting here.'

'Are those robots likely to cause us any trouble?' Thalia asked.

'They can trip you up if they don't get out of the way fast enough, but beyond that . . . you really don't like robots, do you?'

'She's got her reasons,' Sparver said.

It had been a while since they had last seen one of the spindly robots, so perhaps they would be alone for now, their presence registered and noted but otherwise of no further concern.

'I'll level with you, Brig,' Thalia said. 'We're involved in a larger investigation, and Friller's death seems to be a part of it. Knowing that, is there anything else you can share with us about what went on in this place?'

'Everything I know is second-hand,' Brig said. 'What I've picked up since we started clearing it out.'

'Still useful to me.'

'This whole wheel was just a shell. They rented it out, one partition at a time. There were buildings in each partition, sometimes dozens, and they were owned by different people, and run like independent kingdoms – little habitats in their own right. Most of the time what went on inside was kept secret, unless you were a client – and to be a client you needed money.'

'And from what you say, Friller may have been rich enough,' Sparver said.

'Just my guess.'

'Tell us what you know of the individual services provided by the buildings,' Thalia said.

'You name it, from what I gathered. Each of those buildings specialised in something different. Dangerous games, dangerous experiments – any sort of surgery or modification you wanted. Quick and dirty procedures for people in a rush, and not too many questions asked.'

'And the white building,' Thalia asked, with a shiver of insight. 'Did they go in for neural modifications there?'

'Why neural?' Brig asked.

'I'm afraid I can't—' Thalia started.

'I have a question,' Sparver said, cutting across her answer. 'Should those reeds be moving?'

He was pointing across the mudflat at a nearby clump of vacuum-frozen reeds.

Thalia stared at them, wondering what the fuss was about. The reeds were as still and stiff as they had always been.

Until they twitched, buckling back and forth as if being stroked by invisible fingers.

'They shouldn't be doing that,' Brig said.

'Someone obviously hasn't told them,' Sparver answered slowly.

'Air could make them move,' Thalia said. 'But there isn't any air in here. You told us there was no air, Brig.'

Brig said quietly: 'There shouldn't be.'

The reeds were still, then moving, then still again – but the intervals of stillness were growing shorter, the movement more emphatic. The three of them had stopped, bewitched by the moving forms.

Nothing could have felt more out of place than those brittle, twitching reeds. It was as if one element in an otherwise static picture had come to life – a horrible intrusion of animation, where none belonged.

'It was a hard vacuum when we came in,' Sparver said. 'I know – I checked as a matter of routine. Now my suit's picking up a small partial pressure, and it's rising.'

'Mine too,' Thalia said, lowering her gaze to the visor display, and cursing herself for not picking up on it sooner. 'Could some air have come with us in the elevator?'

'Not enough for this,' Brig answered. 'It must be leaking back into this chamber from number eight.'

'Is that meant to happen?' Thalia asked.

'Shit like this used to happen all the time. Lately though . . .'

'Whatever the explanation,' Sparver said, 'it's getting stronger.'

Something buzzed across the suit-to-suit channel they were using. The buzz became a voice, halfway through a sentence. '. . . out of there now, Brig. Bulkhead one is opening. Repeat, bulkhead one is opening.'

'Slater,' Brig said. 'We copy. We can see the air flow. One of the irises must have opened. Can you override and shut it from the hub?'

Brig sounded concerned, but not unduly alarmed. The reclamation crews must have become used to things like this going wrong as the ancient and baroque environmental control systems flickered in and out of life.

An annoyance, and bad timing, but not an immediate cause for panic.

But Slater Virac said: 'This isn't the usual screw-up, Brig. The equalisation doors are opening in sequence, top to bottom. We saw red lights on the status monitors a couple of minutes ago, but none of the usual tricks are working this time.'

'Shit, Virac. You've got to be kidding me.'

'I'm not, and I strongly suggest you get out of chamber one.'

'We're nearly at two. We can be through the connecting tunnel in a few minutes.'

'Too risky – if the overspill floods the tunnel, you'll be in even bigger trouble. Can you get back to the spoke?'

The reeds were buckling over now, snapping one after the other like glass whiskers. Loose debris was starting to tumble across the mudflat – small clumps to begin with, but gaining in size as the force of the draught increased.

Thalia could feel it for herself, a soft pressure against one side of her suit. And through the suit's audio amplification, a faint but rising scream of in-rushing air.

'No chance, Virac – it's going to hit hurricane force long before we'd get back to the spoke.'

'Then find shelter. High ground if possible.'

Larger, heavier pieces of debris were being picked up by the air now; not just frozen foliage, but shards of rubble and building material left over from the clearance process. Thalia pointed to a junction in the raised walkway, one of its forks leading to the shell of a building rising from a nearby island. 'That should do, shouldn't it? Those walls look pretty strong.'

They quickened their pace, Thalia and Sparver breaking into a jog, but Brig's suit was heavier and clumsier and it soon became clear she would struggle to match their speed.

'Go ahead,' she urged, waving them onward. 'I'm slower, but I'm also tougher. I'll see you at those walls.'

'No,' Thalia said. 'We don't leave you. I demanded your presence; that makes you my responsibility.'

'Best not argue,' Sparver said.

They walked as quickly as Brig was able, the force of the wind gathering all the while. They were having to stoop, relying more and more on their suits' locomotive assist just to maintain their footing. Debris shot by on both sides, larger and larger items now being uprooted and carried away by the rising gale. Door-sized flakes of building material tumbled overhead, borne on the thickening air. Something donged against Thalia's helmet, nearly knocking her over.

'Why high ground? What did he mean by that?'

'Just move,' Brig urged.

They were at the junction in the path, a Y-shaped fork leading to two different islands. Debris was raining down almost continually now, hammering against the path, larger and smaller pieces hitting their suits. Instinct had Thalia wanting to reach for her whiphound clipped to the outside of the suit, but there was nothing it could do for her under these circumstances.

'Something new happened,' Sparver said, slowing for a moment. 'Can you feel it? The ground's rumbling under us. It wasn't rumbling a minute ago.'

'Water,' Thalia guessed.

'Nine hundred thousand cubic litres of water,' Brig answered, in a sort of daze. 'Not far shy of a million tonnes. If the doors open in sequence, like Virac said, we'll get the air first, then the water.'

'All right,' Sparver said, with a sort of fatalistic calm. 'There's a lot of water on its way. That island's still the only high ground anywhere near us.'

'Here it comes,' Brig said, twisting around.

It raced towards them across the mudflat, furred with a heavy coating of debris, a mindless stampede of water.

CHAPTER SEVEN

Dreyfus watched as Sister Catherine ambled away, then allowed the other Mendicant to lead him to his wife. Distracted, trying to think of anything but the reason for this meeting, he found his gaze drifting to the pattern of light on the sun-dappled ground, the restless play of the individual specks of brightness.

'Brother Georgi,' Sebastien said in a low, respectful tone. 'I've brought Mister Dreyfus to see Valery.'

Georgi – the Mendicant sitting opposite Valery – had obviously been forewarned of this development. 'Thank you, Sebastien. Tom, it is very good to see you again.'

'It's been too long,' Dreyfus said.

Georgi waved aside this self-criticism. 'Many would sooner forget that they had ever had friends or relatives in our care. In fact, they have been known to have their memories adjusted for precisely that reason.'

Georgi was facing him, Valery still with her back to Dreyfus. They had been engaged in some childlike game, with symbolic cards spread across the table. A rooster. A house. A constellation of yellow stars, drawn five-pointed.

Valery had lost language. She had lost not only the ability to read, but also the mechanisms of verbal expression and understanding. Speech to her was a meaningless, upsetting babble. For years the patient Mendicants of Hospice Idlewild had been trying to rebuild the neural pathways of linguistic function.

For years they had been getting almost nowhere.

But his voice must have drawn some glimmer of recognition in her, for she turned to meet him, her expression open and friendly but also seemingly focused on something beyond him.

'It's me,' he said, scuffing out a vacant chair and lowering himself into it. They were at the thickest point of the habitat and gravity was at its strongest, the chair's wooden ligaments creaking under his frame. 'You look well, my love.' He risked reaching out a hand, extending it slowly until he was able to touch the side of her face. He was cautious because she had flinched from that hand before, and on one occasion struck it forcefully out of her way, as if deflecting a blow.

This time at least she permitted the contact, even if there was something uncomprehending in her eyes.

'Has Sister Catherine told you very much about me, Georgi?' Dreyfus asked, slowly withdrawing his touch, but allowing his other hand to touch Valery's fingers, where her hand lay amid the symbol cards.

'Only that your wife suffered an accident, and that you visit her more often than many. I know of your profession, of course. But that is no business of mine.'

Dreyfus was silent for a few moments, looking into his wife's eyes and trying to find some recognition in them, some sense that she remembered what they had once been. 'When Valery was first taken ill, I didn't have the strength to deal with what had happened to her. In fact, I did exactly what you just mentioned. I had my memories adjusted.'

'I understand that the circumstances were difficult.'

Dreyfus smiled at the understatement buried in that remark, some tension inside him giving way. 'I was responsible for her condition, you see. I took a course of action that brought Valery to this state.'

'Did you intend to hurt your wife?' Georgi asked plainly.

'No,' Dreyfus answered.

'Then I suppose you acted to protect the needs of others.'

Dreyfus nodded slowly. 'That doesn't excuse it.'

'Sister Catherine told me you were placed in an impossible situation.' Georgi moved some of the symbol cards around, flipping a few of them over to show different pictures. 'That's all. If you were such a bad man, why would you come to us now?'

'If she has to bear this, then so should I.'

'It isn't hopeless, Tom.' Georgi selected a symbol card and pushed it into Valery's fingers. 'Say it,' he encouraged, touching a finger to his own lips.

It was a rabbit. Valery moved her mouth, and began to shape – awkwardly and tentatively – something like the opening vowel sound for the Canasian form of the word.

'Good,' Dreyfus said. He squeezed her fingers. 'Very good, Valery.'

But the word died incomplete. Valery swallowed, weariness and puzzlement showing in her face, as if she could not understand why she was being put through this vexing task. If you lose language, Dreyfus wondered, do you also lose any comprehension of the point of it? But he forced himself to smile again.

'These are early days,' Georgi said.

'I can see how much you care. She couldn't hope to be in better hands.'

'Our methods may seem slow, but we have patience. That's our greatest asset. And Valery is content here, I can tell you. She is very good with the flowerbeds. She has an eye for colours and harmony. I'll show you how they're developing, if you have time.'

'I'd like that.'

The three of them went to the flowerbeds, walking along the narrow paths laid out between the beds. Valery walked slowly but steadily, a hand always ready to catch herself if she fell. Around them there was a great deal of patient gardening going on. A male Mendicant was kneeling with a man, showing him how to plant new bulbs. Another Mendicant was watching as a young patient worked along one of the borders with a bright yellow watering can. There were red flowers painted onto the side of the can, daubed on in an exuberant, childlike fashion. The simple innocence of the flowers softened something in Dreyfus and he smiled, this time without putting any conscious effort into the gesture. Then he caught Valery's eye and saw that she was smiling as well – either at the happy colours of the watering can, or at Dreyfus's reaction.

'Show me what you've done,' he said, beckoning at the beds in case the intent of his words was lost.

Valery gave him a tour of her work. She said almost nothing, either because she had no means of voicing her thoughts, or was ashamed at her own limitations of expression. But her gestures were precise, the lesson she was giving him – in the arrangement of colours and patterns – one that she clearly expected him to heed, and so he did, nodding and stating aloud the things he believed she meant him to hear. Once or twice a frown of confusion or irritation troubled her features, but for the most part she did not seem displeased.

Afterwards, they returned to the outdoor tables and drank tea. They held hands again. Dreyfus attempted to coax Valery into calling out the things on the cards, but she refused him, not unkindly, with a firm but serene shake of her head. He understood. The lessons – the hard path she was following – were a private trial best kept between herself and the Mendicants.

Georgi came back to the table after helping with some minor carpentry, a saw still in his hand.

'You see that she's making progress, Tom. You don't need to imagine it.'

'I don't.'

'But she needs encouragement. A sense that there's a world outside these walls, waiting to welcome her back into it. We can't do much about that – some of us barely remember what it's like beyond Idlewild. But you can give her that goal, Tom. You're a busy man, and we recognise that. But try to find time . . .'

'I need to head back,' Dreyfus said, cutting the other man off, and instantly regretting the abrupt tone he heard in his own voice.

'Of course.' Georgi rose from the table and bid Valery to do likewise. 'We'll accompany you to the path, if you're going back that way. I understand you have pressing business. But can we count on you to come back to the Hospice before long?'

'Yes,' Dreyfus affirmed. 'Yes. Very shortly. I won't let it go as long next time.'

The three of them walked slowly out of the sun-dappled area, back towards the picket fence that Sister Catherine had opened. As they approached the open-air clinic, though, Dreyfus sensed there had been a shift in the mood. Voices were raised – one in particular. There was no anger, as such, but a heightened exchange was clearly taking place. Puzzled, he began to pick up his pace, even at the expense of leaving Georgi and Valery to follow behind.

Sister Catherine came around a corner, planting her stick determinedly.

'Oh, I'm too late,' she said, her face sagging with instant regret. 'I'm sorry, Tom. I was hoping to encourage you to spend a little more time in the language compound.' She gave the other Mendicant a beseeching look. 'Georgi – why don't you take Tom and Valery back to see the flower-beds, and then take the high path, via the three falls?'

Dreyfus prickled, sensing that all of a sudden he was an unwelcome presence. 'Is there something I shouldn't see, Sister?'

'We trust each other, don't we?' she asked.

'I thought so.'

'Then take my advice and go with Georgi. Nothing bad will come of it.'

Dreyfus prickled again – but not because of Sister Catherine's words, which he was sure were sincerely meant. But because of that raised voice, from just out of sight. It was impossible, it cut against all logic, but he knew beyond any doubt to whom it belonged.

'He's here, isn't he?' Dreyfus said slowly, barely believing his own words. 'Devon Garlin's here.'

Thalia watched the encroaching water with a peculiar detachment, fascinated and horrified in the same moment. It was a broad, shallow, fast wave – they were not going to be swept under between one breath and the next – but it was travelling quickly and Thalia saw no end to the water beyond the approaching front. If anything it was bulging, more water piling up behind the leading wave, like a crowd of people trying to squeeze through a gap.

'This isn't good,' she said, voicing a thought that she knew she should have kept private as soon as she spoke.

'We should brace,' Sparver said, planting his hands on the walkway's railing and gripping it tightly.

Thalia and Brig followed his lead. The surge licked its way closer, seeming to pounce forward in the last moments. Thalia took a final look down at the still-dry ground, three metres below the level of the planks on which they stood. Then the water arrived, still moving with a clearly defined front. It had seemed like a liquid thing until that moment, but as it surged under the walkway its nature changed to something solid and dense, carrying a fearsome momentum of its own, more like a landslide or avalanche, sweeping a tumbling cargo of boulders and debris in its passage. The water rammed into the stilts supporting the walkway, jarring them to their foundations, and that angry, juddering vibration transmitted itself through to the planks and railings, threatening to shake them loose. Steadying herself, dizzy with the motion of the water, Thalia looked down again. The three-metre gap between the deck and the ground was half-submerged, and the level was still rising. There was no hope of accurately measuring the rate of the rise, not with the surging chaos of waves and debris as the water forced its way between the stilts. Maybe a metre a minute, she decided, which meant a minute and a half before the water was going to be flowing over the walkway, rather than under it.

It was enough time, she decided. All they had to do was get to the section of walkway that climbed up to meet the island, and then they would have metres of extra height, and still more if they reached the highest ground on the island. If that proved insufficient, she would still have bought time to explore further survival options. Her situational training emphasised immediate practicalities: what it took to remain alive for the next minute, and the minute after that, rather than concerning herself with ten minutes or an hour from now. It was hard-won pragmatism, distilled from hundreds of real-world scenarios faced by earlier generations of prefects. The lesson was that it worked – most of the time.

So be it. She held her breath, slowly released it. Water continued to pass under them, a black conveyor belt dotted with industrial rubbish, lapping higher now, but no faster than her earlier guess.

They kept moving. The walkway continued to vibrate, shaking violently every few seconds as some substantial item struck it. Every now and then the force came close to knocking them off their feet. There were sheets of material, lightweight construction blocks, cargo hoppers and pallets, some of them as large as a Panoply cutter. Thalia fixed all her attention on the island, and the hoped-for sanctuary of the elevated ground. It would be enough, she told herself, and they ought to be onto the sloping section within half a minute.

'How deep was this water?' she asked Brig. 'Before you pumped it out, I mean.'

'Waist-deep. You could stand in it, here, anyway. But there were deeper lakes in some of the other partitions, and all that water was pumped into chamber eight.'

'Can we expect all of it to drain out?'

'No . . . I don't think so. There are multiple locks in all the bulkhead walls, at different heights from the floor. They can't all have opened.'

'Why not?' Sparver asked.

'Because there'd be a lot worse than this,' Brig said.

Now the flood was a racing black carpet licking just under the level of the deck, with surges occasionally racing over the planks. On top of that the winds were still lashing, still pelting the walkway, waters and exposed areas of ground with an assortment of dirt, rubble and building materials. The bombardment was increasing in severity – presumably what had been a slow leak of air was now a raging dam-burst as the connecting lock opened to its fullest extent. It would ease eventually – there had to be an equilibrium at some point – but they were obviously nowhere near that moment.

Then, between one step and the next, the walkway jerked, tilting sharply. Sparver, always steadier on his feet, managed to stay upright but Thalia was sent sliding into the open gap between the deck and the railing. Brig grabbed at her flailing right arm, and then Thalia managed to fumble for a grip of her own. Something large had rammed them underwater, knocking out one or more sets of stilts. Along its entire length, the walkway had developed a nauseating twist, and now metres of it were pitched below the level of the water.

Awkwardly but steadily the three of them made it back to a level section. By now the water was welling up through the gaps in the decking, and the bombardment of debris had become a continuous vibration.

They carried on, Brig pushing her suit to the limit, Thalia and Sparver doing all they could to assist, and then in the last hundred metres the walkway began to slope up out of the water, becoming a connecting ramp that took them up to the ground level of the gutted building and took them three or four metres above the still-rising water.

The wind might have been peaking. Thalia's suit registered two atmospheres now, but the rate of increase had been slowing and there seemed little chance of it climbing much higher. Even if it did, the suits could cope – and oxygen at least was not going to be in short supply.

'It looks as if the gale's easing off,' Thalia said, as they neared the top of the ramp. 'We'll still look for shelter, but at least we don't have to worry about being hit from above.'

'We were just in time,' Brig said, pointing to the lower section where they had just been. The walkway was severed now – broken into several pieces. One of the sections was riding away on the tidal surge, completely detached from the stilts.

Only now that she was on firm ground – or what counted as firm ground – did Thalia give any thought to contacting Panoply.

'Prefect Ng,' she said. 'Requesting emergency extraction.'

A thin, distant voice answered her. 'Panoply, Prefect Ng. What is the nature of your emergency?'

Thalia swallowed, looking around. The water had enclosed the island completely by now and was already well over the level of the walkways. Debris surged past like a vast flow of traffic, heading on urgent business.

'Prefect Bancal and I are in the outer rim of the Addison-Lovelace Concordancy, along with a civilian witness. There's been a containment breach from the eighth partition – air and water re-entering vacuum. It could be deliberate sabotage. We're safe for the moment, but we expect the water level to continue rising.'

'Reviewing your situation now, Ng. If it was deemed necessary to drill or blast through from space, could you tolerate a rapid decompression event?'

'Yes . . . we're suited. Whatever it takes. Send in weevils if you need to.'

'A Heavy Technical Squad has been tasked to your coordinates. They should be on station within sixty minutes. In the meantime, can you call in local assistance?'

She conferred with Brig for a few seconds, discussing options, before returning to the Panoply operative. 'No good, I'm afraid. They're not set up to deal with this sort of emergency, and they haven't got anything that could cut through the outer wall in much less than thirteen hours. This is a skeleton crew of clean-up technicians, not a Heavy Technical Squad. Even if they could send more workers to us from the hub, there isn't anything they'd be able to do in the time available to us.' She eyed the water level. 'Is there any way they can get to us sooner?'

'Negative, Ng. They will be on an expedited burn as it is.'

Thalia accepted this without rancour. 'If that's the best you can do for us, so be it. When they arrive, tell them to liaise with the reclamation team in the hub – they know this place better than we do. We've arrived at a partially demolished building – the walls should protect us if there's another air surge.'

'Prefect,' said Brig, touching Thalia's arm.

'Wait a moment,' Thalia told Panoply, following Brig's direction of gaze.

A second surge of water was approaching from the same direction as the first, moving across the already flooded areas like a steep kink in a carpet. For a second or two Thalia studied it with a kind of disembodied detachment, as if she were only playing witness to a catastrophe involving some other hapless individual. If the first surge had easily swamped the three-metre height of the walkway, then this second influx contained a lot more water, perhaps three or four times as much again.

'The lower doors must have opened,' Brig said.

'So it would seem,' Thalia said. But she fought to keep her voice steady and clear as she continued speaking to Panoply. 'This is Ng again. I have an update on our situation. There's a lot more water coming our way.'

'How much is a lot more, Ng?'

'I don't know, maybe three or four times the initial surge volume. I thought we'd be safe on this island, but it won't be enough. You'd better get that extraction squad speeded up . . .'

'Your urgency will be communicated, Ng, but they were already on an optimum crossing time. Nonetheless I am sure that if there is anything that could be done to shave some time off that estimate . . .'

'They'd do it, yes. I understand.'

'It's going to overwhelm the land,' Brig said, staring with mesmerised fascination at the approaching water-wall.

'We'll have to ride it out,' Sparver said. 'Find something that floats, something we can use as a raft.'

'When you find us a raft, tell me,' Thalia said.

'Would that do?' he asked, indicating an out-jutting spur of land which had trapped a section of the walkway. 'All it needs to do is float. It should work for long enough for the swell to subside. We just need to get to it in time . . .'

She heard the heaviness in Brig's voice when she replied – not optimism, just a stone-cold certainty that they had no other options. 'He's right. If it doesn't sink, we'll stand a chance.'

'Do you have a plan, Ng?' Panoply asked.

She was about to say that they had nothing resembling a plan, just an act of last-ditch desperation. But she bit back on those words and said:

112

'We have a contingency. We'll still need that extraction squad as quickly as possible.'

'Understood.'

'Good. If you hear from me again, our contingency worked.'

They moved quickly, negotiating a vague, barely defined path that led them down to the spur. Only the final, sloping part of the walkway now stood above the water level, and that was slowly being submerged. Thalia guessed the initial surge had already reached five metres above the former ground level. By the time the secondary surge arrived, they would be under fifteen to twenty metres of water.

Thalia thought of the hundreds of thousands of tonnes of water building up behind that step change. She had faced killer robots once, and that had been bad enough. But robots usually had a will and a purpose, or were at the very least operating at the behest of some other intelligence. There was always the faint possibility of negotiating with something that had a mind.

The section of walkway Sparver had identified was only the size of a large door. It bobbed on the rising swell, only snagged at one corner by the spur. Thalia would have preferred something bigger, given the three of them, but they were lucky to have any raft at all. The planked decking was intact, and it still had parts of its railings on either side, which would give them all something to hold onto.

'Get aboard,' Sparver said. 'Water's rising so quickly it'll lift free any moment.'

They climbed aboard one at a time, the raft tilting under their weight but maintaining buoyancy. Thalia squatted down onto her haunches, knees raised before her, and hooked her elbows into what remained of the railing, Sparver and Brig doing likewise.

The black surge was almost on them.

'Here it comes,' Thalia said, tightening her grip as best she could.

Her fear had been that the rising wall would break before it hit them, but the one mercy was that mass of debris riding the water made it travel sluggishly. The angle of water tilted ever steeper, and with a jerk the raft broke loose from the island. The tilt increased – Thalia strained to hold on, the railing feeling looser than she would have liked. She felt a sickening sense of elevation, butterflies playing in her belly. All around them was a jostling, crashing confusion of waterborne debris, some of it much larger than their little raft. Huge, empty cargo pallets loomed over them, their glossy sides like sheer, weather-polished cliff-faces. The swell carried them higher, lofting them with an almost insouciant disregard for mass and physics and the intrinsic frailty of small humanoid organisms.

Things crunched against the raft from all sides, ramming from below, raining down from above. Water crashed across the deck with iron force. The swell crested, and then dipped with sickening speed, before cresting again. Then another dip, a terrible jawlike trough opening up in the water before them, and Thalia did the only thing she could think of, which was to close her eyes, hold tighter than ever, and trust that the universe was not quite done with her today.

The upswells and downswells continued for what seemed like hours, but was probably only a minute or two, and then – imperceptibly at first – the chaotic motion began to die away, as the water that had flooded into the chamber found its natural level. The entire floor was completely submerged, with no visible trace of any of the walkways. The islands were all underwater as well, with only the upper parts of the buildings pushing out of the swell.

The water gradually calmed. Thalia surveyed her companions, gratified that they were both still on the raft. They seemed uninjured. If they felt the way she did, they would have their share of bruises and torn muscles, but given the stakes they had come through the flooding remarkably unscathed.

She drew a breath, and realised she had not been breathing for some time.

'That has to be all of it,' Thalia said. 'Right, Brig?'

'I think so,' Brig said. 'It shouldn't get any worse. I think this must be all the water that was in the eighth chamber. We were lucky.'

'I wouldn't call it lucky. I'd say we were pretty damned unlucky to have this happen at all. It's sabotage, I'm sure of it. Those robots must have been monitoring us, acting as eyes and ears. Someone detected Panoply interest in this place and decided to snuff us out.'

'If they were hoping it would make us less interested,' Sparver said, 'I'm not sure they thought that through.'

'No,' Thalia agreed. 'It's odd – clumsy, at the very least. And all that'll happen now is that we'll double-down with our investigation. Are you all right, Brig?'

'Yes – bashed around a bit, but my suit's holding.'

'So is mine. Sparver?'

'I won't look any prettier by the end of the day. But I'm all right.'

'You did well. If we hadn't got to the raft—'

'Wait,' Sparver said, interrupting her with an edge in his voice that she did not care for.

'What is it?' she asked.

'We've started drifting. We were floating around on the swell just now,

114

but now we're moving again, heading towards the other bulkhead.'

'That isn't possible,' Thalia said. 'It's just a piece of walkway. It doesn't have an engine.'

'No,' Brig said. 'But he's right. I can track our movement against the ceiling. We've definitely picked up a drift, and it's getting faster. There's only one explanation: the water's on the move again.'

'But you said it must have emptied out of the other chamber.'

'Equalised, at least. Now there's only one thing that could make the water move again.' Brig looked past the prefects, in the direction the raft was moving. 'It's the lock into partition two. It must have opened on its own. The flood's draining straight through.'

'Is that good or bad for us?' Thalia asked.

'The water level will go down once it's spread into the other chamber. But I'm worried about how it's going to get from here to there. Those connecting doors aren't large, and with the amount of water trying to force its way through, and with us going along for the ride . . .'

'What she means is,' Sparver said, 'it's going to get bumpy.'

'Maybe it's just the lower door,' Thalia said. 'If that's the case, then the flow's mostly going to be under us. We just have to sit it out, wait for the levels to settle down again.'

'No,' Brig answered. 'With the way this current's picking up speed, they must have opened one of the higher doors, at or just below the existing water level.'

'You think it's someone trying to help us?' Thalia asked, conscious now that their motion was gaining, the water on either side moving with them, but only because they were caught in its rush.

'If they are, this isn't how I'd do it,' Brig said.

A roar was growing, carried to Thalia's suit by the air that had not long returned to the chamber. It was a thunderous, waterfall roar. The swell they were riding was beginning to tilt in the direction of movement, while on either side steepening embankments of water were starting to flank the flow on which they were being carried. The bulkhead wall was coming nearer by the second. At the point where the water met it Thalia saw a dark circular aperture, the bottleneck they were shortly going to be squeezed through. The raft would fit, but there was no telling what sort of turbulence it would encounter as it made the passage. She dared not think what lay beyond. Let there be some sort of continuing flow, however treacherous, rather than a waterfall.

She made herself hang on even tighter than before, pushing body and will to their limits, but just as she identified the connecting door as their most immediate difficulty, Sparver nodded urgently to one side.

'Brace yourselves!' he called.

It was one of the cargo pods, shouldering nearer as the water flow began to constrict on the approach to the lock. Another was looming in on the other side, with more beyond. They looked as huge as houses now, and just as sturdy. The debris had been moving almost sedately until then, caught in the deceptive stillness of the flow, but now objects were beginning to clang and jostle each other, fighting for space like frightened animals.

The pod knocked them, then came rebounding back, seeming to gain momentum between strikes. Thalia tensed; each impact was stronger than the last, each one lifting the raft, until on the heaviest collision so far the raft flipped until it was nearly vertical.

Everything slowed down.

Thalia had her back to the water, her helmet dipping in and out of the flow. With a lurch she felt the railings buckle and then begin to give way. She sensed herself beginning to slip off the raft, into the sucking water. She unwrapped her elbows and threw herself belly down across the raft as far and fast as she could, scrambling her heels on the decking to gain some tiny purchase. She let out a groan of desperation – more scream than groan, when it burst from her mouth. And then Sparver had her, hooking his free arm around her right elbow, using all his strength to haul her over to his side of the raft. The pod that had struck them had rebounded again, and Sparver's weight was causing the raft to tilt back to the horizontal once more. Thalia grabbed a railing and felt her heart hammering in her chest.

'Thank you,' she said, her voice hoarse. 'If you hadn't caught me . . .'

They were through the worst of it. They had traversed the lock, and now the flow was calming, the obstacles in the water moving further apart, not closer.

It was only then she noticed that Brig had gone. She met Sparver's face, glanced back along the raft's length – to the section of railing that had been ripped clean away – and then back to Sparver. He shook his head.

'Maybe she'll be all right,' she said.

'I saw her go,' Sparver answered, and his tone told her everything she needed to know.

The squad would arrive soon, she knew, and they would do all they could to find Brig, but that process would be strictly one of formality. Thalia's mood hardened. It was one thing to be threatened in the course of her investigations, but the death of an innocent civilian put a cold fury right through to her.

The water level eased as it redistributed itself between the opened partitions. It continued to shake them back and forth, but each time a little less violently than before, until it was safe for both of them to relax their holds on what remained of the railing. Sparver was the first to stand, his low centre of gravity giving him an advantage. He looked out beyond the raft, further into the second partition. Then he touched a hand to Thalia's elbow and said: 'Look.'

She looked, staring out across the eddying, debris-filled chaos of the water. It was quite obvious why Sparver had demanded her attention.

'The white tree,' she said.

Sister Catherine had interposed herself on the path, blocking the way.

'We didn't invite him,' she said. 'He just came. He arrived half an hour after you. Said he only wished to speak, to present his opinions, and then he'd be gone. You know we can't – won't – turn anyone away.'

Dreyfus made to squeeze by. She raised her stick, just enough to remind him of her authority.

'Let me see him.'

'You'll make trouble, Tom.' There was a steely resolve in her eyes. 'We saw what happened a few days ago, when you went to his speech.'

'I didn't think you took much interest in the news.'

'I don't – but I do take an interest in you. I won't judge you for the past, but we won't have a similar scene happening here.'

'I'm sorry,' he said, pushing past as gently as he could.

'Tom!' she called out.

Dreyfus twisted around. 'He didn't arrive here at the same time as me by chance. It's deliberate provocation.'

'Then don't rise to it,' she said, with a note of dwindling expectation.

Dreyfus came into sight of the speaker. Garlin was standing before a small gathering of Mendicants and some of their more lucid patients. He had stepped onto a wooden chair, leaning slightly with one hand planted on the chair's back, the other outstretched, smiling as he spoke about the benefits of life beyond the Glitter Band. Two suited civilians flanked Garlin, standing with their hands behind their backs. Dreyfus recognised the faces from some of the public broadcasts he had studied. They had a hard, single-minded look to them, like former soldiers or mercenaries.

'You have their respect, and that's all very well,' Garlin was saying. 'The citizens of the Glitter Band, if they give you any thought at all, know that you serve a public good. But still you depend on handouts and fa-vours, barely keeping the air inside your world while the rest of the Glitter Band drowns in prosperity. But the breakaway habitats would value your services very highly. A tithe, applied across all the habitats in our new community, would pay for the upkeep of the Hospice a hundred times over . . .' Garlin trailed off, his smile hardening. 'I don't believe who it is.'

'I don't either,' Dreyfus said, drawing the gazes of the Mendicants and most of their patients. 'Get down from the chair, Garlin. Whatever game you think you're playing, it ends here.'

Garlin remained on the chair. His two bodyguards straightened up and puffed out their chests. 'Game, Prefect Dreyfus? Aren't you the one playing a game?' Garlin looked out to his audience, their attention split between the speaker and Dreyfus. 'I've come here freely, as is my right as a citizen of the Glitter Band. The Ice Mendicants very kindly allowed me to speak, on the understanding that I would state my case and then leave. That was my intention – it was all very amicable. I was just coming to my concluding remarks when you stormed into the proceedings.'

'I was already here.'

'As you were already present when you interrupted my talk a few days ago?'

'I didn't interrupt. You picked me out of the crowd.'

Garlin nodded sagely. 'At least you were wearing civilian clothing that day. Unlike now, with that uniform and weapon of yours. Well, if the purpose is intimidation I feel suitably intimidated.' He narrowed an eye, squinting at Dreyfus. 'Are you *worried* about something, Prefect? You certainly look like a worried man.' He straightened up, standing fully erect on the chair, once more the focus of attention. 'We've all begun to pick up on the rumours, haven't we? There's something loose – something they can't control. But rather than treat us as adults, men like Dreyfus would rather bask in their secrets. People are dying, I hear . . .'

Dreyfus unclipped his whiphound. He held it in his hand, the filament not yet extended.

'Julius Devon Garlin Voi, I am detaining you under the articles of public order, on authority of Panoply.'

'What?' Garlin said, throwing his hands wide, looking around with a mask of plausible astonishment. 'What have I done?'

'You have committed actions detrimental to public order,' Dreyfus said. 'Step off the chair, please, dismiss your helpers, and accompany me to my vehicle. We'll continue this conversation in Panoply.'

He felt a hand on his wrist. A soft voice said: 'This is a mistake, Tom. Stop before it's too late.'

He tugged his wrist away from Sister Catherine's grasp. 'I'm sorry,' he said. 'It shouldn't happen like this. But I have my responsibilities. He can spread his lies about the breakaway movement as much as he likes, but when he starts spreading dangerous rumours . . .'

118

'Even if they're true?' Garlin asked, still on the chair. 'Is it against public order to state the truth?'

Dreyfus stepped nearer the speaker. 'Come with me, Garlin. You wanted a reaction from Panoply – you've got one.'

'You've got witnesses now, Dreyfus – don't do anything you might regret.'

Dreyfus touched the control on the whiphound which deployed the filament. Touching the ground, the filament formed a traction spool and allowed Dreyfus to release his grip on the handle. The whiphound tracked alongside him, waiting for an instruction. The two bodyguards moved in front of the chair, shielding Garlin.

'Get out of my way,' Dreyfus said.

'They're going nowhere,' Garlin said. 'They know full well that you're exceeding your mandate.'

'Track my gaze,' Dreyfus said in a low voice. 'Mark and aquire three subjects.' He looked at the two bodyguards in turn, then Garlin, holding his focus for a short but definite interval. 'Confirm acquisition.'

The whiphound nodded.

'Minimum necessary force. Incapacitate subjects one and two. Proceed.'

The movement was almost too fast to track. The whiphound coiled and uncompressed, throwing itself through the air, flinging out its filament just as it landed within reach of the first bodyguard. In a fluid extension of the same explosive motion, the whiphound wrapped its filament around the lower left leg of the bodyguard, and then yanked it out from beneath the guard, hard and fast enough that the guard gave out a yelp of pain, even as the whiphound was executing a similar operation on the second man. In an eyeblink both men were on the ground, on their backs, staring out along their legs as if they were surprised to find them still attached.

The right-hand bodyguard had caught Garlin off-balance as he toppled. Garlin leapt off the chair, just barely catching himself. He wobbled, threw out his arms, started backing away, then turned and broke into a semi-jog, as if he hardly dared run faster than that.

'Nothing's broken,' Dreyfus said, striding up to the two fallen bodyguards 'That's how it'll be, if you're smart enough to keep out of my way.' Then he turned his attention to the fleeing man. 'Garlin! You're already marked! Make it easy on yourself.'

Garlin looked back. The whiphound was swivelling its handle to track him. For a moment, barely gathering his breath, he seemed to find a calmness.

'I should thank you,' he said. 'You've just proved every point I was trying to make.'

'I saw him again,' Julius said.

'What?'

'Spider-fingers. I saw him on that bed, the way he was before. Just lying on his back, dressed in his black clothes, with that bag on the floor. Asleep. Except he looked half-dead. That hair of his was all lopsided. I think it's a wig.'

Caleb looked scornful. 'You were imagining seeing him the first time.'

'I wasn't. I told you I'd seen him in that room and he showed up that day, didn't he? So I wasn't making it up.'

'You overheard something, is all. Or caught a glimpse of him moving around and made up a story about him being asleep. Or got lucky.'

'He was in the house then, he's in the house now. You'll see.'

'What made you go back to that room in the first place, brother?'

He looked at Caleb, fixing him with a pitying expression. 'You know what. We've both felt it. We've been building up to something for weeks. There was a strange atmosphere about Mother and Father yesterday, and even worse this morning. They're only ever like that when Doctor Stasov's due.'

Julius waited for Caleb to deny it, but even his brother would not have been that dishonest. There had been a heavy, apprehensive mood around the Shell House in recent weeks, as if the boys were being subjected to some quiet scrutiny, watched and measured in readiness for the next step in their education. Usually these build-ups led to a visit from Doctor Stasov.

Julius had a tingle in his belly just thinking about what might be coming.

They had been called to one of the main drawing rooms. Its walls were lavishly plastered and painted in pastel shades. It was full of antique furniture, old glass-domed clocks and writing desks, even a very strange kind of holoclavier that had solid black and white keys that you had to press down to make a sound.

The boys were invited to stand on gold carpeting while Father and Mother delivered a lecture.

'It's time for you to learn a little more about the family name you've been blessed with,' Father said, puffing himself up with overdone solemnity. 'Great things will come your way, because of that name. Doors will open and opportunities come your way. You will go through your lives feeling the respect and gratitude of a whole world, and many beyond this one. Your great-grandmother, Sandra Voi, was the architect of our very way of living.' He nodded at her portrait, set on one of the walls above an elaborate settee. 'She made us who we are, and who we are capable of becoming.'

Julius and Caleb regarded the portrait. There were similar ones all around the house. A severe, old-fashioned woman in severe, old-fashioned clothes, standing at a metal-framed window with one hand on the sill under the window, a book in the other, and the curve of a red planet visible beyond a window. Julius struggled to think of anyone having warm feelings towards the regal-looking woman in the picture, with her unsmiling features and a peevish, judgemental look to her eyes.

'Sandra Voi died too soon,' Father was saying. 'But not before her great work was set in progress. Under the ice of Europa, she founded the first of the experimental Demarchist communities. There people explored new modes of participatory democracy, eventually circumventing or dismantling almost all the traditional structures of hierarchy and government. Rule by the people, for the people, with neural implants to facilitate rapid polling and decision-making.'

The boys took this in with only mild interest. None of it was entirely new to them. They had soaked up enough about Sandra Voi to know her place in history, just as they had more than an inkling of how society worked beyond the environs of the Shell House and its dome.

Outside were hundreds of millions of people, living on the surface and in orbit, going about their lives, content for the most part, guaranteed a high degree of safety and security. In return all they had to do was vote. Many times a day, questions would appear in their heads – matters both large and trifling – and the people had only to register their opinion. They did it whether they were living in the height of luxury or in the self-inflicted hardship of a Voluntary Tyranny. This was the way human society had worked around Yellowstone for over a hundred and fifty years. There was no central authority, no government; no ministries, no chambers of power. There were only the citizens, participating in democracy at such a seamless level that it almost became an autonomic process, no longer – except in very rare circumstances – requiring conscious intervention.

Such a system had to be watertight, of course. In many ways, the brilliance of Sandra Voi lay not in her advocacy of real-time democracy – it was hardly a new concept, even in the early days of Europa – but in the envisioning of the neural processing architecture that made it both efficient and inviolable. The implants, the abstraction, the polling cores – these were her true and enduring gifts. Mathematically ingenious methods of voter authentication, vote tallying, relentless error-correction and bias-elimination. It was as beautiful and intricate as watchwork, and it functioned. Flaws had been discovered over the years, certainly, but they were subtle enough that no real harm had been done before they were plugged. That work continued, for no system as complex as Yellowstone's could ever be said to have reached a state of perfect culmination. What mattered was that Sandra Voi's foundations were still at the heart of the system, for all it had been embroidered and filigreed. In all significant respects she had achieved her goal.

'But no idea,' Father said, 'can be left to chance, without guardianship and protection. All ideas meet resistance – even those that are demonstrably good and true. And even the strongest ideas need nourishment, cultivation – protection and stewardship in times of crisis, when good men and women may lose confidence in that which has served them so well before. Sandra Voi understood this, and it has been central to the family ever since. Chandler Prentiss Voi understood it, during the early years of Chasm City. No change was made to the abstraction architecture without Chandler's direct and careful oversight. The changes have been fewer in recent years – the system works so well now that there has been little need for adjustments – but still we Vois recognise our burden of responsibility. A delicate, fragile thing has been entrusted to us, and we are obliged to pass it forward to the generations to come.'

The boys' attention was wandering. They knew that being a Voi came with strings; that the price for growing up in a place like the Shell House was that they would have to Do Their Bit when they got older. Neither boy was all that troubled by this coming burden, though. If their parents' leisured lives were any barometer, Doing Their Bit wasn't going to prove particularly onerous.

'You are boys now,' Father said. 'But soon you must become citizens. When you are a few years older, you will be free to move beyond the Shell House, into Chasm City and the wider world. Your mother and I have done our best to equip you for that transition. You have learned to shape and conjure the immaterial and the material environments – to don plumage, and command quickmatter. You have learned well, and we are proud of you both. There is more to citizenship, though.' Father looked at Mother, waiting for the merest nod of acknowledgement before continuing. She seemed to withhold it at first, before giving in. 'Now you must accept the mental architecture which will permit your full participation in Chasm City democracy – opening your minds to the polling cores.'

Their father closed his fist, then opened it again, a grey tetrahedron floating in the cup of his palm.

He offered the tetrahedron to Caleb. 'You understand a symbolic exchange,' Father continued. 'This will feel no different – to begin with.'

'What's going to happen?' Caleb asked, reaching out to accept the tetrahedron, but stilling his hand at the last moment.

'It will seem like waking,' Father said. 'Like knowing the world for the first time, with clear eyes. Like finally being alive.'

'But it won't be sudden,' Mother said, striking her usual cautious tone. 'Like everything else it takes time.' Under her breath, Julius thought she muttered: 'Thank goodness.'

Caleb took the symbol and closed his own small fist around it. The tetrahedron fizzed into nothingness as his fingers punctured its surface.

Father closed and re-opened his own fist and offered a second tetrahedron to Julius.

'Take it, son.'

'I like it the way it is now,' Julius said, looking at Caleb for support. 'We're not old enough to vote, so can't we wait until then?'

'Are you frightened?' Father asked sharply.

'No,' Julius asserted. 'I'm not frightened. The polling system can't hurt us. Millions of people have this, so there can't be anything bad about it. It's just a way of voting.'

'Among other things,' Mother said.

'The sooner you get used to it, the better,' Father said. 'Look at Caleb, how ready he is. Why can't you be more like him, Julius, instead of hanging back all the time?'

'Maybe he's happy to be a child,' Mother put in darkly. 'They went through enough, Marlon – why can't he have this for a little longer?'

Father controlled it very well, but there was no missing the anger that flashed across his face, or the fact that it was directed squarely at his wife.

'They've had loving childhoods,' he said, speaking the words as if she were the one who needed persuading. 'No two boys have ever been better looked after. No two boys have ever been better equipped to take their places in society. Caleb is willing. Julius must make the same commitment to the life of a Voi.'

Julius made a lunge for the tetrahedron and squeezed it hard, spiting his father even as he obeyed him. 'I said it wasn't fear. But I don't understand why there's this stupid rush to make us ready. First the plumage and the quickmatter, now this.'

Father stepped back, as if all of a sudden he feared Julius. 'These aren't simple skills.'

'People come in from space all the time,' Julius said. 'On the ships, from other systems. Ultras and their passengers. Sometimes they haven't got implants at all, and still they adjust and become citizens.'

'But they aren't Vois,' Father countered. 'They don't have that name to live up to.'

'What if I wanted a different name?' Julius asked, with a defiance that made him feel a bit giddy. 'What if I wanted to call myself something else? What if I wanted a different life?'

'You don't get to make that choice,' his father said.

Later that day, when the boys were in their bedroom, long after they should have been asleep, Caleb said: 'I was right and you were wrong, Julius. You made it up about Doctor Stasov.'

'I didn't,' Julius said softly.

The lights were out and the house still. Their parents slept in the other wing, the one they were rarely allowed to enter, but the boys had learned to keep their voices low anyway. If they spoke too loudly, especially if they argued, Lurcher would hear them and come up the stairs. The robot would never punish them directly, but it would report back to their parents and there were always consequences.

'If he was here we'd have seen him, wouldn't we?' Caleb went on.

'Maybe he was here,' Julius said. 'Something happened to us today, didn't it? Doctor Stasov's always here when something changes. But he didn't necessarily need to show himself, not now there's all that stuff in our heads. You know he's got things in that bag that can pick up on what we're doing, even if he's in another room.'

'Now you're just making things up,' Caleb said, turning over in his bed. 'Imagining things that aren't real, like you always do. Do you want Doctor Stasov to come into our room and take us away, is that it?'

Julius thought of the ghost-faced doctor stealing into their bedroom while they were asleep, that sweep of hair hiding his eyes as he stood in the doorway, a study in monochrome. Then coming to the side of Julius's bed and drawing back the bedclothes with his spidery fingers, each of them too long and thin, brittle as a tree branch. He imagined the doctor taking him out of bed while he was still asleep, and stuffing him into the black bowels of his bag. Julius couldn't be sure a boy would fit into the bag, and he didn't care to put it to the test.

'He'd take you, not me,' Julius said.

'I bet you'd rather he took you. Then you wouldn't have to face up to those commitments Father was going on about. I could see your face. You looked as if you were about to cry. Poor little Julius.' He made an exaggerated bawling sound.

'Shut up, Caleb.'

'Why, don't you like hearing what you sound like? What if I want a different name? What if I don't want to be a Voi. Pity Julius, boo hoo hoo!'

'Shut up!' Julius hissed.

Somewhere in the silence of the house a door closed. The boys froze instinctively, straining to hear what came next. It was exactly what they feared: the slow, rhythmic plod of Lurcher's footsteps.

'Now you've done it,' Caleb said, squeezing deeper into his bedclothes.

But Julius listened more carefully. 'He's not coming this way,' he said, once he was certain of his judgement. 'If he was, he'd be on the stairs by now. He's going along the main hall, to the entrance.'

Julius slipped out of bed. As quietly as he could he made his way to the bedroom window. Only a year or two earlier he had needed to stand on a box to look out, but now he could easily manage without it. He eased aside the curtains, peering out through the glass to the nocturnal scene below. At night, the dome's facets turned dark to block out the glow from Chasm City, and the lights high in the dome's apex threw down a pale silvery cast, just enough to define the edges of the terrace and the start of the gardens, with gravel paths radiating away from the Shell House, forging into increasingly dense greenery.

All was colourless and still.

'What?' Caleb asked irritably.

Julius was about to pull the curtains back together and return to the bed when a moving shadow came into view. It was travelling away from the house, ticking back and forth like a clock's pendulum. He watched it with an eerie sense of foreboding, until the cause of the shadow came into view. A pale gleam of silver showed. It was Lurcher, walking slowly away from the Shell House. The robot had gained that nickname because of its slow, top-heavy gait, but there was more to it this time. Lurcher was carrying a dark form, stretched limply across two of its arms. Two legs dangled from one end, a hand, a sleeve and a silver flash of hair from the other. Lurcher was also carrying a heavy black medical bag.

Julius watched the robot recede along one of the paths, soon lost in the darkening gloom of overgrowth.

He returned to bed, and said nothing to Caleb.

CHAPTER EIGHT

Aumonier was in the tactical room, accompanied by a small, weary retinue of prefects and analysts, when a chime diverted her attention from the current topic of death forecasts and response projections.

'One civilian casualty,' she said, reading aloud from the scrolling transcript. 'Bancal and Ng both safe, and assistance should be on-site within a few minutes. It seems some safety interlock failed and the entire contents of the reservoir chamber were allowed to spill into the adjoining partition – enough air and water for the entire wheel, all released in one go.'

Robert Tang scratched under his eyes. 'An accident?'

'Conceivably,' Aumonier said, without much conviction. 'These old habitats tend to be bug-ridden, and particularly prone to failures when they're being gutted for re-occupation. But in view of the timing I'm not minded to view it as anything so innocent.'

Mildred Dosso fingered a lock of lank hair. 'Sabotage, then?'

Aumonier gazed at her levelly. 'That this event should happen just as two of my operatives are inside the wheel . . . how else should we consider it, Mildred? Bancal and Ng could very well have died – from what I'm reading it's a miracle they didn't. As it is, I'm not going to take this lightly. We'll pick this incident to the bone.'

Tang and Dosso looked down as further updates scrolled across the table's display surfaces.

'Ng is reporting an object of possible interest,' Dosso said.

'Yes,' Aumonier said, speed-reading ahead of her peers. 'A white structure, in the second chamber of the wheel.'

'Does it mean anything to you?' Tang asked.

Aumonier reflected. It was a reasonable question and it demanded a considered answer. She studied the single, murky image that Ng had sent via her goggles' record-and-transmit facility. The light in the chamber was low, lending the white structure the ghostly aspect of a lightning-struck tree standing alone in moonlight, its angular limbs seeming to reach out

126

as if in embrace, or even the offering of some terrible warning against approaching further.

A parade of shapes and patterns flitted across her mind's eye as her brain searched for a match against the white structure. No human being could know the Glitter Band in its totality, much less the dazzling range of environments and structures contained within the ten thousand habitats. Even to know it once was to hold only a single, futile instant in a waltz of endless change.

But Aumonier had learned to trust in the correlative accuracy of her memory, and a faint, familiar intuition told her she had not seen this shape before. Perhaps it had meant something to her predecessors, but she had studied the major case files and thought it unlikely.

No: she was certain. Whatever this thing was, it had managed not to draw Panoply's interest until now.

'I want a name, an owner, and a purpose,' she said. 'Mildred: feed the image to Vanessa, tell her to start running it through the Search Turbines.'

Dosso nodded.

'Ng hasn't given us the slightest explanation as to why the object is of relevance,' Tang said.

'She hasn't,' Aumonier said. 'But she's also had to deal with the small problem of managing not to die. I imagine she'll enlighten us in her own good time.'

By the time she met Dreyfus at the vehicle dock, the events in Hospice Idlewild were all over the public networks. He was her friend, and she guessed he had his reasons for what, on the face of it, seemed like a serious professional miscalculation. She still boiled with fury at the thought that Dreyfus had brought this on them all with everything else that was pressing for her attention. It looked bad, Aumonier had to admit. There were no surveillance feeds in Hospice Idlewild – the Mendicants refused it – but Garlin's bodyguards had filmed the whole spectacle anyway, and it hadn't taken them long to distribute the recording across the public networks.

Lillian Baudry, next to her in the pressurised area of the dock, said: 'Try to look on the bright side, Supreme Prefect. At least he used minimum necessary force.'

'Is that an attempt to excuse his actions?'

'Hardly. But everyone has their breaking point. That place is sacrosanct to Dreyfus.'

She ground her teeth. 'I know what it means to him.'

'And no matter what Garlin might say, it looks like calculated provocation. To show up there, just when Dreyfus is paying a visit to Valery . . .'

'He can't have known,' Aumonier said. 'Dreyfus was on Panoply business at the Parking Swarm.'

'Then you're saying it was a just a wild coincidence?'

Beyond armoured glass, the cutter settled into its docking cradle. Connections closed around the hull. Aumonier grimaced, thinking how curious it was that the universe could make any prior situation seem only mildly troublesome, when at the time it had seemed to encompass all conceivable woes. She longed to be sitting back in the tactical room, listening to Sparver, thinking only of exploding heads.

'I forgot to mention,' Baudry said, pausing as if to judge Aumonier's mood. 'That woman's been trying to reach you again.'

'Woman?'

'Hestia Del Mar. The one from Chasm City. Marshal-Detective, or whatever she calls herself. She called again just now, reminding you about those three fugitives.'

'I told her we had nothing. We don't retain records of citizen movements.'

'She seems persistent.'

'She's a fool.' And too much like me for my own tastes, Aumonier added silently. 'She doesn't understand the scope of our operations, or the threats and emergencies we face on a continual basis. I'd kill to have nothing but three fugitives to keep me awake at night.'

'I thought you put Jirmal onto the problem?' Baudry asked.

'I did,' Aumonier said, curling her lower lip as she tried to push away feelings of guilt and duplicity. 'I also told her to use her discretionary powers.'

'Which is a polite way of saying "give the impression of taking the query seriously, but stall for as long as possible".'

'No . . . Jirmal understood. She definitely understood.' She looked at Baudry, waiting for reassurance. 'I wanted the query looked at . . . but not at the expense of diverting our time and energy from the real emergency.' She set her jaw determinedly. 'I'll make sure Jirmal understands the delicacy of the situation. But Hestia Del Mar has to understand we're not—'

Clearmountain joined them at the lock.

'Dreyfus has really exceeded himself,' he said, shaking his head, but very clearly taking a certain morbid delight in this latest turn of events.

'Perhaps, in hindsight, it was a mistake for him to continue with field duties after the Aurora emergency,' Baudry ventured. 'I've always respected him, but . . .'

128

'But what, Lillian?' Aumonier demanded. She was still thinking of Hestia Del Mar, oddly troubled by her own lack of helpfulness towards the woman, and the vague way she had delegated the matter over to Jirmal.

The lock sequenced.

Devon Garlin came out first, helped by a gentle shove from Dreyfus. His hands were secured behind his back, but he showed no signs of injury or maltreatment, and if his clothes had been damaged or scuffed in the arrest, they had repaired and self-cleaned on the journey.

Garlin looked at Aumonier. Doubtless he recognised her. All of the senior prefects involved in the Aurora crisis had become public figures, at least in the immediate aftermath of the emergency.

'I owe you a debt of gratitude,' he said, his face oddly composed. 'You've done more for my cause in the last two hours than I've managed in months.'

'I wouldn't be so cocky,' Aumonier said, staring into his ice-blue eyes without blinking. 'If you're found to have violated the articles of public order, you won't have a cause to go back to.'

'Then there's some doubt about culpability, is there?' He twisted around to look at the man behind him. 'That's odd, because Dreyfus couldn't have sounded more certain.'

'The stability of the Glitter Band depends on social cohesion, Mister Garlin. We don't have standing armies, we don't have a citizen militia. Even the local constabularies constitute a vanishingly small proportion of our population. But this system only functions in the absence of malicious fear-mongering. I have no time for those who disseminate lies and half-truths for their own ends.'

'Either there's a crisis or there isn't, Supreme Prefect. Or are you seriously suggesting that you've arrested a man because he had the temerity to repeat a rumour? What's next – a moratorium on gossip?'

She nodded at Clearmountain. 'Take him to a debriefing room, please, Gaston. I'll be along shortly.'

'I brought him here for interviewing, not debriefing,' Dreyfus said.

Aumonier fixed him in the eyes. 'I'd like a word, Tom. It won't take long.'

Near the middle of Panoply a modest area had been set aside as a miniature forest, a steamy, rambling maze of dense greenery and dripping, burbling waters.

Aumonier had designed the space. The hothouse's confusing, beguiling geometries had been laid out in her mind during her long convalescence: those weeks before she regained motor control of her limbs and had little to do but stare at the ceiling. It was meant for all of the prefects and analysts, irrespective of rank. The winding, branching paths were supposed to encourage non-linear thought processes and counter-intuitive jumps of logic. By some silent consensus, though, it seemed to have remained Aumonier's personal space. She rarely encountered anyone else during her walks, and after some initial misgivings she had gradually come around to an acceptance of the arrangement, even quietly welcoming it.

Now she walked with Dreyfus, a brook bubbling alongside the path, filling in the silence that had prevailed since they had started their stroll.

'I thought better of you,' she said, finally speaking. 'I still think better of you.'

'It was an act of provocation.'

'Of course it was. Do you think I'm a fool? He knew exactly where, and when, he needed to be to extract that response from you. And you should have had the professional detachment to ignore it completely, to turn the other cheek—'

'I—' Dreyfus started.

'Speaking. And before you say you don't like demagogues, I don't like political embarrassments that gift the moral ground to our enemies. You were right to be angry, Tom – I don't blame you for that. But you should have exercised the discretion and good judgement I normally feel able to count on.'

Dreyfus walked on in silence, clearly thinking very carefully about the next thing he was about to say.

'He knows more than he should. You can excuse his knowledge of the Wildfire deaths, if you wish. Maybe he really is just picking up on rumours and using them to stoke public unrest. But that doesn't account for him showing up in Hospice Idlewild.'

'He'll say it was chance.'

'And will you believe him? It's part of a pattern – of a man with knowledge he shouldn't have. We're not just dealing with a well-connected agitator here. It's something more than that.'

'All right,' she said. 'Let's take what you're saying at face value. Garlin has access to information channels he shouldn't have – at least according to your theory. But he's just a man.'

'From a wealthy background.'

'The Voi fortune was frittered away years ago. After Aliya died in her shuttle accident the Shell House fell into a ruin. Being born into that family may have given Devon Garlin an early advantage, but now his whole operation is self-financing.'

'What we know of it.'

'Don't make this into more than it is, Tom. He's one man with a few deep-pocketed sponsors and a little more influence than we'd like. That doesn't mean there's some sinister, shadowy cabal behind him, feeding him secret information.'

'There are other things we can't sense,' Dreyfus said. 'Distributed intelligences, spread across the networks.'

'We've heard nothing from Aurora or the Clockmaker in two years. That's because they're so preoccupied with their slow war against each other that they can't spare even a fraction of their energies to bother with our little affairs. So why would either of them start now?'

'I don't have the answers. I'm saying it looks as if there's something looming behind Garlin – some agency or power that's providing him with this information.'

'I can't hold a man on that basis, Tom.'

'From what I gathered, you're not planning to hold him at all.'

'I won't delay the inevitable. I have no grounds for detaining Garlin and the longer he stays in Panoply, the more ammunition we will give him. So I plan to lance the boil immediately.' She walked on, Dreyfus following. 'The immediate damage is containable. No one was hurt, and Garlin will have his liberty back within a few hours. There'll be a fuss, of course, and it will play against us. But I can make a case that you were entitled to detain him under a very literal reading of the articles. Zealous – that's the word. My officer may have been over-zealous in his duties, but there was no irregularity in his interpretation of the law, and I stand by his actions.'

Dreyfus evidently felt it safe to smile. 'So, no demotion – yet.'

'No – not just yet. It's your tactical judgement I prize, not your ability to give a few commands to a whiphound.' Keeping a stony face, she added: 'How did it feel, though, to take down the snivelling little shit?'

'I've had worse moments,' Dreyfus said.

She patted his back. They walked on in silence.

Ghiselin Bronner looked up as Dreyfus entered the interview room, pushing back her sleeve to rub the skin above the wrist where the Painflower had been attached.

'If you've come to apologise for the way my security arrangements were bungled, Prefect, you can . . .'

Dreyfus eased into the seat opposite her, and placed a large black evidence box on the table between them. He left it unopened for the moment.

'I haven't come to apologise, no. But I thought I'd set your mind at ease in one respect. Grobno – the man who fixed that thing onto you – is no longer a concern. I've delivered him to the Ultras, where he'll face their justice.'

'Their justice?' She slid her sleeve back down. 'Is that your idea of a joke, Dreyfus? They sent him in the first place. He'll be rewarded, not punished.'

'What I mean to say is that Grobno acted alone. There'll be no further repercussions as far as you're concerned. I've had a personal guarantee from Harbourmaster Seraphim to that effect.'

'That name's supposed to mean something, is it?'

'He's a man I happen to know and trust.'

'Trust an Ultra.' She made no effort to hide her sneer. 'You really haven't had much experience with them, have you?'

'Enough.' Dreyfus reached over and began to undo the lid on the evidence box. 'Sufficient to know that if you don't try and get one over on them, they'll leave you well alone. They have their own ideas about honour and loyalty, exactly as we do. Just a pity you and Antal didn't take that lesson to heart, isn't it?'

'I have no idea what you're talking about.'

'Spare me the routine, Madame Bronner. Grobno told me everything I need to know. You were playing one faction of Ultras against another, faking goods, inflating margins – swindling the last people in the universe you really want to make enemies of.' Dreyfus set the lid aside and removed the protective wadding from inside the evidence box. 'Still, that's water under the bridge now. You'll be audited, every transaction you've ever made looked into anew. But that won't concern me. Fraud's a criminal matter, but not something Panoply needs to waste its valuable time pursuing.'

'Well, then—' she began.

Dreyfus pulled the white candelabra from the evidence box. He set it on the table by its base, then pushed the box to one side. 'This, on the other hand . . . this interests me quite a bit.'

'You're insane.'

'Do you recognise it?'

'Of course I recognise it. It was in our home. There were others like it. Why have you brought it here?'

'My operative thought it might be of interest, so she flagged it for evidence collection. Can you explain the significance of the design?'

'Yes. It holds candles. Should I tell you what candles are for?'

Dreyfus paused and reached for the compad at the far end of the table. He called up an image and tilted the compad so Madame Bronner had a clear view of it.

'You're looking at a structure, presently being investigated in relation to an ongoing enquiry. Your husband's death also relates to that enquiry. Do you recognise the structure?'

'No.'

'Would you like to reflect on that answer a little longer?'

'I don't recognise it, so why should I? It's just a white building. Where is it?'

'I'm not at liberty to say.'

'What do you mean, my husband's death was part of an ongoing enquiry? We know why he died, and the people behind it.' She paused, as if she might also have admitted too much, but then some belated acceptance seemed to come over her. 'You even had the man who did it. What more is there to say?'

'Grobno didn't kill your husband,' Dreyfus stated. 'I doubt he was even aware of your husband, until after his death. But that death was part of a larger pattern. This building may relate to that pattern—'

'If you know where that building is, why don't you just go there and find out?'

'My operatives are already investigating it. But I think your husband may have known about that building, or had some contact with it.'

'He'd have mentioned it.'

'Can you explain the similarity with the candelabra? The narrow stem, the branching structure, these globe-like candle-holders.'

'Ask Antal. You can speak to his beta-level, even if you won't let me.'

'Was he responsible for the candelabra?'

'I never liked them, all right? He had them made. They were meant to be sold on to the Ultras, faked up to look like something more valuable than they were . . . but Antal decided to keep them. He wanted them in the house.'

Something softened in Dreyfus, if only for a moment. 'Do you know why?'

'Like I said – ask him.'

'Perhaps I will. But there's someone else I could speak to as well.' Dreyfus tilted the compad again, so that they both had a clear view of it. 'Madame Bronner?' he asked, raising his voice.

'I'm sitting right here, you idiot.'

On the compad, a lone figure turned slowly, eyes searching in various directions as if hearing a noise in fog, a sound that they could not immediately localise. They continued looking around in confusion, lost in a cloying silvery whiteness. 'Who's there?'

133

'Madame Bronner? This is Prefect Dreyfus. You've been sequestered by Panoply. I'm with your living instantiation at this very moment. You've both been brought in for interviewing in relation to an ongoing investigation.'

'You can't sequester her,' the seated widow said. 'You have no right. I've done nothing wrong; I'm not even *dead* . . .'

'This is an affront,' said the simulated widow, stepping nearer to Dreyfus.

'When our lawyers hear about this—' began the living widow.

'He has no right,' the simulation said.

'Well, I'm glad you can agree on something,' Dreyfus said, eyeing both versions of Madame Bronner. 'Because it may make this a little easier. I suspect that the living instantiation of you was engaged in commercial fraud. If it's found to be the case, she'll be prosecuted under the usual civilian laws of the Glitter Band.'

'What does that have to do with me?' asked the simulation.

'Quite a bit,' Dreyfus said. 'Whatever sentence is decided, it would be fully applicable to both the living and beta-level instantiations of you.'

'That's completely unreasonable!' the beta-level interrupted.

'I didn't draft the laws,' Dreyfus said, managing to sound suitably unmoved. 'A beta-level shadows and mimics its primary instantiation very closely – that's the whole point, after all. Close enough to embody knowledge of criminal activity – to become a tacit or active accomplice? Who can say? But if there are reasonable grounds for suspicion . . .'

'I was brought here for protection, not to be treated like a common criminal!' the living widow said.

Dreyfus slid the candelabra until it was in clear view of both the versions of Madame Bronner. 'Here's the deal. I can't offer immunity from prosecution, but I can make a case to the civil authorities that one or both of you were of assistance to Panoply in a wider investigation. But I'd need to be persuaded that you were offering me genuinely useful information – especially where that information relates to your recently departed husband.'

'What are you talking about?' asked the beta-level.

'I want to know why Antal had these candelabra commissioned. What they meant to him – and anything you can tell me about a white building that shares a similar form.' Dreyfus flashed a smile. 'I'll give you time to think it over, shall I? Half an hour?'

He rose from the table and left the living and unliving versions of Ghiselin Bronner to consider their decision.

*

Aumonier stepped through the passwall and conjured up a chair, sitting down opposite Devon Garlin. He started to speak, but Aumonier raised a cautionary finger and said: 'Save yourself, Mister Garlin – this needn't take up much of your precious time. I have a high-speed corvette ready and waiting to take you back to the Glitter Band – name your destination and we'll have you safe and dry before you can blink.'

'I was brutalised.' He touched his throat, as if he had been throttled. 'Set upon for speaking freely – for exercising my rights as a free citizen of the Glitter Band.'

Aumonier pinched her features in mock contrition. 'It's a shame things happened the way they did.'

'A shame?' He looked at her with startled disbelief. 'Is that the extent of your apology?'

'Oh, it's not an apology – nothing of the sort. You were detained, as was our right, and now you are being released. This sort of thing happens all the time, Mister Garlin, so please don't make it all about you.'

'This won't end here.'

'I think it will.' Aumonier leaned forward. 'You'll go back to being the low-level irritant you have so far proven to be. I have every confidence that your breakaway movement will burn out of its own accord, like a weak fever. You may continue to spread populist, rabble-rousing nonsense as you see fit. As far as I'm concerned, the local constabularies can deal with you. You're not enough of a problem to keep me awake at night – and believe me, I'm a *very* light sleeper. But you will never go near Hospice Idlewild again.'

'You can't forbid—'

'Did I say I was done?' She elevated her chin, looking down at him along the length of her nose. 'Don't talk to me about what is and isn't forbidden. You scuttle into the protection of the laws of the Glitter Band when it suits you, but at the same time you hold the entire institution in utter, loathsome contempt. You're dirt, Mister Garlin – and if I didn't respect those laws and conventions as much as I do, I'd gladly find a way to silence you. But I won't. I will, though, tell you that you'd be very ill-advised to test my patience in the future – and going near Hospice Idlewild without excellent reason would be a very effective way of doing so.' She allowed herself a breath, giving him the full cold stare. 'Beyond that, you'll show no more interest in Dreyfus. You've made an enemy of him and frankly he has my complete sympathy. Dreyfus doesn't like demagogues. I'll confess I take a harder line. I despise you. I'd like to smear you out of existence before you damage something very precious to me.'

Garlin leaned as far back as his seat permitted. He swallowed. 'This is an outrage.'

'No, this is off the record. You're still below my threshold of interest, but you should be aware that you're buzzing around dangerously close to it. Consider your moves very wisely, Mister Garlin – you'd hate to make an enemy of me.' Aumonier rose from the chair and dismissed it back into the floor with a flick of her wrist. 'That's all I wanted to say. Enjoy your trip back.'

Cassandra Leng had her favoured haunts in Necropolis, away from the gathering places of the other Wildfire cases. Dreyfus had learned where best to look for her, preferring to seek her out rather than invoke her presence, even if it cost him a few minutes of wandering.

He watched her now from a distance, studying her seated form. She was on one of the benches near the lakeside, hands settled in her lap, her posture one of contemplative repose. She wore a dark red outfit today, with a long skirt, full-length sleeves and a stiffened collar that flared up into a sort of bonnet. What he could see of her face was in profile, like a cameo. She was looking out across the greying waters, her expression cryptic. He found himself wondering what was going on inside her head in these intervals when she was not required to engage in conversation. Then he chided himself, because even to think of her having selfhood, let alone an interior existence, was a fallacy he had sworn he would never allow himself to fall into again. He had known a beta-level once, witness to an apalling crime, and despite the opinions of the theorists she had come close to convincing him that she had a private consciousness, a true inner life. He had believed it, too, for a time – the force of her personality dismantling his convictions. Later, for the sake of his own professional detachment, he had tried to go back to his old way of thinking, treating the betas as merely elaborate, filigreed shadows of a life once lived. It was easier that way – simpler to go about his business.

He told himself that he had put the doubts to rest. But as he approached Cassandra Leng he still felt as if he were intruding on some private reverie, trespassing on the thoughts and feelings of another human being.

'Prefect,' she said, roused from her stillness, turning to look at him as he neared. 'Come to grill me again, is it? Aren't some of the others starting to get a little jealous of the attention?'

'They'll cope.'

'Goodness, practically an admission.' A teasing half-smile appeared on her face. 'You don't deny it then. You have been singling me out.'

'Hard not to, Cassandra. You'll always be the first. You've also been one of the more cooperative witnesses.'

She touched her throat and the bonnet collapsed down into the collar, tidying itself away with a snap of air.

'It's easy when you've nothing to hide.'

Dreyfus sat next to her on the bench. He said nothing for a few moments, reflecting on her words and the unarguable proposition that he had been drawn to her beyond the other cases. It was true, and if part of it was indeed for the reasons he had stated – her primacy, her willingness to speak bluntly about her former life – then there was also the part that he was less comfortable with: the similarity to Valery he saw in her. That openness, that unflinching lack of sentiment. But more than that. The down-curve of her lips, when she was thoughtful. The set of her jaw, the green of her eyes, made more obvious by the dark red fabric of her outfit.

He wanted to stop himself, to treat her with the same ruthless indifference he reserved for the others, but whenever he came close to acting on that intention he would only end up sitting or walking with her again, deepening the groove of their relationship, making things worse.

He said: 'Did you hear much about Devon Garlin, before you died?'

'That man? Yes, he was hard to miss.' She looked at him sharply. 'Why. What has he done now?'

Dreyfus sniffed, smiling at his own foolishness. 'It's more about what I've done, Cassandra.'

The sharpness turned to a frown, then an amused puzzlement that had some trace of concern in it.

'And you feel that I'm the one to talk to?'

'You're as good an audience as any. You'd be surprised how hard it is to find a neutral pair of ears in Panoply. People are either for me or against me, but there's very little middle ground.'

'You must have some friends.'

'They're busy, and much too willing to see my side of things.'

'Family, then. I once asked you about that. You said you had a wife, and that was the end of the discussion. I didn't press.'

'I do have a wife,' Dreyfus said, looking down at his shoes, the gravel of the path, the shape and texture of each piece of stone, the astonishing verisimilitude of it all. 'As it happens I went to visit her recently.'

'You're estranged?'

'No . . . not exactly. But my wife isn't well. Years ago she was involved in something that left her very damaged. There are some people looking after her, seeing if they can help her to become a little better . . . they're very kind, and I believe them when they say they see signs of progress. But I don't know if I really believe there's any difference.'

'I'm . . . sorry, Dreyfus.'

'There are worse things, Cassandra. I still love her, and I think she recognises me enough to have reciprocal feelings. But it's a hard road. One day, they say, she may get back the power of language. Until that happens, though . . .' He paused, collecting himself. 'It's not my wife I mean to talk about. But when I was visiting her, I ran into Devon Garlin.'

'This place . . . did he have any business there?'

'None that I can see. It was an odd coincidence, if that's what it was. I preferred to see it as a goad.'

Her eyes narrowed with interest. 'Did he know about your wife?'

'I don't see how he could have. But he was there. I either accept that it was an unlikely coincidence, or that the encounter was somehow engineered. Given that Garlin and I had already had one run-in, you can guess which view I'm inclined to take. What matters, though . . .' He paused, nodding slowly to himself. 'I lost it, Cassandra. Allowed my personal feelings to cloud my professional judgement.'

'You didn't go looking for a fight.'

'No, I didn't. But I should have just logged his presence, left him with a few words to remember me, and allowed him to get on with his rabble-rousing.'

'And instead?'

'I used force to bring him in. I was within my technical rights, but it was poor decision-making and it put the Supreme Prefect in the embarrassing position of having to de-arrest Garlin, then send him back home on our ticket. All of which plays very neatly into his hands.'

Cassandra Leng's answer was delivered after a solemn interval of judicial consideration. 'No way to sugar this one, Dreyfus: you screwed up.'

He smiled at her candour.

'That was my assessment as well.'

'But you're also only human. I don't believe in coincidences like that either. Garlin obviously wanted you seeing red.'

'That doesn't excuse what I did.'

'No, but I'm not going to blame you for it. I didn't like that man when I was alive and I'm not minded to change my view of him now. The first time I saw him, it was hate at first sight. That look of his, those pale blue eyes, those golden curls, that calculated boyish twinkle . . . can't they see it's an act?'

'It works for some.'

'Not me. I'd have wiped that smirk off him, given half a chance. He makes my blood run cold now, just thinking of him. Well. Were there repercussions for you?'

'The Supreme Prefect was very forgiving.'

'She ought to be, the time you spend on your work. Some advice from a dead woman, Dreyfus. If it comes to the point where you depend on me for absolution, you're in trouble.'

'It wasn't absolution I was after. Just . . . a second opinion.'

'Well, you got one. And I think I like you a little better, knowing you have your limits. Was that really all you came to talk to me about, Dreyfus? I'm almost flattered. It makes me feel useful.'

'You are. You will be,' he said.

'You're not a bad man, Prefect. A little driven, a little morose . . . but you can be forgiven for that. You're a policeman of sorts, after all. Now that we've been honest with each other, though . . . you'd tell me if anything was happening, wouldn't you?'

Dreyfus thought back to the white candelabra. 'There's something I'd be interested in showing you, but I have to tread carefully. It might relate to the Wildfire deaths, or it might be a random connection that has no bearing on the larger investigation.' He refrained from mentioning the patterning he had noticed on her earlier clothing, but he was certain there was more to it than coincidence. 'We'll know soon enough, but in the meantime . . .'

'There you are, back to business.'

It was not Cassandra Leng who had spoken. The words had come from the person next to him on the bench, but it was not the same woman he had been addressing only a moment earlier.

Now his companion was a child-woman, a girl of teenage looks wearing a green brocade gown, gold-trimmed, over a dress of gold and fire-red. Her hair was auburn, parted centrally, framing a face that evoked both commanding serenity and a certain lofty disregard.

Blue eyes regarded him: a very particular deep blue, warmer and deeper than the eyes of Devon Garlin, and nothing at all like the green of Cassandra Leng.

Dreyfus fought hard to keep his composure.

'Aurora.'

'You shouldn't be startled. It's only been two years.' She cocked her head to one side, studying him with increased intensity. 'My, you really *are* taken aback, aren't you? And here was I, thinking this would be the ideal place to meet.'

'Who was I just talking to?'

139

'Oh, that was *her*, the poor soul. I'm not so unthinking as to spoil such an intimate exchange.'

'Then what are you doing now?'

'You'd said your piece, and I was bored with her.' She patted his knee. 'She's all right, Dreyfus – relax. I've just relocated her beta-level to somewhere else in this environment, with a local memory reset so she doesn't sense any oddness in the transition. Can't have her listening in on us now, can we?'

'How the hell are you here?'

'I haunt the living worlds; why shouldn't I extend the same courtesy to the dead?' She gave a little pout of displeasure. 'I thought we had a higher regard for each other's capabilities by now.'

'Your capabilities included attempted genocide.'

'Let's not dwell on ancient grievances. I thought we'd put all that unpleasantness behind us – moved on. Haven't we?'

'There'll never be any moving on. If I could catch you now I would.'

'No,' she said sternly. 'You wouldn't – not if you've an ounce of sense left in that meat-stuffed head of yours. You couldn't defeat the monster you imagined me to be, so you let loose another monster to divert my energies. Or had you forgotten about that?'

'What's your point?'

'That I mean to put your mind at ease. The Clockmaker and I remain . . . engaged.' She gave him a strained, lopsided smile. 'Worthy adversaries. Of course we despise each other. But we must also acknowledge what we have in common. Two compromised experiments in the extension or prolongation of human intelligence – two victims to hubris and over-reaching ambition.'

'Two psychotic ghosts, locked in endless stalemate.'

'Don't be so complacent, Prefect Dreyfus. One of us will win eventually, and you'd better hope it's me. At least we have *some* common values. At least I retain some lingering regard for the value of human lives. That's more than I can say for that mad machine you turned against me. If the Clockmaker wins there won't be enough meat-hooks to go around.'

'I'm surprised you can spare the energy for this conversation, in that case.'

'I very nearly can't. You were shrewd, when you set us against each other – forcing us to become distributed across the networks. If I concentrate enough of my resources in one location, as I must do to speak to you now, in what you laughably call real-time, then I become vulnerable to the Clockmaker's detection-attack algorithms. Already they are alert to this change in my posture. Sensing and probing my countermeasures. So we'll keep this necessarily brief, shall we?'

'Suits me down to the ground.'

'You have a difficulty. I am aware of it. People are dying inexplicably and your projections point to a rising curve. Doubtless it's crossed your mind that I might be the cause of it?'

'Not exactly your style, murdering people in their ones and twos – but then who knows?'

'Mm.' Her eyes glittered with a fierce and lively disdain. 'It is not my doing. You can accept my word or not. But know this: I depend on the integrity of your networks, on the continued stability of the Glitter Band, for my very existence – and I am rather attached to that existence. Anything that threatens that integrity is of paramount concern to me. And I will not sit back while you bumble your way through this crisis.'

'Is that an offer to help?'

'I'd put it differently. An intervention to limit the damage to myself brought about by the limits of human competence. How does that sound?'

'As if you're scared.'

'I am,' she said, nodding earnestly. 'Scared of anything that does not fit into my understanding of things – and this most certainly does not. Someone or something is out there, Prefect Dreyfus – something neither you nor I have dealt with before.'

Dreyfus absorbed her words, thinking it wise not to doubt the essential truth of it. 'It's not the Clockmaker, playing some double bluff against you?'

'I don't think so.' Her fingers tensed on the ends of the armrests as she leaned forward. 'It tastes different to me, Prefect Dreyfus. There's a mind behind it, a will – I might even say a human will, amplified though it is. But it's not Our Mutual Friend.'

'You don't know much more than me, in that case.'

'Oh, but I want to.' The blue in her eyes seemed to flash. 'I've come this far – reached this deeply into your security layers. Now let me go further. Open the deep archives. Let me into the Search Turbines. I'll do no harm, and I can tease out patterns and inferences a thousand times more efficiently than your stone-age algorithms.'

'You infiltrated our deep layers once before,' Dreyfus said. 'You've got to be insane if you think I'd let you back in.'

She leaned back in the seat, a pitying look on her face. 'Then you'll just have to solve this emergency on your own, while the bodies pile up. It's a pretty little pinch you find yourselves in, isn't it?'

Dreyfus shrugged. 'Is it?'

'From where I'm sitting. Show restraint, and you'll be accused of betraying the public confidence in your promised security. Act forcefully, take the necessary measures to protect the civilian population – do the very job you were tasked with – and you'll play into the hands of the secessionists. You'd better hope there's a path somewhere between those two possibilities.'

'I'll find one.'

Aurora nodded. 'I have to disperse myself now, but we'll speak again before long. And my offer stands. If you want assistance with this difficulty, you'll have to consider the unthinkable. You can't stomach the thought of it now, but it's a wonder what a few more bodies will do. It'll be a hundred soon, and a thousand before you can draw breath. How will that sit on your conscience, when you were offered help?' She smiled once. 'Well, sleep on it. You know where to find me. Oh, and Prefect Dreyfus?'

'Yes?'

'I'd keep this conversation to yourself, if I were you.'

CHAPTER NINE

A day passed.

Jane Aumonier slept a little. Thalia Ng and Sparver Bancal agreed to remain on-site at Carousel Addison-Lovelace, accompanied by two Heavy Technical Squads and a number of Pangolin-rated Field Prefects. They were beginning to investigate the white structure, moving into it with extreme caution and thoroughness. Meanwhile a corvette returned Terzet Friller's body to Panoply, allowing Doctor Demikhov to confirm that the cause of death was indeed Wildfire. Antal Bronner had been the fifty-fourth direct victim of Wildfire; Friller could now be entered into the records as the fifty-fifth, and the forecasts adjusted accordingly. Elsewhere in the Glitter Band a probable fifty-sixth case came in, flagged at a high likelihood by Panoply's event-detection triggers. As with Friller, there was no chance of recovering a head before the neural structures were hopelessly compromised. Nonetheless, prefects were dispatched to bring back the body for inspection.

Another day passed. A probable fifty-seventh case arrived barely twenty-eight hours after the first – an ominously short interval. This time a Field Prefect was near enough to attempt head capture, but the neural patterns were again too degraded to offer any significant leads.

The forecasts were re-computed. Depending on the statistical weighting applied to various factors, the fifty-seventh case appeared to hint at a marked steepening in the death curve. This left Aumonier disconsolate, but she refused to leap to premature conclusions. She would wait for the fifty-eighth, fifty-ninth and sixtieth cases, before revising her expectations. She hoped that, when those deaths arrived, they would drag the forecasts back to their earlier slopes – as if those were not already bad enough.

Internal Prefect Vanessa Laur, meanwhile, had executed a preliminary search on the white structure, finding only exceedingly sparse priors. The name of the structure was Elysium Heights; it was registered as a private medical facility, and behind it stood a murky chain of ownership. From a legal standpoint, everything that was obliged to be disclosed about the structure had been, but beyond those terse requirements there was not a single shred of reliable information.

But again Aumonier resisted the urge to jump to conclusions. Although it looked suspicious, there would have been thousands of facilities running under similar conditions of confidentiality, and it did not necessarily imply dark motives. A commercial clinic, tending to a wealthy client-base (she speculated) would have been within its rights to run its affairs very stealthily.

Dreyfus, meanwhile, had extracted a valuable joint confession from the primary and beta-level instantiations of Ghiselin Bronner. The entire statement had been recorded, but Dreyfus had summarised the essentials to Aumonier in person.

Ghiselin Bronner admitted to her part in the scam to defraud the Ultras. But the principal architect had been her husband, Antal Bronner.

'She said he was drawn to risk,' Dreyfus said. 'Always had been. Doing legal business with the Ultras wasn't enough for him, even with a modest profit. He had to up the stakes, and drew his wife into the scheme. He knew there was a chance they'd be found out, but living like that was part of the thrill.'

'Then we're back to your theory that a propensity for risk-taking links the Wildfire cases. All right. I'm inclined to give it more credence. But Ng sent that candelabra back to us for a reason, and you thought the widow might have something to say about it. Did she?'

'Antal was driven by something,' Dreyfus answered. 'Haunted, more like. If the Bronner instantiations aren't lying, then he never spoke about it in depth to either of them. But over the years Ghiselin pieced together a partial picture. Something had happened to Antal before she knew him – something he either barely remembered, or was barely capable of speaking about. He'd been involved in something. On the few occasions when it slipped out, all he'd say was that it was a kind of game. Whatever this game was, it took a dark turn. Something very bad happened. Antal got out, but it had left its mark.'

'And the candelabra?'

'Somehow related. That's all she knew. Antal was troubled by flashes – night terrors, daydreams, half-forgotten imagery. A white tree, or something like a white tree, standing alone. It seems he commissioned the candelabra to confront his fears, or familiarise them to the point where they no longer had a hold over him.'

'Have you searched for a similar link in the backgrounds of the Necropolis betas?'

Something played across Dreyfus's face then, some fleeting thing which she almost read as guilt or regret.

'I've made some enquiries. Some of the betas seem to be drawn to similar imagery. Cassandra Leng, for instance, had a pattern of interlocking trees on her clothing. Paulette Stang had a neck brooch with a tree-like form. Lucas Clay spends his time circling a bare white tree in one of the parks in Necropolis. There were others. But if you push them on it, there's no overt recollection. I think it's most likely that the betas are picking up on subconscious cues displayed by their primaries, without any deeper understanding of what that imagery signifies.'

'Perhaps we should ask them directly about Elysium Heights. A simple question, with no contextual explanation. There'll be a risk of cross-contamination, but at this point I'm not sure I see an alternative.'

'I'll ask,' Dreyfus said.

'Good. When you're done, I'd like you to go to the building itself. Ng and Bancal are due a break anyway, and a fresh pair of eyes won't hurt.'

'I agree.'

'I'm glad you do. It'll keep you out of trouble with Devon Garlin, if nothing else. I may as well mention that he's stirring up trouble again, after we released him.'

'I'm not terribly surprised. Would you like—'

'No, Tom – I think not. If I had a way of keeping you and Garlin several light-seconds apart, I'd take it. It's become personal for both of you.'

'He made it personal. Maybe you don't quite understand that—'

She cut him off before he said something he might come to regret. 'My mind's made up, Tom. I can't afford to take my eyes off Wildfire. The latest forecasts are . . . troubling. I'll say no more until we have a few more deaths under our belt, but even our worst projections may turn out to have been overly optimistic. It makes it all the more urgent to pursue the investigation into Elysium Heights.'

She thought of that conversation now, as she floated free in the middle of the spherical room where the scarab had held her for eleven years. A mosaic of displays wrapped the room from pole to pole, each facet representing a feed or status indication from one of the habitats under her care. All ten thousand were indicated, although most were too small to snag her immediate attention, appearing as little more than coloured, flickering swatches.

By deliberate command, Aumonier had lately arranged for more than two dozen habitats to be under permanent close scrutiny. Their facets were enlarged, their feed summaries comprehensive. Spotted around the room's globe, there were always two or three in her immediate field of view. By long habit, she rotated her viewpoint, and the room occasionally cycled the displays if it detected something that it believed merited her interest.

Eight of these facets represented the habitats that had already declared their breakaway status, formally nullifying their ties with the wider Glitter Band. The remaining facets – around twenty, although the exact number went up and down from day to day – represented the habitats that were most at risk of following the initial eight. For one reason or another they were all associated with anti-Panoply sentiment, making them fertile ground for Devon Garlin's separatist rhetoric. He had visited all of them in the last six months, and if his words could not have been said to have been met with universal approval, there was certainly a groundswell of sympathy among the citizens.

Now, one of those twenty habitats was becoming particularly problematic.

The name of the place was House Fuxin-Nymburk and had she placed a wager with herself as to which of the twenty was liable to tip the earliest, that would have been her choice. It appeared that Devon Garlin – an exceedingly shrewd man, for all his faults – had made exactly the same calculation, deciding that was where he next needed to apply his leverage.

A day or two after his release from Panoply, he had rejoined his loose organisation and travelled to House Fuxin-Nymburk on a private shuttle. That was his right, and Aumonier had made no effort to stop him. She had assumed that after his brush with Dreyfus, it would be back to business as usual. There would be public speeches, public rallies, a slow spreading of the rot, but nothing that demanded her immediate engagement. If she could hold it at the present level, manage and monitor its spread in a controlled fashion, it would give her time to resolve the melters . . .

Aumonier allowed herself a rueful private smile, thinking of the way she had chastised Sparver Bancal for using precisely that term. The 'neural overloads', she corrected herself – much more dignified.

But melters was a lot quicker off the tongue.

The smile evaporated; it would be quite a while before it returned. She studied the feeds, assembling a mental picture of the unfolding events. Garlin had broken from his usual script, she saw. It had started with a public rally – more vociferous than usual, more outraged – and it had drawn a larger, more boisterous crowd than the norm. But that had only been the start. Garlin had recounted his brush with Dreyfus in Hospice Idlewild, giving a self-serving account that made it seem as if he had been the victim rather than the provocateur.

Aumonier sifted through the captured recordings, isolating a fragment of audio-video. Garlin was up on an outdoor platform, grandstanding, shaking a clenched fist, rage boiling off his face.

'This was a direct infringement of my civil rights under the Common Articles. They say free speech is sacrosanct, until the moment it doesn't suit them! I was made welcome by the good people of Hospice Idlewild – but that didn't sit well with Panoply! Perhaps they're afraid of the truth? Certainly they were fearful enough to use physical force against my innocent associates – excessive, painful, physical force – which I myself experienced!' He made a show of rubbing his wrist, as if it was bruised. 'To add to this travesty, I was bundled off to a prison cell and subjected to interrogation and threats from the Supreme Prefect herself. I was told that if I continue saying my piece – merely speaking the truth, friends – then I'll be silenced – and woe betide anyone who shares my convictions!' Then he bent down, leaning in with conspiratorial content, dropping his voice an octave. 'They're listening now, you can be sure of it. Using all the instruments at their disposal. They're in our heads, eavesdropping through our eyes and ears. There's a poison at the heart of the Glitter Band and they put it there. But it's not too late to do something about it.'

Aumonier ground her teeth, sensing what was to come.

'They've humoured us until now,' Garlin was saying. 'Allowed eight habitats to strike out for a better life, unfettered by Panoply's dictatorial rules. But now they've decided enough is enough.' His eyes seemed to meet hers, as if they were staring at each other in real-time. 'I got that message very clearly, thank you – and I understand that the game has changed. From now on, Panoply will use every tool in its arsenal to suppress free debate and deny the public will. I know – I've seen it for myself. Mark my words – they'll soon be on their way. Prefects, ships, weapons. But that's only because they're scared – all too aware of how fragile their hold on us really is. How little it would take to snap the chains. Good citizens of House Fuxin-Nymburk, surely I don't need to remind you of the sort of injustice Panoply is capable of inflicting on its own people? You've seen it for yourselves – you know what they're capable of. The lockdown imposed on you, seventy-two years ago . . .'

There was a murmur of approval, the consensus broken only by a few sceptical voices. Garlin appeared not to hear them. Aumonier could imagine his bodyguards gently encouraging those dissenters to step further away.

She stopped the playback, needing no further reminder of the thorn still in her side.

Dreyfus was wrong about one thing. He thought he was the only one personally affronted by Devon Garlin. Perhaps he had cause to feel singled out, given what had happened in the hospice. But Aumonier had dedicated her life to the preservation of the Glitter Band. She knew its moods, its desires, its hopes and fears. For all its flaws, for all its imperfections, for all that it still contained little knots of darkness and cruelty, she believed there were infinitely worse ways to live. It was not such a bad thing, this endlessly circling river of light and lives. It had given itself over to her care, and she took that singular burden with the utmost seriousness.

No; there was no one alive who took Devon Garlin more personally than Jane Aumonier.

It was a relief to find only the ordinary ghosts in Necropolis, the walking dead of the sequestered beta-levels. Dreyfus walked the parks and lawns until he found Cassandra Leng strolling through an ornamental garden set with elaborate metal and stone sundials, all shadowless on this overcast day.

'Did one of us offend the other?' she asked. 'It's just that I remember we were talking about various things and then perhaps it got a little personal for you. But then I was somewhere else, and you weren't there.'

'It wasn't you,' Dreyfus said. 'Or me, for that matter. Just a glitch in the system.'

'Given that I only exist because of this system, I can't help but find that worrying.'

'I don't think it'll happen again,' Dreyfus said, injecting a warning tone into his voice in case Aurora was listening in. 'Anyway, there's no risk to you or any of the betas. We take very good care of our witnesses.'

'There's something you're not telling me, Dreyfus.' She turned her elfin face to him with a guarded expression. 'I thought we were beyond that sort of thing by now – that we had some basis of trust.'

'I've always told you all I can. And I do trust you. It's why I'm here today, as it happens. Can you help me gather up the others? There's something I need to show you all.'

'A breakthrough?'

'I wouldn't go that far. But a lead, at least. Something we didn't have until now.'

'And how many dead is it now?'

'Fifty-seven. But there's a hint that we're seeing a steepening in the death curve.'

She stroked one of the sundials, frowning at his answer. 'That's not good.'

'If it's real, we'll have a better idea after a few more cases have come in.

It's not that I'm wishing for more dead, but each new instance does help our projections.'

'And how bad does it look, exactly?'

'Right now? We're due to hit a thousand cases in a little under three hundred days. I don't like that, but it does give us time to conduct our investigation and put in place a response plan before the crisis becomes unmanageable. If it steepens appreciably, though . . .'

'Will it?'

'Someone's pulling strings, Cassandra – that's my feeling. Or tightening a noose. I think it's going to get a lot worse before it gets better.'

'You said you've learned something.'

'I don't know how much you remember of our conversation the last time. But I was about to show you an evidential item. We can come back to that later, but this thing I want you all to see is . . . related to that item. It would be good for everyone to see it, I think, then talk about it and see if it jogs any memories.'

'Couldn't you just snap your fingers and have us all magically appear?'

'I could. But it would be better if you went and asked, I think. Like it or not, you're always going to be the first victim. That gives you standing, a position of influence, whether you wanted it or not. I've seen how you talk to the newly arrived, helping them adjust to their new situation. You're kind to them. You might not believe in the point of your own existence, but you believe in them.'

'If being your go-between gives me something to do in the afterlife, who am I to complain?'

'You're more than that.'

'Do you really believe so? I thought all you hard-nosed prefects were supposed to treat us as bundles of evidence, with no more soul than a box of photographs.'

'That's how we're encouraged to think. How we should think, if we're to do our jobs properly.' Dreyfus paused, uneasy with himself, knowing that his world would be a much simpler and more straightforward place if he held to the official line. 'I believe it, too. Most of the time.'

'I would have thought it had to be one or the other.'

'That's generally the idea.'

'Then you are a man of odd contradictions.'

'There was a witness once. A beta-level like yourself. She ... left me with doubts. Her force of personality was very strong. When we spoke, I couldn't shake the sense that I was addressing a living soul, a real person.'

'In which case you might be the last person in the universe who believes in souls.'

Dreyfus allowed himself a smile. 'I don't know if I believe. But I know I'd be a better policeman if I stopped having doubts.'

'Better,' she said. 'But not necessarily kinder. Well, I'll be sure to tell you when I start feeling something in myself.'

'You believed in life once,' he said forcefully. 'That's why you tested yourself to the limits. To give that life meaning, even if it meant taking dangerous risks with your own existence – those suicidal games in the Colfax Orb. That was your right, and I won't judge you for it, especially as it wasn't the games that killed you. All I ask now is that you accept there is still some meaning to what you are.'

'You have quite a philosophical streak.'

'There's nothing deep about me,' Dreyfus said. 'But I like to think I know life when I meet it.'

'And . . . speaking of life, in the real world . . . are you still in trouble for what you did to Devon Garlin?'

'A minor blot on my record, to go with all the other blots on it. I've made mistakes before; doubtless I'll make a few more. No. That little storm has blown itself out, for the time being.'

'Ah. Then you still feel there's some unfinished business with that man?'

'That's up to him.'

'Well, I told you I didn't like him, so you won't hear any argument from me. Have you ever taken an immediate dislike to someone, Dreyfus?'

'Not usually a good idea in my line of work.'

'Hard if you can't help it, though. I'm afraid that's how it was with Devon Garlin. As soon as I saw his face, I knew no good was going to come of him.'

'Almost as if your paths had crossed before?'

She seemed to consider the thought before dismissing it. 'I think I'd remember if a Voi had ever had anything to do with me, Dreyfus. But I know his type, as well as his family background. That casual assumption of power, that easy way of making people see his point of view. Some men are born knowing they're better than the rest of us. Frankly I'm not sorry you got to push him around a bit.'

'I'm afraid it did more harm than good. And I doubt very much it will have changed his personality.' He paused. 'Do you know the terrace, on that outcropping at the end of the lake?'

'I'll round them up, Dreyfus – don't you worry.'

Half an hour later Dreyfus mounted a low platform to address the gathering. He surveyed their faces, all of them familiar by now, their names coming to mind with no great effort. In truth it was only a small achievement to remember them all. There might have been fifty-seven confirmed victims of Wildfire, but there were still only forty-eight sequestered beta-levels. Terzet Friller, for instance, had left no known beta-level, and Panoply's legal apparatus was still working to issue the relevant sequestration orders for the two most recent deaths.

Long before they reached the present number of cases, though, Dreyfus had convinced himself that the solution to Wildfire lay among these walking, talking dead, and not in the over-cooked brains of the recently deceased. But Dreyfus was a man who set his stock in patterns and connections. Once the dead overwhelmed his capacity to hold them in his head as distinct individuals with names and faces and histories, he would have surrendered his usefulness to the Search Turbines.

Yet now more than ever he believed the connection was real and identifiable among these forty-eight betas.

'Dreyfus asked me to summon you,' Cassandra Leng said, addressing the forty-seven other betas, not all of whom were pleased at this unscheduled gathering. 'That's as much as I know, though.' She turned her eyes on Dreyfus, holding his gaze for a private moment before adding: 'So whatever reason he has for moving us around like chess pawns, it had better be a good one.'

'Thank you, Cassandra,' he said, nodding at her. 'And thank you all, for agreeing to meet here. I know that each and every one of you has a desire to see your death explained, and any guilty parties brought to justice. But along the way you have had to be patient with my questions, and there are times when I simply can't be as open with you as I'd wish. I understand the frustration—'

'We've already been over everything,' said Simon Morago, the eighteenth victim. 'Every detail of our past lives, everyone who may or may not have had a grudge against us.'

'Give him a chance,' Cassandra Leng said. 'He's trying hard, trying to treat us as people, not patterns of data. But he only has so much time.'

'Then he'd better hurry up and come up with something good,' Morago said.

'I can't promise miracles,' Dreyfus said, making eye contact with as many of the dead as he could. 'What I can promise is that we won't leave any stone unturned, especially if it hints at a linking factor, something in your past you all share. Now we think we may have found something.'

Antal Bronner, standing near the front of the gathering, said: 'I haven't been here as long as most of these people, but I still feel as if we've been over and over our histories. If there was some secret we all had in common, wouldn't we have stumbled on it by now?'

'Not necessarily,' Dreyfus said. 'My suspicion is that your living instantiations may have had direct dealings with a place, a facility, and that what happened to them there may be connected to Wildfire. Equally, you may have been denied direct knowledge of this link. Your primaries might never have spoken of their involvement with the place, or even taken steps to suppress their own memories. But there may have been bleed-through . . .'

'Bleed-through,' he heard someone murmur, in a mocking tone.

'You were created to emulate your primaries, to stand for them when they could not be present,' Dreyfus said. 'You were also curated. Your primaries got to decide what you did and didn't know, and they also had the option to shape your responses to certain stimuli. You're all idealised in one form or another. A blemish removed here, a quick temper there. An unfortunate or embarrassing episode in your primary's past – why would you ever need to be troubled by that?'

'Is there a point to this?' asked Morago. 'If we don't know, we don't know.'

Dreyfus searched his memories before answering. 'Years ago I interviewed the sequestered beta of a person suspected of involvement in vote doctoring. The primary protested their innocence, as she would. Despite extensive questioning the beta appeared to have no overt knowledge of the crime. But during the sessions the beta kept touching a brooch. The action had no direct significance for the beta; it was merely a learned gesture from the primary, empty of meaning. Later I established that the primary's brooch contained an illegal device that allowed them to submit multiple fraudulent votes. The beta had picked up on the significance of this brooch without any direct knowledge of the crime itself. That's bleed-through.'

'And you think it applies to us?' Cassandra Leng asked. 'We're not criminals, Prefect – just law-abiding citizens who happened to die by some unexplained means.'

'I agree,' he said, meeting her eyes again. 'But there's still a possibility that your primaries had knowledge denied to you. Such as the significance of this building.'

'What building?' Simon Morago asked.

Dreyfus smiled. He had been ready for the question.

'The one behind you,' he said.

It had formed while he spoke, shaped to rise from the island in the middle of the lake. They turned, in ones and twos to begin with, then en masse.

It was an accurate representation, reconstructed from the images and

152

scans sent back by the Heavy Technical Squad. A slender, off-white trunk rising high, with angular branches emerging from its upper levels to support a cluster of globe-shaped secondary buildings, suspended from the branches like fruit.

'Its name,' he said, 'is Elysium Heights.'

CHAPTER TEN

They were returning from one of Caleb's hunting games. It had started well enough, as the games generally did. Soon enough, though, Julius had ended up in a squabble with his brother. Caleb wanted them to have actual weapons, conjured out of quickmatter. Julius had objected, and they had nearly come to blows. Caleb had stalked off in a huff, Julius catching up with him, and now they were walking back to the Shell House in a tense, broody silence.

Something burst in Julius. He stopped Caleb with a hand on his shoulder, feeling hard muscles tense in response.

'What is it?' Caleb asked, turning.

'I had the dream again.'

'No one's interested. No one cares.'

'When we were little you told me you had the same ones.'

'I was lying. Just saying whatever you wanted me to say, to get you to shut up.' Caleb turned away and kept walking.

'No,' Julius said, calm despite himself. 'You weren't lying. Maybe you don't have the dreams any more, but you used to, and it was about the same place I keep dreaming about.'

'You mean the place with the Ursas,' Caleb said mockingly, not looking back. 'Those stupid robot teddy bears, or whatever they were. What else was it you used to go on about?'

'I know you remember it all, whether you want to or not. The metal corridors, the dormitories, the windows looking out . . . do you know where it was, Caleb? Not here, not the Shell House. But it has to be on this planet somewhere. It's Yellowstone outside those windows, but nowhere close to Chasm City. It means we weren't born here, within the city limits. We were brought up in some other place and they don't want us to know about it.'

Caleb glanced back, putting on his best scornful face. 'You're an idiot, Julius. If we'd been raised somewhere else, why wouldn't we remember?'

'We do!' Julius said earnestly. 'It means someone didn't want us to remember, so they tried to scrub away the memory, so we'd grow up here and only ever remember the Shell House. But there's something else behind it, slowly coming through. We were there together. But Mother and Father aren't there, just the other boys and girls, and the Ursas, whatever they are.' He walked on for a few paces before delivering his coup de grace. 'And something really, really bad happened there.'

'It's not a real place,' Caleb said, some of his earlier assurance gone.

'But you dream about it as well.'

'Only because you've put the idea of it in my head.'

'There's blood,' Julius said. 'A lot of blood. And dead boys, and dead girls. All cut up, all lying on the floor. But we're still alive. We're standing up and everyone else is dead.' He swallowed hard. 'There's blood on us, too, but it's not our own blood. We're all right. But we've got knives in our hands.'

Julius and Caleb had learned to make a point of arriving earlier than any given appointment. There was a chance of catching their parents in the strained end stages of some discussion or argument, one that would have been silenced by the time they were meant to arrive. Often all they picked up was a snatched word or sentence, but over time it was enough to assemble a picture of what their parents would never have shared in their presence.

'He has a temper,' she said now, her voice low.

'So does Julius,' their father answered. 'They're strong-willed boys. After what they went through, would you expect them to be any different?'

'It's worse with Caleb. Julius flares up, but he doesn't hold onto things. Caleb does. He's not ready for this, Marlon.'

'If you had a say, he'd never be.'

'I love them both. I want them both to be happy. They already have everything laid at their feet. They can go out into the world and make us proud. They don't need . . . this. Not Caleb, and maybe not even Julius.'

'We've been building up to this moment for years. Why are you having second thoughts now?'

'Because if we don't have them now, there'll never be another chance. You can't take back the gift of fire, Marlon, and that's what you're about to put into their heads.'

'This city needs us. The world needs us. The quiet, guiding hand of a Voi . . . it's always been there, barely sensed, barely used, but always ready. Millions have come to trust in our guiding wisdom. We can't let them down now.'

155

Mother gave a sigh. 'You'll allow me power of revocation. At least give me that.'

Marlon sounded relieved this was the only concession expected of him. 'Yes . . . of course. Full revocation rights. And I have the same. If either us senses that the boys are drifting—'

'Good,' Mother said tersely.

'But we don't give up on them, even then. We'll continue their education . . . bring them back to the point when they can be trusted again. As I know they will be.'

'I wish I shared your optimism.'

'There's no other choice for us, and no other choice for them. But if we have to revoke it, we will.'

Julius knocked on the doorframe. 'We're here,' he said, feigning breathlessness. 'Sorry we're late.'

'Julius is getting better at conjuring,' Caleb said, effortlessly falling into the same lie. 'He wanted to show off what he can do now. I need to look to my laurels: he's starting to get quite good.'

'But no threat to you yet, Caleb,' Mother said, her words carrying a darker implication given what the brothers had overheard. 'Come in, anyway – and try to learn some punctuality, both of you.'

They knew this room well enough, although they had only been allowed in it on a few occasions. It was called Chandler's Room, after Chandler Prentiss Voi, and most of its windowless space was given over to Chandler's Solid Orrery.

Julius had found the Solid Orrery fairly impressive the first time he had seen it. Supposedly it had been a gift from the technicians of Panoply, grateful for Chandler Prentiss Voi's help when its terms of operation were being decided. With the right conjuring commands, any part of the Solid Orrery could be enlarged and inspected, down to an almost insane level of magnification.

Julius had proved that to himself once, by zeroing in on Yellowstone, and then finding the eye-shaped atmospheric smudge that marked the location of Chasm City. He had enlarged the city, making it swell out of the side of the planet like a malignant growth, and he had peeled back the main dome and located the greenish swatch – surprisingly small – that was the open area containing the wooded estates, of which the Voi home was only a small element. The Solid Orrery had only let him go as far as the family dome, though, refusing to let him peel it back to see the Shell House.

All the same, though, he had come to think less of it once his own implants were up and integrated, and he had full access to the consensual information field. Anything made of mere matter looked a little tawdry and limited compared to the sensory riches accessible through direct neural stimulation.

Yet there was something different about it today – a kind of pearly glimmer to its details, an inherent lack of focus, as if he saw it through tear-stained eyes. Fine, glinting threads seemed to bind its elements, as if a spider had been crawling around it overnight, trying to fix a web to its endlessly shifting geometry.

Caleb glanced at him, his look confirming what Julius was seeing.

'Why does it look like that?' Julius asked.

'It's an abstraction layer,' Father said. 'A separate visual overlay, augmenting the quickmatter realisation.'

'We realised that,' Caleb said.

'The purpose is to indicate the flow of abstraction packets,' Father said, looking at the boys in turn. 'Trillions of packets flowing from world to world, from core to core, from mind to mind. Abstraction queries, polling results, communications, even the basic instructions underpinning the shaping of quickmatter and the consensual field. The gears that grind behind every human thought, every human whim. The great work of Sandra Voi, laid bare.' He grinned at his sons, while Mother looked on with nothing but apprehension. 'Beautiful, isn't it? I don't think there's anything lovelier.'

Julius and Caleb glanced at each other, Julius certain that his brother shared the same thought. It was pretty enough, but if their father expected them to be bowled over by it, he had underestimated both of them.

'I see you need some convincing,' Father said. A soft smile creased his lips. 'A ballot is pending in the Glitter Band – some minor matter of inter-habitat relations. The cores are beginning to return the results as each citizen registers their vote. Packets flowing between worlds, from the cores to the hubs and routers, to the central collating systems. All under the supreme and watchful eye of Panoply, ensuring that democracy proceeds without friction or impediment.' Father stretched over, reaching an arm into the Solid Orrery. His fingers tweezed at one of the fine, twinkling threads. He pulled with thumb and forefinger. The thread stretched, as if it were on the point of breaking, and then snapped back to its original configuration.

But something glinted between his fingers. He relaxed back to a normal standing position, still pinching a dancing, silvery spark between thumb and forefinger. He brought it close, studying it with a certain lustful fascination, the way an ogre might regard a fairy.

'This is a packet,' he said, his eyes crossed together and gleaming with the reflected twinkle of the tiny spark. 'Or more accurately, a linked bundle of packets, signifying a returning vote. Perfect, integral, self-correcting. But for the moment it's not going anywhere.'

The boys looked on. All of a sudden Julius had a thousand questions. But one thing was already clear to him. Father was not making some theoretical point about something that could or might happen. This was real; this was now. His father had actually reached into the Solid Orrery and stopped a vote in its tracks.

'No one can do that,' Caleb said.

'He's right,' Julius put in. 'The system's foolproof. That's what Sandra Voi gave us.'

'Sandra Voi gave *us* a little more than that,' Father said.

Julius was beginning to feel quite disturbed by that dancing glint. He wanted Father to put it back, to let it go on its way, to restore the right and proper way of things. He had the feeling Father had unpicked some vital thread from the corner of reality, and if he kept tugging at it the whole thing was in danger of unravelling.

But it was Mother who took up the explanation. 'Sandra Voi was a genius, but she was also a pragmatist. Our demarchist system is as perfect as it can ever be. Flawless, instantaneous mass democratic participation. The will of the people, without interference. No government, no hier archies, no vested interests, no possibility of bias or corruption.'

'But—' Julius said.

Mother raised a gentle, silencing hand, and he let her continue. 'But true democracy embodies the possibility of its own dissolution. If a ballot were put to the people to abandon our demarchist principles, and the votes carried the day . . . what then? You may say that no such vote would ever be cast. But that is to neglect the pressures that may apply during times of crisis, during emergencies and times of economic hardship, or when wild and seductive new ideas run rife. Sandra Voi took the long view. She knew that even the most perfect system must contain a self-protecting contingency.'

'We are that contingency,' Father said.

'Sandra Voi designed a safeguard into her system,' Mother said. 'Not a loophole, or a weakness, but a deliberate feature. It allowed Sandra to guide the hand of democracy, to keep it from undoing itself – or from making choices it might come to regret. It was a subtlety, built into the neural architecture at a level that would allow it to pass all scrutiny. Each generation of Vois has known of this contingency, and each has borne that knowledge with dignity and restraint. Ours is not to use this power flagrantly, but always to be ready to use it when the moment calls.'

'Please put that vote back,' Julius said.

Father smiled tightly, but obeyed Julius. He reached back into the Solid Orrery and the glint sped from his fingers, losing itself almost instantly in one of the twinkling threads.

'The system will know something went wrong,' Caleb said. 'It will sense that that vote was delayed.'

'No,' Father said, not without a swell of pride. 'That's all taken care of. The contingency passes all error-handling routines. Deceives them, you might say. I could have snuffed that vote out of existence, made it never reach the collating systems, and no error would have been detected at any level.'

'This isn't right,' Julius said. 'No one's meant to interfere with the system – not even us.'

'It's not interference,' Caleb said, surprising him. 'It's self-preservation. Isn't that right, Father?'

'It's a necessary duty – an obligation,' Father said. 'One to be treated with the utmost respect. And so it's been. In the years since the founding of this city, the contingency has been evoked only a handful of times . . . and on each occasion with a heavy and reluctant heart.' His attention shifted from Caleb to Julius. 'Something still troubles you, son.'

Julius swallowed. He was still shocked by what he had seen, but he took it at face value, not for a second doubting that the show of power had been genuine. Now, though, his mind was flashing ahead, evaluating the implications.

'You delayed a vote, and you say you could have stopped it registering at all. I believe you. But a vote here and there never makes enough of a difference to matter.'

'He's a smart one,' Mother commented.

'Julius is correct,' Father said, nodding at both of his sons. 'What I just showed you was only the simplest demonstration of our capabilities. But if that were all we could do, we would still be powerless. When the worlds poll, even the most closely contested results often hinge on majorities of many millions.'

'You can't affect that many votes,' Julius said.

'Not the way I've shown you,' Father agreed. 'Not by picking at a packet here, a data-bundle there. But we still have influence on the scale necessary to effect change. If the shimmer is the weather, then we can shape the way the weather varies.' He returned his attention to the Solid Orrery, but instead of dipping his fingers into it, this time he held his hands before him and made a sort of conjuring gesture, the way one might persuade a chair to assume one form rather than another. Julius and Caleb studied the results, watching as an invisible breeze seemed to play across the web of data-threads, buckling and trembling them. 'Now there's a delay across multiple core returns,' Father commented, concentration tensing his facial muscles. 'But again the error-correction routines see nothing out of the ordinary. No word of a problem begins to reach the ordinary monitoring systems, let alone Panoply.' He relaxed his hands, letting out a sigh. 'And the vote proceeds as it would have done, except for a barely detectable delay in processing the returns. But I could easily just have cast a portion of those votes into oblivion, or transformed a million returns from one type to another. Enough to swing the result, had I so chosen.'

'I want to know how to do it,' Caleb said.

Julius felt obliged to go along with his brother's enthusiasm, even though he had decided misgivings. 'Yes. Me too. That's why we're here, isn't it? You wouldn't show us these things if you didn't mean for us to be able to do them. And I know we can.'

'You have the talent,' Mother said. 'Both of you are very good at shaping. But there's more to this than technical ability. It's about judgement, responsibility – restraint. Knowing when not to act, as much as knowing when. Sandra Voi did not mean for this gift to be used for our convenience. It was always a tool of last resort, to safeguard that which she held most precious: democracy, freedom, the universal will of the people.'

'We're ready to take on this responsibility,' Caleb said solemnly. 'Aren't we, brother?'

'We can be,' Julius said. But the truth was that he felt as cowed by the idea of that burden as he was stirred by it. It was one thing to carry this name; another to be told he was now expected to save society from itself. He felt as if was being made to grow up between one morning and the next, denied all the carefree years he had counted on.

'Julius has caution,' Mother said, giving her son an admiring nod.

'Caution is good,' Father said. 'Laudable. But the boys have been readied for this responsibility, and they must rise to it.' He was addressing Julius and Caleb now. 'The transition need only be gradual. Your mother and I have many years ahead of us, many good decades in which we hope to be of service. If the contingency must be invoked, then it will be our decision. But you will learn from us, and under our close supervision you will be entrusted with certain obligations.' He spread his hands grandly. 'This will be your classroom from now on, the Solid Orrery your only subject worthy of study. You will immerse yourselves in the shimmer, learn to feel its moods, its tides, its great and silent heartbeat. You will sense the coming and going of votes, but that will only be the start of it. The entire flow of information through the abstraction is yours to sample, yours to swim in – yours to shape. You will see more, and know more, than anyone alive. And through that seeing and knowing you will become wise beyond your years, understanding more than anyone what is at stake – what glories would be lost, if this were to fail. The bounty of contentment that would slip from our grasp, where once our hold on it seemed unassailable.'

Julius had the sense that his father was repeating words that must have been said to him at a similar age. But he straightened his back, listened hard, and tried to measure up to the job expected of him.

'How will we know?' he asked. 'When it's right to intervene, and when it's wrong? How are we meant to know?'

'You are a Voi,' Father told him. 'That is all you need to remember, Julius.'

Caleb took his arm, not ungently – it was more brotherly affection than he had shown in quite some time. 'It's all right. I know we'll be all right. It's hard, but we'll never let anyone down.'

'Don't give us cause to be disappointed,' Mother said.

Caleb raised his chin; it was on the calculated edge of defiance. 'We won't, Mother. Julius and I are good on our own, but we're much stronger together. Aren't we, brother?'

Julius nodded. But he did not meet his mother's eyes while he did so. He was thinking of blood, and of knives.

By the time Dreyfus docked, four days had passed since Brig's death, but from the agitated mood of the other workers it might as well have been a matter of hours. Dreyfus found it hard to blame them for their belligerent mood, with Brig's death coming so soon after the demise of Terzet Friller. They were fed up with being fobbed off with non-answers, and they had his sympathy.

'I'll be straight with you,' he told the restless, aggrieved assembly, raising his voice over their questions and half-muttered insults. 'Brig was the victim of deliberate sabotage, and I don't believe that Terzet Friller's death was any sort of an accident either.'

'You're blaming us now?' asked a huge, muscular individual with an overhanging brow ridge.

'I wish I could. It would make my job a lot simpler.' Dreyfus stared him down, even as he sensed that the man was on the verge of snapping. 'But none of you were responsible. I'm as sure of that as I am of anything. One of the reasons for my conviction is that the death of Terzet Friller is only one of a larger pattern under investigation. Brig died because someone wanted to hamper our enquiry into that death. You'll have spoken to Prefects Ng and Bancal since the incident, of course. They're operating under extreme restrictions of secrecy, limiting what they can say to you. You may have found that frustrating – I know I would. But I know those two operatives as well as any people alive. They'll be burning with fury about the death of your friend. It will have touched them very deeply, and they won't rest until the matter is resolved.'

'But you still won't tell us anything,' the big man said.

'I'm sorry. What's your name, by the way?'

'Mallion Ross. And we're not fools, Prefect. We know the rumours. We've picked up on what people are talking about, all over the Glitter Band. People dying, and you not knowing why. More and more each week. That is what this is about, isn't it?'

'I'm sorry,' Dreyfus repeated. 'I realise how difficult this is. All I'm asking for is that you trust . . .'

'Trust cuts both ways,' Ross said sharply, looking around to the others for tacit support. 'We're citizens as well. We have our votes. We've put our trust in Panoply, just like all the others. What's the word they use?'

'Vested,' someone else said.

'That's it – vested our trust in Panoply. Given them the power of life and death over us. And we know they'll use those powers, when it comes down to it.'

Dreyfus shifted uneasily, but let Ross continue.

'But Panoply doesn't seem to be in any hurry to give any of that trust back to us. We know there's something bad building up, Prefect – we'd have to have our heads in the sand not to. So reach out to us. Tell us what the big, bad secret is. We're not children. We can cope with a little fear.'

'Perhaps you can,' Dreyfus said. 'You're used to danger, after all. Your lives aren't easy. That's the path you've chosen, and I respect it. But there are a hundred million other citizens out there. You're right that their trust has been vested in us. But part of that trust lies in our commitment to spare the citizenry any undue anxiety concerning their present and future security. We conduct much of our work in secret because that is also part of the social contract between Panoply and the Glitter Band. We have the bad dreams so the rest of you don't need to.'

'I was there when we opened up Terzet's spacesuit,' Ross said. 'I've got my share of bad dreams.'

Dreyfus sat in silence for a few pensive moments, his head lowered. He thought about the things that had been said to him and the equally persuasive arguments he had tried to muster.

Something in him gave way. It felt like a slippage, the easing of a strained fault line. He nodded slowly, meeting Ross's eyes. 'All right. Let's take trust seriously. Do you speak for the people in this room?'

Ross looked around at the assembled workers. 'I don't speak for anyone. But if you feel you can trust me, you can trust any one of us.'

'Then I'll tell you what we're facing. Not all of it – I'd be in severe violation of several professional oaths were I to share everything – but more than you've been told, and more than anyone outside Panoply knows.'

Ross seemed momentarily unsure of himself, as if he had leaned against a door that suddenly swung open too easily. Perhaps he now feared what he had been asking for.

Dreyfus eyed him, waiting for his assent to continue.

'Go ahead, Prefect,' Ross said.

The news from House Fuxin-Nymburk was not the sort to give Jane Aumonier cause to cheer. Their indignation suitably stoked, Garlin's audience had split off a small but determined mob, set on taking ownership of the habitat's polling core. The mob was on the move, gathering numbers as it travelled. Garlin was at the front of it, protected by a small cordon of guards, two of whom she recognised as the thugs Dreyfus had dealt with in Hospice Idlewild. There was a bow-legged, chimp-like swagger to Garlin now; he was opening his arms wide as if daring someone to jam a blade into his chest.

Numbering more than a hundred citizens, the mob was already larger than anything the local constables were routinely equipped to handle. They were retreating before it, voicing urgent requests into their cuff microphones, calling for additional support from elsewhere in the habitat. They could handle brawls and unruly crowds, but an organised, purposeful citizen uprising was far outside their usual experience.

For that, they would normally turn to Panoply.

The thought had no sooner formed itself in Aumonier's mind than the first formal request came in. *Emergent civil unrest in House Fuxin-Nymburk – please dispatch priority assistance via all channels.*

They were right. Sending in a squad of prefects was absolutely the correct response to this disturbance. Twenty of her operatives, with full whiphound backup, would send an unambiguous signal.

But that was surely the response that Devon Garlin was counting on.

She opened a direct line to the chief of the constables.

'This is Supreme Prefect Jane Aumonier,' she said, her tone firm but conciliatory. 'You have a developing situation and it was right and proper to bring it to my attention. Panoply stands ready to offer your constables advice and situational intelligence. Our ships and operatives are nearby, and we will maintain a close watch on your emergency. But for the moment I have every confidence in your ability to contain and neutralise this disturbance.'

The chief, a woman named Glenda Malkmus – they had never spoken before this day – could not hide her sense of betrayal. 'Supreme Prefect – we have a crisis on our hands. That mob is one hundred and twenty strong and growing. My constables have shields and electric stun-guns. They're going to be overwhelmed.'

'No,' Aumonier said firmly. 'They won't be, once the mob realises that its objectives are futile. You have the authority to secure the polling core. Raise the emergency barricades, initiate a local lockdown, then declare a binding curfew on the surrounding plaza. Tell everyone to go home. Close your inbound transit terminals, and only allow passengers to board outbound services – you have that means.'

The woman's eyes widened. 'But Supreme—'

'My word is final, Chief Constable Malkmus. The whole point of the local constabulary is to provide a buffer between the citizens and the full might of Panoply. I have my responsibilities, but so do you.'

'You're letting us down.'

'No, I am counting on you to fulfil your civic obligations. As I am sure you will.'

Aumonier closed the link before Malkmus had a chance to respond. The exchange had done nothing for her conscience. The woman was right: she *was* being let down, and so were her constables and the wider citizenry. But Aumonier had to think not in terms of this one habitat, but of all the others. Some would view this non-intervention in a poor light, and that was to be expected. But at least Garlin would not get what he so obviously craved: a direct confrontation between the people and their protectors.

For now, anyway.

The facet remained enlarged, but with a gesture Aumonier reduced its significance a fraction, careful not to let one problem eclipse all the others. Then she resumed her watchful floating posture, a woman at the middle of all things, the restless light of several thousand worlds flickering in her eyes.

Dreyfus checked his environmental indicators then decided it was safe to remove his helmet. He inhaled cautiously. The air reeked. It was like taking a deep breath from a hopper full of week-old kitchen waste. Mud, rubble and shattered buildings stretched away from the elevator terminal into gloomy distance. With most of the ceiling lights inactive, the landscape was defined in deceptive blotches of light and shadow. He made out the curvature of the rim, but not the endcap bulkheads separating one partition from the next. Brightness flooded the path leading from the terminal, making him squint.

A figure waddled out of the glare.

'I know, it smells terrible. You should try being a pig for a day and then you'd *really* know how bad it is.'

'Sparver,' Dreyfus said, smiling. 'Prefect Bancal. Are you all right?'

'A bit battered and bruised, boss, but we got off lightly compared to Brig.'

'Have you found anything in the building?'

'You'd better see for yourself.' Sparver glanced at the worker who had accompanied Dreyfus to the rim. 'Is Mister Ross coming as well?'

'No, I'll get back to the hub now that you're here,' Ross said, placing a hand on Dreyfus's forearm. 'Good luck, Prefect. Thank you for . . . trusting us.'

'I'll do my best not to let you down,' Dreyfus said.

'I believe you,' Ross said, letting go.

'Follow me, boss,' Sparver said, beckoning. 'It's not too far. Still pretty damp in here, even after three solid days of pumping, but we can walk the rest of the way without getting our feet wet.'

The Heavy Technical Squad had been busy, Dreyfus saw. They had helped restart the pumps so some of the excess water could be moved back into the eighth partition, and they had cut through and rewired the control linkages for the bulkhead locks so there was no danger of another surprise like the one that caught Thalia's party out. They had also repaired or replaced sections of elevated walkway, and – with the help of some of the other reclamation workers – were in the process of rounding up the monitoring robots that were still running wild.

It was half a kilometre's walk to the bulkhead that led to the second partition, a semicircular wall looming out of the murk as they approached. Dreyfus stared up at it, searching for the primary lock that had allowed the flood to drain out of the first chamber. There it was, about thirty metres above – an iris only just large enough for a small ship to squeeze through. With the water level now much reduced, it seemed impossible that anyone could ever have gone through it, much less in a raft. He looked at Sparver, leading them on with a confident swagger, and gave silent thanks that both of his deputies had survived.

'What was all that about?' Sparver asked. 'Ross saying you trusted them?'

'We established some common ground,' Dreyfus said, feeling no further need to elaborate.

'I guess it won't hurt to make friends where we can. Have you heard the news from Panoply?'

'No, I was off-line while talking to Ross.'

'Cases fifty-eight and fifty-nine have dropped. Unrelated incidents, but only a few hours apart and for the first time, both deaths took place in the same habitat. Tang's run the numbers. That steepening of the death curve isn't going away.'

'I didn't think it would. Was there any more good news?'

'Lady Jane wants as many prefects as possible dispersed through the Glitter Band, even if that means breaking up some teams.'

'I can see why,' Dreyfus said. 'Maximum dispersion means a greater chance of someone being close enough to harvest a head before there's too much damage. But it isn't ideal.'

'Especially not with the trouble kicking off in Fuxin-Nymburk.'

'Let me guess. Something to do with Devon Garlin?'

'Your new best friend's on a bit of a roll. It's more than the usual rabble-rousing this time. He's got a mob and it's on the move.'

'Then contain it.'

'The constables are struggling. They've asked for assistance, but Jane doesn't want to go in heavy-handed, especially when she wants to concentrate on the Wildfire investigation. She feels that an enforcement action would only work to Garlin's advantage, and we've already given him enough ammunition as it is . . .' Sparver sucked air through his teeth. 'Sore subject, I know. Move on.'

'How about some good news. I bet you're about to tell me you've made excellent progress in tracing the ownership of Elysium Heights.'

'You might want to dial down your expectations a little, boss.'

'I couldn't do it if I tried,' Dreyfus said phlegmatically. 'All right. What's the news, or lack of it?'

'Vanessa's been digging through the ownership chain. But it's a rat's nest. Firms owned by firms that are owned by firms that turn out to be owned by the first firm . . . snakes eating their own tails. It's all just this side of legal, but it's very definitely a smokescreen.'

'Then we're onto something.'

'I think the sabotage may have been a clue as well.'

'Perhaps.'

'You sound less than convinced.'

'If the sabotage was meant to slow down our investigation, it's had exactly the opposite effect.'

'Something made it happen, boss. We saw those robots, and—'

'Yes,' Dreyfus answered. 'And the robots were just a nuisance until you and Thalia showed up. That means someone was waiting for Panoply to take an interest in this place. The robots detected you and by some means your presence was the trigger for the doors to open.'

'By some means?'

'It doesn't mean a person was involved, not directly, just some sort of monitoring routine. A low-level gamma would have been all that was needed. I'll want to look at the control architecture for this place, Sparver.'

'Consider it sequestered,' Sparver said.

There was a service lock at the base of the wall, so there was no need to ascend to the primary one. They went through a short connecting tunnel and then came out into the second partition. Like the first, it was a quilt of light and darkness. But Dreyfus had no difficulty locating the object of interest. It would have been hard to miss under any circumstances.

The curving floor of the second partition made room for about twenty artificial islands, rising from what would have been a shallow lake occupying most of the rim's width. The islands were connected by elevated walkways – or what was left of these paths, after the devastation of the flood. One island was larger and taller than the others, hemmed by a wide expanse of filthy, debris-clotted water. Rising from this island was the single, striking structure of Elysium Heights.

'Do we know what it is yet?' Dreyfus asked.

'It's going to take the technical squad more than a few days to work their way through the thing,' Sparver said. 'But I'll tell you what we already know. It's a kind of clinic. Very high-end. The place is stuffed full of medical equipment, operating theatres, recuperation areas, consultation rooms. What we don't yet know is what they were treating, or why, or for whom.'

'Or why they stopped,' Dreyfus said.

Sparver and Dreyfus climbed a zig-zagging walkway up onto the main level of the island, then went into the base of the trunk via an arched doorway.

Inside was an atrium, its ceiling six stories above, with banks of elevators in the walls and many reception desks and seating areas. The flood must have washed in and out of the main entrance, because there was a tidemark of filth up to the second level, and the desks and chairs were grimed over with muck and debris. Gleaming power lines snaked across the floor, tangled like squid arms. The Heavy Technical Squad had made temporary arrangements to restore power and lighting to the white tree, enabling lights, doors and elevators to regain some functionality.

Dreyfus stepped over one of them and found his way to a desk, where he had already spotted Thalia in conversation with a couple of members of the technical squad. The Panoply operatives were bending down over a tangle of froptic connections, hotwired into the guts of the desk.

Thalia had a compad in the crook of her arm, status code scrolling across it at high speed.

'Oh,' she began. 'Glad you're here, sir. We're just trying to—'

'Save it for the report, Thalia,' Dreyfus said gently. 'The one you're going to submit on your way back to Panoply, before you begin at least fifty-two hours of consecutive rest. The same for Sparver. You've laid the groundwork: the drudge teams can brief me on further developments.'

Thalia looked torn. 'The squad's been really helpful, sir. But this sort of thing is exactly my speciality.'

'You're trying to communicate with the desk?'

She tilted the compad his way, as if it meant anything to him. 'So far it's just scrambled garbage. There might not be anything left worth recovering, but if we don't try . . .'

'All right – an hour or two at most.' Dreyfus looked beyond the desk, to the nearest bank of elevators. A female technician came out of one, pushing a wheeled trolley laden with evidence. 'I'll take a little stroll upstairs, I think.'

'You want a guide?' Sparver said.

'No – I want both of you to keep an eye on each other, and make sure you're both ready to ship out in two hours. No excuses.'

'That's us told,' Thalia said.

Dreyfus walked to the elevator, arriving in time for the technician to come back with an empty trolley. Dreyfus waited for the woman to enter a floor into the crude-looking control box that had been grafted onto the elevator's walls. 'High-level systems aren't working,' she explained. 'And that includes voice recognition. Still, it's not bad for a building that was under hard vacuum only a day ago. Which floor would you like?'

'As high as you can go.'

'All the way up – that's where I'm headed anyway.'

Dreyfus settled his hands before him and looked down at his muddied shoes as the elevator worked its way up the trunk. The walls were a plain silver, blank except for a white tree motif stencilled onto the one opposite the doors. The tree was a stark, minimalist representation of the building itself, with the suspended globes resembling hanging fruit. Dreyfus was forcibly reminded of the pattern he had seen on Cassandra Leng's clothing. There was no doubt in his mind that one was inspired by the other, however deliberately.

168

'Sir . . .' the woman began. 'Prefect Dreyfus.'

He looked up from his shoes. 'Yes?'

'We heard about what happened, sir. About you and Devon Garlin.'

'Did you?'

'I just wanted to say . . . all of us, I think . . . we think you were right, sir. He had it coming.'

Dreyfus raised his eyebrows in an approximation of interest.

'That's your considered opinion, is it?'

The woman looked taken aback. 'I just meant, sir . . .'

'No one has it coming,' Dreyfus said slowly. 'Not even Devon Garlin. And my actions were wrong. They were borne of an error of judgement. I regret them, and I'm fortunate that the Supreme Prefect wasn't harsher in her response. There's nothing to be applauded here.'

'I'm . . . sorry, sir.'

'Good. In future, restrict your observations to the problem at hand. You'll be doing us both a favour.'

At last the elevator reached its destination. The doors opened and the woman pushed the trolley out into a hallway, where two other technicians were gathering and collecting evidence. A corridor stretched away from the hall, mostly dark save for a cluster of lights at the far end.

'May I help you, Prefect Dreyfus?' asked one of the technicians.

'I wanted to get a feel for the place. Is it safe for me to go down there?'

'You should be all right, sir. We've restored partial power to that limb, and we're trying to get some of the clinical systems back up and running for forensic purposes. If there were any nasty surprises, we'd have run into them by now.'

'I'll watch my step.'

Dreyfus walked the length of the corridor, at least a hundred metres beyond the elevator. The flood had never penetrated this part of the structure, so the surroundings showed little sign of disturbance. The trunk was much narrower than this near the top, so he was certain he was moving along one of the high branches. He passed offices and reception areas, finally reaching the lit area. Again, there were power lines and emergency patches in evidence. Dreyfus carried on. The floor dipped down a little, becoming a ramp, but not so steep that it was difficult to walk. At last he reached what had to be the limit of this branch, for the corridor opened up into a circular hub surrounding a central bank of elevators, all going down into what he knew must be one of the globes, suspended below him. None of the elevators were operational, but there was a spiral staircase threading down the middle of the elevator core and he took that instead, his feet ringing loudly on the clattery metal risers.

He went down five or six levels, then found his way back out into the globe. A circular corridor enclosed the elevator core, with radial corridors branching out from it. Dreyfus followed one of them a short distance until he reached the curving outer wall of the globe with angled windows looking out along the length of the semi-flooded chamber, all the way back to the vast bulkhead wall. Leading off from the corridor were more reception areas and rooms. Dreyfus tried a few of the tree-stencilled doors, finding them sealed. He could have summoned one of the technicians to force the door, but he had no doubt all would be opened in good time and the squad obviously had enough to keep them busy. He loitered at one of the reception desks, his attention drawn by a plastic anatomical model mounted on a steel pedestal. It was a human head, with the skull removed so the different brain modules could be undone like a three-dimensional jigsaw. He fingered the waxy parts, imagining the model being used as part of an initial interview or consultancy process.

A flicker of motion showed at the edge of his vision. He turned without panic, noticing an open doorway and a series of readouts playing across a wall. A power line went in through the open doorway. Dreyfus stepped inside, finding himself in a room equipped with desk, chairs, a couch, and what were obviously robotic surgical devices, upright forms parked against a wall and shrouded in chrysalis-like folds of sterile wrap. A trolley sat in the centre of the room, cluttered with equipment, and a fist-thick bundle of froptic cables ran from the trolley to a slot in the wall. Dreyfus picked up a Panoply-issue compad from the trolley, noting that it was displaying the same pattern of readouts as the wall. He remembered what Thalia had said about recovering only garbage, and presumed the same sort of effort was in progress here.

He set the compad back down and moved around the surgical suite. The robotic devices looked clean and well maintained under their translucent shrouds, but they were obviously several decades old, perhaps explaining why they had been left here. Their multi-jointed manipulators were angled up against their bodies, like the limbs of mantises.

He moved to the curving windows, looking out again at the dismal floodscape with its dazzle of light and darkness, and tried to put himself in the place of someone waiting in this room, someone submitting to the tender mercies of those machines. Neural services, he thought. Brain modification – something more complex or delicate than the norm. The elimination of rare diseases, or the augmentation of brain faculties outside the usual scope of orthodox medical services. Nothing illegal, perhaps, but certainly nothing commonplace.

Probably nothing cheap, either.

'You're wondering who would come to a place like this. Wondering why anyone would put their mind under the knife – metaphorically or otherwise. Don't pretend you're not, Prefect. I can read you like a book. A very simple book containing mostly pictures.'

He turned again, but this time with a start, because her voice had been the last thing he had been expecting.

She looked at him from every active display in the room, including the compad he had set down on the trolley. She had not changed any detail of her appearance since their last encounter, but all he could see of her was her face, hair and the backrest of her chair.

'How are you here?'

'Oh, don't pretend it's any sort of mystery. I followed the noise. I followed you, because in a very narrow sense the things that interest you are also of some remote interest to me.'

'Were you responsible for nearly killing my deputies and murdering one of my witnesses?'

She pinched her nose in distaste. 'Hardly my style, is it? If I felt like murdering your deputies I'd make quite sure I finished the job. No, that wasn't my doing – and shame on you for thinking otherwise. But fascinating, isn't it, nonetheless?'

'Not the word I'd use.'

'Whoever was here set up a very deliberate trap. I've eavesdropped on your speculation. You're right – those monitoring robots were definitely part of it. I even found the gamma-level that was task-handling their visual inputs, waiting for Panoply to show up.'

Despite his anger, confusion – and no small measure of trepidation – Dreyfus tried to keep his voice level, his enquiries pertinent. 'You've managed to reach that deeply into the architecture?'

'It's not hard for me. Not much of a challenge. Certainly nowhere as difficult as breaching Panoply's sealed archives.'

'Tell me about the gamma. Who put it there? How long ago?'

'Questions, questions.' Her tone was playfully scolding, the way a child might address a doll. 'Always one way with you, isn't it. Never much give and take. Never much *quid pro quo*. How about we redress that, starting now?'

'You're an all-powerful machine intelligence. What could I possibly tell you that you don't already know?'

'Oh, use a little imagination, Prefect Dreyfus – if it doesn't strain you overmuch. The Clockmaker taxes my resources. I'll beat it eventually, but for the moment it's showing a tiresome resilience, a tiresome ability to outflank my advances. Frankly I'm getting rather *bored* of our little game of hide and seek, and you really wouldn't like me when I'm bored. The truth is, though, that I don't know as much about my enemy as I'd like. But there are secrets in your deep archive – technical files, eyewitness accounts, detailed testimonies. That's all I'm interested in. As you say – I'm a godlike intelligence. The only thing that concerns me is other godlike intelligences.'

'And me, now and then.'

'Don't get an inflated sense of your self-worth. I speak to you because we have some shared history, and you are the key to something I need. And because I know when a man needs help.'

'From you?'

A teasing smile played across her features. 'You'll be surprised how little public information there is to find on this place. They kept their secrets very close to their hearts.'

'I already know more than I did an hour ago. It's a clinic. Elysium Heights. People must have come here from all over the Glitter Band for medical procedures.'

'Yes, well done. That's very good.' Her fingers came into view, making a sarcastic clapping gesture. 'And you suspect a link to your spate of neural deaths. Perhaps the dead were all clients of this facility, is that what you're thinking?'

'It's hardly a leap.'

'Then a patient list would be very useful to you, wouldn't it? Especially if that list included the names of people who haven't yet died, people who are still out there, still walking around, unaware that their heads might explode at any minute. That would be of some small interest to you, wouldn't it?'

Dreyfus forced himself to sound calm. 'If there's a list, Thalia will find it.'

'Provided I don't find it first. Mm.' She touched a finger to her lower lip. 'Provided I haven't *already* found it, and taken pains to make sure no one else will be able to read it.' Lowering the finger, she gave a pout of contrition. 'Oh dear. I've upset you, haven't I?'

'I've no reason to think a list exists.'

'I could give you names.'

'I already know who's dead; I expect you learned the names from us as well.'

'I was thinking of the ones who haven't died yet. I could give you a single name now, but since the neural overloads aren't following any particularly obvious pattern, we might have rather a long wait before the name is confirmed.'

'Then give me all the names.'

Frown lines notched her forehead. 'Why ever would I do that?'

'Because this'll end up hurting all of us, you included. A public emergency plays nicely into Devon Garlin's hands. It proves his point that Panoply can't offer the security we've promised. And that helps the breakaway cause. If the Glitter Band starts fragmenting, you won't have the fully functioning networks you need to keep one step ahead of the Clockmaker.'

'A rather tortuous argument, even by your long-winded standards.'

'Take it or leave it. But a single name doesn't buy you any favours from me.'

'Whereas all the names . . . might?'

'I didn't say that either.'

'It sounded as if you did.' Something mischievous twinkled in her eyes. 'An impasse, then. You won't budge and I won't budge. But we both want something. Let's see if we can't come to an arrangement, shall we? I'll disclose a partial list of the names.'

'All or nothing.'

'Oh, Prefect Dreyfus, *do* try to learn some patience – it would do you a world of good.' She coughed delicately. 'I hadn't finished speaking. I'll disclose a partial list, including all the names on the patient file, but stripped down to only a few characters in each name. That'll be sufficient to confirm that I have the known cases, and you'll also be able to cross-match the next death against my list. The partial list won't give you any predictive powers, but it will confirm that I have the full set of names, if and when you decide to come back and ask for them. As a token of my goodwill, too, I'll be giving you a very significant piece of information: the total number of deaths ahead of you.'

'You could tell me that now.'

'But that wouldn't be fun for either of us. And this is *such* fun, isn't it?'

'Where can I expect this partial list?'

'You'll find it. And you know where to find me, if and when you see sense. Think of the power those names could give you. Find those people, bring them in for emergency surgery, and you've crushed this public emergency in one stroke. Denied Devon Garlin a hand in the breakup of the thing most dear to you. A year from now, he could be history – along with the memory of this unpleasantness. Isn't that attractive, Prefect Dreyfus? Isn't that tempting?'

'To someone else, maybe.'

'You say that now,' Aurora answered. 'But everyone has their breaking point.' She rolled her eyes in quiet exasperation. 'Oh, let me throw the dog another bone – perhaps he'll behave himself then. Your little people are trying to find an ownership trail for this place. They'll struggle.'

'Because of your meddling?'

'Because whoever set this place up went to a lot of trouble to hide their tracks. Shadow companies, double-blinds, that sort of thing. All very clever, all very cunning – for an ordinary mind.'

'And you're not an ordinary mind.'

'We agree on something, at least. Go far enough into that hall of mirrors and you'll find a corporate entity known as Nautilus Holdings. Keep that name in mind – I think you'll find it *very* interesting.'

'Why should I?'

'Nautilus, Dreyfus. Nautilus as in *shell*. Do I have to spell it out to you?'

She regarded him for a few moments longer, then her face dissolved back into scrolling lines of data.

CHAPTER ELEVEN

Thalia looked up as Dreyfus approached from the elevator, plodding across the slick, filth-smeared floor of the concourse. There was a slump to his shoulders, a troubled set to his face.

'Are you still here?'

'You said I could finish off, sir. It's barely been an hour.' She wondered why he took such an interest in her welfare when he never looked far from the ragged edge of exhaustion himself. 'Did you find anything out, sir?'

Dreyfus stepped over a power line. 'Nothing that upsets the picture we already have, that this place was some sort of clinic.'

'The technicians are cataloguing and removing a lot of medical equipment,' Thalia said, nodding at one of the trolleys awaiting collection. 'They say it's state-of-the-art, for thirty years ago. Beyond that, I'm not sure it's going to teach us very much.'

'Which makes it all the more important to get what we can from the clinic's own archives,' Dreyfus said.

'There'll be external records, won't there? Patient files logged with central repositories?'

'Someone obviously wanted to hinder your investigation of the clinic – we can't assume they won't have taken other steps.' He glanced down at the compad she was still holding. 'That's why I'm very interested in what you can get from the local archives.'

'Not much is the answer,' Thalia said, flipping the compad around for his benefit. 'I think I've located the area where we might expect them to have kept the patient files, but if there's anything intelligible left in it, it's well hidden.'

Dreyfus nodded slowly. 'We wouldn't need intact records. Just a fragment, a partial list.'

'I'll see what we can get, sir. Sparver's trying to get something out of the ownership chain, too, but I gather it's not proving very easy. Someone's gone to a lot of trouble to put up smokescreens.'

'All we need is one name – one figure or organisation behind this clinic. Then I can start pulling on that string and see where it leads us.'

'What are you thinking, sir?'

'If I told you, you wouldn't like it. But when I'm confronted with a mystery, I often find it helps to ask one simple question: who is this benefitting?'

'Wildfire, sir?' He watched as a dangerous thought crossed her mind. 'You think . . .' Her eyes widened as the full implication of this line of reasoning became clear to her. 'I mean, I can see how it helps him, but . . .'

'Boss?' asked Sparver, walking over with a compad wedged under his elbow. 'Report in from the Heavies. Reckon they've isolated a gamma-level monitoring intelligence. It seems to have been put there to keep an eye on things until Panoply showed up.'

'Good. Have they sequestered it?'

'That's the thing, boss. There's not much left to sequester. The thing's been corrupted pretty thoroughly. "Torn apart by dogs" is the phrase I heard.'

'When I want colourful metaphors I'll ask for them.' Dreyfus touched his chin. 'If they haven't already done so, tell the specialists to instigate a control and containment sweep for any other active intelligences in the habitat. And I want to know about all communications traffic in and out of this place in the hours before and after your and Thalia's arrival, down to the last binary digit.'

'They're going through it as we speak,' Sparver said. 'I've seen the preliminary breakdowns. Doesn't look as if there's anything out of the ordinary.'

'Losing a witness and nearly drowning's out of the ordinary,' Dreyfus said testily. 'Have you got anywhere with the ownership trail?'

Sparver showed him the compad. 'Must be about nine layers deep by now. But somewhere there's got to be a way through it. It took money to run a place like this, and that money had to come from somewhere.'

Dreyfus reached for the compad. He squinted, tracing a finger along one path of the branching structure. 'These firms – have you verified them all?'

'We're just starting with them,' Sparver said. 'We can run a shallow audit without invoking special measures, but anything more than that needs a one-time mandate, and that has to be signed off by a citizen quorum. It'll take a day or two to work through all these companies.'

Dreyfus hesitated his finger over one of the annotated structures, tapping his nail thoughtfully. 'Nautilus Holdings. Move them up the schedule, would you?'

'Something caught your eye?' Sparver asked, flicking a glance in Thalia's direction.

'Move them up the schedule,' Dreyfus repeated.

For the second time in four days, Thalia and Sparver detached from the Addison-Lovelace wheel and began their return journey to Panoply. Thalia was at the corvette's controls, applying hard thrust as they broke away from the wheel's airspace.

'Maybe it's just me,' Thalia said, when they were safely under way. 'But wasn't that a little odd?'

'What part of this isn't odd?' Sparver had his arms folded across his chest. 'We're on a blind quest to stop heads from exploding, and so far almost all we have to go on is a mysterious and scary white building.'

'I meant Dreyfus, going all tight-lipped like that.'

'Boss's prerogative, Thalia. You'd better start getting used to it, the speed you're going up the ladder.'

She gave him a pointed look, but decided against a direct response. 'You were with him when he arrived at the habitat, weren't you?'

'Some of the way.'

'I saw him too. He was his usual self, more or less. Not exactly bursting with joy and vitality, but . . . then something happened between him arriving and his coming down from the upper levels. He looked like a changed man, Sparver – like he'd just got some very bad news.'

'Perhaps he did.'

'From Panoply, you mean?'

'Lady Jane might have dropped something on him while he was upstairs – you know, some cheerful new development. More deaths, a steepening of the curve, some delightful update on Devon Garlin, who knows?'

'I don't see how things could be much worse than they already are. Anyway, shouldn't he be happier, now we're zeroing in on some kind of common link?'

'We're a long way from that.'

'But closer than we were twenty-six hours ago. That clinic is the key, and we both know it. Dreyfus wouldn't be throwing himself at it if he didn't believe the same thing.'

'So what's your personal theory?' Sparver still had his arms folded, directing a look of expectant interest her way, somewhat in the manner of a tutor unconvinced that she had a thorough grasp of the subject under instruction. 'Enlighten the lowly hyperpig. Let him watch and learn from the higher-ranking prefect.'

'You want to play that game, be my guest.' She seethed for a few moments, before finding a brittle sort of calm. 'Hypothetically . . . what if all the Wildfire cases were clients of this clinic?'

'It would have shown up already.'

'Not if the people involved went to a lot of trouble to hide their involvement. We already know the clinic operated under a smokescreen – that's why you're finding it so hard to trace the ownership. Given that, couldn't the clients have benefitted from the same level of secrecy?'

'Dreyfus has interviewed more than forty beta-level instantiations of the dead,' Sparver said. 'Each and every one of those betas has a vested interest in solving the murder of their living instantiation. Yet not one of them has mentioned any sort of dealings with a super-secret clinic.'

'Maybe the betas don't know what their living versions were up to.'

'Many living witnesses have also been interviewed. Again, no one's brought up any sort of clinic.'

'But Ghiselin Bronner's husband was fixated on those white shapes, and they match the clinic. Memories can be suppressed, Sparver. The people could have had some dealings with Elysium Heights, something that might well have been traumatic, and then had it burned out of their conscious recall. No danger of remembering it themselves, and even less danger of blurting it out to a loved one.'

'And for what reason, exactly?'

Thalia was thinking on the hoof now, but she was not going to let that stand in her way. 'Two reasons, at least. What happened in Elysium Heights was illegal. Or shameful. Or both. Very possibly both. They came here for something, some procedure, and when it was done they didn't want any lasting memory of it. That's why the living witnesses say nothing.'

'And the small matter of the deaths?'

'I don't know. Someone wants to hush it up once and for all, so they're killing off anyone who had a link to the clinic.'

Sparver nodded encouragingly, but there was unmistakable sarcasm in his gesture. 'And in doing so, they're in no way making us even more interested in the clinic, are they?'

'I didn't say I had all the answers. There's something odd going on here, anyway. If that flood hadn't happened, I might have decided the clinic was a dead end, but it's only made me more certain that someone didn't want us to poke around in there. Maybe they were hoping the flood was going to do more damage to the place than it did, destroying what's left of the evidence, but then again that clinic's been sitting there for decades, as far as we can tell, so why wait until now? Something's

178

not fitting together here, Sparver – and I could really use some insights instead of you sitting there with that smug look on your face, looking for holes to poke in my theory.'

'Only doing what a good deputy ought to do,' Sparver said reasonably, before unfolding his arms and polishing his glasses against his sleeve. 'Of course, if you want to suggest—'

The console chimed with an incoming transmission. Gritting her teeth, Thalia reached to respond. 'Ng here.'

'Status, Ng?' asked the familiar but still slightly unnerving voice of Jane Aumonier.

'En route for Panoply, ma'am. Prefect Bancal and I should be docked in just under ninety minutes.'

'Good. You acquitted yourself well, Ng, from the reports I've gathered. Useful leads, and we'll follow them as far as they take us. But I'm afraid I have further need of you.'

'Whatever you want, ma'am – we're at your disposal.'

Next to her, as soon as she had finished, Sparver mimed her saying the same words.

'You may not sound quite so keen when you hear what I have in mind, Ng. We've been monitoring an outbreak of civil unrest in House Fuxin-Nymburk. The local constables are just barely holding the line, and there's a real risk of the mob overrunning the polling core.'

'Civil unrest, ma'am?' she asked, ignoring Sparver.

'Fuxin-Nymburk is one of the habitats most likely to follow the break-away states. Devon Garlin has chosen this moment to apply more leverage. He's there, playing to the gallery, stirring up emotions. If I had grounds for arrest I'd use them, but he's keeping just the right side of legality. The mob is a different matter, though. They must be contained, pacified and dispersed. Normally I'd commit a small enforcement squad, say twenty prefects with dual whiphounds, and a fully armed Deep System Vehicle just to underscore our point. But the present situation requires a more delicate intervention.'

'How might Prefect Bancal and I be of assistance, ma'am?'

'Constable Malkmus has now issued three formal requests for Panoply assistance, and I'm afraid I can no longer ignore her petitions. You and Bancal will detour to Fuxin-Nymburk. Dock, liaise with Malkmus's constables, use your authority, and report back when you have a satisfactory resolution.'

'And if we run into trouble, ma'am?'

'You won't. Your presence alone will send a sufficient message. But should the need arise, additional prefects will not be far away.'

'That's clear, ma'am. Redirecting to Fuxin-Nymburk.'

'Very well, Ng. Just one more thing. Tread lightly around Devon Garlin. He's in the spotlight now.'

One day, only a few weeks after Julius and Caleb had been shown how to shape the flow of information around their world, an odd thing happened with Doctor Stasov.

The boys had been up to their games, playing tricks on Lurcher and hiding from the robot when it went out into the grounds to find them. During one of these bouts, the boys circled back around the Shell House and sneaked inside with the robot still thinking they were somewhere near the dome's perimeter.

That was when they heard the arguing. It was their mother and father, and that was not so unusual lately, but there was a third voice joining the heated conversation and Julius recognised it instantly as belonging to Doctor Stasov.

Caleb and Julius halted in the main entrance hall, not daring to venture into the corridor where the arguing was coming from. The voices had that strained quality of people struggling not to shout, and only just keeping their emotions in check.

Caleb started to say something. Julius, for once the more forceful one, jammed a finger onto his brother's lips. Their own voices would carry from the hall. Even their breathing, fast and ragged from the run-around they had been giving Lurcher, seemed to bounce and amplify off the marbled flooring, the grand metal staircase, the tall, pastel-plastered walls.

They heard snatches of the argument.

Doctor Stasov: '. . . this charade . . .'

Their mother: '. . . treated you very well. Don't take that for granted . . .'

Their father: '. . . undo what has already started . . .'

Stasov: '. . . take a risk every time you bring me here . . . the boys . . . sleeping . . .'

Mother: '. . . ought to be grateful for what we've done . . .'

Father: '. . . know a good thing when you have it. Your reputation . . .'

Stasov: '. . . nothing wrong with my reputation until you took an interest in me . . .'

Mother: 'Don't call it that.'

Stasov: '. . . why not, if blackmail's what it is?'

Then the argument shifted its focus, like the eye of a storm wandering over a landscape. Mother seemed to be making vague conciliatory moves in the direction of Doctor Stasov. '. . . has a small point, perhaps . . .'

To which Father said, turning his venom onto her: '. . . knew what he was getting into. Handsomely rewarded, too . . . if you don't like the arrangement, Aliya, you should have spoken up years ago.'

Doctor Stasov made a scoffing sound. 'Call this a reward?'

Mother: 'Perhaps we should slow down. We're pushing the boys too hard, too fast.'

Stasov: 'Aliya is right. Glad one of you sees sense.'

Father: '. . . have to grow up sooner or later.'

Mother: 'They aren't ready, Marlon. We both know it. Julius still isn't confident of his abilities. Caleb's strong but he's got your temper. We're putting fire in their minds.'

Father: 'Someone has to.'

Doctor Stasov said '. . . this charade . . .' again, followed by: '. . . a lie built on a lie. I won't be part of it. You're making monsters from monsters.'

Mother's sympathies might have been drifting towards the doctor, but this was enough to push her back onto her husband's side. 'Don't call them monsters, Doctor. They're our sons.'

'They're not even that,' Stasov said. 'The games you played with those boys . . . the terrible things you did to them . . . damaged beyond repair.'

'It wasn't my choice,' Mother said pleadingly.

Father's voice grew louder and sharper. 'They'll be back with Lurcher shortly. We'll hear no more of this. You're part of this now, Doctor Stasov. You'd be very unwise to cross us.'

'Oh, don't worry,' Doctor Stasov answered, his low, dry voice barely carrying to the hall. 'I know what happens to people who cross the Vois.'

A door slammed. Julius and Caleb glanced at each other, then backed out of the hall as quietly as they could. They went out onto the terrace, crouching behind a line of large terracotta pots until they saw Lurcher walking back along one of the paths. The robot had a dome for a head, blank except for a single cyclopean eye. It was swivelling rapidly, scanning for the boys.

'We're here, you silly machine,' Caleb called out, pushing over a vase for the spite of it.

While Lurcher cleaned up the mess left by the spilt vase, Mother and Father met the boys in the hall. They were standing apart, tension still showing in their faces.

'Good,' Father said. 'You're here. Doctor Stasov will be with us shortly. He'll run some more tests. Nothing very involved, just to make sure things are moving in the right direction.'

'When can we go into the city?' Caleb asked.

'When you're ready,' Father answered, before Mother had a chance to say anything. 'Which won't be too long now.'

Doctor Stasov emerged sooner after, carrying his bag. Julius thought back to the night he had seen Lurcher carrying the doctor's sleeping form through the darkened gardens, and guessed – presuming he had not been dreaming – that something similar would happen later, and that perhaps, in the early hours, the robot had brought Doctor Stasov to the household as well, laying him on the bed fully dressed, where he would eventually come around from what must have been a deep and dreamless sleep.

The tests, as promised, were simple and painless. For the most part Doctor Stasov worked silently, and even when the boys were alone with him he refused to be drawn into any sort of conversation. Neither Julius nor Caleb were foolish enough to ask him direct questions about what he might have meant during the argument, but they needled around their ignorance with questions about life in Chasm City, what he did when he wasn't in the Shell House, what sort of clients he also visited, and so on. But Doctor Stasov rewarded none of these enquiries with answers.

Only Caleb was brave enough to allude to the conversation. 'What's blackmail, Doctor?'

Stasov twitched up his head from his medical devices. Through his silver fringe his black eyes widened with sudden sharp alarm. 'Why do you ask?'

'I read the word in a story,' Caleb said. 'I didn't know what it meant.'

'Be glad,' Stasov said.

He completed the tests soon after that, but not without delivering more than one lingering look at Caleb, and perhaps Julius as well. Then he gathered his things into the bag, closing its clasp with his spindly, branchlike fingers, and took his leave. They heard him downstairs, communicating in low tones with his mother and father. They were not arguing now, but there was still a coldness in the exchanges.

'You stupid idiot,' Julius said. '*Read that in a book*. When do you ever bother with books? You're too busy thinking of things to shoot.'

'He swallowed it.' Caleb shrugged.

'I'm not sure he did. You can bluff about a lot of things, Caleb, but you're not exactly a born scholar.'

'No, I'd rather leave that to you. It's about all you're good for, isn't it?'

There was some nasty kernel of truth in that, because if one of them was likely to get caught up in reading it was Julius, not his burlier twin. Julius thought of something he had read the night before, something he had meant to share with Caleb, but now he decided to keep it to himself, at least for now.

But not without a tease.

'You think books are worthless, brother. But I know something you don't.'

'How to fall down? How to not catch things? How to miss an animal that's standing five metres away?'

'I know what we are.'

Caleb could tolerate many things, but feeling inferior to Julius was not one of them.

'What?'

'You heard what Spider-fingers called us. Monsters. And I know what he meant by it, too. Something bad happened, Caleb, a long time ago. We're the survivors.'

Caleb hissed his contempt. But there was a splinter of dark curiosity lodged in his eyes. He just couldn't bear to ask Julius what he meant.

Over weeks and months the boys gained instruction in the means by which they could shape the flow of information around their world. The Solid Orrery was always at the heart of these lessons, sheathed over in the pearly ghost-light of the shimmer. Sometimes it was Father giving the tuition, sometimes Mother, sometimes (rarely) both of them. Always the boys were made to feel the press of responsibility upon their shoulders, reminded time and again that this was a grave and terrible obligation, something passed to them in solemnity and trust – a thread of duty and honour stretching back to Sandra Voi. And always the boys nodded and made it clear they understood this was as much a stigma as a blessing, because when the moment came, the calling for which they had been prepared, they would have no one to turn to but themselves. 'The true test will be when we're gone,' Father said. 'Until then, you won't ever know the full force of your burden. But we have borne it, and so will you.'

All they did for the first few weeks was learn how to feel the shimmer's moods, attuning themselves to its music. They learned how to pull information from the abstraction, accessing channels and feeds that were closed to the average citizen. They could break through layers of privacy and security that were considered inviolable, and again all because of the deliberate features rooted deep in the architecture. Sandra Voi had known it was not sufficient just to be able to influence; the influence itself must be predicated on rich, reliable intelligence. Panoply had its monitoring feeds, its eyes and ears, but these were subject to rigorous oversight and constantly scrutinised terms of use. No such limits applied to the contingency. The boys could project their awareness almost without limit, and for a while the thrill of it was intoxicating. Julius had often wondered

183

about life beyond the Shell House; now he realised there was almost no need to leave. Everything he could ever want was already within reach.

But again it was emphasised that this omniscient capability was only there to serve a specific good, and must never be abused. Julius accepted this with equanimity. Caleb, though, continued to test the limits – except when their parents were paying close heed.

Lessons in intervention followed soon after. They began modestly, echoing Father's initial demonstration. The boys learned to delay individual votes, to suppress them, to change their nature. There was never any danger of upsetting a result since they only ever intervened on uncontroversial ballots.

Slowly, though, they were taught to magnify their influence.

If the altering of individual votes was a precise, surgical exercise, then altering hundreds of thousands, or even millions, was more like marshalling the scattered forces of a military campaign, with the details of the engagement much less important than the outcome. Father and Mother watched their progress carefully, rarely showing satisfaction or displeasure. It was not sufficient just to influence the results. The boys also had to show that they had the necessary restraint to achieve their ends with the smallest possible intervention, in a manner that would never have called attention to itself.

'Just because we can act,' Father explained, 'doesn't mean we do – even if the outcome is one that we agree should be changed. Sometimes the public mood is so clearly aligned in one direction that it cannot be resisted.'

Julius frowned. 'Doesn't that go against the whole point of the contingency?'

'What he means,' Caleb said, 'is that we can't go around changing votes if it's expected to be a landslide result. That would look too suspicious, and before you know it we'd have Panoply digging through the polling architecture.'

Father nodded. 'Caleb's right. Our interventions must – except in very extreme cases – be limited to marginal ballots, where a one or two per cent shift is all that's needed.'

'Doesn't that mean our hands are tied?' Julius asked.

'Not if we choose our targets carefully,' Father answered. 'Marginal ballots often have a bearing on key petitions, and we can shift the public mood without ever going near the cases where our intervention might be apparent. Bias a dozen marginals, and we can engineer a landslide that gives us exactly the result we always wanted, without tampering with a single vote in the key.'

Over the weeks Julius had noticed that there had been a gradual shift in the way his father talked about the interventions, from a rare, last-resort thing to an almost commonplace process. If Sandra Voi had meant her power to be used only in constitutional emergencies, when the very foundations of demarchist society were at risk of being undermined from within, then she had clearly underestimated how often those crises came around.

That was the trouble with having a gift, though – however fairly or unfairly it had been acquired.

Sooner or later one felt obliged to use it.

Dreyfus and Jane Aumonier faced each other across the table of the tactical room. They were alone, Dreyfus having taken the unusual step of requesting a private audience immediately after his return from Elysium Heights.

'Case sixty was confirmed just over thirteen hours ago,' Aumonier said, tapping her nails on the table as she spoke. 'We have a high probable on case sixty-one, as of eight hours ago, and our triggers are flagging a possible sixty-second death at this very moment. The curve isn't just steepening, it's turning nearly vertical. There's only one crumb of comfort to be extracted from this latest spate, and that's being generous. Do you know Elspeth Auriault?'

Dreyfus rubbed the corner of his eyes, dry after the air on the cutter.

'I remember her being a satisfactory student.'

'Auriault was close enough to secure the head on case sixty-one. It's with Demikhov as we speak, and there's a chance the implants may be in a slightly better state of preservation than they were with Bronner. A lucky break, if that's the case.'

Dreyfus made a mental note to speak to Demikhov.

'Luck comes in waves. Perhaps we were overdue.'

'You have something to share, evidently. Something you didn't think was suitable for the ears of my other seniors.'

Dreyfus glanced at his lap before answering, knowing there would be no going back once he had voiced his theory.

'It's about Garlin.'

She looked puzzled. 'It can't be. I forbade you to have any further involvement with the man.'

'Something's changed. I'm afraid I've no choice but to resume my investigations.'

'Good of you to make that decision for yourself.'

'I'm only pursuing the course of action you set me on. I was tasked to look into the Wildfire crisis, and now it's thrown up a link to Devon Garlin.'

She eyed him silently for a few moments, as if mentally reviewing every success and failure of his career, every instance when she had placed her confidence in him.

'You've been praying for a link from the moment Garlin humiliated you. Imagining something – wanting it desperately – that doesn't make it so.'

'It's why I had to speak to you in private. Clearmountain and the others would have laughed me out of the room as soon as I mentioned Garlin.'

'They'd have ample reason.' She shook her head, more in sorrow than anger. 'This had better be good. No, better than good.'

'Try this. One of the companies behind the clinic is called Nautilus Holdings.'

'I've never heard of it.'

'There's no reason you would have. Nautilus Holdings was set up by the Shell House. It was an investment enterprise owned and operated by the Voi family.'

Aumonier's interest was unmistakable, even tempered with her natural scepticism.

'You'd better be certain about this.'

Dreyfus slid a compad across to Aumonier, documenting the chain of connections that tied Elysium Heights to the birthplace of Julius Devon Garlin Voi. 'It's all here, in verified transactions. Over a period of about ten years a large portion of the Voi estate's savings was siphoned into Nautilus Holdings, and Nautilus Holdings was the main source of funds for the leasehold and construction of Elysium Heights. No one wanted that to be visible, though.'

Aumonier's finger stroked down the ledger of transactions. 'That ten-year period started in '386. Remind me when Aliya Voi had her shuttle accident?'

'The same year, only a few months before the start of these transactions. The money kept being siphoned off until '395, then the transactions tailed away sharply. The clinic was up and running by then, and entirely self-financing. It continued operating for little more than a decade, closing its books in '407.'

'Someone goes to all that trouble to fund and build a huge, well-equipped clinic, then runs it for only twelve years?'

'Not only that, but they went to a great deal of trouble to hide a link to the Voi estate.'

There was a long silence. More than once Dreyfus sensed that Aumonier was about to speak before she censored herself, as if she dared not put into words the thoughts they were both sharing.

'This is . . . delicate,' she eventually allowed. 'I can't draw a link to Devon Garlin on this basis alone. Rich families sink money into a lot of speculative projects, especially when they're nervous about the future. For all we know the clinic was just one among a spread of investments.'

'There's something else.' Dreyfus kept his voice low, matter-of-fact. 'It just came in from the technicians. They've recovered a list of patient names. The file was badly corrupted, but there's enough in it to make a comparison against the known Wildfire dead. The name fragments correlate with our cases.'

'This is . . . more than I expected.'

'What interests me are the names in the list that *don't* correlate. There are nearly two thousand of them. I believe they're citizens who are still alive, still walking around, and who'll succumb to Wildfire if the pattern continues.'

Aumonier's reaction was guarded, caught between concern and a guilty relief that the terms of her emergency might have been clarified. 'If it really does limit itself to these two thousand cases . . . then at least we're not looking at the end of civilisation.'

'That was my thinking as well. It's a disaster for these people . . . but life goes on. The crisis will burn out of its natural accord. The news will move on, and something else will become our next headache.'

'But we have a duty to these people, if that list is to be taken at face value.'

Dreyfus nodded. 'We can cross-check each case as it occurs, but we can't identify the two thousand people still out there. There are just too many possible matches to the fragments. We'd have to reach out to several hundred thousand citizens, very quickly, all the while trying not to ignite mass panic. Even if we had complete cooperation from all local constables and medical functionaries, we couldn't do it inside a month.'

'And there's no chance of obtaining an intact list? If I re-tasked all available personnel, called in our most trusted constables, we might be able to contain and isolate those citizens in a couple of days.'

'If I knew a way of getting those names, you'd have them,' Dreyfus said.

With a sigh Aumonier pushed the compad back to his side of the table. 'Without that intact list, I'm still powerless. And the rest of your evidence chain remains circumstantial. I trust your instincts, but it's not as if I can bring Garlin in just because of some tenuous link to his family.'

'Someone ought to take a closer look at the Shell House,' Dreyfus said.

'What are you expecting to find?'

'The coincidence of those dates troubles me. Aliya Voi dies, and the funding for the clinic starts soon after.'

'Perhaps it's as simple as Marlon being grief-stricken, and making bad decisions about what was left of the fortune.'

'Are we certain Aliya's death was accidental?'

Aumonier made a long, low nasal sound. 'Since I know how your mind works, I also pulled the case file on that accident. Not our jurisdiction, obviously, but the report was widely distributed between the differing agencies.'

'Leaked, you might say. To help erase any suspicion of complicity where the surviving Vois were concerned.'

'It was a private shuttle returning to Yellowstone from the Glitter Band. Aliya Voi was the only occupant.'

'Did anyone see her leave the Shell House?'

Aumonier frowned. 'You think she was somehow murdered at home and then her body put into that shuttle?'

'It was a small private spacecraft, and with their influence the Vois wouldn't have been troubled by border inspections. It could have flown all the way from the Shell House, out through Chasm City and into space, with no one ever seeing who was inside it.'

'To what end?'

'Someone – say, Marlon or Julius – could have set the autopilot, told it to leave the atmosphere and then come back on a too steep re-entry profile. Made it look like Aliya's recklessness. Body charred almost beyond recognition – just enough left for a DNA sample, so everyone's happy to consider the case closed.'

'Yes, very ingenious. I'll have Garlin bought in on a presumptive murder charge immediately. There's just one snag. Aliya's movements prior to her death are well documented. She visited a number of orbital holdings still linked to the estate – minor asteroids and habitats within the Glitter Band. Witness testimonies prove beyond doubt that she was alive, and in space, only a few hours before the accident. Those testimonies have been triple-checked and verified. There's no way she could have returned to Yellowstone, visited the Shell House, been murdered, and her body been shipped back into space.' Her face fell into an almost sympathetic demeanour. 'I'm sorry. I'm more than willing to accept that there are skeletons in the Voi family, but her death isn't one of them.'

Dreyfus forced himself to accept the obvious facts of the case, realising he had overlooked the significance of the witness testimonies. 'I'd still like to kick over a few stones. Can you get me permission to visit the Shell House?'

'I thought you were done asking special favours of me.'

'Just this one time.'

'It's off our beat, as you well know. I'd need to liaise with the office of the Detective-Marshal in Chasm City.' Something tightened in her face, some awkward recollection. 'This might take a few hours.'

Thalia raised a hand to her brow, shielding her tired eyes from the dusty glare inside House Fuxin-Nymburk. She and Sparver had just disembarked through the docking complex and were now standing on a low-gravity reception platform, staring down the long, tubular length of the cylindrical habitat.

In the open areas that she could see – the public promenades, gardens, parks and lakesides – mobs were gathering and clashing, with clear lines of division beginning to form, as if a hundred ragged armies were massing for some final, bloody settlement of their various long-held grievances. All public transport systems appeared to be suspended, with no trains or trams moving between their stops, and no aerial craft visible. Warning sirens sounded from near and far, along with pre-recorded statements, rendered unintelligible by echoes and distance. Coloured gases – some kind of pacification measure – wafted ineffectually across trees and rooftops. Fires had broken out in dozens of locations, their smoke trails rising, bending and then curdling in accordance with the habitat's spin-generated gravity.

'What is it with mobs and fire?' Thalia said aloud, trying to coax a response from Sparver. 'So you can start a fire. Congratulations. You've achieved the first step to civilisation. Get back to us when you've invented paper and irrigation.'

'Malkmus,' Sparver said, ignoring her.

The Chief Constable was coming up the final flight of steps which led to the platform. She was stooping with exertion, sweat plastering her hair to her forehead. At the top of the steps she paused, hand on the rail, gathering her breath before carrying on.

As was the case with most of the citizen constabularies, she wore no uniform beyond a black armband; no enforcement equipment beyond a few items strapped to a utility belt. The constables rarely had to deal with anything more serious than a domestic argument or the occasional public fracas. Although her clothes were suited to the demands of her assignment, they were civilian garments. Only a double strip of gold on the armband marked her as the chief.

'Chief Malkmus?' Thalia said. 'I'm Prefect Ng. This is Prefect Bancal. Looks like you have a bit of a problem here.'

'We'd have a bit less of one if you'd come sooner,' Malkmus said. 'My constables are only just holding the polling core, and all they have are stun-truncheons and sonic-cannon.'

'We're here now,' Thalia said.

'My deputy's waiting with a car at the base of the stairs,' Malkmus said tersely. 'That only leaves two passenger seats. Can the rest of you follow on foot, if we get the two of you into the main disturbance as quickly as possible?'

'The rest of us?' Thalia asked.

Something dawned in Malkmus's face. 'Don't tell me you're all there is.'

Sparver unclipped the first of the two whiphounds he was carrying. 'We're a lot better than nothing, Chief Constable.'

They descended the openwork staircase, Thalia losing count of the flights as they wound their way down from the reception platform. At the bottom waited a wheeled car in fluted grey metal, open-topped, with only a forward windshield for protection. She and Sparver took their seats behind the two constables, buckling in as the car whirred off. They took a zig-zagging course through steeply graded woodland, the second constable steering via a tiller.

Malkmus twisted around to speak to them, raising her voice over the rumble of wheels.

'I've never had any time for Devon Garlin. Still don't. But when Garlin says that Panoply only offers its protection when it suits it . . . I find it hard not to agree with him.'

'Begging your pardon, Chief Malkmus,' Thalia said, struggling to keep a diplomatic tone. 'But Devon Garlin would be the first to complain if Panoply acted firmly, wouldn't he? He'd say that was a heavy-handed over-reaction, and start going on about his freedom of expression, how we're abusing his rights. Next, he'd be grandstanding about how we've grown too powerful, how we need to be cut back, our numbers reduced. You can't win with men like him. You're either doing too much or too little, and there's never a middle way.'

'So your boss thinks the soft touch is the way to solve it, does she?' Malkmus asked.

Thalia started to answer, but Sparver jumped in ahead of her, leaning forward so his snout was only a few centimetres from Malkmus. 'I don't care what you do or don't think of the Supreme Prefect, Constable Malkmus. But I'll tell you this. One day in her shoes and you'd be huddling in a corner, sucking your thumb and weeping from every orifice you know about, plus a few more that you don't.'

'What my deputy means to say—' Thalia began.

Malkmus swivelled back to face the road. 'There's no need, Prefect. He made himself perfectly clear.'

Thalia turned to Sparver. She glared at him, but with a great force of will managed to hold her tongue.

The car levelled out and they sped through tree-lined back roads, keeping away from the fires and obvious trouble spots. Off in the distance, but looming ever larger, was a silver-coloured, bronze-edged building shaped like a very steep-sided pyramid, surrounded by a cluster of smaller structures like the minor foothills crowding a mountain. Wisps of smoke rose up from several different spots around the complex.

'That's the epicentre of the trouble,' the second constable said, striking a keen, conciliatory note. He was a sandy-haired young man with very pink, almost pig-like ears. 'Devon Garlin made his big speech on the outskirts of the civic grounds, and then started moving in for the core, gathering numbers all the while.'

'Your polling core is located in that structure?' Thalia asked, still bristling at Sparver's tactlessness, which had inflamed an already strained situation.

'Yes, and we've moved as many constables as we can inside to secure the core, as well as implementing a local lockdown. We've also got a squad on the outside, just in case anyone's foolish enough to try and break through.'

'Good,' Thalia said, thinking that if she could keep this one man on her side, that was better than nothing. 'Hopefully the mob will get bored and hungry when they realise they can't reach the core, and start drifting off back to their homes. You've done well here, constables.'

'It's a bit late for the grudging praise,' Malkmus said.

They rode on in silence, skirting around the edges of the worst areas. Now and then Thalia caught sight of elements of the mob, groups of citizens moving in their dozens, many of them carrying improvised implements such as torn-up fence posts or uprooted saplings. Off in the distance, on a patch of lawn between two arena-like civic buildings, she spotted a ragged, shifting brawl going on, involving somewhere between fifty and a hundred individuals. Once or twice, squinting, she made out someone wearing an armband, trying to contain the unrest. But the constables were vastly outnumbered, able to do little more than issue demands for a restoration of order.

The pyramidal building was very much closer now, and Thalia

easily picked up the smell of smoke, as well as the sweeter tang of the pacification gases, now mostly dispersed. The car slowed as they approached a trio of constables waiting out of sight of the trouble. Sparver still had his whiphound unholstered. Thalia unclipped hers, feeling that a show of confident authority could do little harm at this stage.

The car stopped. The still-sweating Malkmus got out without saying a word and bounded over towards her colleagues. The driver shot Thalia a sympathetic look and followed after Malkmus, straightening the hem of his tunic as he walked.

Thalia got out of the passenger seat slowly. They were out of earshot for the moment.

'None of that was called for,' she said in a low voice.

Sparver was looking down at his whiphound handle, adjusting the setting dials.

'It wasn't?'

'We need these people on our side.'

'They're on our side whether they like it or not.'

'Look at the state of this place, Sparver. We're too late to offer more than a token effect. Someone should have gone in sooner.'

'Doesn't give her the right to criticise Aumonier.'

'She was voicing an opinion – and a reasonable one, on the evidence. Couldn't you see how tired she was, after climbing all those steps to meet us? That's after a day of trying to keep this whole place from sliding into all-out carnage.'

'I should cut her some slack, is that it?'

'I think you should cut most of us some slack,' Thalia answered, turning away from him to walk over to the five constables. She heard an unimpressed grunt, then the sound of Sparver's feet behind her.

'Do we have an update?' she called out.

'Chief Malkmus says you're all we're getting,' answered one of the first trio, a scholarly looking man with a high forehead and silver at his temples.

'For now,' Thalia said. 'But you've taken all the essential steps with regard to the core, and Prefect Bancal and I will do our best to help you disperse the troublemakers.'

'With just those little whips of yours?' asked a strong-jawed woman, a heavy fringe of red hair masking her eyes. 'Haven't you got guns?'

'Be glad we don't,' Sparver said. 'Then you'd know you're really in trouble.'

'And this isn't trouble?' Malkmus asked.

192

Sparver flicked out his whiphound's filament. 'Trouble? No, this is a fun day out. All right, point me towards Garlin.'

'We don't touch Garlin,' Thalia said sharply, no longer caring if she gave him a public reprimand. 'The constables were right to show restraint, and we have to abide by the same consideration if we aren't to make things worse.' She flicked out her own filament. 'We'll initiate a soft containment and dispersal protocol. And you can dial back from full lethality, Deputy Bancal – we're not here to draw blood for the sake of it.'

'We're just going to ignore him, are we?' Sparver said, making a bad-tempered show of resetting the force calibration dial.

'No, we'll approach and cordon Garlin. His safety is also our concern, and at least half the people running rampage in this place want to dance on his bones. In the process we'll contain and disperse without resorting to the second edge.'

'Follow us,' said the scholarly man. 'We'll get you close to the main mob, near the main entrance to the core. We've managed to keep the counter-elements away from the immediate area, so at least you aren't dealing with fighting on several fronts.'

'Thank you, Constable,' Thalia said. Then, to her whiphound: 'Forward scout mode. Ten-metre secure zone. Maintain at sub-lethal discretionary force.'

The whiphound nodded its compliance, then slinked away to establish the moving secure zone. Sparver delivered an identical instruction to his own whiphound, the two units coordinating their efforts like a pair of well-trained beagles. Both prefects still had a second whiphound clipped to their belts, and for once Thalia was glad to feel that extra burden.

The prefects and constables walked slowly but confidently. The whiphounds were defining an arc ahead of them, a pair of zig-zagging blurs forming a semicircular space with a radius of ten metres. They would respond if a threat impinged on that moving front, or attempted to cut in from the rear.

They turned a corner, following a broad path along the base of one of the core's outlying buildings. Thalia's hand was never far from her second whiphound, a gesture of intent as much as reassurance for her own sake. They had gone another hundred metres when a group of citizens spilled into view, crossing an intersecting path and engaged in their own business until they noticed the prefects. The citizens halted. There were a dozen of them and at least half of their number carried improvised tools or weapons, with some of them carrying burning torches.

Thalia maintained her pace. But she touched her throat and relayed her voice through to her whiphound at amplified volume.

'This is Prefect Ng. You are under Panoply observance. Lay down your implements and make no sudden or threatening movements.'

She kept on walking, with the moving front of the whiphounds pushing ahead. The citizens were clearly taken aback, two or three of them casting aside their weapons and torches, but the remainder still needed some convincing.

Deciding that this was an outlier to the main mob, Thalia said: 'I repeat, lay down your implements. The whiphounds will respond to an aggressive posture or sign of intent. Go peacefully and you may return to your homes, unprocessed. This is your final warning.'

The whiphounds were now only twenty paces from the gathering. Two citizens broke away, nervously at first, then with quickening footsteps. The whiphounds locked their heads onto them, tracking them until they were deemed to have passed out of the area of interest. Then they locked back onto the remaining citizens.

'Drop them,' Sparver said.

One more citizen complied, lowering a sharp-tipped fence post, but a second made the rash error of tossing her torch at the whiphounds, rather than the ground.

Thalia did not need to give an order; what ensued was well within the whiphounds' permitted sphere of autonomous, discretionary action. Coordinating their response, one whiphound veered to the torch, flicked its tail around it, and flung it away from the path, treating it as it would a grenade or incendiary device. The second whiphound skidded to a halt, gathered itself into a compressed spring and flung itself at the woman, uncoiling as it tumbled through the air. Like a flung skipping rope its arc seemed uncontrolled and haphazard, but that illusion persisted only until the moment of contact with the target. The whiphound curled its tail around the woman's knees, bringing her down with a distinct and gut-wrenching crunch. The woman started moaning. Its work done, the whiphound slithered off her and resumed its zig-zagging patrol, the front encroaching closer and closer to the remaining members of the mob. The entire process, from the flinging of the torch to the incapacitation, had taken perhaps four seconds.

The point had been made, though, and within another few seconds the remaining citizens had seen the wisdom of dropping their tools and dispersing. The whiphounds snapped after a couple of the laggards, but only for a few threatening paces. Then they fell back into the patrol formation. Thalia, Sparver and the constables stepped over the abandoned weapons and torches, Thalia pausing only to kneel beside the still-moaning woman.

'Something to keep in mind next time,' she said, unclipping a medical pouch from her belt and digging out an anaesthetic patch. 'When a prefect gives you a final warning, heed it.'

She administered the patch, stood up, and rejoined the others. They were just turning another corner.

Sparver slowed in his stride, looking ahead beyond the zig-zagging cordon. They were at one end of a broad path which led straight to the front steps of the large pyramidal building, its main doors sealed to prevent access to the polling core somewhere inside. But between them massed a mob that had to be closer to a thousand strong than a dozen.

Thalia scanned the unruly gathering, picking out a handful of constables trying to enforce some kind of order on its ragged periphery. A small number of citizens seemed to be listening to the constables, drifting off in sullen ones and twos, content to lick their wounds back home. But this meagre flow was easily outweighed by random troublemakers swaggering in from other directions, sometimes bloodied and usually equipped with some sort of makeshift weapon.

Thalia spotted Garlin. He was raised head and shoulders above the mob, much nearer to the doors of the building, shouting and gesticulating with all the fist-clenching rage of a baby tyrant. It was her first sight of him in the flesh, although she was all too familiar with his face and body language from the numerous public broadcasts. His voice, too, cut across the noise of the mob and the relentless background of sirens and emergency instructions. There was a loathsome cadence to his proclamations, a certain metrical rise and fall which was as calculated as it was undeniably effective.

Thalia knew what she wanted to do with Devon Garlin. She wanted to squash his face down in the dirt with her boot; she wanted to make him drool and cry and beg for clemency.

She squared her shoulders. The whiphounds pushed ahead. The outer elements of the mob were starting to take notice of the approaching party.

'This is Prefect Ng,' she said again. 'You are under Panoply observance. Stand aside to allow us free passage.'

CHAPTER TWELVE

Dreyfus stepped into the palely glowing cave of the specimen section, waiting a moment for his eyes to adjust to the pastel gloom of the upright glass flasks, their coloured support fluids, and the gentle twinkle of numerous monitoring systems. It was as well, perhaps, that his eyes needed that period of adjustment. It gave his nerves time to settle down after the initial discomfiture of seeing so many disembodied heads and parts of heads, so many brains and parts of brains, many of which were still being fed by oxygen and nutrient flows, still being listened to via a flickering network of wires and probes. There were the parts of sixty-one human heads in this room, and only a little over a year ago each and every one of these heads would have been attached to a walking, talking person, all of them going about their free and easy lives as citizens of the Glitter Band. Now they resembled the pieces of some grisly, barely solvable jigsaw puzzle, made up of flesh and bone and various colourless grades of cerebral matter.

There were sixty-one heads, but more than sixty-one flasks had things in them, and there were still empty flasks stretching away in neat regiments, ready for the cases to come.

'You're either an optimist or a pessimist, Doctor,' Dreyfus called out, sensing that Demikhov must be either in the room or one of the adjoining areas.

There was silence, except for the quiet murmur of pumps and filtration systems.

Dreyfus walked on a bit further, careful not to disturb the equipment set up around the flasks.

'Doctor Demikhov?'

'Oh, do allow the poor man his rest. He's not a machine, unlike some of us.'

He turned around, startled by the voice. It was faint, with a muffled, liquid quality to it. His heart raced, even as his mind rushed ahead and processed the obvious truth of who was addressing him, speaking through one of the flask-bound heads.

'You can't be here.'

'Can't or shouldn't?'

She had selected a woman's head to puppet, but in no other respect was there any similarity between the face and her own. Still, the tone of address was all the introduction he needed.

The eyes were open, but scarcely regarding him. It was just stagecraft, he decided; she didn't need those eyes to be aware of him, but it suited the theatricality of her presence. Nor was the voice emanating from the mouth of the dead woman, although the mouth had cracked open enough to suggest some whisper or dream utterance. No, the sounds were coming from the adjacent equipment, hooked up to the head and brain by some means, and presumably capable of stimulating and reading back nerve impulses and implant signals.

'Get out of her.'

'She doesn't care, Dreyfus. She's past all that. Past everything, come to think of it. Besides, I've come to see she gets justice. To do right by these poor dead people. I gave you Nautilus Holdings, didn't I? A tangible link to the Voi estate, as you now know. That was a gesture of my good intent, just like that list of patient names.'

'A fragmented list, useless to us.'

'But enough to demonstrate that I possessed the relevant knowledge. Your little people never did manage to extract an intact set of patient records from Elysium Heights, did they?'

'They're still trying.'

'You can spare them the bother. They won't find it, ever. The question is, how much do you want that intact list?'

Dreyfus sidestepped her question. 'Two thousand is a scratch compared to the millions you were prepared to burn two years ago. So why is Wildfire still a concern to you?'

She made the dead woman's eyes twitch up in their sockets. 'The dead don't bother me, Dreyfus – I'm one of them. But I do depend on the continued stability of the Glitter Band – at least for the time being. Panoply's mishandling of this whole affair is exactly the sort of thing that gives succour to Garlin and his ilk.'

'Then give me the list.'

'I shall. Gladly. Nothing would make me happier. But only when you've granted the exceedingly small thing I desire. Your archives.'

'No,' Dreyfus stated flatly.

'I'm here already. I've already broken all but the last of your defences. Given time, I'll find my way through your final barricades. And yet, what harm have I done so far? I could have played merry havoc with Panoply, if that were my desire. It isn't. All I wish is to know what you know about the Clockmaker, and there my limited interest in you ends.'

'If you're such a godlike machine intelligence, Aurora, why don't you just find your own way into the archives?'

'Because, in your tiresome way, you have the better of me. I've brushed against your security protocols – I know what's entailed. Three little words will grant me access to the Search Turbines. Unfortunately, all the brute-force computation in the system can't help me if I don't get those words right on the first guess. But you know them. Tell me now, and you shall have your names. I'll make them appear to the technicians you still have in Elysium Heights. They'll think they were being very clever. There won't be a shadow of suspicion in your direction.'

'No,' he said again, but this time with a fraction less conviction than before. 'Not unless it's agreed by Aumonier and the seniors, as a necessary trade.'

'So that your analysts have time to trap me, or in some way comprom- ise the data I seek? No – this remains between the two of us. And do not be so foolish as to think I wouldn't find out if you went behind my back. I could shred those names as easily as I can make them appear. It's your one chance, Dreyfus. I've extended my trust to you with the information I've already provided. Now it's time for some much-needed reciprocity.'

'I'd be a fool to trust you.'

'You'd be a fool not to.'

'Dreyfus?' It was Demikhov, stepping through the adjoining door, snapping a pair of sterile gloves onto his fingers. 'I thought I heard your voice.'

'Talking to myself. It helps me work through the details of a case.' Dreyfus eyed the head that had spoken, watching the eyelids snap shut, the face regaining its earlier slack composure. The change had happened out of Demikhov's line of sight, but only just. 'I was about to ask if you're an optimist or a pessimist?'

Demikhov eyed him with a certain wariness.

'An odd question, even for you.'

'You have all these empty flasks lined up. You must be expecting a lot more heads. That suggests to me that you're not hopeful of us resolving this crisis any time soon. On the other hand, you must think that one of these heads will offer an insight.'

'That's a little too philosophical even for me, Dreyfus.' Still the odd look lingered. 'Were you going to wait here indefinitely until I returned?'

'I got lost in my thoughts. I should have checked the sleep roster before coming here.'

Demikhov strapped a set of magnifying lenses onto his forehead. 'I'll admit to a little greed when it comes to wanting more heads to open. Unless you've come to tell me that the emergency's been resolved?'

Dreyfus produced a weary smile. 'Do I look like a man bearing good news?'

'No, I didn't think so. You'll have heard about case sixty-one, I suppose?'

'That's the one Elspeth Auriault brought in?'

'She did well. We've been refining the detection threshold triggers after each case, and it's given us between sixty and ninety seconds additional lead time, compared to Antal Bronner. No use if the prefect isn't nearby, of course, but Auriault was in the relevant habitat *and* close at hand *and* carrying the containment vessel. That's been another change in the protocol. A difficult call for Jane, since the prefects have to be trusted to carry these things and not ask any questions ahead of time, even without Pangolin clearance.'

'I'd have had confidence in Auriault. Still, even being quicker than Thalia Ng . . .'

'I also made some improvements to the whiphound subroutine and the cryopreservation system. Minor alterations, but enough to make a difference if luck's on our side – as it seems to have been this time.' He gestured for Dreyfus to come around to his side of the table, next to the last flask that had something in it.

It was a man's head, the top of the skull neatly excised, layers of brain tissue pulled gently aside, wires and probes sunk into the exposed neural matter.

'If only they could speak to us,' Demikhov said.

'If only,' Dreyfus agreed.

The man had a thick black beard and moustache, with thick black angular eyebrows that seemed, even now, to be registering surprise and not a little affront at the supreme indignity of his fate. The line of a scar, long since healed, cut from the corner of one eye to the edge of his mouth.

'It's Wildfire,' Demikhov said. 'All the patterns match the previous cases. The citizen's name was Nicholas D'Arcy Moon. No Panoply priors, nothing of interest to the constables. But he had a history of involvement with duelling societies. You'd know more of such matters than me, I don't doubt.'

Dreyfus gave a noncommittal shrug. 'Perhaps.'

'Apparently there are societies and clubs which enable their members to challenge each other's honour, to nurture grudges and feuds and so on, and then settle those disputes by various violent means. Just when I thought I couldn't be surprised by the wilder extremes of human nature . . . but I suppose you like this, don't you, because it fits with your theory about risk?'

'I don't get to choose the patterns, Demikhov. I just follow them. Did they tell you about the clinic?'

'They rarely tell me anything.'

Dreyfus doubted this but played along anyway. 'A private surgical facility, active for a relatively short span of time. Large, well equipped, but operating in near total secrecy. A number of the Wildfire cases may have been clients. Maybe all of them. I think something was done to their heads while they were in there, and this is the consequence.'

'Deliberate action, or medical negligence?'

'Let's say malpractice is looking less likely by the day.' Dreyfus paused, wanting to avert his eyes from the peeled-open skull but unable to resist its macabre attraction. 'What have you got from his implants, that none of the other cases showed?'

'They weren't as badly cooked, and neither was the surrounding brain tissue. Don't get me wrong: he was going the same way as the others. But Auriault got to him just a bit sooner, and that's given us our first glimpse of the implants in a partially preserved state.'

'And?'

Demikhov rattled a little sample tray, laden with tiny gritty-grey specks. 'Other than these neocortical devices, most of them are still in situ. I'm conducting some residual functionality tests while they're still embedded. For the full report, you'll need to wait until C section have got their hands on them.'

'But you can tell me something now.'

'Yes, but you won't like it. These implants seem perfectly normal. There must be millions of citizens walking around with more or less the same combinations of neural devices – tens of millions, even.'

'There's something different. You just haven't found it yet.'

'If there is a difference, it's rooted at the instruction-set level, rather than any change in the physical hardware. But creating such a change would be extremely difficult, if not impossible. There are layers and layers of logical structure inside these things, wrapped around the holy kernel of the Voi architecture, and they're all designed to prevent malicious interference.'

'Someone's obviously breached it,' Dreyfus said.

'A rash supposition, even coming from you.'

'It's been a theoretical concern from the moment we identified Wild-fire. But until we got hold of a set of intact implants . . .'

Demikhov rattled the tray again. 'I wouldn't say these are *intact*, exactly.'

'It proves that there's a way of turning good implants bad, without changing the hardware. An alteration to the instruction-set, as you said. There's thermal regulation built into these things, isn't there?'

'Yes, and a thousand other safeguards. But you're not really hearing me, Dreyfus. The Voi kernel has never been breached. There's no way to get through those additional layers. They've withstood more than a century of human cleverness as well as idiocy, and they're still doing the job they were intended for.'

'Then there's another way in,' Dreyfus said doggedly. 'A way of interfering with the kernel, without needing to bypass those extra layers.'

Demikhov's expression had been growing steadily more sceptical for at least a minute, but now it found a new level of incredulousness. 'You'd be talking about a latent vulnerability, then. A fault which has been there all along, since the time Voi herself put it all together. But which only manifests now, in these last four hundred days?'

'I didn't say I had all the answers,' Dreyfus said.

Demikhov reached to adjust one of these lenses on his magnifying strap. 'If I find anything that fits your theory, I'll tell you. But I wouldn't stake your reputation on it.'

When he returned to his room there was a message waiting from Jane Aumonier, tagged at normal priority. Dreyfus made himself some tea then sat down to listen to it. He had brushed against his wind-chimes and they tinkled gently as she delivered her news.

'I've called in a favour or two – and eaten several helpings of humble pie. A Chasm City liaison will meet you just above the atmosphere. You'll be allowed to visit the Shell House, but only with your liaison. Your powers of investigation will be at their discretion. You'll carry no weapon, not even a whiphound. They expect you to complete your enquiries within thirteen hours from the moment you arrive in the city. You'll be nice to them, Dreyfus – it's my neck on the line over this, not yours.'

'When am I never not nice?' he mouthed to himself.

Aumonier carried on. 'There's no great rush. They'll detect your approach and send up a ship to meet you. You can sleep on it and go there fresh at the start of the next shift.'

Dreyfus swigged half his tea, then poured the rest into the floor. He conjured a mirror and stared into his eyes, peeling down the lids, trying to blink away the redness.

Five minutes later he was at the dock, completing authorisation for the use of an atmosphere-capable cutter.

Sparver was nervous. As their little entourage moved further into the gathering, so the whiphounds had to defend their backs as well as their fronts. The skittering, whisking machines moved quickly, and their presence alone was intimidating. But as they walked on Sparver felt a prickle at the back of his neck, a sense that his options were restricting. The two whiphounds were having to tighten their boundary to maintain it effectively.

'Move your hand away from the second whiphound,' he whispered to Thalia. 'It looks like you're only one twitch away from using it.'

Thalia turned off her voice amplifier before answering.

'Maybe I am.'

'Me too,' he offered. 'But Garlin's mob don't need to know it. If we act like we've already got everything under control, that's half the battle already won.'

'Not too long ago you sounded like you wanted to wring his neck.'

'I wouldn't turn down the chance if it came up. But you were right about our priorities here. Negotiating with Garlin is our best chance of regaining some order here – even if it's going to leave a very bad taste in my mouth.'

Thalia eased her hand away from the second whiphound. It might not have been done with the best grace, but it was enough for him that she had taken his advice.

'We don't have to get into bed with him. I hate him as much as you do.'

Sparver walked on, lowering his voice to the point that his words would have been lost to the constables: 'I think we both have some catching up to do with Dreyfus, where Garlin is concerned. It hasn't even started being personal with us.'

'Give it time,' she said.

The citizens were wise enough not to encroach on the moving front of the whiphounds, stumbling back into the crowd or squeezing past on either side. But that did not mean their mood was in any way subdued. The prefects and constables were faced with a constant barrage of shouts and insults, as well as the occasional projectile hurled from somewhere in the mob. Sparver took a direct hit from a lobbed stone, only just raising his arm in time to protect his face. His sleeve stiffened in time to absorb the impact, but the force of it still had him losing his footing. Next came an uprooted fence post, whirling just over Malkmus's head. Mostly, though, it was clods of dirt, splatting on the ground and only rarely hitting one of the walkers.

Thalia was speaking again on full amplification, telling everyone they were under Panoply observance, but it was hard enough for Sparver to make out her words, let alone most of the crowd.

Garlin was just in front of the broad sweep of stairs leading to the main entrance of the polling core building. Six constables were holding the stairs, four of them nervously sweeping back and forth with stun-truncheons, the other two wearing backpack-mounted sonic-cannon. Behind the constables, a wide set of glass doors had sealed the entrance to the building's lobby.

Garlin had his back to the constables. He was raised up on some sort of platform – only the upper half of his body visible – and he was gesturing to his audience, grinning and making a gradual flapping movement with his arms.

It was having a slow, spreading effect. Waves of uneasy calm emanated from Garlin's focus. The din began to die away, the shouts and insults falling back into a low, expectant murmur. The volley of projectiles subdued, until a last clod of dirt came sailing in.

Garlin made another gesture, this time like a man trying to part a sea, and the crowd pulled apart ahead of the whiphounds, offering clear passage to the raised platform. He was standing on the back of a municipal robot, a cleaning servitor about the size of the constables' vehicle. A loose cordon still surrounded him, but from their vigilant expressions and over-muscled physiques, Sparver decided these were more likely to be part of his travelling retinue than the common citizens of Fuxin-Nymburk.

Garlin flapped his arms again, encouraging the mob into something close to silence.

'It's all right, Prefects,' he said, raising his voice without artificial amplification. 'You'll have no trouble from these good people. This is a peaceful assembly of like-minded citizens. Or are such things now no longer permitted?'

'I am Prefect Ng,' Thalia said, continuing to walk behind the whiphounds. 'I ask you to disperse your supporters. This gathering is in contravention of the Common Articles.'

Garlin looked mystified, but his grin remained. 'How so, Prefect Ng?'

'The constables have determined that your supporters are attempting to reach the polling core.'

'There's never been a law preventing citizens from visiting the core, Prefect. Unless you've just made one up.'

'The core may be inspected by any citizen or citizen delegation under prior arrangement, Mister Garlin. That is not the same as an attempted siege by hundreds of angry people, with no objective beyond petty vandalism.'

Garlin directed his attention from Thalia back to the mob. 'Angry? I don't see any anger. Just decent, concerned citizens, freely expressing their lack of confidence in Panoply.'

'This is a war zone, Mister Garlin,' Thalia said, walking to a halt about twenty paces from Garlin, with the whiphounds still zig-zagging before them. 'You've instigated a riot.'

'Have I? I could have sworn my assembly was lawful and disciplined, until anti-democratic elements began to stir up trouble.'

'We can discuss the right and wrong of it later, Mister Garlin. At the moment our primary concern is your safety.'

'That's very touching.' Hands on hips, he swivelled around to address as much of his audience as he could. 'Did you hear that, everyone? She says my safety is their primary concern. And with a straight face, too! Only a few days ago I was beaten up, arrested and interrogated!' He shook his head scornfully. 'My safety! Here I am, surrounded by friends, and she has the nerve to say that I'm the one in need of protecting?'

'Ask your supporters to disperse, Mister Garlin. Provided they lay down their sticks and stones, they can go back to their homes without being processed.'

Garlin made a show of listening, seeming to give her words consideration. 'They're not my people to order around, Prefect. But I'll gladly relay your terms.' He shaped his hands around his mouth, his chest heaving as he drew breath. 'Good people! The Prefect has given you a choice. She says you can all go back to your homes, and trust that there'll be no further repercussions. Or you can exercise your rights and remain exactly where you are!'

Sparver could hold himself back no longer. 'Don't mistake this for the soft touch, Garlin. Tell your rabble to go home.'

Next to him, Thalia said: 'You've made your point, Mister Garlin. But there's nowhere further for you to go now. The core's out of reach.' She nodded over her shoulder. 'But there are still elements out there who could do you harm.'

'Then do your jobs. Police them.'

'We will,' she said. 'Once you've told your gathering to disperse. They'll listen, Mister Garlin. Just for once, do the right thing.'

Garlin shook his head slowly. 'If you weren't concerned about the core, you wouldn't be in such a hurry to break up this assembly.' He shifted his delivery to the mob. 'Did you hear that? The core is the only hold they

204

have over you. While it's theirs to control, there's nothing they can't do to you.' By some clever projection of his voice he seemed to shift into a low, confiding register, even while his words still boomed out over the gathering. 'But they're worried now. The core is nearly ours. Do you think those constables would be looking so worried if they were sure we couldn't get through those doors?' He twisted around, still grinning. 'Truncheons and loud noises. That's all they've got! They'd be doing well to stop twenty of us, let alone several hundred.'

'Garlin,' Thalia said, anger breaking through the composure she had maintained so far. 'I told you we hadn't come to take you in. But that changes the moment you try and break through to the core. Don't make us turn these whiphounds on you.'

'I see it doesn't take much to have you resorting to threats,' Garlin said.

Up on the steps, the six constables crouched lower, holding their stun-truncheons and sonic-cannons double-gripped, swivelling to cover an inrush from any possible direction. Every now and then one of them let off a warning pulse from one of the cannons: a low, sickening bellow like a dinosaur's death-moan.

'I think it's time,' Thalia said in a near-whisper, unclipping her second whiphound.

Sparver did likewise. He agreed, flicking out his own reserve unit's filament and setting its action threshold. 'Discretionary force. Maintain at sub-lethal, but use second edge as required. Register all constabulary units as cooperative assets.'

The whiphound locked its head onto Malkmus and her associates, nodding with each acquisition, then performed the same swift process with the six constables up on the steps.

'All remaining citizens are to be considered potentially hostile. Identify and mark Julius Devon Garlin Voi.'

The whiphound fixed its head onto Garlin and nodded once.

'Log and retain for possible detention,' Sparver added.

The whiphound confirmed its understanding. Up on the cleaning robot, Garlin's face tightened slightly, perhaps in bruised recollection of the detention he had undergone in Hospice Idlewild in the coils of Dreyfus's whiphound.

Thalia had been issuing equivalent commands to her own second unit. When she was done she opened a channel back to Panoply and issued a terse but efficient status update.

'Sparver,' she said. 'Go and give those constables some moral support, will you? I'm going to establish a safety cordon around Garlin, then bring him in for his own protection. If we lose visual contact I'll see you back at the ship, with Garlin.'

'He won't like it,' Sparver said.

'Nor will I,' Thalia said, disgust flashing across her features.

Sparver allowed the first two whiphounds to maintain their sweep, defining an open area just before the cleaning robot. His second whiphound moved ahead of him, establishing a moving pocket as he pushed back into the mob still loitering between Garlin and the steps of the polling core building. Perhaps the deployment of the second whiphound had sent the appropriate signal, for the citizens were in no hurry to remain in his way. In twenty seconds Sparver was up on the steps, nodding his solidarity at the constables, and taking a low, spread-footed stance before them, with his whiphound patrolling back and forth along the lowest step.

Behind the constables stood the wide glass doors, sealed since the moment Malkmus had issued the local lockdown order. Other than a few artful mud-splats, they remained intact. The lobby beyond was dark, its details hard to make out from the outside. The glass doors looked fragile, but if any structure in a habitat was likely to be well defended it was going to be the place that housed the polling core. Such structures were usually designed to withstand vacuum blowouts and spacecraft collisions, allowing emergency measures to be coordinated even during the direst catastrophe.

But Garlin must know that as well, Sparver thought.

Thalia, meanwhile, was using her second whiphound to disperse Garlin's security people, sending them scuttling back into the mob. If they resisted, the whiphound flicked itself around their legs and brought them down. There were cries and shouts, threats of retribution both legal and physical. The crowd, though, was pulling even further back from the edge of the cordon. They were getting a lesson in what a whiphound could do, even on its sub-lethal setting.

Garlin teetered on the robot. He had his hands on his hips and was looking down.

'You can call this whatever you like, Prefect. It's still an infringement of my right to free speech.'

'Climb down,' she said. 'Climb down before I send the whiphound up to bring you down anyway.'

'This is a violation of my—'

'This is my final warning,' Thalia said. 'You've five seconds to get off the robot. I'm counting. Five . . .'

Behind Sparver, behind the constables, something made a low clunking sound, followed by a continuous whirr. Sparver risked a look back over his shoulders. He hardly needed to. It was obvious from the moment he heard that sound what was happening.

The doors to the polling core were opening.

Aumonier was jolted from sleep – such sleep as she was lately capable of taking – by a soft but insistent chime from her bedside. No anger or resentment stirred in her as she forced sufficient wakefulness to take the call. None of her operatives would have disturbed her without excellent reason.

'Yes?'

'Ma'am,' said the voice of Robert Tang. 'I didn't want to wake you, but under the circumstances . . .'

'It's quite all right, Robert.' She was still half under the sheets, leaning over to answer the call. 'I presume it's something more than just another death, or some more unreasonableness from our favourite man of the people?'

'That's just it, ma'am. It's . . . well, you'd better see it for yourself, I think. It's something the technicals found in Elysium Heights. I can send it straight through to your quarters, if you wish, but you might prefer to come to the tactical room.'

'I'll be there promptly. But send it through to me now as well. At least I'll have some idea what it's about.'

'As you wish, ma'am. It's ready for immediate replay – just say the word.'

'Thank you, Robert.'

She dismissed the call, took a cold but refreshing step through the washwall – banishing the last traces of sleepiness like a blast of sterilising radiation – and wrapped a scarlet gown around herself. Then she sat down on the edge of her bed and conjured at the facing wall. 'Show me whatever it is.'

A portion of the wall brightened into a rectangle. The Panoply symbol appeared, then a Pangolin security rating, then a unique serial number identifying a particular item of evidential significance.

She read:

Evidential docket: 665/3G37/1AA
Acquisition timestamp: 29/9/29 15:04:23 YST
Locale: GB/Addison-Lovelace/Outer rim/Chamber 2/Elysium Heights
Description: data fragment
Embellishment: vision-only recording, partial recovery, 35 second
    fragment

Steeling herself for whatever she was about to learn, however unpalatable it might be, Aumonier voiced a barely audible instruction for the fragment to start playing.

The rectangle crazed over with static before resolving into the view of an interior location shot from an elevated vantage point. It was a lobby or plaza, its clean, sweeping surfaces bathed in a soft, heaven-like glow. Figures were moving through the lobby – citizens in colourful clothing or plumage being met by white-uniformed staff whose outfits almost blended in to the brilliant backdrop of polished floors and walls, so that only their hands and faces were really distinct.

The view drifted down, swooping over the heads of the visitors and staff. The staff had reassuring, friendly smiles. They stood talking with the visitors, going over treatment options on compads. Others were walking their guests over to clusters of lounge chairs and coffee tables, or for a more detailed interview behind the privacy of smoked glass partitions. The smiling staff had the clinic's tree motif embroidered onto their sleeves, the only visible emblem save for small glowing nametags on their breasts.

Now the point of view dived across the lobby, over an ornamental fishpond, then through glass doors – which swished open just in time – into a more functional area of the clinic. The view was still saturated in that soft, white radiance, but in addition to staff and patients there were now treatment rooms, with beds and medical equipment just visible through milky partitions.

The view penetrated one of these partitions. A woman sat on the edge of a bed, much as Aumonier now did. There were flowers in a vase behind the woman. She wore a green gown and was looking up at a tall, authoritative-seeming man in the same white uniform as the rest of the staff. The man was holding a compad and talking, the woman nodding, something in her expression shifting from anxiety to reassurance as his silent words washed over her.

The man turned from the woman, passing his compad to a waiting attendant. Now he was looking directly at the viewer, delivering a monologue – what was obviously a sales pitch for the services on offer.

Aumonier stared at his face, caught between instant recognition and a sense of strange unfamiliarity. It was a handsome, boyish face, plump across the cheeks in a way that suggested vigour and humour rather than ugliness. His hair was a mass of golden curls, rakishly tamed. His eyes were an extremely piercing pale blue.

Aumonier's own eyes tracked down to the man's nametag. She read: Doctor Julius Mazarin.

The man kept speaking. Then the recording broke up into static again and the Panoply evidential summary reappeared.

Aumonier watched the piece twice more, alert to anything she might have missed on the first playback. Then she instructed her clotheswall to provide her with her Panoply uniform, and met Tang and a gathering of Seniors in the tactical room.

She sat in silence for several moments before speaking.

'Is this the only such fragment?'

'It is, ma'am,' Tang said. 'That we know of.'

'Why didn't it come to our attention sooner?'

Tang looked at Lillian Baudry before continuing. 'We nearly overlooked it, ma'am. It was buried deep, and pretty badly scrambled. We're lucky to have these thirty-five seconds. Whoever was running that clinic tried very hard to remove all trace of their identity, and for the most part they succeeded.'

'Can we be certain of the fragment's authenticity?'

'Why wouldn't we?' asked Baudry. 'It's as plain as day, Jane. The man in the recording is Julius Devon Garlin Voi.'

'It's a close likeness but not an exact one,' Aumonier said.

'That's because it would have been made decades ago, when the clinic was active,' Baudry replied. 'Possibly before it was fully up and running.'

'We know of at least one link between the clinic and the Shell House,' Clearmountain said. 'We shouldn't be too surprised to find another.'

'It must be investigated,' said Mildred Dosso.

'Dreyfus is already doing so,' Aumonier replied levelly.

'I mean in a more direct manner. Bring Garlin in again.'

'What do you think Ng and Bancal are attempting to do, Mildred? I already have two prefects with orders to locate and secure Garlin.'

'That's for his own protection,' Lillian Baudry answered. 'Now the terms of interest have shifted. We can't escape the inevitable, Jane. Garlin is both the architect and prime beneficiary of Wildfire.' She made a distasteful puckering of her lips. 'I'm forced to admit it. Dreyfus was right all along, and we should have trusted his instincts.'

He studied the other ship as it approached his own, just above the outer atmosphere of Yellowstone. It was larger than his cutter, somewhat sharper and sleeker in its lines. Whereas the cutter was almost entirely black, this new vehicle was white, except for areas of black chequering.

It shone a hailing laser onto him. Dreyfus accepted the call and a face appeared on his console. It was a woman, age indeterminate but perhaps not far off his own. She had a tight bowl of curled hair and a wide freckled face, with prominent cheek and jaw bones, her mouth a level, unsmiling line.

There was no trace of welcome in her eyes.

'Identify yourself.'

Dreyfus tried a smile. 'I thought I was expected.'

'Identify yourself. I won't ask again.'

'Prefect Tom Dreyfus of Panoply, requesting an inter-agency liaison and escort to Chasm City. I was given to understand that the Supreme Prefect had already made the necessary—'

'You're early.'

'I thought you'd appreciate it if I came and went as quickly as possible.'

'Then you thought wrongly. You've caused me considerable inconvenience, Prefect Dreyfus – forcing a change in my plans at very short notice. Believe it or not we do have work to be getting on with down here.'

'I don't doubt it,' Dreyfus said, straining to keep a friendly and open demeanour. 'And I apologise for upsetting your plans. I could turn around, I suppose . . .'

'You're here now,' the woman said, with a long-suffering sigh. 'And my day is already ruined. We may as well make the most of it.'

'I'm sorry I have to take up any of your time. It's just that I'm investigating a matter which has urgent security implications.'

She looked unimpressed. 'Your breakaway crisis? No concern of mine.'

'It might be about to become one.'

She shook her head once. 'Follow my ship. We'll go in hard. Do let me know if you can't keep up.'

Her face vanished from the screen. The other ship pivoted around with a flicker of steering motors, then daggered itself back towards Yellowstone, its triad of main engines flaring. In a few seconds it had dwindled to a hard, flickering glint, sliding against Yellowstone's marbled cloudscape. Dreyfus forced himself out of a sort of stunned paralysis, establishing a lock on the other ship as if he were in pursuit mode, and allowed the cutter to suspend its usual load ceilings. If she was determined to make a point, he would let her.

'Your host's name is Hestia Del Mar. I thought you might like to know that.'

Dreyfus tried not to look ruffled or surprised.

'I'd have found out for myself soon enough.'

'But now you have one tiny edge on her. Aren't you grateful for that?

I could tell you more, if you liked. Her service history, her disciplinary record, what her colleagues think of her, her private life . . . mm, now *that* is interesting. We have that much in common, she and I.'

'Just the name is fine.'

'You're not cross with me, are you?' Aurora's face had superceded Hestia Del Mar's, but it conveyed no more friendliness. Dreyfus rather preferred the stern-faced Del Mar; at least there was no doubting her feelings. 'Or is it that a troubling matter for your scruples?'

The cutter held its pursuit lock on the white ship. Gee loads rose, and a pinkish nimbus of ionised atmosphere began to curl around the hull, lapping and licking against its surfaces. The surfaces of Dreyfus's acceleration couch pushed through layers of skin and fat to find bones.

He grunted away the discomfort like a man passing a stone.

'Scruples . . . have nothing to do with it.'

'No? Then why were you so careful not to explain your sudden interest in Nautilus Holdings to your colleagues?'

'You provided a lead,' Dreyfus answered, feeling sweat prickle his brow. 'I looked into it.'

'And yet, no mention of where that lead came from – from whose lips it was shared.' Her smile was coquettish, teasing. 'I'm guessing, at least. Oh, relax – I'm not privy to every single conversation you have, Prefect, much as I might like to be. It would mean I didn't have to persuade those passwords from your lips.'

The cutter began to shake as dynamic forces built up. Wings and control surfaces budded from the hull, grown using rapid-response quickmatter. And yet they were still accelerating. Hestia Del Mar was either suicidal, or very, very sadistic.

Possibly both, Dreyfus decided.

'It was a no then. It's a no now. We'll solve this the old-fashioned way, with police work.'

'Yes. Good luck with that. Have you seen the latest death forecasts? Aumonier's tracking another case as we speak. Your triggers are lighting up like fireworks. If only you had those patient names, though. How much easier that would make your task.'

The gee loads were reversing; now at last even Hestia Del Mar was having to slow down as her course took her into the deeper layers of the atmosphere. Determined not to give in, Dreyfus closed the distance between the two ships. On the screens her white vehicle seemed almost close enough to touch as it rammed onward through thickening yellow and brown cloud layers. Engine backwash and re-entry turbulence made for a bone-shaking pursuit.

'If there's a shred of humanity left in you,' Dreyfus said, grimacing out the words, 'give them to me now.'

'Oh, I'd love to – really I would. But there's the small matter of give and take. It's not often I have real leverage over you – I'd be foolish to waste this opportunity. Let go of your inhibitions.'

The two ships began to level out. The hull shutters opened, the hull's visible arc still giving off a faint glow as it surrendered some of the heat gained during the entry. They were moving hypersonically now, and snatches of terrain occasionally opened up below.

'You really don't understand people any more, Aurora. If you ever did.'

Her face blanched, her eyes flaring with wounded pride – a little too theatrically to be convincing. 'Mm. You really know how to hurt a girl, Dreyfus. How unchivalrous of you. How mean.'

'One day you might grow a conscience.'

'Oh, I wouldn't want one of those. I tried it once and it didn't suit me at all.' Her face began to fade out, crazing over with static before sharpening one last time. 'Regretfully, I must now take my absence – but we'll speak again, won't we?'

'No rush,' Dreyfus said, Aurora becoming disembodied eyes and mouth, and then just the mouth, the last part of her to fade.

It was gone for a moment, and then another face appeared on the console.

'Still keeping up, Dreyfus?'

'Yes, Hestia.'

'Good. If you've done your homework, you'll know that my correct title is Detective-Marshal Del Mar. We'll keep it formal, shall we?'

'Absolutely. It's Field Prefect Dreyfus, if we're holding score.'

'Follow me,' she said.

Julius did not care for the new phase in Caleb's hunting game. He went along with it all the same, grudgingly aware that he preferred his brother's company to none at all.

Caleb had grown more adept with the shaping of material objects. One afternoon, visibly pleased with himself, he showed Julius his latest triumph. It was a fully functioning crossbow, formed from a single piece of quickmatter. He passed it to Julius, inviting him to admire it.

'I thought a hunting rifle was more your style,' Julius said. 'Something that works, not just a dummy.'

'I could have shaped a functioning rifle easily enough,' Caleb replied off-handedly. 'I know what's inside a rifle. A few moving parts: nothing too challenging. But you need chemistry to make bullets, and quickmatter's chemically inert.'

'Pity. Poor you.'

'I figured a crossbow oughtn't to be too hard, and it wasn't. It's just a question of designing different tensile properties into the components. The range and stopping power isn't as good as a rifle, but that just makes the game a bit more interesting.'

'Does it?'

'Yes. We'll need to get closer to the animals.'

'They're not real,' Julius pointed out, for all the good he knew it would do. 'They're figments, visual ghosts. We don't need to actually shoot them with a physical object.'

Caleb looked at him oddly. 'There's no fun in making the game too easy. We have to feel as if we're doing our part, and that means we won't be able to kill them unless we're within a realistic range.'

Julius sighted along the crossbow. It felt solid in his hands, well balanced, economical and elegant in its design. It was beyond anything he was presently capable of conjuring, but Caleb already knew that and certainly needed no further encouragement. 'As long as you don't expect us to use knives. What are we supposed to shoot with this?'

'I've already thought about that.' Caleb dug into the pocket of his shorts and came out with a sharp-tipped dart, about the size of his thumb. 'Quickmatter again. I tried a few different forms until I found the right shape. Go on, try it.'

'There aren't any animals nearby.'

'Just shoot at anything. I want you to get the hang of it.'

Julius armed the crossbow, figuring out for himself how to latch it. He placed the dart in the smooth groove that ran the length of the weapon, then raised the crossbow to his shoulder. He swung around slowly, sighting at a grove of trees about fifty paces away. He picked one tree, held his breath and squeezed the trigger stub. The bow jerked a little as it released, but he had been ready for that and it had not upset his aim.

A moment later, the dart embedded itself in the tree with a solid, satisfying thunk.

'I hope you've made a few more of those.'

'A few,' Caleb said. 'But since it's quickmatter, it responds to a homing command.' He gestured in the rough direction of the tree, and the dart gave an unsettling wriggle and dropped to the ground. Julius watched as it began inching through the undergrowth, propelling itself with queasy, sluglike undulations. 'I could have made it fly, I suppose,' Caleb said. 'But as long as it gets back eventually it doesn't matter how long it takes.' Then he patted Julius roughly. 'C'mon. Let's go and hunt. If it goes well we'll talk Father into giving us some more quickmatter, and then I can conjure a second crossbow just for you.'

'I can't wait,' Julius said.

They had been walking for a few minutes, Caleb holding the crossbow again, when he said: 'What did you mean back there, by the way?'

'About what?'

'Knives. You said as long as we're not expected to use knives.'

Julius frowned. 'Did I?'

'I know you, Julius, and nothing comes out of your mouth by accident.' Caleb walked on, swinging the crossbow from its stock. 'It's that dream of yours again, isn't it?'

'I thought we agreed not to talk about my dream.'

'You were the one who raised it, not me.'

'I don't think I ever mentioned my dream involving knives, Caleb. I'd have remembered it if I had.'

Caleb turned around, bringing the crossbow around in an arc so that Julius had to duck back not to be bludgeoned. 'Don't lie to me. You said we were standing holding knives, and everyone else was dead.'

'I didn't.' Julius reached up and snatched the crossbow from Caleb's grip, surprised at his own speed and strength. 'I know, because I made a point of never saying it. But I've caught you out now, haven't I?'

Caleb seethed, but said nothing.

'We both have the same dream,' Julius carried on, meeting his brother's eyes and not flinching away from the menace he detected in them. 'You just don't want to admit it. You prefer the lie you've been sold.'

'And what lie would that be?'

'That you're the son of a Voi. That you're entitled to this power, this responsibility.' He threw the crossbow at Caleb's feet. 'You're not one of them, and neither am I. We're something else.' He cocked his head at the Shell House. 'We weren't born here. Whatever childhood we had, it wasn't the one they want us to know about.'

Caleb stooped down to pick up the weapon. He shook the dirt from it, tension flexing through his arm muscles. 'You can keep trying to tease me, brother, but it won't work. Either cough up or stop going on about it.'

'Do you remember what Doctor Stasov said, the last time he was here?'

'I suppose you do.'

'He said they were making monsters out of monsters. He meant us, Caleb. He meant Mother and Father are trying to turn us into something. He also said we're not really theirs.'

'Here you go again.'

214

'You can pretend you don't remember, but I saw how much you were bothered by his words.'

'If he's so clever, why haven't we seen him since?'

'I don't know.' Julius scowled, not wanting to be side tracked. 'He was having an argument with them, wasn't he? Saying he didn't want to carry on, and they were telling him it wasn't any good. I think they were threatening him, Caleb, trying to stop him going away or whatever he was thinking of doing. It's funny that they haven't found another doctor, isn't it? I mean, there's a whole city out there. How hard could it be to find another doctor to keep an eye on two boys?'

'You already know we have to keep all this secret,' Caleb said. 'Perhaps we don't even need a doctor now, anyway. He hardly did anything the last time.'

'Maybe we don't need him now. But that doesn't change the things he said. He said something bad happened a long time ago, didn't he? Well, I know what it was. They've been careful with the books they leave us, haven't they? There's not too much about the history of the Shell House or the Voi family.'

'No need. We get it rammed down our throats every time we walk past a painting.'

Julius conceded that this was a reasonable point. 'Still, I wanted to see if I could find out about something bad. And I didn't have to look very far. There's a book on Marco Ferris. It goes into a lot of stuff. I think they forgot that it also mentions the Amerikano settlement.'

Caleb fingered the crossbow. 'And?'

'Don't pretend you don't know what I'm talking about, brother. Before they had the fast ships, they sent robots to lots of different planets. Robots with eggs inside them, or with genetic patterns that could be made into human embryos once they'd arrived and started mining raw materials.'

'Get to the point, Julius.'

'In each instance the robots created a batch of children – newborns. But there wasn't anyone around to raise those children except the robots themselves. The trouble is the robots didn't get it right, and the children ended up all wrong. If there was a second generation, it was even worse. Something hadn't developed properly. Empathy, social awareness, call it what you will. They were little sociopaths. Little monsters.' Julius said the word deliberately, watching his brother carefully. 'And most of them went mad. All those settlements, in all the different systems. They all failed for different reasons, but underlying them all was a common cause. They weren't knitting together the way human communities are meant to. No one should have been too surprised, should they? We're just mammals.

That's all we've ever been, all we've known for tens of millions of years. We've evolved to grow up surrounded by other mammals, one or two generations of them, showing us how to behave. But the Amerikano children didn't have that. They came out of metal wombs on an alien planet, with only robots to stand in for their parents.'

'You're an expert of all sudden.'

Julius touched a hand to his heart. 'I don't need to be. I don't need to be told this stuff, because I've known it all along. It's *us*, brother. That's what we are. The survivors of one of those settlements. Those are the dreams we have – being back there, with the other children, and the robots.'

'That's not possible. It happened too long ago.'

'I don't claim to understand it, Caleb. But I can't ignore it, either. The Ursas – remember them? I didn't make that up. It's all in the book. That's what the robots were called, when they were trying to raise the first generation. They gave them arms and legs, like people, and covered them in fur, so they wouldn't be too frightening. It was meant to help the children – like orphans being raised by friendly teddy bears. But it all went wrong.'

'It wasn't us.'

'It *was*. I don't know how, but that's what happened. We killed all the other boys and girls. We weren't meant to remember it, but we do. And now we're here.'

CHAPTER THIRTEEN

It took a few moments for the mob to notice that the doors to the polling core were opening. Until that development, the human tide of Garlin's assembly had seemed to be on the turn, first in ones and twos and then in gathering numbers. Sparver had allowed himself to believe that a peaceful resolution was still feasible, and that he and Thalia would be able to leave the habitat with Garlin in their protective custody and some measure of calm restored.

But the opening of the doors had a profound effect on the mob's state of mind. The retreat lost its impetus, and then, with a roar of collective determination, that tidal surge began to press back towards the steps and the seven operatives attempting to hold them. This was the crowd's moment. Those opening doors were not just an opportunity, but an invitation.

The constables pressed out their stun-truncheons, the ends flickering with blue sparks. The operatives with sonic-cannons began to douse the crowd with continuous pulses, a horrible sound even for anyone not caught in the direct focus of the cannons. Undeterred, the mob was already spilling onto the first couple of steps. Sparver had just enough time to bark an order to his reserve whiphound, instructing it to use maximum force in holding the line.

On the level ground, next to the cleaning robot, Thalia had been in the middle of persuading Garlin down from his roost. Malkmus and the other constables were next to her. The first two whiphounds were still holding a cordon, but the mob was pressing in and he saw when Thalia became aware of the opening doors. As his own whiphound zig-zagged back and forth at high speed, trying to club or lash anyone who dared test its threshold, Sparver watched Thalia glance around and touch her throat microphone, and then her voice sounded in his earpiece.

'Ng to Panoply. Things have just turned here. The core is compromised. Repeat, the core is compromised.' Then, locking eyes with Sparver:

'Malkmus doesn't know what's happening. Those doors shouldn't have opened.'

'She said there were constables inside,' Sparver said. 'Maybe they overrode the lockdown, for whatever reason.'

'Malkmus says no. But there should still be multiple barriers between the lobby and the core.'

'I'm not sure I'd count on them, given what's just happened. Did Garlin send any sort of signal just before the doors opened?'

'I'm looking at him right now. He didn't say or do anything. That doesn't mean he isn't responsible.'

'I agree, but it's nothing we can prove for the moment.' Sparver jerked back as a projectile narrowly missed his shins. Thalia looked small and vulnerable, hemmed in by the mob on all sides. She had two whiphounds defending the cordon, and a third at her side, but Sparver knew all too well that she could still come to harm.

'You have one last chance, Garlin,' he heard her call out. 'Tell them to pull back from the steps.'

'These are free citizens,' he answered, roaring out his words, and snaring the mob's attention while he spoke. 'They don't answer to anyone, Prefect Ng, let alone me. And if there has been such negligence as to leave the core unprotected, why should they be blamed for it?'

'Julius Devon Garlin Voi,' Thalia said, her voice breaking under the strain, 'you are under arrest for the commission of actions detrimental to the democratic process.' She flicked a glance at her whiphound. 'Bring him down and hold him on the ground.'

The whiphound moved in a blur and crack of coils. Garlin had just enough time to register surprise, and to begin moving his hands into a reflex defensive posture, almost a surrender, but it was to no avail. The whiphound had flung itself airborne, lassoed itself around his lower legs, drawn itself tight, and toppled Garlin. That was as much as Sparver saw clearly, but he had little difficulty imagining the rest.

Garlin would have come down hard. By the time he hit the ground the whiphound would have looped a few more coils around him for good measure, preventing him from flailing out or reaching for a weapon. Depending on the orders Thalia gave, the coils would either lock solid – making it feel as if he were imprisoned in a single unyielding restraint – or would tighten under resistance, eventually biting into skin and bone.

'Have you got him?' Sparver called.

Thalia grunted as she knelt down. 'Yes. Contained. Ng to Panoply. Update on the situation here. I've detained Garlin. Things are getting hot here. We could really use that backup.'

The whiphound's zig-zag patrol was growing ever more frenetic. The citizens had gathered up their weapons again and were using them with increasing ferocity, throwing crude projectiles or swiping the air threateningly with sticks and fence posts. Individually, none of these items would have posed the slightest challenge to the whiphound. But sheer force of numbers was starting to make a difference, and Sparver knew that when the defensive line failed it would happen quickly.

He turned back to the constables. 'Fall back and regroup with your colleagues inside.'

'They'll overrun this entrance,' one of the constables said, fear showing in his eyes like a bright new dawn, as if it was an entirely novel emotion.

'I'll hold it as long as I can. But if you can form a cordon around the inner core that'll be a lot easier than defending this entrance.'

'How long do we have to hold it for?' asked a second constable.

'Not long,' Sparver said. 'Chances are there's already a cruiser docked as we speak.'

That was close to a lie, but to his relief the constables accepted his word and abandoned their line, with one of them passing him a stun-truncheon before they left.

Sparver found he was surprisingly grateful for the stun-truncheon. Its end was sparking and he swung it in an arc, even as he stepped back to assume a higher position on the steps.

'Still there, Thalia?'

'Garlin and I aren't going anywhere,' she said, with a sarcastic friendliness. 'Are we, Devon?'

'Hang tight. Don't try and move him back to the ship on your own – it's a job for two of us, even with whiphounds.'

'Advice noted, Deputy Bancal,' she said.

A second later the line fell. A hooded citizen saw their moment, springing onto the steps when the whiphound was at the opposite limit of its patrol. As the citizen crossed the threshold, another risked a swipe against the whiphound's head with the blunt end of a wooden stake, doing no harm to the whiphound but knocking it aside and thereby gaining a precious second or two for more citizens to swarm onto the steps. The whiphound responded with an escalation in the severity of its attacks, using the second edge to draw blood, and whipping and coiling around any limb or extremity unwise enough to stray within its range. Joints were dislocated, bones fractured, skin gashed. Those unfortunate citizens fell back instantly, nursing sudden, bright wounds, but still greater numbers came trampling forward. A few of the wounded fell to the ground, their shocked and moaning forms quickly lost under the advance.

Sparver redoubled his hold on the stun-truncheon. The whiphound was still flailing, still doing all that could be asked of it, but the surge of people had flowed around and past it, and the steps could no longer be defended. Sparver jabbed out with the truncheon, and citizens dropped like sacks as soon as they were touched. But there were always more. Dozens were already on the steps, oblivious to injury or the criminal nature of their actions, and hundreds pressed in from behind.

He stepped back again. The shade of the lobby was at his back. Two or three citizens were already through, their shouts gaining an echoing timbre as they entered the enclosed space. More came at him. He parried with the stun-truncheon, citizens dropping, the smell of burning skin and fabric ripe in his nose. Dozens were inside now, their footsteps drum-rolling into the distance as they sought the core. The stun-truncheon seemed to be losing its effectiveness under this sustained discharge. They were not dropping so quickly, and in any case the rush of citizens was beginning to overwhelm him, their combined momentum causing him to be pushed back, carried along on their seething front. Finally someone wrenched the truncheon from his two-fingered grip and an elbow smashed into his face.

Sparver blacked out.

Dreyfus buckled on his equipment and made his exit from the cutter. His belt felt tight under his belly, as if his guts had shifted during the re-entry. Hestia Del Mar was already striding around on the landing pad, wrinkling her nose as she sniffed at the fumes still lingering under the pad's pressure-tight ceiling. She wore a white uniform with crisp black trim at the cuffs and collar, and carried no weapons or enforcement devices that he could make out.

'Did you push it a little harder than was wise, Field Prefect Dreyfus?'

Dreyfus shrugged. 'I kept up, didn't I?'

She looked doubtful. 'I'd get that cladding looked at, if I were you.'

'I'll make a note of it,' Dreyfus said, looking up into her face. 'Look, Hestia . . . wouldn't it be easier if we just put our professional differences aside for a few hours? I'm sure we'd turn out to have a lot in common. My name's Tom—'

'I know your name.' She started walking away from the two ships, down a shallow ramp. 'As you know mine. But I believe in the professional courtesies, Prefect Dreyfus. I feel it helps to have a clear sense of responsibilities. We'll take my flier the rest of the way. You have fliers in the Glitter Band, don't you?'

'And fire, and the wheel,' Dreyfus said.

At the base of the ramp stood a sleek, black flying machine, shaped like a cat's paw. Del Mar beckoned for Dreyfus to climb into the volantor's cabin and buckle in to one of the padded seats. Then she joined him and folded down the vehicle's aerodynamic canopy, taking a seat next to his own.

Del Mar muttered something into her collar and the volantor took off and sped into a narrow, rock-lined tunnel.

'Before we get to the Shell House,' Del Mar said, 'you should be aware that we take a very dim view of attempts to influence democratic process in the Glitter Band, however much the outcome might not be to your liking.'

'And if I told you that my interest in the Shell House is only incidental to the breakaway movement, would that change your mind?'

'You would need to persuade me first, Prefect Dreyfus.'

Rock walls hurtled by at great speed. Dreyfus's back was sticky with sweat, forming too quickly to be absorbed by his clothing. He leaned forward, unpeeling himself from the seat. 'We have a developing emergency involving random deaths. If your intelligence on us is as good as ours on you, then you'll already know of it.'

'I don't need intelligence. I just need to listen to the rumours.'

'You're right – it's already out there, and it'll soon be beyond our ability to contain. But you must understand why we've tried to keep a lid on it.'

'And the relevance of . . . you call it "Wildfire". The relevance of all this to the Shell House?'

'The dead seem to have had some contact with a private medical facility in the Glitter Band, a clinic calling itself Elysium Heights. We think the money behind the clinic originated with the Shell House.'

She listened and nodded, and for the first time he had the impression he was being treated, if not as an equal, then not with complete contempt.

'It could be an attempt to damage the standing of Devon Garlin, by linking him to your crisis.'

'I've still got to look into the connection. Devon Garlin can hang himself for all I care. It's the Wildfire deaths that I'm here to stop.'

'By identifying past clients of this clinic?'

'That's our hope. We have a lead that suggests about two thousand clients in total, but we're nowhere near identifying unique individuals, let alone figuring out their present whereabouts.'

'Two thousand is rather a lot of people, Prefect. You can't even be sure that all of these individuals still live in the Glitter Band. There'd have been nothing to stop some of them emigrating to Yellowstone.'

'In which case you might have seen a few Wildfire cases of your own by now,' Dreyfus said. 'Which we'd know if you had . . .'

221

'Would you?'

'Of course. You'd have shared that intelligence with us.'

'Well, naturally – but first we'd have to be sure of what we were dealing with. If, say, we were interested in the prior whereabouts of three individuals who had become of concern to us, and we asked for Panoply's assistance with this matter . . .'

Dreyfus blinked against a sudden inrush of daylight as the volantor exited the tunnel into clear air. Mountain-sized buildings slipped by on either side.

'Did you make such a request?'

'You know that we did.'

'I don't, and I'd have pushed for cooperation if I did.'

'Then it's a pity you aren't in a higher position of authority. Our request was roundly ignored.'

Dreyfus made the mistake of looking out and down. The buildings' roots seemed to plunge an impossible distance, with tiered gardens and lakes reduced to tiny swatches of colour. No matter how far down he peered, he could see nothing that looked like ground level or bedrock.

Vertigo had him slumping into his seat.

'I can't believe that Jane Aumonier would dismiss a lead relating to Wildfire.'

'We didn't mention Wildfire. All we asked was that Panoply assist us in backtracking the movements of these individuals.'

'With, presumably, a cover story to explain your interest?'

'It was stated that they were fugitives. It was only a slight untruth. All three had had some involvement in semi-legal activity prior to their deaths. They *had* evaded justice; they *had* been fugitives in a technical sense.'

'If that's your idea of a slight untruth . . .' But Dreyfus relented, knowing he needed to keep his host cooperative, at least for the next thirteen hours. 'Knowing what you do now, would you describe them as risk-takers?'

'Conceivably. Why would you make that connection?'

'Because it shows up time and again in our Wildfire cases. Hedonism, pleasure-seeking, recklessly addictive behaviour, call it what you will. It's the only pattern that was there from the start.'

'And the significance of this pattern?'

'I don't know yet. But something happened to our victims in that clinic. They were treated for something – presumably voluntarily – and years later their heads explode. I'd have put it down to some unlikely side-effect, except that it works so well for Devon Garlin.'

'I see that it puts you in a bind.' Something tightened in her face

– almost a grimace of sympathy, if Dreyfus read her correctly. 'You're of the opinion that Garlin engineered Wildfire as a boost to his separatist movement?'

'I'd have counted it as unlikely, until that link to the Shell House came up.'

'And now you hope to confirm your suspicions with some old-fashioned boots-on-the-ground police work. I'm afraid you may be in for something of a disappointment, Prefect.' She turned to glance out the window, the tendons showing in her neck. 'There was a man making . . . outlandish claims. An embittered former employee. His story was preposterous, but I looked into it anyway, and that meant I had to visit the Shell House.'

'What man?'

'You miss my point. I went there. It's a crumbling, overgrown ruin, and it's been that way for decades. There's nothing there.'

The blood was still running from his nose when he came around, slumped with his back against the wall, the whiphound waiting next to him, loyally alert to his movements. He was in the lobby, exactly where he had fallen, citizens streaming through the open doorway, completely uninterested in him. Sparver reached out to the whiphound, using it for leverage as he regained his footing.

Still groggy, he clipped the retracted whiphound to his belt and staggered along the wall until he reached the doorway. Something had twisted in his knee when he went down, and each footfall sent a precise stiletto of pain jabbing up his thigh.

The area in front of the polling core building was a littered and smoking mess, but there could not have been more than a hundred citizens still out there. Some of them were fighting each other. There were bodies on the ground and fires stretching away, beacons proclaiming some total breakdown of civil order.

The majority of Garlin's mob, without doubt, had gone inside.

He straightened up as best he could, wiped a sleeve under his nose to soak up the blood, and watched as the blood faded back into the stainless black fabric.

'This is Prefect Bancal,' he said, opening a channel to Panoply. 'Request expedited backup. The mob has overrun the polling core building. Ng and I couldn't hold them back. If they break through to the core itself, we may lose abstraction and comms services . . .' He paused, smearing his nose again. 'Panoply? This is Prefect Bancal . . .'

He trailed off, because he had seen something. A single whiphound was defining an exclusion cordon around a curious humpbacked form on the ground, next to the toppled-over cleaning servitor. A second whiphound, outside the cordon, twitched and coiled in a single spot on the ground, like a snake with a severed head. Of the third whiphound, nothing was to be seen.

Sparver limped down the steps. A handful of constables were still trying to impose calm, but as soon as they pacified one group of citizens, a fight broke out elsewhere. Several were kneeling by the fallen and injured.

He hobbled to the cordon around the humped form. The circling whiphound detected his authority and allowed him to step into the area. He moved to the shape on the ground. It was Thalia, pressed down over Garlin, with her back to the sky. He immediately understood that she'd used her own body to protect Garlin, shielding him from any possible advance of the mob. He watched her guardedly, wondering why she had not pulled herself off Garlin now that the time of greatest danger had passed.

'Thalia?' he said.

She neither moved nor responded. Sparver mouthed an oath, realising that she must be injured or incapacitated. He knelt down next to her, praying for an obvious sign of life.

A ragged voice called to him.

He turned. It was Malkmus, looking as if she had just been through a military campaign. Dirt was sweat-plastered to her face. One eyelid was swollen.

She stood at the cordon's edge.

'Prefect. Will it let me through?'

Sparver nodded, even as he reached out a hand to touch Thalia. Malkmus hesitated for an instant then took him at his word, stepping across the line grooved into the dirt by the hurtling whiphound. She joined him next to Thalia.

'Is she all right?'

'I don't know.' He studied her carefully. 'I think she's breathing. What the hell happened out here?'

'They came in fast,' Malkmus said, catching her breath. 'Started picking at the edge of Garlin's crowd. I tried to call in more constables, but I couldn't get a signal through.'

'You won't,' Sparver said. 'They've taken out the core. Everything rides on that – even our own comms back to Panoply.'

'But my constables inside the building – the lockdown shields . . .'

'None of it worked. The core was wide open from the moment those doors opened.'

'That isn't how it's meant to happen.'

'Story of our lives.' He had tugged up her sleeve enough to feel for a pulse, and believed he could feel one, albeit weakly. 'Can you help me with Thalia?'

'Yes . . . yes, of course.' Together, with great care, they lifted her off Garlin's form and laid her down on her side. Her uniform had stiffened across her back, forming a defensive shield from her neck to her hips, hard as a turtle's shell. 'She can't be too badly hurt, can she?' Malkmus asked, touching a finger to Thalia's lidded eyes.

'I don't know. How well do you think you'd feel if a mob had just trampled over you?'

'I didn't mean . . .'

'It's all right,' Sparver said, not wanting to have snapped. 'I know you see two prefects, two of us in uniform, coming to teach you how to run things. But that's not how it was. Thalia's my friend.'

'I . . . understand,' Malkmus said.

Sparver wanted to do something, but he knew that there was little he could offer that was not already being handled by the medical systems embedded in Thalia's uniform. It would be sampling her blood chemistry, administering micro-dosages of tailored drugs, doing all it could to stabilise her condition before help arrived.

Malkmus left, then came back with an item of clothing that had been left on the ground. Gingerly she slipped it under Thalia's head, so her face wasn't in the dirt.

'Thank you,' Sparver said.

'I didn't see much of what happened. I think they ran right over her, even with those whiphounds. And then when the others piled in, all they wanted to do was tear him apart.'

'She wasn't kidding about taking him into protective custody,' Sparver said, shifting her body so she might be able to breathe more easily.

'He's alive, I think,' Malkmus said.

'Good. I'd hate to miss the look on his face when he finds out who saved his life.'

'Yes,' she said, half a smile creasing into her dirt-smeared face. 'I wouldn't mind being there for that myself.'

Sparver unclipped his whiphound. 'Run a medical scan on Prefect Ng and Julius Devon Garlin Voi. Coordinate with all remaining whiphounds and continue attempting to signal Panoply that we need a Heavy Medical Squad inbound at maximum priority.'

'How long will it be?'

'They'll have gone to an emergency posture as soon as the core went down. But I don't know how long it will take. Maybe an hour. Less if we're lucky.'

Malkmus stood up, her hand on her stun-truncheon. She looked around at the chaos and smoke, the slumped bodies and the brawls still continuing. 'Does it look like it's our lucky day? I'm going to see if I can reach some of our own medical functionaries.'

'You'll be safer in this cordon. Call in the rest of your constables, before they get too bruised and bloodied out there.'

'You took a few bruises for us today, Prefect. The least we can do is take our share.'

Sparver spoke to the still-circling whiphound. 'Break cordon and provide protective escort to Chief Constable Glenda Malkmus. Accept orders from Glenda Malkmus under discretionary limits.'

She looked at the whiphound with unconcealed apprehension.

'What about you?'

'I'll be fine,' Sparver said. 'This one will shield us once it's run the medical scans. The other whiphound will stay with you until you dismiss it.'

'I shouldn't be long.'

'Take care out there, Constable Malkmus.'

'I almost forgot to ask. Are you going to be all right, Prefect?'

'Oh, I'm right as rain.' Sparver looked down at his fallen colleague, resting a hand on her side, feeling her breathing, shallow but steady. 'Like I said, just one big fun day out.'

Garlin had come around by the time Panoply's reinforcements reached the habitat. By then Malkmus had returned with as many constables as she could mop up, as well as four fatigued-looking medical functionaries. They tended Thalia, treating her with a sort of wary reverence, as if Sparver might hold them accountable for any lapses. But he had complete faith in them, as he did in the Heavy Medicals who arrived shortly after, accompanied by twenty Field Prefects with dual whiphounds. They made a formidable presence, but Sparver was not a little surprised to see they were still carrying no weapons beyond the whiphounds. Given the severity of the declining situation in Fuxin-Nymburk, he had expected the Supreme Prefect to petition for the use of the heavy weapons still stored in Panoply's vaults, ready to be released to the prefects for a period of exactly one hundred and thirty hours.

Either the petition had failed, or Lady Jane had decided the stakes were still not quite high enough to justify that measure.

Under the moderate restraint binding that Sparver had applied from his belt, Garlin moaned his way into semi-alertness.

'Get this stuff off me.'

'Did you not hear my colleague placing you under arrest?' Sparver asked reasonably. 'And then placing her own life on the line to protect you, when the tempers you'd stirred up turned against you?'

One of the newly arrived prefects knelt down next to them.

'Prefect Bancal. Good to see you, sir.'

'We understand Garlin's been served a detention order?'

'Thalia Ng did it just before the mob closed in,' Sparver said. 'Have you got word back to Panoply?'

'Just now, sir. Partial restoration of core. The constables sealed the doors from the outside and pumped sleeping gas into the building. It took down a few of their own, but they'll make a good recovery and it allowed the rest of them to go in and consolidate the core. Our technicians are down there arranging a full restart. No one's quite sure why the lockdown failed, though.'

'Perhaps Mister Garlin can shed some light on that,' Sparver said.

'Panoply say to bring him in on the arrest order. We can take over from now, if you like?'

'No,' Sparver said, fighting to his feet, and dragging Garlin halfway to standing in the process. 'Mister Garlin and I will be just fine on our own.'

Dreyfus was getting the hurry-up-and-wait treatment. They had stopped off at the offices of the Chamber for City Security, Hestia Del Mar going off to deal with some doubtless urgent administrative business, even though it was on his time, eating into his allotted thirteen hours.

He accepted it stoically, gazing out of a window in an empty meeting room, conscious that Panoply probably put some of its own visitors through a similar process.

Beyond the glass, Chasm City stretched away to the limits of vision, building after building receding into a twinkling, pearly haze. It was the densest urban concentration in human history, vastly larger and more populous than any of the habitats under his responsibility. The size of the place made the back of his neck tingle with a sort of anti-claustrophobia, his innate understanding of the right and proper scale of things constantly mocked and undermined in every direction that he stared. Habitats were contained, manageable. Their cities never had room to sprawl too far before meeting their own edges again. Even if the worst possible thing went wrong in a habitat, it was still just one among ten thousand. But this place was madness. It was a huge, humming, human machine spun up to berserk speed, just waiting to go wrong.

He thought of Devon Garlin being born here, the son of one of the oldest, most influential and respected families, given the metaphorical keys to this city, all its promise and power at his fingertips.

And still that wasn't enough for you, you bastard?

His bracelet chimed.

'Dreyfus,' he said.

'It's Jane,' he heard. 'I gather you've arrived. Are you making progress?'

'They're falling over themselves to help,' Dreyfus said.

'Good.'

'Good? I was being sarcastic.'

'Fine, yes.' He picked up on the distracted edge in her voice. 'I should have . . . look, something's happened, and I feel you should know about it.'

'To do with Garlin?'

'Ng and Bancal got caught up in trouble in Fuxin-Nymburk. Garlin was in danger of being trampled and Ng took him into protective custody, but she got hurt in the process.'

'Hurt?'

'She made a human shield of herself. When Bancal made it back to her she was unconscious.'

Dreyfus sifted through his emotions. Pride that Ng had acquitted herself selflessly. Resentment that he had not been allowed to be there in her place, with all his additional years of experience. Anger that Sparver had not done a better job of looking over her shoulder.

'Why the hell wasn't he with her to begin with?'

'Don't blame him. If anyone's at fault it's me, for not sending in a larger team.'

Dreyfus made an effort to lower his voice. 'Where is Thalia now?'

'Under observation, being transported back to Panoply. They tell me she's stable, but I daren't count my blessings yet. We'll throw the entire resources of the medical section at her when she comes in, but until then we can only hope for the best. It was a mess, Tom – worse than I anticipated. Garlin's mob gained access to the polling core.'

'That's impossible.'

'It happened. And you've been the one telling me all along that Garlin wasn't operating within the usual rules.'

'I was hoping to be proved wrong, not right.'

'Too late for that, I'm afraid. We have Garlin, at least. Barring a few bruises he got off lightly.'

'At least you have reasonable grounds to detain and question him now.'

'More than that. Something came in after you left – a definite link between Garlin and the clinic.'

'It was definite enough as far as I was concerned.'

'The rest of us needed a little more persuasion. Now we know Garlin was posing as Doctor Julius Mazarin, one of the clinic's staff.'

'He confessed to it, did he?'

'No, he's still putting up a façade of ignorance about the whole thing. What we have is a video fragment . . .'

'Send it through to my goggles when you have a chance. But I'm not pinning all our hopes on fragments. No citizen quorum will sign off on an enforcement action on the basis of a video, no matter how incriminating.'

'We'll squeeze Garlin – he may crack any moment. In the meantime, continue your investigation of the Shell House.'

Dreyfus glanced over his shoulder. 'Just as soon as Hestia Del Mar finishes off her year-end tax returns, or whatever else is keeping her.'

'I'm sure she's a busy woman. Oh, and Tom?'

'Yes?'

'Another Wildfire case just came in. Make that our sixty-third victim.'

'Sixty-sixth,' Dreyfus corrected her. 'I just learned about three earlier cases.'

'That doesn't match . . . oh, wait. I see. Obvious in hindsight, I suppose, that Wildfire would show up on her watch, as well as mine.'

'I believe you had a request for intelligence-sharing? Something about tracking down fugitives?'

'Yes, I put Jirmal onto it. I couldn't give her authorisation to use all available resources, though – especially not now. I just trusted that . . .'

'The problem would go away, if we ignored it long enough?'

'That's a little unfair. Jirmal understood the request had to be treated with a realistic level of priority. Not ignored . . . not at all. But relegated, until we're out of this mess.'

'We're not the only ones who could use a helping hand occasionally, Jane. We should have been more cooperative from the outset. I'm trying to rebuild some bridges now, although judging by Hestia's warm and welcoming nature it might be a bit too late. Anyway, I've told her what we know about Wildfire, as little as it is.'

'She doesn't have Pangolin clearance.'

'I'm aware of that. But just for once, I felt a little trust might not go amiss.'

'All right,' she said, with grudging agreement. 'It's risky and I'll probably regret it. But share with her as you see fit. And use your damned discretion, too – she doesn't have to know everything. In the meantime I'll attempt to make amends about her requests. You'll have that feed on your goggles as soon as Tang sends it through.'

'Thank you, Jane. Keep me informed about Thalia, will you?'

'I will.'

There was a cough from behind him as he signed off. He turned around to see Hestia Del Mar placing some items on the room's bare table.

'I was starting to worry you'd forgotten about me,' Dreyfus said.

'It took a little longer than I anticipated to compile these summaries,' Del Mar answered, squaring up the little pile of dossiers she had created. 'These are evidential packages relating to our three Wildfire cases. There are issues of witness confidentiality, so I had to make sure we weren't in violation of our own rules, which meant omitting some of the testimonies. I also had to go up the chain of rank to get agreement, and not all my superiors were happy with the idea of sharing this knowledge in the light of Panoply's recent intransigence.'

'I . . . all right.' Dreyfus was momentarily flummoxed. 'Thank you.'

'Just as long as you didn't think I was wasting your very precious time, Prefect.' She gave him a knowing look. 'You may take these dossiers and examine them as you see fit. In the meantime the contents will be up-linked to Panoply for the eyes of Jane Aumonier and her tactical staff only.'

'I did you a disservice,' Dreyfus said, reaching for the dossiers 'I assumed—'

'Later,' Del Mar said, flicking aside his apology with the disdain it merited.

She had parked the volantor on the roof. They returned to it, climbed in, then swooped off and dived hard. Del Mar had given the volantor a verbal instruction before, but now she was flying it on manual override, making effortless but precise inputs via its multi-mode joystick.

Layer after layer of Chasm City rose up and stacked into a thickening, gridlike pattern overhead. The gold-stained daylight, which had seemed bright from the train, now turned brassy, then sepia, then a dim, effectless brown. Still the buildings' roots plunged deeper. Concourses, shopping plazas, parks, woods, gardens, civic lakes, rose up and were swept into the dense complication overhead.

'So, about your call from Panoply.'

Dreyfus affected no surprise that he had been eavesdropped on. 'What about it?'

'Firstly, the obligatory sympathies concerning your injured colleague. I trust she makes a good recovery.'

'So do I.'

After a silence Del Mar said: 'How could Garlin's people get into the polling core so easily? Didn't you have the place under some sort of lockdown?'

'It failed. We don't know why.'

'Yet your boss made mention of Garlin operating beyond the usual rules.'

Dreyfus sighed, debating with himself how candid he ought to be. It was one thing to share scraps of intelligence, another to voice unverified theories of his own.

'I've been keeping an eye on him since he crawled out of the slime. There are things he can do, things he's able to find out, that can't be easily explained. Call them superhuman powers of omniscience and fore-sight.' He caught her sidelong expression, doubt shading into incredulity. 'Nothing magical. I just think he's able to use abstraction in a way that shouldn't be possible. He can pick up on information patterns – detecting my presence in a crowd, for instance. But it goes beyond that. I think he just willed that lockdown to collapse. I'm not even sure he knows how he does it.'

'And you have an explanation for these . . . capabilities?'

'He's a Voi. I think Devon Garlin must have been let in on a few family secrets.'

'But to be so brazen about it . . . he must expect to be found out?'

'He's careful. There's always an alternative explanation. If he spreads rumours about Wildfire, it's only because he picked up on the gossip him-self. If I bump into him, it's just coincidence. But over time, the pattern becomes clear.'

Gradually the last traces of daylight vanished and the only lighting sources were the artificial colours of neon signs, the busy, strident flick-ering of holographic adverts and slogans, the bright patterning of other vehicles and traffic lanes. Even though he was only along for the ride, Dreyfus felt a definite shift in the volantor's flight characteristics as the air became heavier and more sluggish, humid with updraughts of steam.

'And Wildfire – that's his doing as well?'

'The victims were tied to the clinic I mentioned. Now the Senior Prefect has found another connection.'

'The video fragment she mentioned.'

'I take it you've already had a good look?'

'No – although I can, with your permission.'

Dreyfus fished out his goggles. 'I need these to view the recording.'

'Ah, right – no implants. I'd almost forgotten how backward you people like to keep yourselves. But there's no need for those clumsy things. We'll watch it together.'

A Panoply evidential docket summary appeared on the volantor's console, followed by a lofty view of the inside of Elysium Heights, as it must have looked during its years of operation. They watched all thirty-five seconds of the recording in silence, Del Mar only occasionally flicking her attention back to the outside view, then played it back a couple of times.

'It's him,' Dreyfus said, after a moment or two of contemplation. 'Twenty, thirty years ago, but definitely the same man. He could have shifted his appearance, used a completely different name, but he's barely bothered with an alias, let alone a physical disguise.'

'As if he's playing a game with you,' Del Mar said. 'Taunting you.'

'Even though he wasn't expecting us to find this fragment.'

'Perhaps,' she said, making an equivocal sound. 'All right, take it at face value. He used family money to set up this clinic, posed as one of its senior staff, and now the people who were treated there are starting to die in extremely unpleasant ways. That's bad enough, but since you believe the Wildfire deaths to be deliberately engineered, I think there's a question you're not asking yourself.'

'Which is?'

'You might wonder what those people did to him in the first place.'

Jane Aumonier requested the lock be cleared of all other staff when the corvette came in. It was somewhat against protocol, but then a great many things had been against protocol recently. She doubted one more infraction would matter.

Sparver Bancal came out of the lock first, with Devon Garlin just behind him, his hands bound but with no other restraints applied. One side of Garlin's face was cut and bruised, with dirt already ground into the wounds. A fat medical cuff had been clamped around his wrist. He had already been examined by medical specialists, but she would submit him to an extra round of analysis just to be absolutely safe. Regardless of her feelings about him, she was determined nothing bad should happen to Devon Garlin while he was her guest.

'About Thalia—' Sparver began.

'She'll be taken straight to medical. I'll have Demikhov attend to her personally, no matter how busy he is.'

'I'm afraid we left you a bit of a mess to clean up.'

'It was the best of a bad job, Bancal. You shouldn't blame yourselves for what happened in there.' Garlin was floating just behind Sparver, drinking in this conversation, but Aumonier saw no call for anything but the most forthright honesty. 'Now, I'll take our guest off your hands, if I may.'

'What will happen to him now?'

'He'll be interviewed.'

'You've interviewed me once already,' Garlin said.

'That was a friendly chat,' Aumonier said, delivering the coldest smile she could muster. 'I told you not to make yourself my business again. What part of that wasn't clear to you?'

'I did nothing wrong.'

'You can leave us now, Bancal. I'll make sure Demikhov keeps you up to date.'

'Thank you, ma'am.'

'No need, Field Prefect.' She lingered over the rank, making it plain that his demotion had been rescinded; that he was now back to his former status of Field One. 'I think we can consider that small lesson learned, can't we? I suspect it was instructive for both of you.'

'It was, ma'am . . . and thank you, again.'

'Good. Drop some observations into a report, when you have time. I'll value them.'

'I shall, ma'am.'

Sparver left the reception area, leaving her alone with Garlin. They floated a few metres apart, Garlin bound only at the hands and Aumonier weaponless. For a long while neither said anything. Garlin was bursting to come out with some indignation, Aumonier decided, some mendacious claim that his most fundamental rights had been violated. And yet, there was restraint as well. A certain calculation and shrewdness, despite the battering he had taken.

'For the record,' Aumonier said, volunteering to break the silence, 'Ng was sent in to give you protective custody. I was concerned that you'd stirred up emotions beyond your control. The constables couldn't hold the line, and I was worried one of your many enemies might get close enough to do you harm. It appears I was entirely justified in those fears.'

'She arrested me.'

'Had you submitted to her offer of protective custody, there would have been no arrest – at least while Ng was acting under her original instructions. But you delayed matters, playing to your rabble. Ng knew she couldn't stand by while you were inciting the crowd to attempt a takeover of the core. Despite that, she exercised commendable restraint. But when those doors opened . . .'

'That wasn't my doing.'

'I'm speaking. You were encouraging that mob to make a stampede for the core even while Chief Constable Malkmus's lockdown was in force.

You must have known that no such attempt could ever succeed if the lockdown held. But you persisted, demonstrating to me that you had prior knowledge that those doors would eventually open. Are you going to deny it?'

'Is this an interrogation?'

'No, that will follow. You'll be cross-examined by my senior operatives. We'll move to trawl you if I deem it necessary. But you can spare both of us a great deal of unpleasantness if you cooperate immediately. From the outset Dreyfus—'

'Dreyfus,' Garlin said, with a disgusted sneer. 'Didn't you learn to disregard his stupid fantasies?'

'I should have listened to him sooner. Dreyfus was convinced all along that you were operating with advantageous knowledge and capabilities: information and insights that shouldn't have been yours to have. You know about our crisis, and you've been stoking fears, knowing how well it will play into your breakaway movement.'

'That's paranoid conspiracy-mongering.'

'Dreyfus isn't prone to that sort of thing. Besides, our investigations have turned up a direct and damning connection between you and our emergency.'

He studied her with new interest, surprise and suspicion mingling on his face. 'Whatever you think you've found, Aumonier . . .'

'We have a legal link between your family and a clinic tied to the Wildfire cases. That's proven, and damning enough on its own terms. But we also know about your other identity: Doctor Julius Mazarin, evidently high up in the running of the clinic.'

'I don't even . . .'

'Don't even what?'

He swallowed. 'You're spouting nonsense. There's no clinic, and that name means nothing to me.'

'We have the evidence, Mister Garlin. Very shortly I expect to have even more.'

Something of her certainty must have penetrated his own sense of imperviousness.

'I demand to speak to my legal representatives.'

'They'll be informed of your detention. That's the extent of my obligations. As of an hour ago I have sixty-six unexplained deaths on my conscience, and I'd be very surprised if there isn't a sixty-seventh case before I go off-watch. I have you in the frame for mass murder, Mister Garlin, and I have tools at my disposal to ensure I get to the truth.'

He looked at her with widening eyes. 'Are you threatening me with torture?'

'We wouldn't need it. We've much better methods than that.'

She turned from him, content to leave him floating until the clean-up crew arrived.

CHAPTER FOURTEEN

Below them was the nearest thing to open countryside Dreyfus would ever see in Chasm City. Some small portion of the city had been given over to a series of green estates, each bounded from the other by walls or moats of water. A number of these densely wooded estates had hamlet-like clusters of buildings rising up from them, but most were occupied by only one or two modest structures, usually close to the middle. Modest was a relative term, though. These were still sprawling, mansion-like properties; it was just that they had twenty or thirty floors, rather than two or three thousand.

'Old money?' Dreyfus asked.

'Not far off the mark. The Vois, the Sylvestes, the Swifts, the Nervals . . . a dozen other families you very likely won't have heard of. The oldest of them go back nearly two hundred years. It takes money to develop a city district, but it takes even more to stop someone else developing one. Very few families could afford to retain these pastoral estates, especially with the population pressure we've had in recent years.'

'And even the best of them go bankrupt in the end.'

'All things have their natural cycle – even great dynasties like the Vois.' Del Mar pointed ahead with a free hand. 'There. You can see the Shell House now.'

Dreyfus spied one of the more heavily wooded areas with a low, grubby, green-stained dome blistering its middle. 'That's not how I visualised it.'

'The house is inside the dome. The Vois were very private people, as well as having a morbid fear of a failure of the main dome.' Her voice lowered, taking on a confiding, almost trusting tone. 'That's what happens when you've had great success in life – when you've achieved the one goal you always desired. You lose a sense of purpose. Your smallest anxieties fester and magnify. Your fears turn inward, and attach themselves to irrational concerns.'

They had crossed the walled and moated border surrounding the Voi estate. The volantor dropped altitude and sculled low over the trees hemming in the dome. They formed a wild, dense wood, lapping over the outer wall and pressing hard against the green dome's lower flanks. The dome was about a kilometre across, Dreyfus judged, and perhaps a fifth as high as it was wide. There was a hole in part of it, punched as if by a great fist. Hestia aimed the volantor for this ragged aperture.

'Do you really think the Vois succeeded?' Dreyfus asked.

'Why wouldn't I?' she said sharply. 'Chasm City and the Glitter Band might differ in many respects, but our underlying principles stem from the same template. Two hundred years of peace and stability – two hundred years of not going to war with each other, two hundred years of prosperity and guarded tolerance, two hundred years of benign, controlled experimentation – freedom within boundaries, anarchy within sensible limits. A steadily rising lifespan, a society free from poverty and sickness, and absent of all but the most rare and ingenious forms of crime . . . why should we not consider that a shining success, Prefect Dreyfus?'

'Because freedom demands the giving of voice and liberty to men like Devon Garlin. Because an absolute democracy admits the possibility of deciding to dismantle itself.'

The volantor eased over the dome's boundary and edged through the hole in its side. As they slipped inside, the golden daylight was supplanted by an oppressive, green-stained radiance. The inner surface of the dome was caked in some kind of mould or slime, thick in places but never quite dense enough to entirely block the light.

'That sounds like the start of an argument for doing away with democracy once and for all, Prefect Dreyfus. Is that what you believe?'

'I wouldn't go quite that far.'

Below was the strange, curving architecture of the Shell House, its coiled, chambered form supposedly modelled on the mathematical geometry of shells, but to Dreyfus's eyes more suggestive of a pale turd or some hungry muscular snake, lying in ambush. The house, too, had succumbed to the mouldering infestation, its lower levels furred over in green, and with probing, strangling vines reaching nearly all the way to its sagging, wimpled summit.

The dense woodland persisted this side of the dome, fringing the house and making its exact footprint hard to determine. Del Mar picked out an area of flattened or burned ground near the house and brought the volantor down.

She killed the engines and flipped back the canopy.

'Nobody ever thinks they'll go that far until their convictions are tested.'

'Garlin will fail. He's already lost complete control of his own mob. It's a sign of fracture, of forces spinning out of his hands.'

'And you have complete confidence that those forces won't end up tearing the Glitter Band to pieces?'

'It'll end one day,' Dreyfus answered. 'But not this time, and not on my watch.'

'Fine words,' Del Mar said, stepping out of the vehicle and jumping the last metre to the ground.

Dreyfus was following her, taking care not to lose his footing, when his bracelet chimed. Dreyfus made to take the call, then coughed gently as he met his companion's eyes. 'Detective-Marshal?'

'Yes, Prefect?'

'I accept that you had a right to listen in when I was inside your offices. But I'd very much appreciate taking this call in privacy.'

She looked at him, went through some effort of judgement, then nodded. 'Of course. I . . . hope for the best, concerning your colleague. I'm going to fight my way closer to the house. Catch up when you're done.'

'I shall.'

Dreyfus eyed her, waiting until she was a decent distance away, then answered the call. He was disturbed to hear back from Panoply so soon after his last conversation, troubled by the sense that there could be only one reason for interrupting him now.

'Yes. Is there an update on Thalia?'

'There is.' Aumonier's voice was scratchy, dropping in and out. 'I just wish it were better news.'

His qualms turned to sharp apprehension.

'Whatever it is, I'd like to know. She's . . . still alive, isn't she?'

'Yes . . .' she answered, but without the flat assurance he might have wished for. 'But the crush was worse than we thought at the time. There's head trauma, a possible bleed on the brain. The medicals have brought her back twice now. Demikhov's expressed concerns that there may have been long-term neural damage. I'm sorry to have to drop this on you now . . .'

'You had no choice,' Dreyfus said, walking around in an attempt to improve the signal. 'I know you'll do all that you can . . .'

'Demikhov's assigned half the medical team to Thalia's case. She couldn't be in better hands.'

'Please keep me informed about her condition, no matter what else is happening.'

'Of course – take it as read. I'm having difficulty localising you, by the way – are you still in the able hands of Detective-Marshal Del Mar?'

'Yes,' Dreyfus said, still distracted and troubled by the news concerning Thalia. 'We're inside the Voi estate – what's left of it. It's a jungle. I'm afraid you were right to be sceptical about this lead. I'm not sure what we're going to find here.'

'You have your thirteen God-given hours, Tom, you might as well make the most of them. One other thing – not that you need more worries – but we have confirmation on that latest case, and a possible new incidence breaking even as I speak.'

'Has Garlin broken?'

'Not yet.'

'Then I suggest you keep working on him. Men like him always have their limits.'

Dreyfus signed off. He stood silently for a few moments, his mind reeling, balanced between equally momentous decisions. He tried to ignore the fury burning in his blood, forcing himself to think rationally, to consider only whether it was wiser to act or refrain from acting, knowing that two thousand living souls were still his to save, if he acted decisively. Nothing had changed, he told himself: they had Garlin in custody and Thalia Ng was alive. But she had been hurt in the line of duty, quite unnecessarily, and even if she survived the next few hours – which was not certain, judging by the diffident tone of Aumonier's voice – then she might still be left with neurological impairments which would end her career in Panoply. Even if she had not been his friend, even if he had not monitored and mentored her through the difficult years in which she proved her worth to the doubters and naysayers, those who could never accept Jason Ng's innocence – even then, Thalia's fate would have cut him close to the bone. She was one of the best they had, a trusted colleague in whose hands the future of Panoply was safe. There were a hundred ways in which prefects might be wounded or killed in the execution of their duties, and for the most part Dreyfus would have felt no sense of unfairness at the loss of a colleague, knowing the operational risks. But what had happened to Thalia was the consequence of one man's delusions of grandeur, an act born of narrow-minded vindictiveness, and if one thing was now fuelling Devon Garlin's crusade – leading directly to Thalia's injury – it was Wildfire, and Panoply's inability to stamp it out.

His thoughts flashed back to two faces, both of them instilling a flood of emotions. One was Thalia, green as they came on her first full day as a cadet, yet already learning to wear the mask that would protect her against the jibes and whispers – the mask hardening to a kind of scar tissue that was with her even now. He had seen the promise in her instantly, and despite all the misgivings from his colleagues, he had pushed to steer Thalia into his own training stream, and then – when she became a Deputy Field – into his own operational unit. She had tested his patience on numerous occasions, drawn reprimands and re-education sessions, but never once had he had cause to regret that initial judgement.

The other face was Devon Garlin, branded into Dreyfus's brain like a kind of poison-filled lesion, gathering mass and toxicity, making connections from itself, slowly infiltrating every good thought, taking over his consciousness. It could not continue. He saw it now, what had always been there, always explicit, but which he only now forced himself to acknowledge in all its truth and simplicity. To destroy Devon Garlin – to destroy the enemy of everything he held precious – it was first necessary to destroy Wildfire.

And so he would.

While Hestia Del Mar continued fighting her way through the weeds, safely out of earshot, he tapped his collar microphone, but did not open a specific channel to Panoply.

His throat turned dry. His spine was cold, his belly churning. He knew he was on the edge of something irrevocable, either the gravest error of his career or the hardest right decision he had ever been forced to make.

'If you're as good as you like to boast, you'll be hearing me now. Are we being eavesdropped on by city officials?'

Her voice was as scratchy and distant as the last.

'No. They recorded your earlier exchange, but this one is untraceable. I'm seeing to that.'

'Then you know where I am and you know how things are progressing with Wildfire. I've thought it over. It makes me sick to my marrow, but I'm going to give you what you want. You'll honour your pledge. Those names appear. No ifs, no buts. No sly complications. You'll communicate them to the technical squad working the clinic, and you'll make sure they recognise the names for what they are. Do this one thing for me, extract the information you want on the Clockmaker, and never remind me of your existence again. Then we'll be square. Is that understood?'

'I knew we'd find common ground eventually. And yes, you have my word. Such things do matter to me, difficult as it might be for you to credit. You can have principles without a conscience.'

'You'll get in, find what you need, and leave no trace of your presence.'

'Believe me, I have no intention of lingering. The Clockmaker knows of my interest in your records. I would be very surprised indeed if it didn't try and spring a trap or two on me. But I'll be discreet, and fast, and true to my word.'

'If there's any ambiguity about those names, even—'

'Just do it, Prefect. You've seen how steeply that curve is rising now. An hour wasted could be another life lost. I *want* to help those people – but I must also consider my own needs.'

'Your needs?' he said, almost laughing.

'I've made mistakes – I don't deny it. But I'm something new, something unique, and I value my existence. I think I can do better than I've managed until now. Besides: ask yourself one simple question. When all this is over, would you rather be dealing with me, or the Clockmaker?'

Dreyfus breathed in. Beyond the dome, filtered through facets of dirty glass, the lights of Chasm City spoke of life and potential, of love and death, of the simple teeming business of ordinary people, forcefully reminding him of what was at stake.

As if he needed it.

'The words are Solstice, Mandrake, Plainsong. I don't suppose I need to repeat them.'

'You do not. You've chosen wisely, Prefect – made the correct decision. I'm releasing those names as we speak. I'll make sure your operatives stumble on them in an entirely plausible fashion.'

'Good. I'll be waiting for confirmation from Jane Aumonier.'

'Of course, doubting Thomas that you are. But then I shouldn't expect anything less from a policeman, should I?'

'Are we finished?'

'Such as we ever are.'

Dreyfus closed the communication link, standing still and silent while he ruminated on the magnitude of what he had done. It was impossible not to feel that he had violated something sacred, undoing in a single spasm of weakness the good work of a lifetime. A moment's lapse, and all was lost. But he wondered how much worse he would have felt when another ten lives were lost, much less another two thousand.

'What's keeping you?' Del Mar called.

'Business, Detective-Marshal,' Dreyfus called back. 'But I'm done now.'

The panther was a puzzle in black fragments, a series of disconnected forms moving behind tall blades of grass. Caleb had seen it first, tapping Julius on the shoulder and mouthing him to silence. The boys had crouched low, advancing with the utmost care, Caleb unslinging the crossbow and passing it to his brother in one slow fluid movement, a bolt already loaded.

'Kill it,' Caleb said, pushing the words directly into Julius's head

241

without needing to say them aloud. 'It's near enough, and you'll never get a better shot.'

'It's not interested in us,' Julius pushed back. 'It just wants to get on with hunting.'

'No reason not to kill it.'

By now Julius knew better than to resist. The panther wasn't real, anyway. It did have a sort of will, but only because it was obeying the algorithms Caleb had set up, giving it a form of independence. In this matter at least Julius trusted Caleb not to cheat, not to privilege himself with inside information on the animals' whereabouts. They had been looking for the panther for three hours, anyway, long past the point when they should have been back at the Shell House. Caleb would never have had the patience to string Julius along for so long unless the hunt was genuine.

Julius sighted along the crossbow, tracking the panther's progress. The head was too small a target, so he shifted until he was aimed at the area just behind the animal's shoulders. He held his breath and squeezed the trigger-nub. The crossbow released with a twitch of recoil. The dart flew noiselessly, seeming to disappear into the panther. The panther arched its back, let out a bellow of pain, and slumped over on its side.

Caleb patted him on the back. 'You're getting better.'

Julius handed back the crossbow, feeling he had done enough to placate Caleb for now. Without much enthusiasm he followed his brother to the fallen animal, grass whisking against their knees as they approached.

'Do you think you could do it to a person?' Caleb asked.

'Do what?'

'Shoot them, like you did the panther.'

'It wasn't a panther. It was a figment.'

'But could you, if your life depended on it?'

Julius pushed through the fringe of grass hemming the panther. It was lying with its legs stretched towards him, its eyes still open, making a slow, pained purring. There was a red wound where the dart had hit it. The tableau was so realistic that Julius felt some need of reassurance. He knelt by the animal and scythed a hand through it, his fingers vanishing into the panther without resistance. He could feel the real grass that was being edited out of his visual field.

The panther's laboured breathing grew slower. One eye regarded him with a soft, dwindling focus.

'Why can't it just die?' he asked Caleb. 'Why does it have to have this drawn-out death?'

'Do you want it realistic or not?' Caleb asked, shrugging.

'I don't know why we have to keep hunting things anyway.'

'I've been thinking of something better than this,' Caleb said brightly, as if Julius had made no remark. 'All we've got is this little bit of quickmatter, enough to make a crossbow and a few darts. But there's a lot more out there in the real world. Chasm City's practically made of the stuff. Think what we could do, if everything around us was quickmatter.'

'Maybe you should have listened to what Mother and Father told us. You can't do anything you like with quickmatter.'

'I could,' Caleb said. 'One day I will. I'll make a place like this, and conjure up animals. But they won't be figments. They'll be just as solid as you and I.'

'Just so that you can kill them?'

'They'd be able to kill us as well. Or hurt us, at least. More fun that way.'

'Your idea of fun, maybe. Anyway, you won't have time for anything like that. Neither will I. We'll have responsibilities. The contingency—'

'You really are soft, Julius. You'll do anything they tell you, won't you? Anything to make them pat you on the head and say you're being a good Voi.'

Julius stood up from the dying panther, disgusted by his own feelings of pity towards the mindless figment.

'I don't hear you rebelling – at least not when Mother and Father are nearby.'

'I know my mind. I'll play along with their ideas for a bit. But why should I waste my life doing something no one will ever know or care about?'

'Because that's what we've always done. Are we finished here?'

Caleb shaped a hand in the direction of the panther, narrowed his eyes in mock concentration, and made it give out one last ragged breath before dying.

'Happy now?'

There was a spot at the edge of the dome where Lurcher had been doing some repairs, replacing a damaged panel. The area had been burned clear of overgrowth, allowing the boys to get as close to the dome as they liked. The new glass panel was the only one not filmed over in a fine coating of mossy discoloration.

Through it the spires and towers of Chasm City twinkled with an unnatural clarity, so close that Julius felt his heart hammer in anticipation of the bright, teeming life that awaited them beyond the Shell House. He watched the tiny glinting specks of moving air vehicles slipping between those fabulous structures, thinking of the power and the glamour of their invisible occupants.

He could not say he had ever been discontented with his upbringing within the domed estate, especially if he discounted these last few months, filled as they were with revelations both exciting and troubling. The boys had been given enormous freedoms as they grew up, as well as more room for sport and games than the children in those towers could ever hope for. Their lessons had seldom been burdensome, Mother and Father rarely too strict with their discipline. Even Lurcher tolerated the boys' boisterous excesses most of the time.

But this was not the real world. The real world lapped at its borders, but it did not penetrate them. The Solid Orrery offered the boys a glimpse of what it was to swim in a sea of total information, how they might shape and manipulate the flow of data through that sea, but they would not know the full, immersive experience of abstraction until they were beyond the Shell House. Caleb was right about quickmatter, too. Beyond the dome it was commonplace, not even worth mentioning. And yet Julius trusted that their shaping faculties were already far in advance of the average citizen. He yearned to put that skill to its test, beyond the restricted arena of the estate. He imagined admiring eyes on him, people who neither knew nor cared that Caleb had a slight advantage over his brother. They would need to moderate their talents, of course – Father and Mother had made that perfectly plain. But they could still be just as skilled as anyone else, and that would be no small thing.

'I'll make you a deal,' Caleb said quietly, appearing to be just as transfixed by the view as his brother.

Julius had learned to be sceptical of such overtures. 'Oh?'

'I'll think of a different game for us soon. One that doesn't involve hunting things. To be honest, it isn't as much fun as it used to be. This place is just too small.'

'We'll be free of it before long.'

'Will you come back, do you think?'

Julius was confounded. It had never even crossed his mind not to come back. He had taken it as a stone certainty that the Shell House would always be here, a part of his life to which he was anchored.

'Of course. Won't you?'

'Oh, I expect so,' Caleb said, kicking a stone lodged near the window's base. 'But there's a lot of the world I want to see first. Not just Chasm City, but everything beyond it. The Glitter Band, to begin with, all those pretty little worlds. But I'm not sure I'd want to stop there. We're still fairly rich, aren't we? I'd like to go on one of those ships, travel to another system

– see more of the universe. So what if it takes decades?'

'People don't live for ever,' Julius said.

'I'd say goodbye properly,' Caleb replied. 'And tell them I'd look after the place when I get back. Lurcher will still be around. Robots don't wear out half as quickly as people.'

'You said something about a deal?'

'All right. I'll come up with another game – something more to your taste. Hide and seek or something silly like that. But you'll do something for me, too. I don't want to hear another word about that place you keep going on about. Nothing more about Amerikanos or Ursas or other boys and girls, or us with knives. It's over, Julius – done. A bad dream you can forget about. It never happened, anyway.'

'How can you be so certain?'

'I'm not a fool. I picked up that book of yours when you weren't looking. All that stuff happened three hundred years ago.'

'Maybe they froze us. Or cloned us and gave us the memories of some dead boys.'

'Or maybe it's just something you read in a book that got into your dreams.'

'And yours,' Julius said softly. 'And into yours.'

'Do you want this deal or not?'

Julius weighed the things that mattered to him. 'Yes. I suppose.'

'Then we'll say no more of it. We've both got more important things ahead of us, haven't we? You've heard Mother and Father.' He nodded out to the lights of Chasm City. 'There's a whole world depending on us.'

Back at the Shell House Mother and Father were waiting for them, coldly furious. There was some sharp new tension between the two of them, too, as if they had only recently been arguing. Julius and Caleb exchanged glances, each trying to read the other. They had stretched the hunting game out too long, that was true, but it was hardly the first time they had committed such an infraction.

'What is it?' Caleb demanded, always the first to speak up.

'Come inside,' Father said.

Just for a moment Julius flirted with the idea of outright disobedience. What was to stop them turning around and going back into the grounds? But a neck-prickle alerted him to the fact that Lurcher was coming back to the house, trudging along one of the paths with a wheelbarrow. Was it coincidence that the robot was at their backs now, gently discouraging any thoughts of rebellion?

'We'd better go in,' Julius murmured.

'I almost miss Spider-fingers,' Caleb said back in the same low voice. 'At least they usually kept up a united front when he was around.'

'Until the end,' Julius said, thinking back to the three-way row between his parents and Doctor Stasov, before the abrupt termination of his visits.

They stepped onto the terrace and followed their parents through the main entrance into the Shell House, and then across the clacking tiles of the marble-floored lobby, on to the drawing room where their lessons often took place. It was the one with the solid holoclavier. Insolently, Caleb lifted the lid on its keys and played a painful, discordant triad.

Their mother slammed the lid down, giving Caleb just enough time to snatch his fingers out.

'Have we done something wrong?' Julius asked, Caleb joining him, the two brothers standing with their hands behind their backs.

'No,' Mother said. 'We have. It's been too much, too soon. Your father and I have come to a decision. There'll be a hiatus in your development, while we give you some time to reflect on what's already happened.'

'A hiatus?' Julius asked, thinking that such a thing did not sound too bad.

'Your mother feels . . .' Father began, before drawing an admonishing look from his wife. 'We both feel . . . that you could benefit from a little more maturity, before proceeding with your . . . education.'

'Maturity?' Caleb questioned. 'We're old enough, aren't we? If we were in Chasm City, we'd have almost all the rights of any adult citizen by now.'

'It's not about rights,' Mother said. 'It's about wisdom. You don't have it yet. Certainly not enough. One day . . . maybe. But it's too soon now.'

Caleb frowned so hard a dark trench appeared in his forehead. 'What do you mean, "one day"?'

'I mean that nothing's promised,' Mother answered. 'This is too great and powerful a gift to be bestowed thoughtlessly.'

'There's been nothing thoughtless about it,' Father said. His face was so strained it looked like it might crack into shards at any moment. 'We acted as we saw fit. You are our natural heirs, and this responsibility will be yours, in the fullness of time.'

'If they prove themselves,' Mother said. 'With balance, restraint, empathy, foresightedness. Kindness and fairness. Altruistic instincts. Maybe they will have that in time. Perhaps one of them does, at least. The glimmerings of it. But it's not proven.'

'It's just a question of slowing down,' Father said. 'Of more instruction, more study.'

'Then there won't be a revocation?' Caleb asked.

Julius grew cold. The word had never been uttered in their direct presence, only when the boys had overheard it in a supposedly private exchange between Mother and Father. But they both knew exactly what it meant.

He tried to salvage the situation. 'I don't even know what that means. Revoke what?'

'Oh, don't be naïve,' Caleb chided. 'The thing that they've given us. The contingency. It was put in our heads, it can be taken out again just as easily.'

'There'll be no need for revocation,' Father said.

'I'd be the judge of that,' Mother answered, directing a fierce glance at her husband. 'Yes, we have that power. It could be done. You'd still be Vois, still able to go out into the world with all the advantages of that name. But you wouldn't have the means to correct the world when it's in danger of harming itself.'

'Then who would?' Julius asked.

'We'd continue to,' Father said. 'As we have done. We're not ready for the grave just yet. Many good decades ahead of us, aren't there, Aliya?'

'Oh yes,' she answered, with grim resignation.

'You'd still be the inheritors of this responsibility . . . this prize,' Father went on. 'Even revocation wouldn't have to be permanent. It would just allow all of us time to ensure that things are done properly. Wouldn't it?'

'Anything's possible,' she said, clearly not the answer their father had been hoping for, judging by the continued strain on his features.

'I suppose if it's just temporary,' Caleb said, 'it wouldn't be too bad.' He looked to his brother for support. 'We understand the responsibility, don't we, Julius? It's a big thing. If it takes a little more time, it'll still be worth it in the end.'

'You'll continue as you are,' Father said. 'For now. We'll be watching, considering. But I have faith in both of you. It's time to show us that you have the moral stature required of you. I know you do . . . as does your mother. But we need to see it.'

Caleb swallowed hard, looked to his brother with a sudden false humility, as if on the point of tears.

Julius saw through it in an instant. But he said nothing.

'We'll show you,' Caleb said.

Aumonier invited Doctor Demikhov to take a seat opposite her, in the position around the tactical room table that Thalia Ng occasionally occupied. A smattering of seniors and analysts were already present, but the pressures of recent days had begun to take a toll on the usual shift patterns, leading to vacant seats, slumped postures and expressions of near-exhaustion.

'I won't detain you unduly, Doctor Demikhov,' she said, settling her hands together before her, and trying to look and sound unflappably composed. 'You have something for us, I believe.'

'Where is Garlin now?'

'Being prepared for soft questioning. Is there a particular line of enquiry you felt we should pursue?'

Doctor Demikhov was still wearing surgical gloves. 'Dreyfus told me he thinks someone may have breached the Voi kernel. I was inclined to dismiss any such possibility, given how secure that architecture has proven itself over the years.'

'Just as well, given that it's inside the heads of around one hundred million citizens.' Aumonier glanced at her fellow prefects, calibrating their various states of fatigue and sharpness. 'I'll remind us all that Auriault brought back a head in an unusually good state of preservation. It's been our best shot so far. What has it given us, Doctor?'

'I can't see what's been done to the kernel. That's lost for good – too much thermal randomisation. But there's a solid state update register. Until now, we've never had a clean look at it in any of the victims.'

'And in the case of this man' – Aumonier had to snatch a look at the Wildfire list to bring back the relevant name – 'Nicholas D'Arcy Moon?'

'Many updates. But a major change logged in '399. Someone went deep into his implants – maybe as deep as the Voi kernel.'

'That fits within the period of full operation of the clinic – '395 to '407. But we don't know where it was done.'

'We do – or at least, we can be very sure. The neural updates were unusual, but they were performed using proprietary medical devices. There are commercial fingerprints . . . subtle, but traceable. They match the surgical equipment already logged and extracted from Elysium Heights.' Doctor Demikhov began to pick at his gloved fingertips. 'There's next to no doubt. Moon was a client of Doctor Julius Mazarin.'

'And you believe he was set up as a victim of Wildfire from that very moment?'

'It's hard to say. Wildfire could be an intrinsic process, with a pre-set clock. Or it may still require an external trigger, something transmitted to the implants. In that case, the clinical procedure would have primed the implants into a receptive state, but there'd still need to be an external stimulus.'

'There were no verified cases prior to Cassandra Leng,' Aumonier reminded her gathering. 'What we have is a slowly rising pattern of deaths beginning about four hundred days ago, which happens to be of indirect benefit to Devon Garlin. I don't see that as consistent with an intrinsic clock. Much more likely to me is that Garlin has begun hatching eggs he set in place twenty-eight or more years ago, knowing as he does that now is the ideal time to push his separatist agenda. He's been biding his time all this while, waiting for us to be at our weakest.'

Lillian Baudry, the most senior person present besides Aumonier herself, said: 'We'll push for a confession using all available means. But in the meantime we should ensure he won't trigger any more cases.'

'There's an easy way,' Demikhov said. 'Remove his implants. You have reasonable grounds, don't you?'

'Reasonable grounds,' Aumonier replied. 'But not the moral authority.'

'We could petition for it,' Baudry said.

'But not without clarifying the reason for our proposed action. Then we'd definitely have a panic on our hands.'

'What if we make it clear that we're only anticipating two thousand deaths across the whole Glitter Band?' asked Ingvar Tench. 'If the citizens are reasonable, they'll understand that there's no reason for mass panic.'

'Until we have a solid patient list that figure is speculative,' Aumonier replied.

Baudry looked nonplussed. 'Call in a citizen quorum, then, if you won't petition.'

'I've already initiated one. But not to give me consent to open up his head. I just want the questioning and trawling to be completely transparent and accountable.' Aumonier paused, tiredness hitting her like a slow rolling fog bank. 'We're not out of legal options. Isolate Garlin. Nobody with an implant speaks to him, nobody with an implant goes near him. No communications equipment, no whiphounds – nothing that he might be able to reach. If we're right, we should see a flattening in the death curve.'

'Then we'll have him,' Baudry said, with a sharp, retributional gleam in her eye.

Aumonier gave the woman a dutiful nod. She wondered how evident her own feelings on the matter were. It would be good to have him.

Rather good indeed.

After an hour chasing sleep, Sparver had surrendered to the inevitable – washing, dressing in full uniform and making his way to the refectory to shovel some food into his system, even though he had no appetite. A dozen or so other prefects were scattered through the room, most of them engaged in low, weary conversation. He took his tray to a vacant table near the wall, neither inviting nor disdaining company, but glad enough to be alone with his thoughts.

Inevitably it was Thalia Ng who swam most readily to mind, and the complications the last few days had brought to their professional relationship. Deep down he recognised that he had blamed her for his demotion, even though he had never really doubted his reduction in rank was a temporary affair. And when Thalia had tried to make friendly amends for the reversal in their status, he had given her short shrift. He regretted that now, just as he regretted the error in judgement that had left her to handle the Garlin detention alone. Not that Aumonier appeared to blame him for anything that had happened in Fuxin-Nymburk, recognising perhaps that the dice had already been loaded from the moment she sent in just two of her operatives. He was back to a full Field now, his demotion no more than a brief aberration that would not even enter his formal service record. He doubted very much that it would hamper his chances of advancement through the higher grades of Field, and on to the hallowed rank of Senior, presuming he lived that long.

But there would always be a shadow between him and Thalia. They could carry on working together, they could agree never to mention the demotion, they could act as if it had never happened, but it would always be there between them.

Sparver felt disappointed in himself. The one consolation lay in knowing how much worse he would be feeling if she had died in Fuxin-Nymburk.

Gradually he became conscious of something impinging on his thoughts. Someone had left a transmission feed playing on the nearby wall, cycling through the same loop: one of Garlin's legal spokespeople, agitating against his completely unjust and undemocratic detention, and warning Panoply of the grave consequences of standing up to the will of the people.

Sparver watched it silently. He took his time with the small amount of food he had gathered onto the tray, pausing every now and again to sip from a glass of water. Periodically he dabbed at his lips with a napkin. His reading glasses were folded neatly next to the tray.

Now the loop was showing an earlier statement from Garlin himself, delivered to an enthusiastic but doubtless carefully curated audience. There were whoops and wild flourishes of applause at predictable moments, even though nothing about the speech was in any way original or surprising. Garlin was recycling the same tried and tested lines, regurgitating the same beats, the same moments of apparent intimacy and sincerity. Sparver reflected on how much Garlin loathed Panoply, and yet how much he had owed to Thalia when the opposing mob finally closed in. He wondered if there was a shred of remorse or contrition in the man now, or whether he was even capable of examining his own contradictions that objectively. Perhaps there was some loop or circuit missing from the brains of people like Garlin, some absent process that prevented them from seeing themselves from outside their own skin, in all their ludicrousness. But to a degree, Sparver reflected, it must also be absent from those they swept up into their movements.

Garlin went on. His face loomed larger as his pronouncements became more blatantly threatening and divisive. Sparver studied the interesting symmetries and proportions of that face. Human features were still something of a conundrum to him, but he was getting better at mapping their essential elements, and he believed now that he would have little trouble identifying Garlin in a crowd.

He took another sip of water and pushed his tray forward. Leaving his spectacles on the table, he walked over to the wall where the playback was showing.

He removed his whiphound, extended sixty centimetres of filament, set it to sword mode, and jabbed it into Devon Garlin's face. He dragged it down, leaving a violent, flickering wound in its wake. Blue and pink flashes spangled from the point of contact. The malfunction spread in branching cracks, radiating away from the line of damage. The cutting edge met increasing resistance as the wall's own structural quickmatter tried to contain and rectify the attack. Finally the whiphound jammed rigid. Sparver released the handle and left it there, sticking out of the sparking, crackling display.

He rubbed his palms, turned from the chaos and went back to his table. He sat down, scraped his chair forward, drew the tray closer, and took another mouthful of water from the glass.

There was a silence from the rest of the refectory. The conversation, low as it had been to start with, had ceased completely. All eyes were on him. The other prefects had been aware of him before, but now he felt the electric prickle of their unblinking, astonished attention.

Then someone began to applaud. It was a slow, lone clap to begin with, but it was soon joined by another, and another.

Sparver continued eating. It was an odd thing, but he had begun to get a small part of his appetite back.

Fighting hard not to shake, Dreyfus wandered through the soupy, green-stained gloom until he caught up with Del Mar.

She studied his face, reading something in it.

'News about your colleague?'

251

'Something like that.' He swallowed, tried to marshal his words into some sort of coherence. 'Not the good sort. Her condition's worsened.'

'I'm sorry.' Del Mar was kneeing her way through dense weeds, sweeping it apart like someone swimming through mud. 'Beyond our line of work, they don't really understand how it is.'

'Our line of work?'

'What we do, the both us. Policing.'

Dreyfus forced himself to fall back into the pattern of discussion they had been enjoying before his call. 'Steady on, Detective-Marshal: that almost sounds like an expression of solidarity.'

She unclipped a dainty little sidearm, adjusted a dial, and began to scythe away the worst of the overgrowth with some sort of optical beam. The weeds crackled and burned, giving off a smoky tang.

'What will happen to Garlin now?'

'He'll be answering some questions.'

'And if he's less than cooperative – as I'd expect?'

'Then he'll be made uncomfortable.'

'A nice euphemism.' She paused to tweak the dial setting. 'I must remember it the next time we need to apply our own enhanced interrogation package.'

'It's not a euphemism. He'll be interrogated, and perhaps trawled, but only after a medical assessment. He won't be hurt, and he won't be threatened.'

They walked on, the sagging contours of the Shell House looming larger. Dreyfus had seen the dome from the air, but once they were inside its dimensions seemed to relax, like some great green lung expanding beyond its former limits.

'Damn this grass,' Del Mar said, the sidearm giving a blinking red error light, which presumably meant it was overheating or in danger of draining its power.

'Yes, if only we'd thought to bring a sharp cutting tool, possibly one with autonomous capabilities. Are you sure no one uses this place now?'

She holstered the sidearm, resorting to brute force to push her way through the grass, Dreyfus following just behind.

'You'll be aware of Aliya's death in '386. Julius left a few months later. He was legally of age by then, and I don't think he cared to stay around a place with so many memories of his mother. Marlon stayed on, but by then he was a broken man, his money draining away, his wife gone, his only son abandoning him to his grief.'

'They say Aliya was coming back from space when she died.'

'Yes. Marlon rarely left the estate, in those latter years. He relied on Aliya to visit the remaining Voi holdings.'

'Which were?'

'A scattering of minor habitats and asteroids. Nothing of consequence. There was a property slump around that time. It was a bad period for real estate investment.'

'Do they still own those places?'

'A lump of rock called Lethe, one or two other minor pebbles. Chances are they'll be just as derelict as this estate.'

'I'm not surprised money was tight,' Dreyfus said. 'Most of the family wealth was being siphoned into Elysium Heights.'

'Do you think Marlon had a hand in that?'

'I doubt it happened willingly. Julius seems to have been the one pulling all the strings here, not the father. But that makes me wonder what Julius had on Marlon, that he could exert that sort of control.'

Del Mar let out a yelp. 'Damn this as well.'

'What is it?'

'Caught my shin on this. There's a step up to a terrace – mind yourself.'

She reached back to offer him a guiding hand.

'Thank you,' Dreyfus said, feeling that in some small way the ice had been broken.

The terrace had been invaded by weeds, covering it in a dense green carpet, but beneath the springy growth the stonework felt firm and level. They picked their way to the front of the building, where a pair of ornate, scrollwork doors lay partly closed on what must have been the main entrance. The doors were half off their hinges, sagging at an odd angle like a pair of buck teeth. Del Mar eased open the gap and produced a torch from her belt, shining it into the gloom. Dreyfus unclipped his own torch, glad to be doing something useful.

They squeezed through into the interior of the Shell House. Dreyfus swept his light around, picking out small areas at a time. The overgrowth had only managed to push its tendrils a few metres beyond the doors. Other than that the place was dusty, cobwebbed, grey with neglect. Black and white tiles led away from the entrance, down a long, grand lobby towards a metalwork staircase. The curving walls bore traces of ornate plasterwork, some of the pastel coloration still showing despite layers of mould, moss and dust. Doorways and arches led off into other rooms and corridors.

'The place is bigger than you'd think,' Del Mar said, as they advanced into the lobby. 'Many rooms and floors. But I can't vouch for the structural integrity of the upper levels. If you wish to poke around, you're on your own. But if you're expecting a blinding insight into Devon Garlin's character, a confession note left here decades ago . . .'

Her torch went out. So did the one Dreyfus was carrying. There had been two white flashes, almost simultaneous, just before the torches failed. From his own, Dreyfus felt heat and an acrid burning. He dropped it before it stung his fingers, knowing it was useless.

For a moment the two of them waited in darkness. Dreyfus was certain that Del Mar was assembling the same speculative train of thoughts as he was. Something had attacked them, something in the shadowed reaches of the lobby. He had no weapon, and Del Mar's little sidearm had already proven itself next to useless.

Light flooded the lobby. It was hard and blue. Dreyfus squinted against it, throwing up an arm in instinctive self-defence.

A robot was coming at them, emerging from the cover of one of the side rooms to their left. For a second Dreyfus was stunned into paralysis. The tall machine walked on two legs, its metal feet loud on the marble. Four segmented arms swung from its torso. Its head was a dome, with a single blue eye putting out that dazzling light.

'Halt,' Del Mar said.

The robot kept coming. She drew out her sidearm, levelled it in a single fluid movement and shot at the robot. The laser pulse flashed off the robot's mirrored hide, leaving only a scorch mark.

'No power!' she hissed.

The robot kept advancing, walking slowly but determinedly. Wordlessly they arrived at the same joint conclusion. They spun around and broke into a heavy jog, both encumbered by belts and uniforms.

'Were you expecting—' Del Mar began.

'No,' Dreyfus said, barking out the word between breaths. 'I wasn't expecting to be attacked by a robot.'

The robot was at their backs, its blue light blazing against them, lighting up the lobby and pushing their own shadows towards the entrance. Feverishly Dreyfus considered what they would do once they were outside. The going would be much slower in the undergrowth, but he doubted that would trouble the robot. Even if they reached the volantor, they would need precious seconds to get aboard, power it up, and achieve a safe elevation.

Two more white flashes came. The lobby became a brief negative of itself. Masonry and plaster crumbled from the ceiling just ahead of them, showering onto the floor. Two more flashes followed, directed at the area above the door. Rubble and dust crashed down. Some structural beam gave a groan and the ceiling buckled lower, riven by a broad, dark crack. Debris slurried through the widening fissure.

Dreyfus and Del Mar slowed. They had not been touched by the damage, but even some of the small pieces of broken masonry could have done them real harm had they been under the point of collapse.

The message was clear enough.

They halted and turned around slowly. Del Mar still had the sidearm in her hand, its red indication blinking. Very slowly she inched her aim back onto the robot, levelling the barrel in the direction of the blue eye.

The white flash came again. It was a beam, lancing from the eye. It connected with the sidearm and exploded it instantly, leaving only the scorched stump of a handle and trigger grip. Del Mar let out another yelp and flung aside the useless item.

'Worth a try,' Dreyfus said, breathing hard.

The robot had stopped, at least. It was a good metre taller than either of them, slender at the legs and broadening to a wide pair of double-shoulders, the segmented arms nearly reaching the floor, each tipped with a three-fingered claw. The domed head was featureless save for that eye, which now locked onto them with a fierce, unblinking scrutiny.

'Who sent you?' Del Mar asked.

'I don't think it's here to answer questions,' Dreyfus said, when the robot gave no answer. 'How's your hand?'

'Scorched.' Slowly she raised her fist to her mouth and sucked at her thumb. 'I'll live.'

'I'm going to draw a crumb of comfort here. It could have killed us easily by now. Do you need an anaesthetic patch?'

'I'm all right.' There was a pause. 'But thanks for asking.'

Dreyfus lowered himself onto his haunches, and then sat cross-legged on the hard marble floor, facing the robot with his belly squeezing against his belt.

Del Mar looked at him. 'What are you doing?'

'Sitting down. I've a feeling we'll be here a little while.' He touched his collar. 'Dreyfus. Is anyone reading me?'

There was a silence, a crackle, a silence.

'Let me try,' Del Mar said, lowering herself down next to him. 'Hestia. Pick up, someone. I need a suppression team, escalation level amber . . . no, make that red.' She listened, frowned, repeated herself – not once, but twice, and with steadily lessening confidence. 'Blocked,' she confided. 'Either the dome, the house, or that robot.'

'You have a headful of implants, Detective-Marshal. Can't they get through to someone, or find a way to tell that robot to stand down?'

'I've tried those things, and about a dozen more.' She sucked at her scorched hand again. 'I should have come in with some support. This will reflect very badly on me. Like it or not, you've been under my protection from the moment you arrived.'

'We all make mistakes,' Dreyfus said. 'Comes with the job, I'd say.' He shifted his buttocks, the cold ground growing uncomfortable under him already. The robot seemed to take this as challenge, stepping forward by one menacing stride. Dreyfus raised a calming hand.

'Do you think Garlin sent it?'

'Thugs and hired muscle men are more his line. But you've poked your nose into this place before. Did you ever run into a robot?'

'No . . . not like this.' After a short silence she added: 'I studied your record, Prefect. I know you went up against the Clockmaker. This . . . isn't the Clockmaker, is it?'

'No, you can rest easy on that score. If we were in the presence of the Clockmaker . . . well, we'd know it, if only for the relatively limited amount of time it allowed us to remain alive.'

Again she was silent. Once or twice a new flurry of dust came down from the ceiling. The robot remained still, its arms dangling at its sides. But its eye swivelled occasionally, as if tracking some distant presence.

'I lost someone too. Different circumstances to your own. But not without a certain ambiguity as well. You know of the Eighty, of course.'

Dreyfus found his interest piqued more than he cared for. 'Hard to avoid. We're still living in its shadow.'

'I was fifty when Calvin began putting his first subjects through the destructive scanning apparatus. I was married then, in a triple valency. My husband and wife were Tyrone Lyall and Clemence Mersenne. Perhaps the names aren't unfamiliar to you. They were among the Eighty, among the earliest failures.'

Dreyus had reviewed the names often enough during his background investigations into Aurora, and he recognised the people of whom she had spoken. But there was a reason the name Hestia Del Mar had not sparked off any sort of memory. She had not been one of the direct victims.

'Tell me what happened.'

'Late in the day I had second thoughts. It was a serious matter, to back out. Money had been committed, reputations nailed to that particular mast. Media attention around the clock. Calvin was very persuasive, confident of his theories, brushing aside our petty doubts. Most of us fell for it. But my qualms surfaced once the scans began. I liked life rather too much to chance everything on an unproven route to immortality. I backed out, about a month before we were due to be put through. Of course there was a scandal. But within the valency, we'd had an agreement. It was all or nothing. If one of us decided to withdraw, then so would the others. It was something we'd all agreed to – as serious as a marriage vow.'

'But they didn't,' Dreyfus said softly, finally understanding – and at last realising why Aurora had claimed something in common with Hestia Del Mar. They were both, in their different ways, victims of Calvin Sylveste.

'Tyrone and Clemence went through with it anyway. Calvin moved them up the list and they were scanned within two days of my decision to withdraw. I wasn't even there when it happened. Calvin knew I'd have used every emotional appeal, every legal means, to stop it.'

Dreyfus chose his words carefully. 'I'm sorry you were betrayed. But you've done more for Chasm City in one honest day's work than you'd ever have achieved as part of Calvin's botched experiment.'

'You barely know me, Dreyfus.'

'We're police. Different uniforms, different traditions. But not so far apart.'

The robot swivelled its eye again, tensing its body as if it meant to pounce. Dreyfus flinched in response. But he had heard something as well. It was a repetitive dull tone, like someone striking a cracked bell over and over, and it was coming slowly nearer.

Very gingerly he allowed himself to swivel around until he was facing the entrance to the lobby. Del Mar did likewise. The sound gained in volume, even while the interval between the tones remained unchanged. The robot's eye brightened, casting a confusion of shadows and highlights. Dreyfus tried to peer beyond the ruined entrance to the green swelter of the dome. A dark form loomed into view. It was a low, crouching figure, moving in a lopsided fashion across the terrace. Dreyfus stared, trying to fit this new apparition into his half-formed theories of Wildfire and the Voi family.

The figure reached the doorway, a smudge of black against the green background of the dome. The figure tapped something long and hard against one of the sagging doors, then made a spiderlike incursion through the irregular gap into the dust and debris of the lobby. Then it resumed its lopsided approach, ramming a walking stick against the marble, the tone shifting now that it was inside.

'Is this your robot?' Del Mar called out. 'Answer me.'

'You're in no position to be demanding answers from anyone,' the figure called back, voice creaking with age.

Dreyfus continued staring. The man was hooded and gowned in black, no part of his face yet visible. He walked with a stoop, but there was also a boldness in the way he placed the stick, as if he had been using it for so long that it had become fully part of him. The robot tracked him with its blue eye, but clearly it had decided to tolerate the man's presence.

'I am Detective-Marshal Del Mar of the Chamber for City Security. We are being detained here against our will. This is a serious crime.'

'And your accomplice?'

Dreyfus answered for himself. 'I'm an operative of Panoply, here as a guest of Detective-Marshal Del Mar. I'm investigating a series of deaths that have a link to this estate.'

'Your authority begins and ends in orbit, Prefect. Here you're nothing. You didn't even tell me your name.'

'You didn't tell me yours.'

The figure worked its way around the debris piles, glancing up at the ceiling as if it might crash down at any moment. Dreyfus caught a glimpse of a sharp, pale face, with eyes like thumb-holes. 'My name needn't concern you.'

'I think it does,' Dreyfus said. He made to push himself up from the ground and the robot lurched forward threateningly.

The man waved the stick at the machine. 'He may stand, Lurcher. As may the woman. But don't allow them to leave.'

'Who are you?' Dreyfus asked, feeling it couldn't hurt to ask again.

'I know who you are,' Del Mar said in a low, confiding tone. 'The doctor. The family physician. It's you, isn't it? Doctor . . . something. Strelnikov. Stresov.'

'Stasov,' the man answered. 'Doctor Balthasar Stasov. How well you remember me, Detective-Marshal, for all my troubles. How well I lodged in your memory.'

'You know this man?' Dreyfus asked.

'The former employee I mentioned? This is him. Dismissed from service due to some form of gross professional misconduct. After Aliya died he was interviewed as part of the routine investigation surrounding her death.'

'Tell the man I was innocent of any wrongdoing in that matter, Detective-Marshal.'

She sighed. 'He'd left the service before she died, so there was no suggestion he was involved in her murder. Naturally, he was interviewed in the aftermath of her death. The files say that he was tight-lipped, but otherwise cooperative. Vouched for the family, gave credence to Marlon's account of the accident – said she'd often gone away on business, and was prone to cutting corners when she was in a hurry to get back home. The case was closed soon after.'

'But you reviewed it.'

'He came back to us, years later. Wanted to change his story. That's when he crossed my path; why I looked into the older files. He wasn't credible, though. His new story didn't make any sense.'

'Don't feel you have to spare my feelings, Detective-Marshal. Tell him what you really thought of me.'

'You were a broken man, Doctor Stasov. Ruined. Your reputation had been fragile to begin with – it was hardly a glittering career. The family took you on out of charity, hoping to give you a second chance. Then they had to dismiss you. You've been nursing your resentment ever since, desperate to get back at the Vois.'

'Is it true that you were dismissed?' Dreyfus asked.

The hood slid from Doctor Stasov's head. He was bald; his skin waxlike; his eyes two dark, unblinking voids; his lips colourless; his mouth a black gash. His face contained a great many vertical wrinkles, his cheeks like drawn curtains.

'I made an error,' Doctor Stasov said. 'I attempted to learn the location of the Shell House.'

'You were in the service of the Voi family,' Dreyfus said, confused. 'How could you not know where you were?'

'Things were never as they appeared, Prefect,' Stasov answered. 'Not to begin with, and even less so as time went on.'

CHAPTER FIFTEEN

Sparver was called into the tactical room. He took his seat next to the one normally occupied by Thalia, and swept his eyes around the assembled gathering, trying to judge the mood. The atmosphere was expectant, a nervous energy present despite the obvious tiredness of the prefects and analysts. The Seniors were leaning over to the analysts, whispering exchanges, tapping fingers at scrolling lists, mouthing agreement or framing careful queries. Gaston Clearmountain and Jane Aumonier were studying the same compad, trading clipped observations. Lillian Baudry was talking to someone via a microphone and earpiece, nodding in quiet, frowning concentration. Over in the room's left-hand corner, the Solid Orrery was in an unusually complex configuration, bristling with numerous enlarged habitats and dense thickets of annotation, the whole thing knotted in a mad tangle of orbits and trajectories. Mildred Dosso and Robert Tang were standing next to it with their backs to the table, engaged in a deft display of dual-conjuring.

'Ah, Bancal,' Aumonier said, finally noticing his presence. 'Someone close the doors, please.'

'Has Garlin cracked?' Sparver asked, trying to uncover the reason for the heightened atmosphere.

'No, not yet. I'm putting him through a series of soft interviews, trying to root out inconsistencies. Claudette and Miles are with him at the moment. We'll go harder soon, but I want to know where his weak points are first. Oh, this is yours, I think.' She reached down for something beneath the table, rolling his whiphound across to him. 'You misplaced it, I gather. Normally that would be a disciplinary matter, but . . .' Aumonier gave him the tiniest nod, the slightest forgiving smile. 'You won't make a habit of it, will you?'

Sparver took the whiphound and clipped it to his belt.

'I got it out of my system, ma'am.'

'Good. I believe you may have helped get it out of one or two other systems as well.'

Assuming this was an end to the matter, and the reason for his summoning, Sparver made to leave.

'Wait,' Aumonier said, raising her hand. 'You're still needed. We're all still needed. We have the opening we've been hoping for, Bancal. A breakthrough from the team at Elysium Heights.' She glanced down, some urgent new report or analysis showing on the table. 'Would you brief him, Ingvar?'

Ingvar Tench cleared her throat. 'Does Bancal know about the link to Julius Mazarin?'

'Julius who?' Sparver asked.

'An apparent alias of Julius Devon Garlin Voi, when he was involved in the operation of the clinic. We have a video fragment, a sort of sales document. All the implications are that Garlin was a senior figure in the clinic, more than likely the head of operations if not the owner of the clinic itself. Of course he denies the connection.'

Sparver frowned. 'Wouldn't we know if he was running around operating a clinic?'

'The recording could be thirty or more years old,' Tench answered. 'Garlin wasn't a public figure then, and under the terms of provision of the Common Articles his movements aren't on record. Other than financing the clinic, and monitoring its operation, his day-to-day involvement needn't have been close, anyway.'

'Then why risk blowing his secrecy by appearing in a sales document?' Sparver asked.

'He was trading under the alias, and his clients wouldn't have had any *a priori* reason to suspect a link to the Voi family,' Tench said. 'In any case, whoever mothballed the clinic must have thought they'd covered all their tracks pretty thoroughly. As they did, apart from this fragment and the patient list . . .'

'Which is corrupted to the point of uselessness,' Sparver said.

'Was,' Tench replied. 'It seems the technicals overlooked an intact record during their initial search. It came to light a little over an hour ago, giving us just enough time to begin adjusting our response strategy.'

'They overlooked something? That's not like them.'

'Something about a search algorithm hitting some memory threshold, and then it cleared.'

Sparver nodded, accepting this at face value, even though it struck him as highly uncharacteristic of the Heavy Technical Squad to have allowed such an oversight, no matter the technical reasons.

'I have a question. How many names are there?'

'One thousand, nine hundred and thirty-one,' Tench said. 'But some have died by other means, and some have either left the system or vanished to the margins. That leaves one thousand, seven hundred and fifteen citizens who are still alive, still within the vicinity of Yellowstone and the Glitter Band, still walking around. Eighty-five are believed to be within Chasm City or one of the outlying settlements. That leaves sixteen hundred and thirty citizens on our immediate watch, sprinkled more or less randomly around the ten thousand.'

Sparver understood the reason for the Solid Orrery's unusual configuration. It was undoubtedly showing the present locations of those citizens, and the habitats they were in.

He thought of them going about their daily lives at this very moment, sleeping or awake, busy or idle, each utterly unaware that they had become the subject of Panoply's immediate and pressing interest.

'Can we get to them?' he asked.

'That's what we're evaluating,' Tench answered. 'Supreme Prefect – you've seen the most recent coordination plans.'

'Yes, Ingvar,' Aumonier said, looking up from her readouts. 'Our aim is to secure each of those citizens as quickly as possible. We're liaising with local constables as I speak – where possible they'll approach and isolate the citizens, without causing undue distress. Meanwhile, medical functionaries are being placed on immediate standing alert, and tasked into areas close to the citizens. Our threshold triggers will maintain their vigilance. The medicals will be ready to intervene if any of the citizens show signs of imminent Wildfire.' The lines around her mouth tightened. 'Of course, beyond cutting their heads off there isn't a lot they can do . . .'

'But we have other options,' said Gaston Clearmountain. 'Priority number one, after the citizens are located, will be to screen their implants for outside influence. Abstraction services will be reduced to emergency levels in the relevant habitats, turned off completely in some instances, and that may help a little. But we can't rely on that as a solution.'

'Why not?' Sparver asked.

'You saw it yourself, Bancal,' Aumonier said. 'The lockdown failed in Fuxin-Nymburk. That means we can't depend on absolute control of abstraction or polling services. Even if we thought we had a block in place, a hidden signal might still be able to slip through. What's required is some form of physical barrier.'

'Some of the habitats already have the means to establish isolation cages,' Clearmountain said. 'Where they are lacking – or can't be manufactured in a useful time – the citizens will be moved to other habitats or conveyed to our own facilities. Estimates suggest we can move to isolate around six to seven hundred citizens within the next thirteen hours, with the rest following over another twenty-six. That buys us a little time – maybe as much as we need. But it's only a temporary measure until we can get in and disable those implants. Again, medical functionaries are being tasked to lay the necessary groundwork. Our powers also allow us to requisition civilian surgical facilities, and to delay any non-essential procedures while we clear the backlog.'

'And all of this without causing a panic?' Sparver asked, raising a sceptical brow.

'It's all but unavoidable now,' Aumonier said. 'But I have one advantage I lacked before: now I know the exact scope of our problem. If we act firmly, and efficiently, we can declare the crisis contained and neutralised almost as soon as the panic breaks. The people will see it, too. I have a duty to protect them from undue distress, but ultimately I believe in their reasonableness.'

'I do like an optimist,' Sparver said.

Thalia had the sense he had been watching her for a while before she became fully aware of his presence. She waited for her eyes to find focus, and when that failed to happen she made to touch her forehead, wondering why her skull felt as if it had swollen to the size of a balloon, monstrous and throbbing and huge, the rest of her no more than a limp, useless appendage.

'Easy, Prefect Ng.'

She made to speak and nothing came out except a senseless guttural croak. Sparver's still-blurred form reached out to a steely, skeletal thing that might possibly have been a trolley or bedside table, and then he was pressing a stiff white surface to her lips, a gesture which struck her as both surreal and unwarranted until she realised it was a cup and she was expected to drink from it.

'You can nod for the time being,' Sparver said. 'Demikhov says he's spoken to you a couple of times, but you were groggy on both occasions and he's not sure how much sunk in.'

She had to work hard to puzzle his words into a form she could understand. It was as if he spoke a twisty, difficult language that she had once studied and then allowed to grow rusty.

'Mm . . .'

'Just nod, Thalia.' Sparver watched her reaction. 'You were as close to being dead as most of us get before the big day. But you got us Garlin. He came in with hardly a scratch on him.'

With a substantial effort of will she placed these jumbled facts onto the murky, fog-shrouded terrain which she knew to represent the larger picture. Garlin, the breakaway movement, the clinic, the polling cores. She remembered crowds and shouting. She remembered whiphounds and glass doors. She remembered walking around with someone's head in a box.

'What . . .' she started again.

'Garlin's here. Aumonier's putting the slow squeeze on him. He can't weasel out now, not after what happened in Fuxin-Nymburk. Not sure I'd have believed it myself, if I hadn't been there, but I saw that lockdown fail with my own eyes and things like that just don't happen.'

'Sparver.' She forced his name out, a minor miracle, and took more of the water, cradling the cup with her own fingers. 'I feel a mess.'

'Concussion. I think a skull fracture, too. But beyond that you got off lightly. I mean, not that I'd call those bruises nothing, but . . .'

'And you?'

'I'm all right. Got knocked out, too, but only for a minute or two. I wanted to see you now because I'm going back out again.'

'Didn't we both do enough?'

'It's not as unjust as it sounds. I've had some rest, got one or two things off my chest, and now I'm ready to finish this off. Did Demikhov mention the names?'

'I don't even remember Demikhov speaking to me.'

'We have the remaining Wildfire cases – all the citizens who are ever going to pop. Now it's just a question of rounding them up and defusing them. It's all hands on deck. They're giving me a cutter and a list of targets, and I expect it'll keep me busy for at least another thirteen hours. I just wanted to drop by now, while they're turning the ship around.'

'Is it safe work?'

'Compared to our last couple of assignments? A walk in the park. The constables and medics are rushing around trying to pin down the citizens. All I need to do is ship them back here as quickly as I can.'

'I'd come with you if I could.'

'You've earned an exemption on this one, Ng.'

Something floated up from the base of her memory. 'Are you still . . . what I mean to say, are you working for me, or am I working for you?'

'I got my rank reinstated.'

'I'm glad. It should never have happened the way it did.'

'Well, don't cut yourself about it too much. A sudden reversal of roles, like that . . . it was bound to be difficult.'

'I meant your demotion. That's what I mean should never have happened.'

'Of course.' Sparver shifted. 'I'm glad you're going to be all right. I don't have too many friends in this place – need to take care of the ones I do have.'

She studied his face, lingering over the strangeness in it, but also the humanity, reminding herself of the times when he had shown her loyalty and support, even when he had borne some cost to that support. A true colleague, in other words, but more than that. A friend she had turned to more than once and knew she would have cause to rely on in the future.

'I . . . feel the same way.'

'I'm glad. That would have been a hell of an awkward speech if it turned out you couldn't stand the sight of me.'

She managed a laugh.

'Thank you for dropping by. You didn't have to, and I appreciate it. Have you heard from Dreyfus?'

'No, he's still down in Chasm City trying to find some more dirt to shovel onto Garlin's reputation. Not that we need it now. We've got the patient list, and we've got a younger Garlin showing up under an alias in the clinic itself.' Sparver tightened his belt, making a quick patting inventory of his equipment. 'He'll crack sooner or later. Then it's just a question of making him stop the deaths.'

'Do you think he'll give in so easily?'

'He's got some fight in him still. But maybe not as much as he did before that mob trampled his smirking face into the dirt.'

Thalia nodded, her thoughts still foggy, but something nagging at her with the odd and troubling insistence that often came with waking to a half-glimpsed connection, some clue or link furnished by her unconscious link.

'Sparver, will you do me a favour?'

'Only if it's the sort that doesn't get me into trouble again.'

'I don't think they'll let me have a compad in here, not when I'm supposed to be resting. But I've still got Pangolin clearance and I want to see the files on the Terzet Friller death again.'

'It was open and shut – or as open and shut as any of the Wildfire deaths. Wasn't it?'

She gave him her best pleading look.

For the third or fourth time Dreyfus attempted to get up from the cold marble floor, only to have the robot stomp towards him with sudden and menacing intent, flexing its arms and spreading wide its three-clawed hands.

'Do you mean to kill us, Doctor Stasov?' he asked. 'I only ask because you might want to get on with it. Both of us will soon be missed by our respective agencies. Enforcement squads will arrive – more than you or that robot are capable of resisting.'

Doctor Stasov leaned in on his stick. Dreyfus and Del Mar had turned to face the robot again, and now the doctor was to their left, carefully avoiding interposing himself between his prisoners and the machine.

'Are you trying to provoke me, Prefect?' he asked.

'He's just trying to get at your plans for us,' Del Mar said, giving Dreyfus a narrow, warning eye. 'You had this robot waiting here to ambush someone. It took you a little while to arrive, though, so I suppose you were somewhere else, waiting for a signal. What did you hope to gain by capturing a police officer?'

'You were never the object of my interest, Detective-Marshal. The truth is I'm disappointed to find you here instead of one of them.'

'Them?' Dreyfus asked.

'The Vois. I hoped one of them would come back eventually, if only to burn this old place down, erasing the last trace of the old falsehood. The robot was theirs, did you know? Lurcher. The family retainer, guardian and grounds-keeper. When it was no longer of use they sold it to a third party. Better that they should have destroyed it, or left it to rust, but no Voi has ever turned down the chance to make a small profit, even at their own eventual cost.'

Del Mar asked: 'Were you that third party?'

'No – that would have roused immediate suspicion. The robot passed from hand to hand over a period of years, until I had the means to acquire it. I badly wanted access to Lurcher's security settings. I was hoping there might be a clue in them . . . some vital data fragment which hadn't been properly erased or reset.'

Dreyfus looked into the doctor's lavishly wrinkled and ancient face, trying to read the sunken, voidlike eyes. 'And was there?'

'No, they'd been more thorough than I hoped. But the robot retained some basic knowledge of the estate's layout and that at least allowed it to serve as my watchdog. I set it here to wait and report. Trespassers came and went, the occasional city official. But it was *them* I wanted to find.' Spittle ejected from the bloodless gash of his lips. 'I confess that lately I placed the robot on a higher degree of alertness, thinking a visit all the more likely. Otherwise it would have concealed itself more effectively, and allowed you to complete your pointless investigation in peace.'

'Julius Devon Garlin Voi still has the deeds to this place,' Dreyfus said. 'It's still his, in a legal sense, even if he downplays the family connection. Why would he allow you to come and go?'

'The place is of no concern to them. They've left it to fester. An informational dead zone. The abstraction doesn't penetrate here, by design. The dome rebuffs it. The family craved their privacy, their insularity. My alert was a simple radio frequency trigger, with just enough power to reach beyond the estate. A risk even in that, but one worth taking.'

'You keep saying *them*,' Dreyfus said.

'For a reason,' Stasov answered.

'There's only one living heir. Aliya died, than Marlon. Now there's just Julius, calling himself Devon Garlin.'

'There were always two sons,' Stasov said. 'I have every reason to think they are both still alive.'

'No,' Dreyfus said, shaking his head. 'If anyone knows that family inside out it's me. Julius was an only child. He grew up here with his mother and father, and when Aliya died he set out on his own. There was never a sibling.'

'You're wrong on two counts,' Stasov told him. 'There was a brother. His name was Caleb. They were non-identical twins. I know because I was often called to the household to monitor their progress. The boys were being groomed . . . shaped for greatness. And they didn't grow up here.'

'Julius certainly did,' Dreyfus said.

'I assure you he didn't,' Stasov said. 'There's another one, you see. Another Shell House.'

'I told you he had a story,' Del Mar whispered.

Stasov leaned in as if he had only just caught her words. 'Yes, and I came to you with it often enough, didn't I? I asked only to be given the benefit of the doubt, but even that was too much.'

'You weren't the most credible witness.'

'And perhaps there was just too much at stake to risk challenging the reputation of a powerful man of the people such as Devon Garlin. Perhaps the sacred name of the Vois couldn't be allowed to be tarnished – even when a terrible crime had been committed.'

'You mean Aliya's death?' Dreyfus asked.

'Before that.' He jabbed the stick against the floor for emphasis. 'I don't mean to belittle her death. For all I know, maybe it was an accident after all. Between her and Marlon, she was at least the more cautious one, maybe the only one with a shred of human decency left in her soul. Although they were both implicated in—'

'We looked into his claims,' Del Mar said, allowing her voice to rise defensively. 'We're not so blinkered that we'd dismiss someone with a story about Devon Garlin, even when they had every reason to loathe that family. But the doctor's accusations couldn't be verified.'

'Were they disproven?' Dreyfus probed.

'No . . . but they couldn't be verified.' She glanced away, almost as if she didn't wish him to see the guilty look on her face. 'We observed due diligence. Would Panoply have acted any differently, if you had a hundred other problems demanding your attention?'

Dreyfus fixed his gaze on Stasov, forcing himself not to blink or flinch from those dead black eyes. 'Are you a man of conscience, Doctor?'

'Why do you ask?'

'Because I want to trust you.'

Doctor Stasov regarded him for several long seconds, judgement and calculation flitting across his ancient and cavernous face like cloud shadows on rock. 'I am not a good man,' he said slowly, a strain opening in his voice. 'I would never pretend to that. But I always tried to do right by those boys. I thought, for a while, that they had it in them to rise above the circumstances of their origin. I thought they could become better men . . . good custodians.' A dark tongue licked the pale margin of his mouth. 'I was wrong.' Then he turned his eyes to the robot. 'Let them stand, Lurcher. They're not the ones we were waiting for.'

Doctor Stasov reached out a hand to Dreyfus. His fingers were extraordinarily long and thin, and they seemed to have too many knuckles and joints about them. Dreyfus took the hand warily, as if it might break into brittle twiglike shards at the first touch.

He was mistaken. It was stronger than it looked.

'Who's with him now?' Aumonier asked, while she was being inspected – at her own insistence – for concealed devices. 'Saint-Croix and Jaffna?'

'No, ma'am,' answered the fresh-faced duty prefect, newly promoted from Field III, and visibly nervous at having to perform a sweep and pat-down of the Supreme Prefect. 'I understand they didn't get very far. Senior Prefect Baudry's in there now. Would you like me to tell her you're ready to take over?'

'That won't be necessary, Chin. Am I clear?'

The flustered, sweating Chin stepped back from the inspection. 'You're clear, ma'am.'

'That's a relief to us both. Extend the bridge, and then pull it back when I'm inside. I'll need about thirty minutes.'

Chin operated the controls that pushed out the pressurised bridge, connecting to a door in the side of the cube. 'You'll be out of contact once the bridge withdraws. Any emergencies, you can always hammer on something. The braces will pick up the acoustic signal.'

'Thank you, Chin. You'll be astonished to hear that I've done this once or twice before.'

The bridge completed its extension. Aumonier walked across, mentally preparing herself, running through the things she was prepared to discuss and the things she had decided to withhold, until – if – they proceeded to trawl.

She closed the airtight door behind her, then went through the lattice-work of secondary doors that led through to the interviewing suite. It was a simple affair, after all the external technicalities. A windowed partition divided the space into two rooms. The partition was fitted with one-way glass, composed of inert material rather than quickmatter. One room was an observation area, so that one or more prefects or citizen observers might witness an interview in progress. On the other side of the glass was a bare room containing a table and three sturdy grey chairs. Power, illumination and life-support was provided by rugged, self-contained systems entirely independent of the rest of Panoply.

Garlin was on one side of the table, Baudry on the other. Aumonier rapped her knuckles on the partition's connecting door and admitted herself into the interviewing cell.

'Where is my citizen quorum?' demanded Garlin sharply, breaking off from whatever he had been saying. 'I have my rights. You can deny me access to my legal representatives, but you can't deny me my citizen quorum.'

Aumonier eased herself into the vacant seat next to Lillian Baudry. 'Under executive clause six-slash-one, sub-paragraph five of the Common Articles,' she explained in a pleasant, obliging tone, 'that's exactly what I can do. We are under emergency conditions, and as such it wasn't feasible to locate and deputise a standing quorum, each of whom lacked any sort of neural implant.'

'That's a twisting of the laws to suit your own ends,' Garlin said.

'It isn't,' Aumonier clarified, still in the same friendly spirit. 'The onus is on me to ensure the safety of that citizen quorum, and I couldn't in all conscience guarantee I'd be able to protect them.'

'Protect them from who?'

Aumonier blinked, feigning surprise. 'From you, Mister Garlin. Who else did you think I had in mind?'

'Don't be absurd. What are you expecting me to do – reach through that glass? Wait. *Wait.*' He shifted his gaze onto Baudry now, something tightening in his brow. 'What she was asking me, about those citizen deaths. The Wildfire rumours . . . that clinic you kept going on about . . . are you seriously suggesting I had something to do with all that?'

'Then you admit to your knowledge of Wildfire,' Baudry said, in a smooth, judicial tone.

'She mentioned it!' he said, eyes widening as he looked back at Aumonier. 'When she dragged me in. Aumonier was the one who mentioned Wildfire. I'd never heard of it until that moment. You can't blame me for knowing you had a problem. The rumours have been flying around for months. But that doesn't mean I knew what it was.'

'The trouble is,' Aumonier said, 'you seemed to know rather too much for a man who just happened to have his ear to the ground. Not only about Wildfire, but other things. You seemed to have an almost preternatural ability to anticipate the movements of my operatives . . .?'

'When a man has a vendetta against you, you get pretty good at guessing his moves,' Garlin said.

'How do you explain the failure of the local lockdown in Fuxin-Nymburk?' Aumonier asked, still keeping her manner ruthlessly civil. 'Your gathering couldn't have broken through into the polling core by force alone. Yet you seemed content to bide your time, knowing that the doors would open.'

'Don't blame me for your mistakes.'

'It wasn't a mistake,' Aumonier answered. 'It was the unprecedented breakdown of a system that shouldn't ever go wrong. Unlikely as it seems, I'm forced to one conclusion. Someone was able to reach in and disable the lockdown using channels reserved for high-level security operatives only, yet at the same time leave no trace of their intervention.'

He folded his arms, lifting his chin to her. It was finely stubbled, making him look a little older than his usual public guise. 'And have you found this mythical individual?'

'I think I'm looking at him,' Aumonier said.

To his partial credit, he did a good job of looking astonished, flustered and utterly enraged, all in the same quick blizzard of reactions. 'What? *What*? Are you out of your mind . . .

'You're a Voi,' Aumonier said.

'I've never made any secret of it.'

'No,' Baudry chipped in. 'But you've never advertised it either. It doesn't fit very well with your image as the strong man of the people, does it, being born into one of the oldest, wealthiest families in the entire system? You couldn't be more part of the establishment if you tried. You've had every advantage in life – including access to the deepest secrets of the Voi clan.'

'Your ancestor laid the template for our entire society,' Aumonier said. 'Drew up the blueprints for everything we hold dear. Abstraction, polling, transparency . . . freedom of access to information. The doors of perception, flung gloriously wide. But all of it built around the Voi kernel. It's uncrackable. Sacrosanct. But if there was a flaw in the Voi kernel – maybe a deliberate one – who'd be in a better place to know about it than a Voi?'

'I didn't have much faith in Panoply to begin with. Now I think you're unhinged.'

'I'd hardly credit it myself,' Aumonier replied. 'But we have a proven link between the Wildfire victims and your family. We think it happened under the auspices of a clinic, called Elysium Heights, which was run by you under the alias of Doctor Julius Mazarin. Nearly seventy people are now known to be victims of that deliberate action. But there are many more who were programmed to die in the weeks and months ahead.'

Garlin's face had hardened into a fixed mask of staring dismay. 'How much more absurd do you want to get, Aumonier? You can blame me for the economy if you like as well. Or the fact that black's in this year.'

Baudry bent down to retrieve something between her knees. 'I brought images,' she said, laying a cardboard dossier onto the table. 'Some of the early dead. Should I show them to him?'

'A few,' Aumonier said. 'But we'll hold back the rest for the trawl.'

Baudry opened the dossier and extracted three shiny images. Rather than display them on a compad, she had taken the precaution of having them embossed directly onto paper by some ingenious chemical means. Each picture showed the face of one of the dead. The first was Cassandra Leng, the earliest victim known to Panoply.

Baudry slid the picture across to Garlin. He kept his eyes level, refusing to glance down.

'Look at it,' Aumonier said.

'Don't be ridiculous. You can't force me to look at anything.'

'Ah, but I can. It's fully within the permitted scope of my interrogation methods. It's not an especially pleasant procedure, though, so I suggest you spare yourself the trouble.'

He kept his eyes fixed on her for several seconds, strain showing in his neck muscles, but some unconscious reflex or twitch soon broke the spell. It was a momentary glance, but perfectly sufficient for her purposes. She watched him carefully, comparing his expression before and after that glance, vigilant for the tiniest betrayal of recognition.

She had to hand it to him. Devon Garlin did a good job of seeming not to know Cassandra Leng.

'One or two more,' Aumonier said.

'Before I accompany you,' Doctor Stasov said, his stick clacking on the hard ground beneath the weeds, 'perhaps you'd clarify the terms of our association.'

'What do you think needs clarifying?' Dreyfus asked.

'Is this an arrest?' Stasov asked. 'You have the authority, I suppose, and despite appearances Lurcher would not use violent means to prevent my detention.'

'You've already interfered in the course of an investigation,' Del Mar said, raising a hand to her volantor, signalling it to begin preparing for departure. 'Forcefully, too. That's grounds enough for me to bring you in, before we start with trespassing.'

'If you can be of service to us,' Dreyfus said, 'then I'm minded to set aside any earlier misunderstandings. But you're going to have to work hard to convince me that we're not in the Shell House.'

'Of course this is the Shell House,' Stasov said. 'Just not the only one. The Vois' wealth and influence brought great freedoms. They could come and go as they pleased, flying in and out of Yellowstone with nothing but the most cursory of checks. On the rare occasions in later life when they needed to entertain, this is where it happened. This is also where Marlon returned with Julius after Aliya's death, and where he saw out his grief, playing the role expertly.'

'And the other place?' Dreyfus asked.

'In space, located in another piece of Voi real estate. Spun up to simulate Yellowstone gravity, and rendered exactly, down to the last crack, the last grain of dirt, so that you couldn't tell one from the other. To begin with, when I first started visiting the boys, I came here. By then Julius and Caleb were eight years old, or so I was informed. They had kept them out of the way until then, but I think Marlon and Aliya were growing nervous. The estate was private enough, but still much too close to Chasm City for their liking. They were worried that something beyond their control might result in the boys being discovered.'

'Why—?' Dreyfus started.

Del Mar touched a hand to his shoulder as she set a foot on the volantor's boarding steps. 'Let him continue.'

'Marlon and Aliya decided to continue with the boys' development in space, where their privacy could be more easily controlled. But they didn't want it to be any sort of upheaval. So they created a second Shell House and grounds, and the boys were drugged and shipped there without anyone being the wiser. They went to sleep in one bedroom and woke up in another, and even the boys couldn't tell the difference. It was the perfect solution. There was just one irritant.'

'You,' Dreyfus said.

'They had grown dependent on my services – as I had grown to need their flow of funds, small as it was. They knew some of my secrets and I knew some of theirs. A mutually beneficial symbiosis. So they elected

272

to continue hiring me. Once every few months I was obliged to visit the boys. But I was not permitted to know the whereabouts of this second Shell House. In fact no mention was ever made that there had been a change. I was to go along with the charade, never questioning it. The only complication was that I, too, was required to be drugged and put to sleep. So I went along with it, across numerous visits. I would come here, and awake there. I guessed soon enough that it had to be in space: there were too many missing hours from my life for it to be anywhere else. But I wasn't permitted to know the whereabouts.'

Dreyfus climbed in after Del Mar, then extended a hand to help Doctor Stasov.

'I'm guessing you tried to find out.'

'Yes – my ultimate undoing. I concealed a small inertial tracking device about my person, disguised as one of my ordinary medical instruments.'

They were all aboard. Del Mar closed the door and took the volantor into the air, aiming it for the gap in the dome by which they had entered.

'And did it tell you where you'd been taken?' Dreyfus asked.

'It provided a set of orbital coordinates, with a margin of error. I would have needed to make several trips to obtain a definite fix. What I had, though, was convincing enough for my purposes. Tell him, Detective-Marshal. I think it would be far better coming from your lips.'

'Lethe,' she answered, not without a moment's reticence. 'The last significant piece of orbital real estate still tied to the Voi family.'

Dreyfus stared at the doctor, astonished at what he was hearing. 'You checked his story, didn't you? He gave you a place, a name.'

'Not our jurisdiction,' Del Mar said, turning around sharply in her seat now that the volantor was in open air.

'So you asked. You went through the usual channels. Tell me you did that much.'

'We . . . felt that discretion ought to be exercised. Our request was framed as part of a larger investigation into minor tax irregularities concerning a number of orbital holdings.'

'And I can bet *that* was top of Jane Aumonier's list of priorities,' Dreyfus said.

'Even if Stasov's story is true, what they did is weird, not illegal. There's no law that says you have to tell the truth to children.'

'She's never really believed me,' Stasov said.

'It would have helped if you'd been able to show me some physical evidence to back up your account. But you couldn't even produce the tracking device.'

'They confiscated it as soon as it was discovered. I was dismissed short-ly afterwards.'

'You're lucky they stopped at dismissal,' Dreyfus said. 'Those big fam-ilies can be ruthless.'

'Better to keep me on a long leash with blackmail and threats. For all they knew they might have had some need of my services again.'

'Did they?' Dreyfus asked.

'No. There were tensions growing. Aliya felt that the boys were being given too much power, too soon. She didn't trust them with it, and as time passed her doubts grew and grew. I was party to some of the disagree-ments between her and Marlon.'

Dreyfus wanted to ask about the powers granted to the boys, willing for the moment to indulge Doctor Stasov's conviction that there was another son besides Julius. But he had a more pressing question. 'Then Marlon might have had a motive to murder Aliya, if the two of them were arguing over the boys?'

'I have no love for either Marlon or Aliya,' Doctor Stasov answered. 'What they did was indefensible. But neither was capable of killing the other. If suspicion should fall on anyone, it would be one of the boys. I studied them carefully, before my dismissal. Both showed rapid devel-opment, a keen ability to wield their new gifts. But Caleb was generally the quicker, stronger one. There was a meanness in him, as well. Perhaps it would have flowered in Julius, given time, but Caleb was the one who most concerned me. And the one about whom Aliya had the most doubts, as well.'

'Could Caleb have done it?' Del Mar asked, addressing Doctor Stasov.

'Most certainly,' he said. 'Especially if she tried to take away his toys. He wouldn't have cared for that at all.'

Sparver docked the cutter at the first of his pick-up points. He had come in fast, ramming the habitat so hard that they must have felt the bump all the way to the far endcap. A little rude, a little discourteous, but he had dispensation, and the local constables were expecting him to exercise all haste. He just hoped they were playing their own parts with the same sense of urgency.

He need not have worried. They were waiting on the other side of the airlock, constables and medical functionaries, his jolting arrival not only forgiven, but entirely excused given the nature of the emergency. They barely seemed to notice that he was a pig, so novel was the situation. The constables and functionaries seemed glad to have finally been let in on the secret, even if it was only in the bare details. They had their citizen with them, the one Sparver had been sent to collect, a worried-looking man of apparent middle age with a tall, flat-topped bristle of grey hair rising back from a high, agitated brow.

'The Supreme Prefect's still determined to avoid unnecessary citizen distress,' Sparver said, as he checked off the pick-up details on his compad. 'So you'll understand that the details of the emergency must be disclosed on a need-to-know basis only. That said, I'm authorised to inform you that we have a clear idea of the total number of citizens who need protecting, and it's well within our combined response capability. One or two more fatalities are probably unavoidable over the next couple of days, but the risk to any individual citizen on our target list is much less than one per cent.' He nodded at the man they had brought to the dock, hoping to strike a note of professional reassurance. 'You're one of the fortunate ones, Citizen. We'll have you back at Panoply very shortly, and there's no safer place for you in the whole Glitter Band. You'll be looked after, and when the emergency has passed – which should only be a few days – you'll be returned home.'

'I don't know why I've been brought here,' the man said, looking around with widening eyes. 'No one's telling me anything.'

'Citizen . . .' Sparver glanced down at the name, the first of the ten individuals he was required to ferry around. 'Mister Deverer. This is upsetting for you, I appreciate, but it's all for your own good. The Supreme Prefect has determined that you may be at risk of a sudden and serious illness. Luckily, the cause of this illness is understood and we have the means to both protect you and remove any possibility of danger in the future. But to do so we have to act quickly and efficiently, and that means you need to come with me.'

'Have I done something wrong?'

'No – you've done nothing wrong. But we have a duty to protect you, whether you wish it or not. Come with me, Mister Deverer. I've a busy day ahead of me, and you're just my first pick-up.'

The handover was completed. Sparver thanked the constables and medical functionaries for their assistance, promising them that they had the gratitude of Panoply and the Supreme Prefect in particular, and that they would be kept fully informed of ongoing developments. He could feel their excitement starting to sag by the second, as they realised their moment of intense usefulness was already drawing to a close. He felt for them, too. This was one of the many thousands of decent, unexceptional habitats that just got on with being a part of the Glitter Band, abiding by the Common Articles, seldom making the news and almost never testing the patience of Panoply. Its citizens lived contented if uneventful lives, generally happy with their lot. Being a constable in such a place was not exactly the most demanding of callings. He imagined the conversations that might go on later, as the constables and functionaries relayed developments to spouses and loved ones. *Today we had to collect a man and take him to the dock. A prefect came all the way from Panoply for him. Can you imagine? A prefect – and a pig, as well!*

Sparver made sure his charge was buckled in, then undocked with the same haste that he had come in.

'Bancal, inbound to Panoply,' he said, calling ahead. 'One down.'

CHAPTER SIXTEEN

Caleb was the first to notice the change. The boys were out in the grounds, entertaining themselves with contests of quickmatter shaping and manipulation of the consensual visual field. Julius lacked his brother's competitive streak, but he was happy to go along with any sort of game that did not involve hunting and death, no matter how illusory the sport.

They were standing close to each other in an area of cleared ground, struggling to assert their individual wills on the quickmatter staff, each brother trying to force a certain shape onto the staff and trying to deny the other the means to distort that form. The staff lay on an upturned bucket between them, safely out of arm's reach. As the quickmatter responded to the more dominant will, so the staff squirmed and shifted from one mercurial form to the next. Adding complexity to the challenge was the fact that each brother was using every means at their disposal to bias the other's visual environment, such that the apparent shape of the quickmatter staff was no guarantee of its absolute state.

Time was when Caleb would have easily bested Julius, but the contest was not so uneven now. Caleb still had the edge in terms of brute force, his shaping will being stronger in overall terms. But Julius had learned to wait for the slips in Caleb's concentration, the predictable moves, the moments of over-confidence. He had become very good at slipping his own shaping commands into those narrow opportunities, wasting no effort until there was a likelihood of success. Then his interventions were quick and dagger-like.

Something was off today, though, and at first Julius thought it was his own inadequacy reasserting itself. He felt slow and clumsy, his shaping commands coming out ill-formed and imprecise, the quickmatter resisting his will just as if he had unlearned all the lessons of recent months. When he tried to distort the consensual visual field, dropping an illusion over Caleb, his efforts were lacklustre and easily dismissed.

It would have meant defeat for Julius but for one thing: Caleb was similarly afflicted.

They played on in increasingly desultory terms, Julius unwilling to voice his suspicions, until with a snarl Caleb made the quickmatter staff spasm and twitch so violently that it flung itself off the bucket.

'What's wrong?' Julius asked, not too sorry that the contest had come to a conclusion.

'Don't tell me you don't feel it. Something's holding us back.' Caleb tapped the side of his own head. 'Control filters, brother. Blockades. They've dropped them in overnight. Or rather, she has.'

'We can still shape,' Julius said, puzzled.

'Oh, she wouldn't be so silly as to remove everything, not after all the work they've put into us. That wouldn't go down well with Father, for one thing. But she's frightened we've come too far, so she's put the brakes on us.'

Julius went to collect the quickmatter staff, frozen in the buckled form in which Caleb had left it. 'I don't understand. Shouldn't it be all or nothing?'

'No, not the way they've arranged it. They both still want us to go out there and be good citizens, and it would be a bit strange if we couldn't shape at all. I think she's put a restriction on the speed we can generate shaping commands, or some sort of sense-feedback time-lag. Don't tell me you don't feel it as well. It's like we're trying to think through treacle.'

'I thought it was just me,' Julius admitted. 'To begin with.'

'No,' Caleb said, looking at his brother with grave intent. 'It's both of us. And having gone this far, she might go further.'

'If that's what they want for us . . .' Julius started saying.

Caleb narrowed his eyes in pity and disgust. 'Do you know what your problem is? You give in too easily.' He stepped forward and snatched the quickmatter staff from Julius. 'Why should we accept this, after all the hard work we've put in?'

'It's just a setback,' Julius said, gazing down at his empty palm. 'She just wants time for us to develop a bit more, I think.'

'You think,' Caleb said, the corner of his lip curling in contempt. 'Well, I'm not going to stand for it. Father's on our side. He'll see this is wrong.'

'She won't have done this without his agreement.'

'You mean, she'll have bullied him into accepting it. But we don't have to.' Caleb nodded at the ground. 'Grab that bucket. We're going back to the Shell House.'

Their parents were in the parlour room, caught in some tense exchange when the boys burst in, Caleb flinging down the quickmatter staff like a challenge. It clanged against the marbled flooring.

'What have you done?' he demanded, his voice harsh with rage, jutting out his jaw and straining his neck so hard that the tendons stood out. 'We can't shape, can't conjure, can't project images . . .'

Father raised a calming hand, making to say something. But Mother was already rising from her chair, locking her eyes on Caleb.

'Do not dare speak to me that way. You were given a gift, one that you were not ready for. And if I had any doubts about my decision, you've silenced them with this outburst. You aren't ready – not now, and maybe not ever. That temper of yours . . .'

'Why me?' Julius asked, his own voice sounding timorous. 'I was doing all right, wasn't I?'

'Go ahead,' Caleb said. 'Betray me, you little Judas.'

'I didn't mean—' Julius began.

Father closed his eyes, making a slow fanning action with his hands. 'Please. Some calm. Your mother is correct. We pushed you too hard, too fast, and now we need to slow down, take stock, and review the progress you've made. Nothing has been taken from you – merely a modest curtailment of some of your recent capabilities.'

'We worked hard for this,' Caleb said, in no way placated. 'Sweated blood to become the sons you wanted, the heirs to this stupid throne. We were ready to go out and do our bit for Chasm City – become good little public servants, upholding the family tradition – meddling when needed. But that wasn't good enough, was it?'

'Don't over-dramatise,' Mother said, still angered. 'You still retain most of your new faculties. You haven't been impoverished. You haven't been turned out into the streets and forced to find a living, like all the other little people.'

Caleb grimaced, gesturing at the quickmatter staff. 'I can barely make it move! Don't you realise what you've done?'

'Nothing has been blocked that can't be unblocked,' Father said. 'In time. When you've proved yourselves. And when you' – he was pointing at Caleb – 'learn a little self-control, son. Because if you can't demonstrate it now, you aren't fit to take the reins of this city. Do you understand?' He waited an instant, repeated, louder this time: 'Do you understand?'

Caleb worked his fingers, then slowly adopted a more relaxed posture, softening his expression. He nodded slowly, shooting a complicit glance at Julius. 'Yes . . . I understand. If this is what it takes.'

'Credit to you, Caleb,' Mother said, giving him an admiring nod. 'I didn't think you'd see sense so readily.'

'I didn't mean to be angry. It was just a shock, after all the hard work we've put in.' Caleb's chest heaved up and down as if he were on the verge

279

of tears. 'But I mis-reacted. It has been quick, I agree. Maybe Julius and I do need a little more time before we're ready to accept this responsibility.' He offered Julius a conciliatory smile. 'I didn't mean to be nasty just then. I shouldn't have called you Judas.'

Julius accepted this apology with a nod. 'It's all right.'

'Your mother and I may differ on some of the details of your development,' Father said, relieved that the heated exchange had blown itself out. 'But whenever we arrive at a decision like this, it's one we agree on. And no matter what you may think at the time, it is always in your best interests.'

'Yes,' Caleb said, a little too earnestly for Julius's liking. 'We realise that. And we're sorry. I mean, I am, in particular.'

'Then you'll take this as adults – as the grown men you're soon to become. Consider it a test, not a setback.'

'We will, Father,' Julius said.

'And in case it wasn't clear, this decision was unanimous. You'll attach no blame to your mother.'

'We wouldn't dream of it,' Caleb said. He stooped down and collected the malleable staff. 'I'm sorry about throwing it down the way I did. But is it all right if Julius and I keep practising, even with the blockade in place? There can't be any harm in that, can there?'

'I don't—' Mother began.

But Father smiled tightly. 'We can't deprive them of everything, Aliya. Working with these restrictions will help them learn resourcefulness – and maybe a touch of humility. It will be for the best in the long run.'

'Thank you,' Caleb said. Still holding the staff, he adopted a mask of avid concentration, pressing his will into the quickmatter. Julius felt the turbulence of his shaping commands, like a cold wind blasting out from his temple. The staff quivered and took on the look of some knotty, gristled piece of meat, far from the smooth functionality of the crossbow. 'I'd forgotten how hard it used to be,' Caleb said, with an abashed look.

'It won't hurt to have this reminder,' Mother said. Then, with a flick of her hand: 'Take it. Do with it as you will. In a month or two, we'll review matters.'

Julius nodded, accepting this state of affairs. But there was something in Caleb's own nod that put a chill through him. Too accepting, too submissive by far. It was not like his brother at all. Caleb's rage was like a sleeping fever, only just contained beneath his skin.

He waited until they were alone again.

'That was good,' he said. 'Very convincing.'

'I'm sorry?' Caleb said, as bad at feigning innocence as he was at meek acceptance. 'Very convincing in what sense?'

'You gave in too easily. I know you better than that. What do you know?'

Caleb was silent for a few seconds. He studied Julius, some private calculation whirring behind his eyes. Then he allowed himself a smile. 'She thinks she's pretty smart, our mother. Maybe she is, by the usual standards. Smarter than Father, in some ways. She got us both with that blockade. But she doesn't know our heads half as well as we do.'

'What's that supposed to mean?' Julius asked, with a dark suspicion that he already knew.

'I found a workaround,' Caleb said breezily. 'A way to make her think the blockade's still in place, even when it isn't. I did it, just standing in that room. It was that easy.'

'I don't believe you.'

Caleb shrugged. 'But you'll believe this, won't you?' He held up the malleable staff, making it transform back into the crossbow, just as elegantly conceived as it had ever been. 'I shouldn't have been able to do it, not that quickly, and not that easily. And do you know what I'm going to do next?' He didn't wait for Julius to answer. 'I'm going to unblock you as well. No fun in being the only one, is there?'

Julius did not have time to react. He felt Caleb push a shaping signal into his head, jabbing in as cold and precise as an ice-pick. It unlocked something that he did not even know had been locked. Experimentally, Julius formed a conjuring command and applied it to the staff. It shifted into his desired form: a model of a spacecraft, one he had been practising in quiet moments.

'It won't make any difference,' Julius said. 'She's limited our powers for a reason. If you go around showing them off, she'll realise you've broken the blockade.'

'Oh, I know,' Caleb said, as if the point were trivial. 'And she'd find out eventually whatever happened, I'm sure. This workaround isn't watertight, either. If she took sufficient trouble over it, I'm worried she could lock us out for ever.' He smiled, all reasonableness. 'We can't let her do that, can we?'

Skin hairs prickled on the back of Julius's neck. 'What are you saying?'

'It's may be time to make sure she never gets the chance to stop us.'

'No. You won't hurt her.'

Caleb's smile turned to a smirk. 'Would you stop me if I tried? Do you really think you've got it in you?' Then he shook his head, reaching out to place a hand on Julius. 'It's all right, brother. I wouldn't dream of hurting her.'

Jane Aumonier had long ago learned to recognise and trust that first tingling intimation of disquiet. It was a faculty that had served her well over the years, although there had never once been a time when she welcomed its calling.

It only ever meant bad news.

'There's an error,' she said, as if voicing that assertion might somehow bend reality to better suit her wishes. 'There must be. There's no other explanation. Either she wasn't in the Faraday cage or the cage hasn't worked properly.'

She had taken the fact of the first new Wildfire case with regret and anger but also a certain bruised equanimity, knowing it had always been a question of where and when, rather than if. There was nothing she could do about that now, other than honour the death of that hapless individual by making sure that not a breath was spared saving those still alive.

But now this. A second Wildfire case, within thirty minutes of the first. Statistically improbable, even given the steepening curve. And all but impossible, given the fact that the citizen in question had already been secured and protected.

Let this be an outlier, she told herself.

'Ma'am,' said an analyst holding a compad, barely raising her voice above a timid whisper. 'We've got . . .'

'An explanation, already?' Aumonier snapped, before the woman had a chance to finish her sentence.

'No, ma'am.' The analyst had to swallow before continuing. 'It's Prefect Dreyfus. He's asking to be put through to you. Under the emergency footing we're filtering direct communications through to tactical.'

'Where is he?'

'Still in Chasm City, ma'am, but back in contact. He says it's urgent.'

'So urgent it couldn't wait until this exact moment?' Aumonier asked, not in any expectation of an answer.

The analyst made a valiant show of pretending not to hear this unwarranted and uncharacteristic outburst. 'Ma'am?'

'Put him on.'

Aumonier took the call via earpiece, preferring not to disturb the discussions playing out around her. She waited a second for the connection to finalise, and for his voice to buzz through.

'Jane?'

'Who else? I see you've decided thirteen hours was more than enough time to be out of the kitchen.'

His voice was scratchy, faint against a background of vehicle noise and rushing air. 'I'm on my way back. Is there any more news on Thalia? I've been fearing the worst ever since we spoke.'

Aumonier bit down on her irritation. She could not begrudge Dreyfus his concern for his immediate colleagues, but his priorities struck her as a little misplaced.

'I told you she was in good hands, didn't I?'

'I thought . . .' She had the sense that he was censoring himself. 'I believed it was serious.'

'It *is* serious. I never pretended otherwise. But no one's in better hands, and she seems to be out of the worst of it. She's responsive, answering questions lucidly – a little foggy about what happened, but nothing that we wouldn't expect. In fact Demikhov's having a hard time keeping her in bed. She keeps trying to get back to her duties.'

'That sounds like Thalia.'

'You can take the blame – you instilled it in her.' She frowned, wondering what it was she had heard in his answer. 'Are you all right, Tom? You sound . . . less relieved than I'd have expected.'

'I am relieved,' he said. 'Totally. I just wish she'd listen to Doctor Demikhov.'

'I'll pass on your instructions.'

'And my best wishes, too. Tell her . . . well, tell her I'm very glad she's all right, and this is no longer her fight.'

'I will, and—' Aumonier broke off, because another analyst had just shoved a compad under her nose. It was scrolling with what she instantly knew to be confirmation of her worst fears. 'Tom, I have to tell you that we're in the middle of something very concerning – as if things weren't already bad enough. How much did the analyst tell you?'

'Nothing. I just asked to be put straight through.'

'Then I'll give you the bare facts for now. While you were out of contact we recovered the complete patient list for the clinic.'

'That's good.'

'So we hoped. And we've been acting on it ever since, mobilising all available resources to gather up and safeguard the remaining citizens. Our plan was straightforward, if ambitious. Get those citizens into complete isolation, then schedule them for surgery. It's not perfect – it'll take time, and given the pattern of Wildfire deaths to date, some are bound to die before we get to them. But we're now seeing the one thing I wasn't counting on. We've had two confirmed instances of Wildfire *after* the citizens were already supposed to be safe . . . the second one just came in.'

Dreyfus took a few seconds to answer. 'Perhaps there's a latency. The triggering signal arrives, but Wildfire doesn't happen immediately. That might explain why they're still dying, even after you get them into isolation.'

She nodded, desperate to cling to such a hope, but knowing in her bones that it could not be the whole answer. 'Yes, that's feasible. But there's something else, too. The curve is still steepening. We might have expected two, possibly three instances across the first twenty-six hours of our operation. But we lost one before anyone made contact, and two after they were already in our protection. Our supposed protection. That's three deaths in barely an hour.'

'Are you still holding Garlin?'

'Yes . . . no reason to let him go. Even less now. But he's under the same isolation as the citizens. Maybe you're right about that latency idea . . .'

'I'll be back at Panoply in a few hours. I'd like to speak to him.'

'Of course. We'll keep working him. I'm moved to go to trawl sooner rather than later. Would you have any objections if I didn't wait until you were back?'

'Do what you think is right. I'll back you all the way. Can you spare me an asset or two, though?'

'Depends what sort you had in mind. We're not exactly sitting on our hands here.'

'Pull a corvette, or better still an HEV. Put a good squad on it, and give them a full armaments dispensation. There's an object we need to look at.'

'An object,' she repeated.

'A lump of rock, in the Glitter Band. An abandoned former asset of the Voi family, called Lethe. I've checked. There's no other asteroid or habitat with that name.'

'And the significance of this place – the reason you want me to divert valuable resources away from a rescue operation that's already straining at the seams?'

'I can't be sure. Not just yet. I just feel it would be useful to take a closer look at Lethe.'

'Because of something you learned in the Shell House?'

'Yes,' Dreyfus answered, after a moment's hesitation. 'I'm returning with a material witness, too. And Detective-Marshal Del Mar will be accompanying me.'

She steeled her jaw, thought of a hundred instantly regrettable things she might say, but with great force of will found the strength for a decorous reply.

'Then . . . inform the Detective-Marshal that she will be made more than welcome in Panoply. You'll come here directly?'

'Yes. In the meantime, proceed with the trawl. But try and leave Garlin in a state where he can mumble a few answers. I'd still like a word or two.'

'Don't worry,' Aumonier said. 'I'd never deprive you of that satisfaction.'

Thalia knocked, waiting for someone to let her into the tactical room from within. After an interval Robert Tang opened the doors, staring at her wordlessly before swivelling on his neat polished heels to call out to the Supreme Prefect.

'It's Thalia Ng, ma'am. Should I let her in?'

Aumonier was standing next to the Solid Orrery, her hand on her chin, debating something with Baudry and Clearmountain. 'Is there any reason you wouldn't, Robert?'

'I wasn't sure if she was still running Pangolin clearance, ma'am.'

Aumonier turned around, giving Thalia a doubtful look. 'Did Doctor Demikhov give you permission to leave the clinic, Ng?'

'No, ma'am. I discharged myself.'

Aumonier's features sharpened. 'Was that wise?'

'Probably not, ma'am. My head's still throbbing. But I couldn't sit around being useless for any longer, especially after Prefect Bancal told me what he's doing. I realise I'm in no fit state to resume field duties . . .'

'No, the bandaged head doesn't exactly inspire confidence.'

'I thought I'd see if I could be of assistance. Either with Garlin or the Wildfire operation. My Pangolin boost still seems to be holding.'

'Go,' Aumonier said.

'Ma'am?'

'To the refectory. Fetch us all a dozen strong cups of coffee, freshly brewed. I can't abide the conjured stuff we get in here. When you're back, you can help Lillian and Gaston revise the forward planning for the next thirteen hours. A fresh pair of eyes might be beneficial. We're running into some . . . headwind.'

'Ma'am?'

'Coffee, Ng.'

She was back in ten minutes, but it might as well have been ten hours for the palpable shift in mood. If it had been tense before, now it was apocalyptic. All the prefects and analysts present were crowded around the Solid Orrery, the table abandoned, its updates scrolling past unnoticed.

285

The voices from the assembled staff were hushed but urgent, exchanges being delivered in rapid, clipped abbreviation. Thalia felt as if she had stumbled into the middle of some desperate, difficult surgical procedure that was going increasingly wrong.

'Re-evaluate, damn it,' Aumonier said.

'No improvement. Still holding at thirty.'

'What if we abandon—'

'Tried it. Makes no improvement.'

'Two new instances breaking. Revising to thirty-two as best-case.'

Thalia set down the tray of coffees on the main table, hardly daring to breathe, let alone speak. She straightened her uniform, trying to look presentable and engaged despite the bandage and her lingering feelings of fogginess.

Her throat felt tight.

'Ma'am?'

Aumonier carried on talking to her subordinates, trading one dire-sounding estimate after another. Thalia had enough of her wits to guess that the figures being bandied around were predictions for how many citizens would still succumb to Wildfire, even as the protection operation tried to get them into isolation. Clearly the figure had risen compared to the initial predictions. Which was bad, she thought – very bad. If they lost thirty or thirty-two, that was almost half as many people as had already died via Wildfire, but squeezed into a day or two rather than stretched out across four hundred days. Still, she told herself, trying to take the analytic view, they were trying to save more than one thousand seven hundred citizens, and even if they lost fifty that would still have to count as a triumph, not a failure . . .

Then she caught someone say 'per cent' and the shock of it was enough to have her reeling, steadying a hand on the edge of the table.

'Ma'am,' she said again. 'I brought the . . . did I understand it right, that we're looking at thirty per cent losses?'

'No,' Aumonier said, finally noticing her return. 'That was the good old days. Now we're facing thirty-two as an absolute best-case option, and almost total certainty that the figure will rise sharply.'

'It's a response, then,' Thalia said. 'Someone's reacting to our rescue initiative, raising the stakes. But we've got Garlin in detention, haven't we? He's supposed to be isolated from the outside world – just like those citizens.'

'He's screened,' Baudry said. 'Triple-layer Faraday isolation. Even if he has theoretical access to secret abstraction channels, they won't get through to him. He shouldn't be able to send or receive a single bit of information beyond those walls. He shouldn't even know about this operation, much less be able to adapt to it.'

'Dreyfus thinks there might be a latency,' Aumonier said. 'A delay between Garlin initiating a Wildfire event, and the death itself. That would explain a long tail of deaths after both Garlin and the victim have been isolated. But unless Garlin had extraordinary foresight, it's hard to see how he could have anticipated our plan. We should be witnessing a slowing fade-off, not a steepening pattern.'

'Could there be any way he's getting around that isolation?' Thalia asked. 'Some special implant or something, that cuts through the screening?'

She half expected to be mocked for the rank implausibility of this suggestion, but what was more disquieting was that Aumonier appeared to have already given it ample consideration.

'Demikhov says his implants aren't putting out any form of soft microwave radiation we wouldn't expect. Beyond that, he's taken the trouble to look for signals across the whole electromagnetic spectrum, as well as neutral particle emissions that might be slipping through our mesh. You can send and receive almost anything you want, if you have the right equipment and power supply. But there's a limit to what you can squeeze into a set of ordinary-looking implants, inside a human skull.'

'Then it isn't Garlin,' Thalia said. 'At least, he can't be responsible for what's happening right now, from hour to hour. There has to be an accomplice, doesn't there?'

'Constables have detained all known affiliates of his extended organisation,' Baudry commented, not dragging her eyes from the Solid Orrery. 'Common thugs and bully-boys, for the most part. They've been processed and isolated along with the citizens. A few fish might have slipped through the net, but . . .'

'Something's not right,' Thalia said.

'Thank you, Ng,' Aumonier replied. 'None of the rest of us were capable of that dazzling leap of insight.'

'I meant to say, ma'am . . .'

'Did you fetch the coffee?'

Thalia looked over her shoulder. 'Yes, it's on the table.'

'Good. Bring it over. Then see if you can help Gaston and Lillian dig us a way out of this mess. If we must lose a third of the people we're trying to save, I'll accept that if there's no other alternative. But my fear is it will only get much worse than this. And to top it all Dreyfus wants me to reallocate a whole corvette or cruiser . . .'

Thalia brought over the coffees. 'To do what, ma'am?'

'Dreyfus likes looking under rocks, Ng. You'll have learned that by now.' Aumonier took one of the coffees and drank it slowly, closing her eyes for a few seconds as if savouring the last rare pleasure of a lifetime. 'He wants to investigate something in the Glitter Band, connected to the Voi estate. I just wish his timing were a little better.'

Thalia looked to the Solid Orrery, scribbled over with orbits and trajectories.

'Some more citizens will end up dying, won't they, if you divert a ship?'

'Dreyfus knows that, too,' Aumonier answered, with grave resignation. 'I explained the situation to him, and he still made the request. And that was before things got really bad.'

'What are you going to do?'

'What else can I do, Ng? I'm giving him his damned ship.'

Aumonier had not been lying when she told Garlin it had been impossible to assemble a citizen quorum made up of people who lacked implants. Under better circumstances, perhaps, it might have been possible to scour the Glitter Band for the necessary deputation, and bring them all to Panoply in time to witness Garlin's soft interrogation. The emergency measures, her own concern for the citizens' safety, and the high demand on prefects and their vehicles, made that quite impractical now. But she had still been determined to abide by the Common Articles to the limit of her capabilities, and that meant that a citizen quorum had indeed been convened.

She went to see them now. They were in a wood-lined room which was smaller and brighter than the tactical room and furnished with a few minimalist ornaments to offset the austere claustrophobia of the windowless space.

The citizens were not happy. They had been unhappy from the moment they were deputised and assembled, not least because Aumonier had – until now, at least – felt obliged to disclose only the essential facts of the crisis.

'You're frustrated, and I understand that,' she said, addressing them from the concave side of a crescent-shaped table, the twelve members of the quorum facing her in an almost semicircular arc. 'But there have been aspects of this crisis which, for reasons of security and intelligence, I have felt it unwise to share with you. I hope you will accept that none of my decisions have been taken lightly. No one is more concerned with Panoply's ethical transparency than I am. But we have also been dealing with a matter that impinges on some of the oldest and most trusted institutions of our entire circum-planetary society. Reputations don't matter to me.

288

If someone violates the law, no matter how elevated their standing, no matter how sacred their family name, I will act without compunction. But I do have a responsibility not to cause the wider citizenry unnecessary distress or anxiety.' She tapped a nail against the table. '*That* is also enshrined in our charter. The Common Articles require that Panoply conduct its business with the minimum intrusion into the ordinary lives of our hundred million citizens. Engendering fear and panic would be counter to my mandate – a reckless and irresponsible abdication of my duties.' She settled her hands together, blinking some focus into her eyes, grateful for the energy spike that had been provided by Ng's coffee. 'But now we are at a crux. I must be frank with you. We were dealing with an emergency, but we believed we had a strategy in place for resolving the situation with only a fractional loss of human life – a few citizens, compared to the one thousand seven hundred we expected to save.' She glanced down. 'I was wrong. Our control is slipping. For reasons we don't yet understand, something – someone – is circumventing our rescue operation. We are now seeing an active, escalating response.'

'You have your suspect, Supreme Prefect,' said the woman sitting directly opposite her. 'That's what you've been assuring us, from the moment we were convened. That this prominent public figure, this man who has been openly critical of you and your organisation, is also behind an epidemic of unexplained deaths. Are you now telling us you might have the wrong individual?'

'I still have grounds to suspect culpability,' Aumonier said. 'The evidence trail is too clear to ignore. But the latest developments indicate that Devon Garlin cannot be acting alone.'

'This evidence trail you'll barely discuss,' said another citizen. 'These deaths we're barely allowed to ask about. And now this unprecedented interference in the freedoms of the entire population, justified by little more than rumour and half-truths.'

'You'll need to excuse us for drawing the obvious conclusion,' said a third speaker, softening his remarks with a sympathetic smile. 'Panoply has every reason to feel threatened by Devon Garlin and his breakaway movement. Shallow populism it may be, but it's hitting you where it hurts. Your job would be a lot more straightforward if Garlin and his ilk disappeared, would it not?'

'I won't lie,' Aumonier said.

'You'd better not,' said the first woman.

'I detest him. If I had the moral and legal means to make him go away for ever, I'd have done so long ago. But he's also one of us – a free citizen of the Glitter Band, to whom I owe a duty of protection. That's why Prefect Ng was prepared to lay down her life for him.'

'Exaggeration,' someone muttered.

Aumonier kept her voice level, refusing to be baited. 'I wish it were so. Ng nearly died. She suffered a skull fracture and ought now to be recuperating under close medical observation. But she isn't. She's in the tactical room, barely able to stand, in obvious discomfort, and yet still trying to save some lives. Ng's one of us as well, you see. She won't rest while she knows that there's an existential threat to the Glitter Band. And while she has no more love for Devon Garlin than I do, she'd have given her life to execute her duty of care to a fellow citizen.'

'Fine words—' someone else began.

'They're more than words, Citizen,' Aumonier answered, still fighting back the tide of rage and self-justification which she felt rising inside herself. 'They're all that we live for. We've sacrificed our lives for the sake of a promise. Invest your trust in us, and you'll sleep well in your beds. We'll keep the monsters from your windows. We'll let you have your easy dreams. And while a single one of us still breathes, you'll know there's still someone willing to make that final stand. Still someone guarding the gates of utopia.' She paused, gathered her breath, stared at her fingers before continuing, certain that if she had not already made her point, no further persuasion would make any difference. 'I need to trawl Devon Garlin. I have my reasons. I need to establish the exact degree of his knowledge and involvement in our present crisis, and I need to establish it quickly.'

'Then . . . let us see him,' said the sympathetic man. 'Let us see him, and speak to him, reason with him if at all possible. Perhaps in the face of a citizen quorum he will see sense . . .'

'He won't,' Aumonier said wearily. 'We've spoken to him at length. Studied his reactions. Body language, subliminal cues. These are expert analysts and prefects, trained in non-coercive intelligence-gathering. And they might as well have been speaking to a blank wall, for all they've got out of him. Besides, I can't let you near him.'

'For these vague reasons—' started the first woman.

There was a knock at the door. Aumonier thanked her stars; the timing could not have been better. She craned round in time to see Doctor Demikhov coming through into the room, propelling a trolley before him. The trolley contained a number of bulky, upright items shrouded under a green cloth.

'I've tried to spare you this,' Aumonier said, returning her attention to the quorum. 'But in truth, you do deserve to know the full facts of our case. Devon Garlin has some impressive capabilities. We're certain of that, and equally certain that these powers stem from his implants. He's able to bypass the normal limits of data exchange, gathering knowledge far beyond his expected means. He's been able to outflank us, anticipating our movements, our intentions. That in itself would make him a serious threat to public security. His powers undermine our confidence in everything from abstraction to the inviolability of the polling cores. If he was able to get into your heads – and that wouldn't be a problem for him, if you were near enough to see and talk to him – he'd be able to access your Voi kernels, enabling him to corrupt or bias the voting process at any level, as well as – quite feasibly – manipulating your very perceptions of reality. He could adjust your reactions, your responses, to suit his immediate needs.' Aumonier looked around, satisfied that this disclosure, risky as it had been, had gone some way to making her case. But she was not done. 'It wouldn't stop there, though. Doctor Demikhov – would you oblige?'

'Are they ready, ma'am?'

'I doubt that they'd ever be ready, Doctor. Do it all the same.'

He whisked aside the green cloth with a magicianly flourish, taking a brisk step backwards in the process. Aumonier had steeled herself – indeed, it had been her suggestion in the first place – but the sight of eight severed human heads could hardly fail to be upsetting, especially as those bottled heads were all facing in the same direction, with their eyes open, their mouths slightly parted, as if no less startled by the audience facing them.

There was a shocked silence. Aumonier regarded the quorum, content to let one of them speak.

'If this crude and provocative stunt—' began the woman facing her.

'There was no call for this,' said another. 'We were perfectly capable of listening to reasoned persuasion, without this base appeal to tawdry emotion.'

'Do you think about death very often?' Aumonier asked, sweeping her gaze from left to right, taking in all twelve members of the quorum. 'I doubt that you do, any more than these eight people did. You're all able and in full possession of your faculties, or you wouldn't have been selected for this role. Provided you make some intelligent choices, most of you can expect at least another hundred years of life, perhaps more. And who knows what might come along in that interval? These eight people were no different. They were going about their daily lives, utterly unaware that something was about to go very wrong inside their heads. It would have begun without warning, almost innocuously. A breakdown of normal implant functionality, preventing their usual interaction with quickmatter, plumage, the polling cores. They'd have tried to report the breakdown, but the notification channels would have stopped working. Quickly, things would have worsened. The malfunctioning implants would have begun to exert a chaotic influence on their brain function. The victim would have fallen into a hysterical, panicked spiral of lessening self-control, even as they tried to seek help. Think of them stumbling into some public arena, seemingly drunk or confused – reaching out in desperation. Then begins the discomfort, as a growing thermal overload starts to damage tissue and turn water into steam, creating a pressure build-up, literally cooking the brain from within. Think of the worst headache you've experienced, then imagine it doubling in intensity from minute to minute, pressing against the backs of your eyes, squeezing the auditory nerves, causing terrible hallucinations. But by then you hardly care. You're dying, and on some primal level you realise as much, and there's nothing that anyone around you can do to help. Not even us. Even if by some miracle we're able to get there while the victim's still alive, there's nothing we can do for them except preserve the evidence as best we can. That's all we've ever managed. And this has happened over and over, more than sixty times before we initiated the rescue operation, and each of these victims has a direct link to the clinical facility operated at the convenience of the Voi family. Devon Garlin put time bombs into the heads of two thousand citizens, laying the groundwork for a crisis that he knew would put us to a severe test, exposing our limitations for all to see. He murdered these people, and there are still many, many more who are in immediate danger of the same fate. He can still reach them, even now – and if it isn't him acting directly, then we need to locate and isolate his accomplice. Not in days, but in hours.'

'Forgive me, Supreme Prefect,' said the reasonable man. 'You make a persuasive case with these poor people. But none of us have ever visited this clinic of which you speak. I cannot therefore envisage any great risk in our contact with Devon Garlin.'

'Nor can I,' Aumonier said, drawing a sharp surprised look from the man. 'But equally, I can't rule it out. Simply put, Devon Garlin's capabilities are beyond our present understanding. For all we know, any close contact with him could expose you to danger. Until I know his exact relationship to this ongoing crisis, I can't guarantee your safety – and that is paramount.'

'My fellow citizens and I might be moved to grant reluctant consent to trawl,' said the first woman, glancing at the others for expressions of assent. 'But only after the usual precautions have been taken. His implants must be removed or protected against—'

'There isn't time,' Aumonier said. 'Not for him, not for the people already dying while supposedly in our care. I don't have thirteen hours or twenty-six or however long it would take to satisfy you that Devon Garlin won't be harmed by the trawl. It must be done now. All I can offer are my assurances that we'll proceed as quickly and cleanly as possible.'

'If I know anything about trawling,' said the reasonable man, 'you'll be exposing him to a milder case of the experience these people went through.'

'It won't be pleasant,' Aumonier replied. 'I'd be lying if I said otherwise. But we'll stop long before there's any chance of permanent neurological damage. He won't die, and he won't have much to remember the experience by. But we'll have gained intelligence we couldn't have obtained by other means. I must have this assent, citizens. There are people dying now that we can't help. This is our last and best chance to find a solution.'

'Would you leave us for a moment, Supreme Prefect?' asked the first woman. 'And please – take those heads with you.'

Sparver was halfway back to Panoply when the re-routing order came in. He accepted it without question, assuming – as he had done on the four or five previous occasions – that there had been a recalculation in rescue priorities, his services suddenly needed in one place rather than another.

'Complying,' he said, barely registering that the new destination was a Panoply ship, not Panoply itself or another civilian habitat. But even had he paid heed to that, he would have reasoned that the brains in the tactical room had a sound reason for the rendezvous; that the ship was urgently needed elsewhere, perhaps, and someone or something on board it needed to be ferried to another destination, and he was the designated courier.

He had locked in his new course, and was debating whether to try to grab a few minutes' sleep on the way, when the Supreme Prefect called through directly.

'Prefect Bancal?'

'Ma'am.'

'I'm relieving you of the rescue operation. You've done very well so far, and I've no doubt of your continued dedication to the cause – even though I've asked far too much of you already.'

Sparver pushed aside his half-formed fantasies of rest. 'It's all right, ma'am. I'll sleep when we're done. And we are going to be done, aren't we? It's just that I keep seeing reports of new victims . . .'

'The picture is complex and changing, Bancal. Our initial assumption, that it would be sufficient to move these citizens into isolation . . . appears to be flawed. At the moment the only sure-fire remedy is complete removal of all implants, but we simply don't have the means to process the citizens quickly enough. And our death toll is rising. We've had five confirmed cases in the last sixty minutes, and indications that the curve is steepening further still. Even with the optimum utilisation of our assets, we now expect to lose thirty-four . . . no, thirty-five per cent of those we were hoping to save.' He heard her mouth a near-silent and highly uncharacteristic oath. 'The estimates are climbing almost as I speak, Bancal.'

'Then the last thing you should be doing is pulling me from the operation.' Sparver reviewed his statement, decided it was somewhat lacking in the necessary formalities, and added: 'With all due respect, ma'am.'

'It's all right, Bancal. You and I know each other well enough by now. The truth is we're losing the race so badly that an asset here or an asset there isn't going to make much difference. That's why I'm taking perhaps the biggest risk of my career, and reassigning both you and an entire Deep System Vehicle to a parallel operation. You'll take immediate command of its operations.'

'That's . . . begging your pardon, ma'am. Are we sure about this?'

'Dreyfus requested that I re-task the ship. Does that go some way to sugaring the pill?'

'I suppose it does, but . . . what would he want with a ship like that? We're trying to move people around, not blow them out of the sky.'

'Dreyfus is on his way back to Panoply. In the meantime he's asked that I send a ship to investigate a long-standing Voi asset in the Glitter Band. It's a lump of rock called Lethe. No, I doubt that it means very much to either of us. And frankly I ought not to be distracted, especially when Dreyfus has a proven grudge against the Voi family. But he has his hunches, and on the few occasions when he's asked me to place my faith in them . . .'

'What are we expecting to find in this rock, ma'am?'

'I can't say, just yet. I don't doubt that Dreyfus will oblige us with an explanation when it suits him.'

'It'll cost lives. But then he knows that.'

'He wouldn't make such a request lightly. And this is a parallel operation, but we must presume it's connected to our larger emergency. You'll take the cruiser, investigate the rock at your own discretion, and report back. If there's nothing of interest, we'll consider this line of enquiry closed.'

'If you think it worthwhile, ma'am.'

'I do, Bancal. There's one other thing – a minor technicality. No prefect below Field Three has ever been assigned control of a Deep System Cruiser before. I don't propose to undo that tradition today.'

'Then you have a difficulty, ma'am.'

'I don't think so, Bancal. We'll complete the formalities when the dust has settled. But consider yourself promoted as of immediate and binding effect. Let's not make this one temporary, shall we?'

The Deep System Cruiser *Democratic Circus* was ninety metres long, sleekly finned and bladed, all sadistic edges and barbs, like some hard-forged instrument of war that was meant to do as much damage being yanked out of a victim as it was being shoved in. The design considerations were entirely deliberate: this was the physical expression of Panoply's authority, a forceful reminder that – while rarely exercised – its powers could and did extend to the complete destruction of entire habitats.

Sparver docked at its ventral lock, exited his cutter, then sent it away on autopilot, so it could be utilised by some other prefect as part of the rescue operation.

Even a Field Three – however long in that rank – lacked the expertise to pilot such a complex and powerful craft as the *Democratic Circus*. All DSC/HEVs retained dedicated operational crews, Panoply operatives of supernumerary status. The normal complement was three: a captain-pilot, an auxiliary systems specialist and a weapons master, with some functional overlap between the roles. Accompanying this operational crew might be additional specialist staff, and depending on the mission requirements, anything up to fifty prefects and their enforcement equipment.

They were nowhere near that loading today. There simply weren't enough prefects to go around, and since the *Democratic Circus* had been functioning largely as a high-capacity taxi, there had been no need for more than a skeleton staff.

Captain Pell welcomed Sparver aboard, offering him a firm handshake and an immediate offer of coffee. The whiskered Pell was a veteran of several crises, with a reputation for steadiness under pressure. Sparver and Dreyfus had worked with Pell during the Aurora emergency, and there was a mutual respect between the captain and the hyperpig.

'The ship's at your disposal, Field Bancal. We're pretty much in the dark about this reassignment, though.'

'If it's any consolation they haven't told me much either,' Sparver said, glugging down the bulb of coffee in one hit. 'I'd like you to lock in a high-speed crossing to an object called Lethe. We'll make a normal approach and stand-off just beyond the anti-collision volume.'

'Are we likely to expect trouble, sir?'

'Your guess is as good as mine, Captain Pell.' Sparver gave the man an encouraging pat on the shoulders. 'But I'd stand ready to pop out those guns.'

Pell took Sparver forward to the command deck, where the two other supernumerary operatives sat visored and gloved in acceleration couches. 'This is Prefect Bancal. Prefect, these are operatives Grolnick and Dias,' Pell said, introducing the young woman and man wearing the visors. 'We're going to be taking a quick look-see at an object called Lethe.' Pell eased into his own seat and began conjuring navigation facets and tactile input surfaces, his hands and fingers moving with the effortless speed and precision of a master musician. 'Minimum crossing time, military power, and an attack-readiness posture on final approach. Mister Dias: would you go back and instruct the prefects to secure for imminent gee loads?'

'A question,' Sparver said. 'How many are we carrying?'

'Four fields, plus tactical armour and dual whiphounds. No sidearms, though. We don't have dispensation, and even if it came in now we'd have to run back to Panoply to re-equip.'

'Then let's hope we don't run into anything problematic,' Sparver said.

The field trawl was an upright contraption mounted onto a horseshoe-shaped base, equipped with a swooping neck and a dome-shaped scanning helmet. Aumonier stepped aside as the technicians wheeled the cumbersome object along the bridge that led to the isolation cube.

'And you can guarantee me he won't be able to use this thing as a means to reach beyond Panoply?' Aumonier asked Tang.

'I can't make any such assurances, ma'am,' Tang replied, with the understandable annoyance of someone who had been asked a similar question at least half a dozen times in the last half-hour. 'If the trawl can read Garlin, then there's at least a chance that Garlin can push back. We've done what we can, though. If you were prepared to lower Garlin into a subconscious or semi-conscious state during the trawl . . .'

'I need him awake and receptive,' Aumonier said. She gestured with the folder clamped between her fingers. 'Wheel it through. The sooner we're done with this the better.'

Tang and the technicians propelled the trawl into the observation area of the triple-lined cube. Aumonier signalled for the bridge to be retracted. The trawl team began to power up their machine, studying a stream of data and graphics on a built-in screen with a privacy hood.

Aumonier opened the partition door and went into Garlin's interrogation area. He was still sitting with his arms resting on the table, staring up at her with a blunt, unyielding defiance.

'This has gone beyond an infringement of my basic rights. You'll be facing an interrogation of your own before long, Supreme Prefect.'

'I've addressed the citizen quorum,' Aumonier said, placing the folder on the table and slipping into one of the two chairs facing Garlin. 'They had grounds for concern over the conditions of your detention, and my refusal to allow them physical access.'

'Then you admit you've crossed a line.'

'I admit I've been forced into unusual measures. I was still able to persuade them that my position had merit. More than that, I was able to obtain permission to trawl you.'

'Trawl as much as you like. You'll find you've been persecuting an innocent man. Of course, I don't doubt that you'll bury that evidence, and then concoct something that incriminates me . . .'

'I'm not in the business of concocting, Mister Garlin.' She turned around, nodded to the mirrored window.

The trawl team wheeled the apparatus into the room. The humming machine gave off a faint tang of ozone.

'Wait,' Garlin said, his façade beginning to crack. 'It doesn't work like this. You don't just put someone's head in that thing. They have to be prepared . . . their implants taken out, drugs administered . . .'

'That's normally the way,' Aumonier agreed, as the technicians eased the trawl into position, the two prongs of its base fitting either side of his chair. 'And for good reason. Inductive heating can do a lot of damage. But then you'd know all about that sort of thing, wouldn't you?'

'You can't do this to me.'

'You've put me in this invidious position, Mister Garlin. I'm not digging for deep memories here, so we don't have to go in at high-resolution. But I do need you to be fully conscious.' She lifted her head to the analysts. 'Strap him down.'

Garlin resisted, but she had expected as much and couldn't swear that she would have been any more submissive in the same circumstances. Restraints were applied at his cuffs and elbows, and then the dome-shaped scanner was lowered down until it reached the level of his eyes.

'Ready when you are,' Tang said.

'Commence initial read.'

The trawl's hum intensified. Garlin tensed, his hands stiffening on the armrests.

'Sub-cranial,' Tang reported, his eyes to the hooded screen. 'Resolving bulk cortical structure.'

'Stop now,' Garlin said.

'Vocalisation will only confuse the read,' Aumonier said gently. 'Better for you, and better for us, if you refrain from any utterances. We'll be done much faster that way.' Carefully she opened the folder and slid out one of its chemically printed images, face down.

'You showed me the people already,' Garlin said.

'It's not the faces I'm most interested in now. I don't know how much contact you ever had with those victims. Perhaps you were always at one remove from them, even when you were operating the clinic.'

'The what?'

'Bloodflow normal. Synaptic firing strength normal. Resolving functional neural modules.'

Aumonier flipped the image and presented it to Garlin, giving him no chance to avert his vision. It was a picture of Elysium Heights, captured by the Heavy Technical Squad only a couple of days earlier. She held the image for a few more seconds, studying his reactions, then placed it face down on the table and selected another from the folder. It was another recent view of the clinic, taken from a fresh angle and under different lighting conditions.

'Is this supposed to mean something?' Garlin asked, still tense but fully able to speak.

'I'm establishing your visual familiarity with this structure, Mister Garlin.'

'I've never seen it before.'

Aumonier offered a third view, this one a still frame from the thirty-five-second video fragment, showing the elevated view of the main lobby. 'It doesn't matter how you answer me. You may even think you don't recognise this place. That's entirely possible. Memories can be suppressed, deliberately or otherwise. Some of the targeted amnesia therapies are extremely effective, so I've heard. But the trawl sees beyond conscious recall. There'll be traces lodged in your long-term memory.'

'I think I'd know.'

Aumonier presented the fourth and fifth images. They were further stills from the video, showing deeper areas of the clinic: waiting rooms, friendly staff, gleaming equipment.

'Don't glance away, Mister Garlin. If you resist the recognition test, I'll just end up clamping open your eyelids.'

She carried on with more images. By the eighth, she risked a glance at Tang, hoping for the clear signal he was meant to send if the trawl was picking up unambiguous evidence of deep-learned recognition. But Tang's face was pensive, his frown deepening.

Aumonier had been warned they might not pick anything up at the low settings. To be sure of a result – even a null result – they would have

298

to push deeper into the brain structure, at a more fine-grained resolution setting. That would mean a higher risk of induced damage.

She looked to her colleague.

'Crank it up a little, Mister Tang.'

Tang did as he was instructed. The humming grew more intense. Garlin clenched his hands on the seat rest, his jaw straining, the tendons in his neck beginning to stand out.

'Stop,' he said, but with difficulty this time.

'Work with me, Mister Garlin,' Aumonier answered, selecting another tranche of images, more pictures of the Wildfire victims. Perhaps he had never met any of them in person, but she would be a fool to pass up this chance to test him. She turned over the images one at a time, presenting the faces to the man under the trawl.

By now Tang was giving her a tiny twitch of his head, signalling 'no' for each instance.

Aumonier had dropped three control images into the list of faces. One was Sister Catherine of the Ice Mendicants, but presented in civilian garb. The second was Constable Malkmus, again in full civilian clothing, and the third a randomly selected citizen known to have been present and visible during one of Garlin's recent rallies.

Aumonier interspersed these controls with more images of the Wildfire cases, including some of the citizens who had not yet succumbed. Tang found no clear traces of recognition, except when the controls were tested. Then he nodded at Aumonier, seemingly pleased that at last a result had been obtained. But she had deliberately not mentioned the control images to Tang.

'Go deeper,' she told him.

'He'll feel it,' Tang replied quietly.

'Go deeper.'

Tang nodded peremptorily. 'Increasing resolution. Inductance effects now exceeding safe threshold.'

The trawl increased its humming. Garlin jolted in his restraints, his spine flexing. He let out a grunt of discomfort or shock, his nostrils flaring, his eyes still wide and alert as they met Aumonier's. Something twitched in his cheek. A sweat bead ran down the side of his face. His breathing hastened to sharp, sawlike inhalations.

Aumonier turned over a fresh image of Elysium Heights, presented it to the subject.

'Maybe you can fool the machine, Garlin, but not me. You've got a breaking point. It's just a question of finding it.'

He straightened his jaw, made a strained guttural sound that only bore a distant, debased relationship to language. Aumonier had to struggle to assemble the noises into words.

'Never . . . liked you. But thought . . . you were better . . . than this.'

Still Tang was reporting an absence of recognition. She worked through some more pictures of the clinic, Garlin juddering now, a seizure-like tremor in his muscle tone. Tang was right to warn her that they had crossed the safe threshold. But there were margins of error. The trawl could be continued at this level for some while without risk of irreversible damage.

But not indefinitely.

She turned over another image. According to the label it was an interior shot, the inside of one of the elevators in the main lobby, with the clinic's stylised motif of a lone white tree.

Tang glanced at her.

Recognition – a flicker of it at least.

Sensing she was making progress, Aumonier moved to her trump card. It was a still frame of Doctor Julius Mazarin.

'This man, Garlin. Do you see anything in his face that might ring a bell?'

'I . . . don't know who that . . . man is.'

'Take a closer look,' Aumonier said.

'You think it's me. It isn't me.' Garlin made a choking sound, forced out the rest of his words. 'Not me. Someone else. Look at—'

'Go deeper,' Aumonier said.

CHAPTER SEVENTEEN

Sparver would have welcomed time to gather his thoughts ahead of their arrival at Lethe, but the *Democratic Circus* had only needed thirty minutes to complete its rapid dash through the Glitter Band, all civilian and non-emergency traffic re-routed to allow the heavy ship unrestricted passage. Sparver had spent most of the time back with the four prefects, giving them as much of a briefing as he felt able to.

He leaned on a bulkhead, bracing himself as the cruiser commenced its bruising deceleration burn.

'All I can tell you is that this came down from Lady Jane, and she's acting on credible intelligence supplied by Tom Dreyfus. There's a piece of rock that might relate to the Wildfire emergency. You've all got Pangolin clearance so I can tell you that this object belongs to the Voi family, and that fact alone ties it to Devon Garlin, presently a guest of ours. You can see what a powder keg this could be if it isn't handled properly.'

'Is this going to turn into an enforcement action, Prefect Bancal?' asked the most senior of the four, a Field Prefect named Dalia Perec. Like the others she was wearing full tactical vacuum armour, buckled into deceleration webbing, only her visor yet to be snapped down. Her name was stencilled onto the black skin of her suit, but Sparver knew her well enough from routine work in Panoply. She had fine angular eyebrows and very pale green eyes, surprisingly expressive for a baseline human.

'Depends if we find anyone who needs enforcing, Dalia. Most likely there'll be nothing there but dirt and stale air.'

'But if we did run into trouble . . .' She made an open gesture with her palms. 'We weren't expecting to need sidearms on this operation, Prefect Bancal.'

'And we might not have got them even if we'd asked, Dalia. But we've got the weapons on this ship, if anyone feels like proving a point.'

'If there's something we can stick to the Vois, I'm happy going in there naked,' said the prefect jammed in next to Dalia Perec. 'Just give me a whiphound.'

301

'We might not be going in at all,' Sparver told the eager young Field One, a recent promotion from Deputy Three by the name of Kober. 'If the rock checks out, we'll be back on rescue duty without ever touching vacuum.'

'Is it true, sir, about Prefect Dreyfus?'

Sparver turned to the questioner. It was the prefect sitting opposite Perec, on the other side of the cruiser's aisle. 'What did you hear, Prefect Singh?' he asked, reading the name stencil.

'Only that it's personal between Garlin and Dreyfus . . . I mean Prefect Dreyfus, sir.'

Sparver tightened his grip on the bulkhead as the cruiser made a sharp course adjustment. He guessed they must be on the final approach, nosing up to the rock's legally designated anti-collision volume. 'Garlin made it personal. But all Dreyfus has ever done is execute his duty according to the rulebook. He didn't go looking for this connection to the Voi family – it dropped into his hands.' Sparver studied the expressions – Perec, Kober, Singh and the fourth of them, Gurney – deciding that their reactions all fitted somewhere on the spectrum between doubtful and sceptical. 'All right, I'm going forward to talk to Captain Pell. Maintain readiness.'

The ship had become weightless by the time he pushed back into the command deck. Pell, Dias and Grolnick were whispering observations to each other, so quietly that it almost seemed there might be a risk of their words carrying across vacuum.

A large area of the forward part of the flight deck had turned transparent, affording an excellent view of the nearby Lethe. It was an unremarkable-looking lump of cratered rock, muddy ochre in colour, fifteen kilometres across at its widest point, and about seven at its narrowest. It tumbled slowly, the elongated poles cartwheeling around once every three minutes. Beyond it oozed a moving river of more distant rocks and habitats, and beyond that the half-shadowed face of Yellowstone.

Sparver studied the rock wordlessly.

'We're standing off at seventy-five point five kilometres,' Pell said. 'Just outside the nominal anti-collision threshold. So far we haven't been scanned or signalled.'

'Do you have any readings on the rock?'

'Orbit's regular, the spin stable.' Pell enlarged a schematic for Sparver's benefit. 'The surface is plastic-sheathed rock, for the most part. A scattering of docking points, airlocks and routine communications equipment: ownership beacons, transponders, and so on. Nothing you won't find on a few hundred similar boulders.'

'Then it's just a dead lump of rock with some flags stuck into it?'

'A bit more than flags,' Grolnick commented. 'There's a thermal excess, more than you'd expect if there was nothing going on inside it. House-keeping systems of some kind, buried under the visible crust.'

'Something must feed power to those transponders,' Dias said. 'And correct the drift if the orbit starts deviating. But it's not a large signature.'

'Can you localise it?' Sparver asked.

'Closer to one of those poles than the other,' Pell said, pointing to a pink smudge on one of the readouts. 'Beyond that, we're a little too far out for a detailed sub-surface scan.'

Sparver rubbed his chin, debating whether or not to report back to Panoply before taking further action. On balance, he decided that Jane Aumonier probably had enough on her plate for the time being.

'Take us in, Captain – not too fast, not too slow. And go to maximum weapons readiness.'

Pell applied thrust again. The cruiser edged forward and an automated voice warned them that they were about to cross the anti-collision threshold.

'We've been painted,' Pell said, noting that a proximity radar had picked up the cruiser.

'Nothing out of the ordinary about that,' Sparver said, but not without a certain skin-crawling prickle of anticipation, the way one felt sticking one's hand into a dark sealed box. 'Keep taking us in. At the very least I'd like a better idea of what's putting out that heat signature.'

'Holding at one hundred metres per second and transmitting continu-ous approach requests,' Pell answered.

'Weapon ports cleared for immediate dilation,' Grolnick reported. 'Warheads dialled to standard yield. RD racks showing green on all boards. Solutions locked in for a target spread. Shall I assign fire control to autonomic?'

'Hold on manual for now,' Pell said, still sounding as ice-cool as ever. 'Agreed, Prefect?'

Sparver nodded his assent, seeing no reason to risk an over-reaction. 'Take defensive action as required. But we don't start shooting until Lady Jane pulls the trigger.'

'Ma'am,' Thalia said, turning from the Solid Orrery. 'You ought to see this. If it's half as bad as it's looking . . .'

Lillian Baudry had been pulled back to the main table, putting out one or more fires only peripherally related to the ongoing effort. Citizen dis-turbances were cropping up all over the Glitter Band, sometimes beyond the ability of the constables to contain and pacify. With great reluctance, Panoply was still having to divert some of its prefects to deal with these panicked outbreaks, further hampering the Wildfire operation.

'Yes, Ng,' Baudry answered testily, barely glancing up from the scrolling reports on the table. 'We know that things are difficult. Dwelling on it won't make it any better. Your job is to optimise our response, not to . . .' Baudry trailed off, her brittle attention finally settling on the Solid Orrery. 'No. That can't be real.'

'I think it is, ma'am. The threshold triggers are only getting more reliable, not less, as we gain more cases.'

Baudry turned to Clearmountain, who was equally deep in concentration, leaning over a spread of compads with Claudette Saint-Croix and Ingvar Tench. 'Gaston. Drop what you're doing.'

'I'd like to, Lillian, but—' He fell silent, taking in the changing status of the Solid Orrery. Then he pushed himself up from the table, even that simple action seeming to be a triumph of supreme will over fatigue. Silently he walked over to join Thalia and Baudry by the Solid Orrery.

'Ng says they won't be false triggers,' Baudry stated, in a low, reverent voice.

'We thought five cases per hour was bad,' Thalia said.

Across the Solid Orrery, red status call-outs were popping into life like the first new blooms of spring. Each signified a probable instance of Wildfire, either in a citizen yet to be reached or in someone already within protective custody.

'Summary, Ng. You were monitoring,' Clearmountain said.

'The curve's been steepening for days,' Thalia said, fighting to organise her thoughts despite the light-headedness she still felt after her concussion. 'But at least we had a handle on that. We knew it was going to be bad, but even our worst projections said we'd be able to save more than half of the afflicted citizens. Somewhere in the last ten minutes, though, it's gone through the roof. I'm estimating one new instance every sixty seconds.'

'This is . . . impossible,' Baudry said.

'We're tracking it, ma'am,' Thalia answered. 'It's real.'

'I know it's real, damn it. I'm just saying this doesn't fit with any of our existing theories. It can't be a latency.'

'Not now,' Clearmountain agreed.

Baudry turned to one of the harried-looking analysts. 'Call the Supreme Prefect. She needs to be aware of this shift.'

'She's with Garlin,' Clearmountain said. 'Running a trawl. Maybe not a coincidence.'

'You think the trawl's allowing him to steepen the death curve?' Baudry asked.

'Theoretically . . . no.' Clearmountain scratched at the day-old stubble bristling against his collar. 'But this is unequivocal. We've missed something. Given him a channel, a means to send signals to their implants.'

'Maybe it's not what it seems,' Thalia ventured.

'I'd say there wasn't much room for misinterpreting *that*,' Baudry answered, as another red flag popped into existence.

'I mean, maybe we're looking at it from the wrong angle, ma'am.' Thalia swallowed hard. 'We've taken all necessary measures with Garlin, haven't we? Isolated him, and done the same thing to hundreds of the citizens. And yet something is still getting through to their Voi kernels. A signal where a signal shouldn't be possible. So I'm thinking, maybe there *isn't* a signal.'

'We're back to the idea of a latency, then,' Clearmountain said, tolerating her outspokenness for the time being. 'But this new cluster proves—'

'I don't believe in the latency theory either, sir. But I do believe in physics. Unless Garlin's walking around with a neutrino transmitter in his skull, there's no way for him to be able to send any sort of signal through to those people, whether or not he has access to private abstraction channels.'

'You're being needlessly oblique, Ng,' Baudry said.

'What I mean is, ma'am, we might have made a mistake by locking him away. I keep thinking back to Terzet Friller, the worker who died in a vacuum suit.'

'What about Friller?' Baudry asked sharply.

'The other workers told us there was an intermittent fault with the communications in Friller's suit. That nagged at me, so Sparver helped me access the case file to make sure I wasn't misremembering.'

'You were meant to be resting, Ng.'

'I knew I was onto something, ma'am. Friller was out of contact with the other workers when Wildfire kicked in. It didn't happen until Friller's suit went off-line for an extended period of time, screening out any chance of an abstraction signal getting through. That made me wonder if we'd got the cause of Wildfire the wrong way around. It's not due to a triggering signal reaching those implants, it's due to a safeguarding signal not getting through.'

'None of the other victims were wearing spacesuits, Ng,' Clearmountain said.

'I know, sir, and I've thought about that as well. It doesn't rule out my idea. It just means that Friller might have died ahead of schedule.

I think the safeguarding signals were deliberately withheld from the others, but Friller jumped the queue by accidentally isolating themself from abstraction.'

'The clinic ceased operation more than twenty years ago,' Clearmountain said. 'That would mean Garlin's been actively suppressing these Wildfire cases . . . all two thousand of them . . . until a little over four hundred days ago?'

'I know it sounds difficult to accept, sir. But it would explain why the cases are rocketing now. He can't get those suppressing signals out.'

Lillian Baudry made to issue a flip answer, but something checked her response. She creased her lips, some desperate, weary calculation going on behind her eyes.

'You think there's something in it?' Clearmountain asked.

'I don't know. It doesn't quite fit the timeline. We've had him in that isolation cell for hours, and yet that new spate of deaths only started showing up a few minutes ago. I also wonder why Garlin didn't use this as a bargaining chip, if he knew we'd be cutting off the suppressing signals. But damn it all, she's right to voice her theory. It's an angle we hadn't considered.' Baudry's expression hardened. 'I don't like it, either. How can we squeeze Garlin, if we need him to keep sending out those signals?'

'We can't,' Thalia said. 'Can't kill him, can't risk making him unconscious, can't risk trawling him, can't even isolate him from abstraction.'

'It's too soon to act on a doubtful hypothesis,' Clearmountain said.

By then another red flag hag appeared on the Solid Orrery. 'Then what?' Baudry asked, with a terrible apprehension in her voice.

'I don't know,' Clearmountain whispered, as if that admission was a confession of the utmost shamefulness.

A draught played across the back of Thalia's neck. She turned around in time to see Jane Aumonier coming through the main doors, accompanied by Robert Tang and a couple of supernumerary analysts. Aumonier had the stricken look of someone who had just had the last of their certainties shot out from under them.

She strode to the Solid Orrery, snapped her eyes to it, nodded once. It was clear to Thalia that she had been briefed on her way from the interrogation room.

'When did this uptick start?'

'About thirteen minutes ago, ma'am,' Thalia said.

'And you didn't think to inform me until now?'

'I wanted to be sure it wasn't random clustering,' Thalia said, refusing to be cowed. 'You wouldn't have appreciated being dragged up here for a spurious pattern.' She ran her tongue along the back of her teeth. 'Ma'am.'

Aumonier turned to Clearmountain. 'Bancal should be approaching Lethe around now. Do we have a report?'

'Negative,' Clearmountain said, conjuring an enlargement of the relevant area of the Glitter Band. 'But we still have a hard fix on the cruiser's location, and no reports of anything adverse.'

'I'd call this adverse,' Aumonier muttered, taking away from Clearmountain's conjuring, swelling Lethe and its surrounding volume to the size of a watermelon, with the cruiser as a tiny pulsing speck off to one side of the slow-tumbling object. 'They've entered the anti-collision volume.' She nodded at one of the analysts. 'Get me Bancal. Immediately.'

'Just a moment, ma'am.' The analyst held up a compad, Sparver's face looming large, backdropped by a sweep of controls and readouts.

'Bancal,' Aumonier said. 'We have a development. Confirm that you are now inside Lethe's anti-collision volume.'

'Well into it, ma'am. We're getting near enough to investigate a power source under one of the poles. Captain Pell says we can drop some forensic packages once we're a little closer.'

'When did you cross into the volume?'

Thalia heard the voice of Captain Pell, well known to her from cutter and corvette instruction classes. 'Fifteen minutes ago, ma'am.'

'Have you provoked any sort of reaction?'

'Nothing, ma'am,' Pell continued. 'We were swept by anti-collision radar, but that's to be expected. We're at weapons readiness, but I'm not anticipating any sort of hostile action. Prefect Bancal will confirm, but this doesn't look like anything out of the ordinary.'

'You mentioned a power source.'

'Probably just low-level housekeeping. We'll take a closer look for completeness's sake, but—'

'No, you won't. Execute an immediate retreat, Captain Pell. I want you out of that anti-collision volume as quickly as possible. But do nothing that might be construed as threatening action.'

'I . . . very well, ma'am. Initiating hard reverse burn.'

Aumonier's order countermanded any sort of instruction Sparver might have given, so there was no need for Pell to consult with the senior-most prefect on the cruiser. Thalia could imagine that smarting with Sparver, but he knew the ropes as well as any of them. Under any circumstances, at any time, the word of the Supreme Prefect was the ultimate authority.

'We're backing off,' Sparver said. 'Nice and casually. But we'll keep our claws sharp, if no one objects.'

'Provided they're not yet visibly deployed,' Aumonier answered. 'How long until you've cleared the volume?'

'At this rate,' Pell answered, 'ten minutes.'

'Halve that,' Aumonier said.

'Complying,' Pell said.

'Ma'am,' Sparver said. 'What sort of development were you talking about?'

'A spike in the deaths, Bancal. The start of which was uncomfortably close to the point where you crossed into the volume. It might be nothing, but it's not a chance I'm willing to take. I'm concerned that you may have tripped some monitoring system, somehow linked to the Wildfire incidence.'

'Do you think backing off will help?' Sparver asked.

'If it does or doesn't, Bancal, we'll know very shortly.'

If Lethe was a boulder-shaped clock hand, then according to Sparver's reckoning, by the time it completed two whole revolutions they would be on the safe side of the anti-collision volume. They were still backing away, keeping the nose of *Democratic Circus* aimed at the tumbling rock, Pell determined to keep the cruiser's scanning systems garnering as much data as possible. That pink smear of sub-surface heat had got a little sharper since they began, like a thumbprint coming into slow focus, but Sparver was still none the wiser about the exact cause of it. Something was drawing power, to be certain, but it was an excessive signature for a few housekeeping systems.

As they backed up, a proximity monitor read out a slowly increasing series of numbers. Grolnick continued to report on weapons readiness. Dias was running a sweep on any nearby space traffic, as well as feeding routine updates to Panoply. The flight deck illumination was at condition red, the rhythmic cycling of master caution tones and status chimes creating a lulling, womblike ambience.

'As soon as anyone is ready to explain what this rock might have to do with Wildfire . . .' Pell began.

'You heard Lady Jane,' Sparver said. 'We just poked our noses into something, and now there's a new spate of melters. She's not one to buy into coincidences and, given the Voi connection, neither am I.'

'I thought we had Garlin?'

'We do. But Garlin can't be the whole story. Dreyfus was supposed to be looking into the family background down in Chasm City. Whatever he turned up made him think *this* was worth our time – and Lady Jane obviously thought it was worth listening to his hunch. Now this has happened, I'm inclined to think Dreyfus must have been onto something.'

Pell looked disgruntled. 'I hope you're right. It's not that I don't trust

Dreyfus – I don't need to tell you that. But if all we were ever going to do was knock on a door and scuttle away, we didn't really need a ship this big.'

'But I'm glad we brought it,' Sparver said. He eased out of his fold-down seat, still weightless as the cruiser backed up at a constant speed. 'I'm going back to talk to the prefects. They've got their blood up. They were expecting a little more than this.'

'They won't be too sorry to be told the hunt's off,' Pell said. 'We aren't exactly equipped for an enforcement action.'

'Ten kilometres from threshold,' Dias said. 'No change in Lethe or its proximity systems.'

'Good,' Sparver replied. 'I'll feel a lot easier when we're the other side of that line.'

He went back and spoke to the four prefects, all of them armoured-up with their visors raised, making them look like a clutch of baby birds, gape-mouthed and black-feathered. He explained the new order to them, saying that it was too soon to speculate about returning to the earlier operation, but that in his opinion there was only a small likelihood of an immediate enforcement action. He watched their reactions, detecting a definite easing in the collective mood. It would have been an exaggeration to say that they were relieved at the prospect of being stood down – these were experienced field operatives, all of whom had already seen action – but equally they knew they would not normally have been sent into a high-risk investigation without additional weaponry and equipment.

'I won't second-guess the brains in tactical,' Sparver said. 'But if they decide this place really does demand a closer look, chances are they'll want some additional operatives and firepower.'

Kober glanced down at his whiphound, the handle appearing small and ineffectual in the heavy gauntlet of his armour. 'Should we stand down from tactical readiness, sir?'

'Let's not count our chickens just yet,' Sparver said, giving Kober an encouraging pat on the shoulder.

A general address chime sounded. 'Pell to all stations. We've crossed out of the anti-collision volume. We'll continue at our present rate of drift until we receive revised instructions from Panoply.'

Sparver went forward again. Grolnick was holding the cruiser's weapons at their alert status, but with every kilometre that they backed off, the chance of a hostile intervention became less likely.

A minute passed, then five. Lethe was becoming just another slow-tumbling rock, beginning to fall back into the broader flow of orbital bodies.

'Incoming transmission from Panoply,' Dias said. 'It's the Supreme Prefect, sir. Shall I put her on general display?'

Pell glanced at Sparver, received a nod, then told Dias to go ahead.

'We put you safely clear of the threshold, Captain Pell. Can you confirm?'

'Safely beyond Lethe's volume, ma'am. No change in status at our end. We've got a slightly better idea of that thermal excess, and it could be consistent with something more than routine housekeeping systems. Equally, someone could just be wasting power unnecessarily. Do you want us to move back in and take a closer look?'

'Negative, Captain. We'll make no rash movements on this one until we see a trend in the Wildfire incidences. Maintain your posture until I say otherwise.'

'Understood,' Pell said.

Slowly the *Democratic Circus* continued its retreat.

Tang checked the restraints then lowered the trawl back into place, Garlin squirming against the straps but unable to offer any physical resistance.

'You went in once.' His speech was slightly slurred, one lip swollen where he had bitten it under the earlier trawl. 'Wasn't that enough for you?'

'I never said I was done,' Aumonier answered. 'Just that you needed a little time off between sessions.' She directed a curt nod at Tang. 'Begin. We can dispense with the niceties this time.'

'Show me as many faces as you like, as many pictures of that building . . . it isn't going to make any difference.'

The trawl started humming. Tang quickly pushed through the lower power settings.

Aumonier took out the still frame of Doctor Julius Mazarin, the one she had already tested on Garlin.

'You showed clear recognition when I presented this image to you.'

He shot her a scornful look. 'Hard not to recognise my own face.'

'Then you accept that it's you?'

'What are you trying to prove here, Aumonier? Anyone could fake up a picture of me in that place. It proves nothing. Whoever did it didn't even take the time to get all the details right. Haven't you noticed the scar under my eye?'

'I thought it was an affectation, designed to make you look tougher than you really are.'

'I've had it since I was young, you stupid . . .' He paused, some doubt or troubled recollection showing in his features for an instant. 'A boy did it, that's all. A game that went wrong. I never had it fixed, because why should I?'

Aumonier withdrew the picture of Julius Mazarin, annoyed at herself for not noticing the absence of that scar, but equally refusing to rush to judgement about the significance of that detail. Perhaps the scar had been removed from the video, or cosmetically concealed when the recording was made. Perhaps Garlin was lying when he said he had possessed the scar since his youth.

Perhaps many things. But she still had a tingle of doubt.

She returned to one of the earlier frames. It was the motif of the white tree, on the inside of one of the elevators. She slid it across the table, waiting until his eyes snapped onto it.

'Forget the face for now. You still knew what this was. It had some prior significance to you.'

She nodded to Tang, instructing him to increase the power.

As the trawl took a firmer hold so Garlin tensed and began to have increasing difficulty forming words. 'It's a white . . . tree.'

'It's emblematic of something, Mister Garlin. You based the architecture of your clinic around this motif, didn't you? The tree has some personal meaning to you, something you can't hide from the trawl . . .'

'Haven't you . . . ever seen a . . . white tree?'

'That's more than just a white tree. It's an idiosyncratic symbol, something of profound personal significance.' She glanced at Tang again, gave a nod.

Tang whispered: 'We're at the safe limit now, ma'am.'

'Higher.'

After a fractional hesitation Tang adjusted the settings. The trawl's humming escalated in an almost musical fashion. Garlin stiffened, a low strangling sound coming from the base of his throat.

'Let me make myself plain,' Aumonier said, selecting another image from her portfolio. 'I'm at the end of my patience. The Wildfire deaths are coming in at more than one a minute now. In the guise of Julius Mazarin – the face I showed you; your face – you primed their Voi kernels to behave in this way. Now you're going to tell me how to resolve this emergency. Starting with the significance of this object . . .'

She presented an image of Lethe to him.

He looked at her with a mad bemusement. 'It's a rock. A . . . fucking . . . rock.'

'The death curve steepened after we approached this object, too sharply for me to accept that it was coincidence.' She flicked her attention to Tang, hoping for the tell-tale marker of prior recognition. 'Lethe, Mister Garlin. It's a family asset. What's there?'

'I don't . . .'

Tang's expression had not shifted since he started the trawl, and still there was no private signal to suggest that Garlin had any prior knowledge of Lethe.

She moved to present another image. But as she was touching the folder, she felt a soft bump pass through the room. She twisted in her seat, anger flaring. She had given express orders that she should not be disturbed while conducting the trawl.

'Reduce the power,' she mouthed to Tang, rising from her chair, intending to step through into the observation partition and give merry hell to whoever had countermanded that order.

She had barely left the chair, though, when the connecting door opened from the other side.

'Pull him out of the trawl,' Dreyfus said, without preamble.

'I'm in the middle of—'

'Pull him out. He's innocent.'

Aumonier shook her head, denying this truth before its wider implications had time to uncoil themselves. 'You've been arguing exactly the opposite for months. Even if I had any lingering doubts, the newest wave of deaths has banished them completely.'

Behind Dreyfus were two other individuals, neither of whom had any authority to be in this part of Panoply. One – she recognised, almost guiltily – was the Detective-Marshal from Chasm City. The other was a thin, ghost-faced man who meant precisely nothing to her.

'Devon Garlin is a threat to the public order,' Dreyfus said, while Tang waited for an order from Aumonier. 'I'm confident we can build a solid case against him, purely on the basis of his public deeds and pronouncements.'

'And?' she asked.

'He isn't responsible for Wildfire. You can trawl him until steam comes out of his ears and you won't find the link you're looking for. He had nothing to do with Elysium Heights.'

Someone was breathing heavily and it took Aumonier a second to realise that it was herself. Her skin tingled. She felt as if she had been slapped hard across both cheeks.

She looked at Tang. 'Power down. Get it off him.' *For now*, she added, for her own silent benefit.

'Ma'am,' Tang said, not without a blush of relief. He deactivated the trawl, elevated the hood, and wheeled it back from the chair.

'Loosen the restraints,' Dreyfus said.

CHAPTER EIGHTEEN

Julius and Caleb approached the fallen form. The lion was still breathing, but that was only to be expected given Caleb's refusal to allow any of his animals a quick, clean death. Given where the bolt had gone in, Julius had no doubt the wound would prove fatal. The lion had been shot in the neck, blood emerging in bright, crimson pulses.

Still, he approached the lion warily, conscious that Caleb was holding back for some reason. Julius glanced at his brother, sensing some deception, some shift in the rules of the game which Caleb had not yet disclosed. The lion could not be physically real, Julius told himself: there wasn't nearly enough quickmatter in the environs of the Shell House to produce a three-dimensional form as large as a lion. But even if the lion remained an illusion, as it had to be, Julius began to wonder if Caleb had still found a way to make it harmful.

'You aren't as bored with this game as you make out,' Julius whispered to himself.

'Wait,' Caleb said with a sudden urgency.

Julius halted at the instruction, looking back impatiently. 'What now? I shot it, didn't I? Wasn't that what you wanted?'

'Something's not right. You were meant to shoot the lion. You weren't meant to shoot—'

'No,' Julius said, denying what he now saw before his eyes. 'No. That's not real. It *was* the lion. I shot the lion.' His mouth had turned very dry. 'I saw the lion and I *shot* the lion. I didn't—'

'What have you done?' Caleb said, in an awed, horror-struck tone. 'My god, Julius. What have you done?'

The lion had been lying on the ground a moment earlier. Julius was sure of it. But where the lion had been was now their mother, slumped on her side, strangely still, the bolt embedded in her chest, a spreading blood pool already forming a dark, forbidding cordon around her body.

Julius approached a few paces nearer, then halted. 'It's a trick,' he said, hating his brother for the cruelty of this stunt but relieved he had seen it for the illusion it was. 'If you can make me see a lion, then you can put a figment of our mother in its place. You're sick, Caleb. Twisted. Why would you even—'

'It's not a figment,' Caleb said, coming to stand next to Julius. 'I swear it. That blood's soaking into the ground just like real blood.' He drew breath, shuddered. 'It's real. She's real. You really shot her. And it looks like—'

Something broke in Julius, overriding all other concerns. He dashed to the fallen form and reached out, fingers slowing as they neared the side of her face, clinging to one last, desperate hope that she would prove a figment, as the panther had been, as every other hunt had been, and that his fingers would scythe through that substanceless surface and find nothing but air beneath it. Then his fingertips touched flesh: colder than he had expected, but real flesh for all that.

It could still be a trick, he thought. Caleb could have found a way to manipulate his senses that comprehensively, so he felt the figment as a real thing. But as he pressed his fingers against her face, he felt a yielding subsidence of bone and muscle, her body shifting against the pressure. It was his mother, real and present and dying on the ground, where he had shot her.

'Lurcher!' Caleb called, throwing himself back and bellowing the robot's name. 'Lurcher – it's an emergency!'

Julius crouched lower. He wanted to press a hand against the wound, to staunch the blood, but he was afraid of doing more harm than good, of inflicting distress when he meant to provide comfort. He knew nothing of emergency medicine, nothing of first aid. Those scraps of knowledge had no place in the modern world.

But they were not in the modern world, not just yet. They were in a strange sheltered bubble, where some rules applied but others did not. And his mother was dying.

Her eyelids fluttered. He had the sense she was on the edge of consciousness. He brought his own face next to hers, as if both of them were staring out at the same odd spectacle, viewing the world sideways on.

'Please don't die,' he said.

She made a sound that could have been 'Julius', a polysyllabic gasp and hiss that he chose to hear as his own name. Then her eyes closed tightly and a more profound and permanent stillness seemed to take hold of her.

'Lurcher!' Caleb called again. 'Quickly, Lurcher!'

There was a terrible silence. Julius touched his mother's face again, moving a lock of hair away from her cheek, then turned to look at his brother.

'You did this,' Julius said.

'What are you saying, you idiot? You were the one with the crossbow. You were the one who thought you were shooting a lion.'

Julius was surprised at how calm he sounded. He was outside himself, hearing his own words, impressed by the force of certainty he heard in them. They sounded as if they were coming from some other, more assertive version of himself, a Julius who had crossed the gap between childhood and adulthood in the time it took a crossbow bolt to murder his mother.

'You made me see a lion,' Julius stated, the mechanics of Caleb's deception becoming clear to him with the dreadful clarity of hindsight, like a blueprint that had just snapped into focus. 'You could edit my visual field. I already knew that, and I should have seen it coming.' He rose up from the ground, content to leave his mother where she was while he addressed Caleb. 'You wanted her dead, because you were afraid she'd revoke our powers. But you didn't have the guts to do it yourself.'

Caleb took a step backwards. 'You're not thinking straight. I didn't make this happen. I told you to be careful with that crossbow . . .'

'*This* is why you wanted one last game,' Julius said.

Caleb must have seen something in his eyes, some new and wild anger. 'Brother . . .'

Julius still held the crossbow. He glanced at it for a second, wondering why Caleb had not considered this detail. Then he looked back at their mother, and extended a hand to the crossbow bolt. For once, the conjuring command came to mind without effort; indeed, he formed and executed the order so fluidly that it seemed to happen at an almost autonomic level. The bolt wriggled and popped itself out of the wound, a weak, sticky-looking pulse of blood following it. The bolt began to inch its away along the ground with wormlike undulations.

Too slow. Julius reached for it again and sent another conjuring command. Again, it required little or no conscious will. It was as if, after months of struggle, he had finally broken through into the realm of effortless expertise that his brother seemed to inhabit so naturally. He knew what he wanted the quickmatter to do, and the quickmatter fell into immediate, eager obedience. All the intermediate steps – visualising the state changes, thinking of them in terms of geometry and physics – now felt superfluous and clumsy – beneath him.

The shock and fury of his mother's death had opened a door.

The bolt shattered into a hundred ant-like specks. Julius opened his fist and the specks swarmed through the air, only congealing back into the form of the bolt at the last instant, as his fingers tightened.

The bolt felt cold, solid, clean.

He primed the crossbow. He slipped the bolt back into the crossbow.

'No,' Caleb said. 'Put it down, Julius.'

Julius levelled the crossbow at his brother. 'You're so good with quick-matter, why don't you make me?'

Caleb stumbled back, raising a hand. In his own hand Julius felt the crossbow trying to become something other than its present form, a kind of restless shudder passing through the entire object. Julius resisted his brother's intention, again more by reflexive instinct than the considered, deliberate issuing of a counter-command. Caleb responded in turn, the crossbow squirming and writhing like some distant thing seen in a mirage, Julius just managing to maintain the weapon's functional integrity. If their earlier games had been as sequential and cerebral as chess, now the struggle felt more like wrestling: a continuous, fluid, bruising engagement.

Julius surprised himself at how well he resisted Caleb. But the toll was intense and with an instant's inattention he would lose control. While he was still able to hold the crossbow's form, he released the bolt in Caleb's direction.

Time slowed.

The crossbow liquefied, sluicing through his fingers like thick black oil. The bolt's course began to bend, as Caleb tried to shift its aerodynamics. Then he tried to shatter it into a multitude of components, as Julius had done before. But Julius was imposing a reinforcing command on the bolt, compelling it to stay whole.

It broke into five or six blunt, sluglike components. Deflection wrenched most of them past Caleb's face. One part struck him under the eye, before spinning away.

Caleb stood like a statue, shock and amazement on his face, even as blood began to flow from the wound. He reached up, touched his face, stared down in mute astonishment at his bloodied fingertips.

'You've gone mad,' he said, raising his voice as if he expected an audience. 'First Mother, then me.'

Most of the quickmatter had formed a twitching puddle at Julius's feet. Caleb grasped for it and the puddle began to stretch itself towards him, like an amoeba searching for a food source. Julius snarled and issued a sharp, violent, dispersing command, flinging the constituents of the puddle away in all directions.

Caleb, as weaponless as Julius, took another stumbling step backwards. The blood scribed a line of red warpaint down one side of his face. He raised his palm at Julius again and Julius's world exploded with a chrome brightness so vivid that it became hot pain.

'If you can do that . . .' Julius said, blinded under the visual overload. 'So can I.'

Even without sight he felt he could see the inside of Caleb's brain, its layered mysteries as glassy and translucent as a paperweight. He knew where to make Caleb hurt, where to make Caleb scream. It was just a question of reaching inside and doing bad things.

It was easy for him now. The wonder was that it had ever been difficult.

Julius could see again. Caleb was still trying to blind him, but Julius was stronger, deflecting his brother's intentions. Julius mirrored and amplified the same commands and Caleb buckled to his knees, then dropped to the ground, drool loosening from his mouth.

Julius was the master of his brother now. With each breath he seemed to draw strength from Caleb, even as Caleb became weaker. He knelt as close to Caleb as he had been to his mother, staring into Caleb's eyes as they rolled back.

'I could kill you,' Julius said softly. 'You see that now. You were the stronger of us, once. But you released something in me today. And now it's like swimming. I can't imagine how there was ever a time when I didn't have this power.'

Hearing something, he stood taller. Undergrowth shifted and Lurcher came striding into the scene, silver limbs scissoring as the robot assessed the scene and moved immediately to their mother's side. Lurcher examined the body with an efficient, meticulous detachment, while the single eye of its domed head swivelled onto Caleb and then Julius, regarding him with an odd, accusatorial intensity.

More movement. Their father was hard on Lurcher's heels, already out of breath as he sweated his way through the overgrowth, comprehension breaking on his face as he took into the bloody tableau, Julius the only one still standing.

'My god . . .' Marlon Voi began.

Julius raised a silencing hand. 'She's dead, Father. It's much too late to do anything for her now. But I didn't kill her. I'd never have done that. I *loved* her. I may have shot her, but that's only because Caleb tricked me.'

Father almost pushed Lurcher aside in his haste to reach his fallen wife. He touched her on the forehead, shock and grief already making an unfamiliar mask of his face.

'What have you monsters done to her?'

'I said it wasn't me,' Julius persisted. 'It was Caleb. That's why I've punished him. He was stronger than me, but only up to a point. When he pushed we found out who was really the stronger of us.' Then, with sudden reasonableness: 'Shall I kill him, Father? Once and for all?'

'Put them to sleep,' Father said, his voice breaking. 'Now.'

It was an order meant for Lurcher. The robot straightened itself up, extending one of its arms, a needle sliding out from a hidden pocket in the robot's wrist. Lurcher took a bounding stride towards Julius.

Julius willed the robot to halt. It was as transparent to him as his brother, its levers as easy to pull.

'I like this,' he said, marvelling at it. He knew he ought to be feeling the same shock and grief that his father was, and to begin with, in the moments after the kill, there had been a little of that. But it had been a weak signal soon drowned by something much stronger, much less ignorable.

Instead of grief, what Julius felt was release. Release and possibility and the giddy exhilaration of testing his own limits.

'She was right about you,' Father said.

'About both of us? Or just Caleb?' Julius frowned, touching a finger to his lip. 'I know she didn't trust him, but I was never like him, was I? I was always the better brother.'

Father was sobbing now, bending over the still body of their mother. He dabbed at the wound in her chest, his fingers coming away sticky and red.

'I should have listened,' he said, as if that admission was meant for the woman on the ground, rather than either of the boys.

Julius stood watching, a cold spectator to his father's melodramatics. He was content to give his father a little more time with his dead wife before getting to the matter at hand. Then he coughed gently.

'This is a bit of a mess, isn't it? You've got a dead wife on your hands. Of course, you could go straight to the authorities, but then you'd have some awkward explaining to do. Us, to start with. Where we're from. What those dreams of ours are about. The Ursas, the other boys and girls. The knives. Doctor Stasov. The contingency . . . yes, there's quite a lot that it might be best to keep out of the public eye, wouldn't you agree?'

Father looked at him. Hate welled behind his tear-clotted eyes.

'What do you propose, you little shit?'

'I propose,' Julius declared grandly, 'that it's time for me to make my way in the world. I think I'm ready.' He grinned, cocking his head in the direction of the dome and all that stood beyond it. 'I think I'm more than ready.'

Dreyfus reached down and undid the straps himself. It brought their heads close. Garlin turned his face to meet Dreyfus, a sneer lifting the corner of his mouth.

'It's a nice try,' he said, still slurred. 'But I know a stunt when I see one. You've set this up. You're hoping you'll get me off my guard.'

'It's not a stunt,' Dreyfus said. 'There isn't anyone in Panoply who's staked more on your guilt than me. I went down to Chasm City to find the final piece of evidence that would tie it all together. Instead I found Doctor Stasov.'

'Would you mind explaining this man's involvement?' Aumonier asked. 'Or what he's doing deep inside Panoply?'

'Might I?' said the woman.

Aumonier dredged her memory for the woman's name. 'Yes . . . go ahead, Detective-Marshal Del Mar. I'd be very grateful.'

'Doctor Stasov has been known to me for some while, Supreme Prefect. He was the family physician to the Vois. He was called into their service when the boys were eight years old—'

Aumonier made to speak. Dreyfus raised a cautioning hand. 'Hear her out, Jane. You won't be asking anything we haven't already gone over.'

'There were two sons,' Del Mar went on. 'Two brothers. Julius Devon Garlin Voi and his brother Caleb. You have no record of Caleb, and neither did we. But Doctor Stasov helped with their development, observing the boys as they were initiated into some of the inner secrets of the Vois. You suspect that Julius has access to forbidden layers of the Voi kernel, a way to sift and manipulate abstraction data, reaching into others' heads, bending the consensual reality field to suit his aims. You're nearly right. Julius does have unusual capabilities. But he's closer to an idiot savant, blessed with gifts he barely recognises that he possesses. Caleb, on the other hand . . .'

'This brother no one's heard about until now,' Aumonier said, making no effort to hide her scepticism.

'He's real enough,' Doctor Stasov said, speaking for the first time. He had a high, quavering voice, shot through with fractures, like some old piece of pottery that had been broken and reassembled too many times. 'I visited that household many times. Caleb was always the faster of the two. The more dominant – the crueller, too, if you want my opinion.'

'And you're saying he's behind all this?'

'It fits,' Detective-Marshal Del Mar said. 'Caleb has the same capabilities as Julius, except in Caleb's case they're directed, purposeful. Caleb knows what he's doing, what he wants, and how to achieve it. His brother's only ever been an unwilling instrument.'

'And this . . . objective?' Aumonier asked, still not willing to surrender her doubts.

'Punishment,' Dreyfus said. 'That's all. Retribution. Directed at the two thousand Wildfire cases in particular, but the rest of us in general. And if we all go down in flames, if everything burns, Caleb won't mind at all. He doesn't want to live. He doesn't want to make things better for himself. He just wants to destroy.'

'I don't have a brother,' Garlin said. 'Do you think I'd forget that I had a brother?'

'Lethe is the river of forgetting,' Dreyfus answered. 'I think it's very likely that you did forget – or were made to. Tell them, Balthasar.'

Doctor Stasov – Balthasar must have been his first name – said: 'The family had the means. The boys had already been put through at least one round of forced amnesia treatment when I entered the household service. Their entire environment was shaped to enforce one narrative: that they were the natural sons and heirs of Marlon and Aliya Voi. But for as long as I worked with them, the boys were troubled by fleeting recollections of an alternate past. They rarely allowed themselves to speak of it, because it was so disturbing to both of them. At best, they tried to pretend it was just a particularly upsetting recurring dream. But it seemed to me that something that powerful, that vivid, must be rooted in an objective reality.'

'And this troubling past?' Aumonier asked, feeling herself being drawn down a rabbit hole despite her natural reluctance.

'I tried to find out. The boys – Julius in particular – were drawn to a particular historical episode. It nagged at them in a way that can't be down to chance. I began to wonder then if this was a hint of their true memories, breaking through the forced amnesia.'

'What episode would this be?' Dreyfus asked.

'Something too impossibly remote for it to be true. The Amerikano settlement. The failed colony, the children raised by machines. But that was three hundred years ago . . .'

'Could the boys have been kept in hibernation since then?' Aumonier asked, with a direct and level gaze.

'No one's ever been frozen for that long,' Doctor Stasov answered. 'Besides, when I had my suspicions . . . I took a liberty. I managed to obtain genetic samples of all four individuals: Marlon, Aliya, Julius and Caleb. The boys are the natural heirs of Marlon and Aliya.'

'Then that rules out any possible link to the Amerikano era,' Aumonier said.

'He's raving about something that makes no sense,' Garlin said. 'I also don't have the faintest idea who this man is.'

'You don't *know* that you know him,' Dreyfus said. 'But if we put you back under that trawl, I'm sure we'd pick up a clear memory, suppressed or otherwise.'

'Go ahead, if you're so certain.'

'We wouldn't have the right,' Dreyfus said, directing his answer as much at Aumonier as the man in the chair. 'When it seemed that you were directly responsible for Wildfire, a case could be made. I suppose the citizen quorum gave their assent?'

'She'd have got them to say whatever she wanted,' Garlin said. 'If they even existed in the first place.'

'Precautions had to be taken,' Aumonier said, instantly detesting the pleading, self-justifying tone she heard in her answer. Grow a spine, she thought, and stop sounding like a child caught stealing cookies. She had only ever acted on the basis of the best intelligence available to her.

'Sit down with him, Balthasar,' Dreyfus told the doctor. 'You were with him until he was sixteen, according to your account. Whatever happened to bury his memories of your involvement, there'll still be some latent recall. Tell him what you remember about the Shell House – and what you discovered. Hopefully that'll jog some memories. And Julius?'

His hand free, Garlin stroked his swollen lip. 'What the hell do you want with me, Dreyfus? Forgiveness?'

'Not yet,' Dreyfus said bluntly. 'But you can start by listening.'

There was a knock at the partition door. Irritated by yet another interruption, Aumonier opened her mouth to demand an explanation. But the person who had arrived was Senior Prefect Mildred Dosso, not someone to test her patience without good reason.

'Supreme Prefect – we need you back in the tactical room.'

'What is it, Mildred?' Aumonier asked.

Dosso looked around, clearly uncertain how frank she could be in such unusual company.

'The cruiser, ma'am. The *Democratic Circus*.'

'What about it?'

'It's heading back to Lethe, ma'am.'

Dreyfus, Aumonier and Detective-Marshal Del Mar arrived at the heavy bronze doors to the tactical room. Doctor Stasov had been left with Garlin, free to speak to him under the close supervision of Robert Tang and Mildred Dosso.

Aumonier hesitated before opening the doors. 'I shouldn't allow you into this room, Detective-Marshal. Better people than me have lost their positions over lesser security lapses.'

'But I think we might make an exception here,' Dreyfus said.

'Yes,' Aumonier said, nodding slowly. 'I think we might. I owe you some kind of apology, Hestia. May I call you Hestia? Formalities seem a little . . . superfluous. I gave you the run-around, when I should have heeded your requests.'

Detective-Marshal Del Mar appraised this answer and seemed to give some considerable thought to her response.

'A little more clarity and open-mindedness wouldn't have hurt . . . from both of us. You have my word that I'll respect the confidential nature of anything I see or hear beyond these doors. Now – shall we see what the difficulty is with your ship?'

Pressing open the double doors, Aumonier said: 'Pell is a trusted operative. Bancal's on that ship as well. He's . . . reliable.'

'I've heard that you can be sparing with your praise,' Del Mar said, bending her mouth into half a smile. 'From which I take it that you have a very high opinion of the professionalism of that crew.'

'They were given a clear order to retreat. There's no reason for them to have disregarded it,' Dreyfus said, following the two women into the darkened hush of the tactical room.

'A situation might have developed,' Del Mar speculated.

'Then they'd have notified Panoply after taking action.' Aumonier moved to the table and invited Del Mar to take one of the seats facing her. 'I'm afraid the coffee's cold, but you're welcome to whatever you can stomach.' She turned her head to Clearmountain. 'Did you get any warning, Gaston?'

'Nothing,' Clearmountain said, hardly raising an eyebrow at the presence of the Chasm City operative. 'Pell's not answering. But our tracer diagnostics show no fault in the comms chain between here and the cruiser.'

'Where are they now?' Dreyfus asked.

'Over here, sir,' said Thalia Ng, next to the Solid Orrery.

Dreyfus moved over to Thalia, overjoyed and conflicted in equal measure. At last he had the proof that she was well, or at least capable of being of service. But the doubts he had nurtured since the Shell House now crystallised into cold, piercing certainty.

'Are you all right, sir?'

'It's good to see you up and about,' he said, trying to smile away his awkwardness. 'I was prepared for . . . something worse.'

'I'll mend, sir. It's Sparver I'm concerned about. He's on that ship.'

Dreyfus forced his mind to the immediate practicalities.

'So I gather. Are they back inside the anti-collision volume?'

'Well into it, sir. Current fix has them less than twenty kilometres from Lethe's centre of mass.'

'Pell wouldn't contravene an order,' Dreyfus said, musing aloud – and following a train of thought that could only lead somewhere unpleasant. 'So he must still think he's following orders.'

'Pardon, sir?'

'Could we get another ship into that area?'

Thalia conjured some configurations through the Solid Orrery. 'Not quickly, sir. Thirty minutes if we re-task one of these assets, longer—'

He shook his head. 'No. It would need to be a ship starting from here, with pre-assigned orders and instructions to disregard any transmissions that come in after they've departed.'

Thalia looked at him oddly. 'Are you saying we can't trust our communications, sir?'

Dreyfus's face tightened. 'Something like that.'

'Then we're stuck. All operable craft are now in-field, other than the cutter you came back with, and that's being refuelled ready for turnaround.'

'Hold it for me.'

'It still won't get you to Lethe in time to do anything about the *Democratic Circus*, sir.'

'We're not exactly spoilt for choice here, Thalia. I'll take that ship as soon as it's ready to move out.'

Lillian Baudry had joined them next to the Solid Orrery, standing with her arms folded and one hand propping up her chin. She watched the enlargement of Lethe, with its splinter-sized representation of the cruiser. 'This will turn out to have a simple explanation, Tom. All our services are under strain at the moment. One shouldn't read too much into a temporary drop in communications.'

'That's a Deep System Cruiser, Lillian. It has the capability to take apart an entire habitat, or turn Lethe into rubble. I can't say I'm entirely comfortable with the idea of it going rogue.'

'And I'm equally uncomfortable with throwing another ship into your side-investigation. I hear you've had a sudden change of heart concerning Garlin.'

'He's the puppet, not the puppet master. I think his brother's in Lethe.'

'His brother. Did you just say—?'

Aumonier raised her voice. 'Lillian. Might I have a quick word? With all of you, in fact.' She stood up, her expression reflected back from the shiny surface of the table, ghosted through with the endless scroll of status summaries. She waited a beat, allowing the room to focus its collective attention on her. 'Whether or not there's a brother is something we'll get to the bottom of. But I have a witness who strikes me as credible, and Detective-Marshal Del Mar will – I think – agree with me in that assessment. Am I right, Hestia?'

Del Mar seemed reticent. She cleared her throat before speaking, rising only at Aumonier's invitation.

'There may be a brother called Caleb, raised under identical circumstances to Julius. But something drove them apart – most likely the death of their mother, Aliya Voi. It's my belief that Caleb's been alive all these years, more than likely using his Voi privileges to slip from one assumed identity to another. This clinic you've all been interested in – Elysium Heights. Caleb could well have been behind it. He'd have been in exactly the right position to siphon away the family funds and lay the ground for Wildfire.'

'After all these years?' Baudry asked, making no effort to conceal her disbelief.

'Yes,' Del Mar affirmed. 'Caleb's patient. He waited for the right time to unleash this emergency – when the public confidence in your organisation was at its lowest ebb; when the Supreme Prefect was already restricted in the range of responses open to her. None of that was accidental.'

'Sirs,' Thalia said, raising her voice from the Solid Orrery. 'I think you should all see this.'

CHAPTER NINETEEN

The forensic packages popped away from the belly dispenser in the *Democratic Circus*, each one a monkey-sized, spider-shaped probe with autonomous guidance and decision-making capability. They selected a variety of landing sites on Lethe and guided themselves down, springing out capture barbs and tongue-like sticky coils at the last moment. Once locked onto the rock, the packages drilled through the plastic integument and began to use precise seismic mapping tools to assemble an increasingly detailed picture of Lethe's interior.

Sparver was on the flight deck, watching as vague impressions of sub-surface structure hardened into crisp, pink detail. Most of his focus was on the volume around the thermal excess, Sparver barely remembering to breathe as the images grew sharper and more provocative.

'That's an awful lot of space to give over to basic housekeeping,' Pell commented. 'Seems like someone's hunch was on the money, Prefect.'

'Not mine,' Sparver said. 'And believe me, I'd take the credit if I could.'

Grolnick was expert in the interpretation of the forensic package data. Sketching a gloved finger across the images, she lingered over a cystlike void tucked under the same pole where there was a thermal excess. 'This is a low-density volume, about three kilometres across. Maybe vacuum, maybe pressurised. But it's definitely not rock, ice or stabilising plastic. It could be a habitable space, Prefect Bancal.'

'Do the power requirements add up?' Pell asked.

'Depends what they're doing in there,' Grolnick said. 'But it's feasible. In fact, I'd say there's more than enough capacity to manage an ecosystem about that large.'

'There's nothing like this on the official schematics,' Dias said, overlaying everything that Panoply thought it knew about Lethe. 'But deviating from official schematics is a civil matter, not a violation of the Common Articles.'

It was true, Sparver reflected. If Panoply bothered itself with every change in a habitat or rock that wasn't properly registered and notified, they would have no time for anything else.

'But this isn't any old rock,' he said. 'It's Lethe, and we already had grounds to be suspicious of it. Well, Dreyfus did, at least. Can you squeeze anything more out of those packages?'

'No,' Grolnick said. 'We're at the resolution limit now. It's like knocking on a door to a sealed room and trying to work out where the furniture is, based on the echo.' She tapped at a faint, spinal trace. 'There's a suggestion of a connecting spur here, running back up to Lethe's centre of gravity . . . that would probably be how you got in and out, if you didn't want to land upside down under a negative gee of down-force.'

'Mister Dias,' Pell said. 'Signal Panoply that we're sending back the forensic imagery, as requested. We'll make one close approach to that pole, run a deep-terrain scan, then reverse back out again. Mister Grolnick: hold at our current threat posture, and be ready to interdict any anti-collision measures.'

Lady Jane had been in no hurry to explain the reasons for sending the cruiser back in again, but Sparver took it as read that there had been a shift in intelligence at Panoply's end, necessitating a closer look at Lethe. He had explained the new orders to the prefects, and they had accepted the revised plan without question, taking it as read that no such order would have been issued without good reason.

More than likely they would complete their deep scan, find there was nothing worth investigating, and be pulled back into the rescue operation – however well or badly that was going.

Sparver returned to the flight deck, some small, distant voice in his head insisting that something, somewhere, was not entirely as it should have been, but Sparver reasoned that since very little had seemed right for several days, this disquiet was merely the new normal, and he had better start getting used to it.

'I'm a little clearer about that access duct, sir,' Grolnick said. 'It has to be an elevator shaft, something like that, so that you can dock as close to the centre of grav as possible.'

'And that chamber?' Sparver asked. 'What sort of gravity would they be feeling in there?'

'Close enough to a gee as to make no difference, sir. Can't be accidental. The whole geometry and spin of this rock is just right to provide a habitable volume under that pole.'

Democratic Circus was holding station now, allowing Lethe to rotate under it. It only took three minutes for the rock to complete its spin, and after a few such cycles Pell said that the deep-terrain sensors had gathered as much information as was possible, given the layers of intervening rock.

The interior chamber was roughly hemispherical, with a domed ceiling about a kilometre high, and a gently curving base about three kilometres in diameter. Surrounding this volume were layers of insulation and life-support management. The connecting thread came in at an offset angle, joining the chamber at its rim, rather than piercing the dome. At its other end, seven kilometres away, was a right-angled connection to a surface lock and docking emplacement.

'We can just about resolve some interior features,' Pell said. 'Enough to say that the chamber looks mostly empty, except for a structure near the middle of the floor. Could be almost anything: a ship, a building, a machine. It's warm in there, though, and our best guess is that there's some kind of atmosphere. Do you think they'd like us to dock and take a closer look?'

Sparver opened a channel to Panoply and the Supreme Prefect. 'Bancal here, ma'am. We think we've identified a way into Lethe, if you'd like us to conduct a meet-and-greet.'

Her reply came back almost immediately. 'Yes, we see your imagery, Bancal. Proceed with caution, but dock and investigate.'

'Just a reminder that we don't have tactical armament, ma'am – just armour and whiphounds.'

'I'm sure you'll use whatever is available to the best of your abilities, Bancal. If you run into difficulty, I shall be prompt in tasking assistance.'

Sparver nodded to himself as he closed the connection, his qualms in no way dispelled by this latest communication with Jane Aumonier. He wished he knew her better: at least as well as he knew Dreyfus. Then he would have known if that paradoxical sense of interested detachment was in some way typical.

'Well,' he said under his breath. 'Orders are orders.'

It was time to go back to the prefects and swallow his pride.

Dreyfus, Thalia, Aumonier and the others watched from the tactical room as the cruiser dropped its forensic packages, then swung in close for what could only be a deep-terrain scan. Several more minutes passed, the cruiser maintaining communications silence, neither issuing transmissions nor responding to requests for a clarification of its actions.

Then it swung away from its holding position, making a slow but unmistakable vector for one of the surface docks.

'I could use that cutter,' Dreyfus said.

'This isn't the work of someone misconstruing an order or responding to changed conditions,' Aumonier said. 'Pell's acting as if he's following a script, one order after another.' Then a dark intuition clouded her features. 'Is it possible, Tom? Given what we know about Garlin and his brother – or don't know – could either of them be using their Voi privileges to intercept our own signals and feed Pell false orders?'

Dreyfus phrased his answer carefully, thinking how easily Aurora had already tricked and manipulated him, firstly by mimicking Aumonier and then by feeding him lies. 'Pell can only be following false orders. I have to get out there and instruct him to stand down.'

'It might be a little late for that,' Lillian Baudry said, casting a despairing glance at the Solid Orrery. 'The new wave of cases isn't easing off. If anything I believe we might be seeing a further steepening. We've had six threshold triggers in the last four minutes . . .'

'Look on the bright side,' Clearmountain said. 'At this rate the entire emergency will be over in less than a month.'

'Because they'll all be dead,' Aumonier answered. 'That's not my idea of a consolation, Gaston.' She coughed, straightened her spine, forced some final spark of authority and confidence back into her voice as she once again addressed the room. 'We've still got a job to do here. I want a revised update on those clinical throughput estimates. It's no good taking people into our custody if we can't get their implants out for days to come. If you see a corner, cut it. We're not striving for perfection.'

'I'll . . . see what we can do with the surgical throughput,' Clearmountain said.

'*Democratic Circus* is on final docking approach,' Thalia said. 'No weapons interdiction so far.'

'We take our blessings where we can find them,' Baudry said.

Dreyfus turned to Aumonier. 'If the deaths are still spiking, that at least shows we were right to be interested in Lethe. Caleb's in there, I'm sure. He's aware of our presence and he's sending a message.'

'Not a very bright one, if he wants to avoid being found out,' Aumonier said.

'He knows we know,' Dreyfus said. 'Now he wants to make it very plain that we can't use force against him – not while he has direct control of Wildfire.'

'Ng had a theory, Tom,' Aumonier told him, nodding to Thalia. 'It was about Julius, to begin with, but if she's right it could just as easily apply to Caleb.'

Thalia seemed reticent. 'It's just a theory, ma'am.'

Dreyfus gave her an encouraging look.

Thalia swallowed. 'I wondered if whoever was behind this wasn't causing Wildfire, but in some way actively suppressing it, with some sort of safeguarding signal. I know it's difficult to imagine anyone doing that, but if half of what we know about Julius or Caleb is true . . . you see what it would mean, don't you?'

'Our isolation measures won't make any difference,' Dreyfus said, the full and terrible implications of her idea opening up in his mind like some vast mansion. 'Not just that, but we could easily be making things worse. And we can't neutralise Caleb, even if we were sure he was the only one alive in Lethe.'

'That's my fear, sir.'

Hestia Del Mar had risen from the table to join the gathering by the Solid Orrery. 'This is the endgame Caleb's always known would come. That's why he's so unconcerned about you discovering his location. He knows you can't touch him – can't even risk closing off his communications.'

'You almost make it seem as if he's guided us to this confrontation,' Aumonier said, with morbid amusement in her voice.

'I think he has, all along. Dreyfus told me about the sequence of events in Addison-Lovelace, when the partition was flooded. I thought there was something odd about that whole drama even then and I'm even more certain of it now. You were being steered to the truth about the clinic, prodded into making the apparent connection to Devon Garlin. That was Caleb trying to goad you into a reckless over-reaction. But you did the one thing he wasn't counting on. You showed restraint, good judgement, wisdom.'

Aumonier almost blushed at this unexpected praise. 'Unfortunately my supply of good judgement is running a little low.'

'I don't blame you. But the facts still apply. If Ng's correct, and he stops sending the suppression signal, all the citizens on your list could be dead within the day.'

'Then tell me how to get that cruiser to retreat.'

Something chimed. Thalia lifted up her bracelet, spoke quietly to someone on the other end.

'Thyssen, sir. By the time you get to the dock they'll have that cutter ready for immediate departure. With an expedited burn you can be at Lethe in just under thirty minutes.'

'There's still not much chance of you reaching Pell in time to make any difference,' Aumonier said. 'But if you think it worthwhile . . .'

'I'd like to make an additional request,' Dreyfus said. 'No one's going to like it very much.'

The prefects were visors-down and ready for immediate vacuum operations. As the cruiser completed its final approach, Sparver clambered up and down the aisle, offering such encouragement as he felt able to give.

'We've mapped a route in, a shaft that will take us from the dock to what looks like a habitable volume. If there isn't an elevator, it'll be a clean drop. You'll have a tactical overlay compiled from the deep-terrain scans.'

'Will you be accompanying us, sir?' asked Kober.

'I'll be right behind you. I came without tactical armour, and the ship can't fabricate me a set at short order. But it can give me an m-suit.'

'You won't be very well protected, sir,' said Gurney.

'No, but if we do run into trouble I'll have you to hide behind, won't I?' Sparver had meant it as a joke, but the nervous silence that followed made him wonder if they took him at his word. 'Now, let's go over those whiphound settings one more time.'

The ship jerked without warning. Sparver, weightless until that moment, slammed against the nearest wall. The surface softened itself just in time to make the impact painful, rather than bone-breaking. The prefects' couches had swelled up to provide cushioning cocoons. The ship jerked again, and a series of clangs rained along the hull. An instant later Sparver felt a low, tooth-grinding vibration, which he knew to be the the cruiser's rapid-deployment Gatling guns, giving back some part of whatever had just been dished out to the *Democratic Circus*.

The return salvo lasted three seconds at the most. Then the ship was silent and still again.

Sparver said: 'Captain Pell. Anything I should know?'

Pell's voice sounded from the flight deck. 'The closest ring of anti-collision guns took a disliking to us getting so close, Prefect Bancal. But we took them out before they managed to do much damage. Grolnick says we're out of the sight-lines of any remaining hazards. Do you want to back off and deliver an asymmetric response?'

'Tempted, Captain – sorely tempted. But Lady Jane gave us a job to do. Force us in if you have to, but complete the docking.'

'Stand by,' Pell said.

It was a jolting touchdown, by the standards he was used to, but Pell was taking no chances and if Sparver had asked him to ram their way into Lethe, he felt sure the captain would have obliged.

With the attack neutralised, the prefects were released from their impact cocoons and able to continue checking their whiphounds and armour.

Sparver went forward.

'Docked and secure,' Pell said. 'Standard airlock interface, green on all capture seals. You can stroll right in. We'll hold at immediate departure readiness.'

'Appreciate the show of solidarity, Captain, but I'd sooner you undocked and pulled out to a safe monitoring distance. Use your discretion regarding those remaining anti-collision defences. If you feel like neutralising them ahead of time, you won't hear any complaints from me.'

'I didn't see you bringing tactical armour aboard,' Pell remarked.

Sparver touched his forehead absent-mindedly. 'Knew I was forgetting something. But you can stretch to an m-suit, can't you?'

'You know where the suitwall is. Go easy in there, all right? None of this is sitting right with me, not since we got those revised orders.'

'We're all a little on edge,' Sparver said. 'Comes with the times.'

While Pell double-checked the docking arrangements, Sparver stepped through the quickmatter membrane of the suitwall and allowed an m-suit to mould itself around him, forming to his contours and fashioning life-support, communications and navigation systems within itself like quick-growing organs. Parts grew transparent, parts grew opaque, parts hardened or formed flexible joints and detachable seams. A spray of status symbols fed across his faceplate.

Sparver fixed two whiphounds onto the adhesive attachment points on the outside of the suit. He would have felt happier with something he could point and aim. But like the m-suit itself, the whiphounds would have to suffice.

He met the four prefects in the staging area on this side of the lock, the m-suit automatically establishing a common communications protocol with the other suits.

'Reading vacuum on the other side, sir,' said Perec, her stencilled name glowing gently against the dull black of her inert-matter armour.

'I'm set,' Sparver said. 'Proceed at your discretion, and be ready for surprises.'

Kober had already opened the cruiser's airlock, clamped tight against Lethe's counterpart, with only a quickmatter membrane holding back the cruiser's air. Sparver had been through several thousand similar locks and nothing here looked out of place or in any way remarkable. It was an old, sturdy and reliable design, exactly the sort of thing one would expect on a piece of mothballed real estate which might yet still have some capital value.

Kober reached through the membrane and worked the other lock's manual controls. After a second's hesitation it opened, grinding back into a recessed slot.

All was dark beyond it. Then sets of red striplights flickered on, revealing a cylindrical chamber more than large enough for the five of them, with a secondary door at the other end of it.

'Whiphound,' Perec said.

Singh unclipped her whiphound, keeping the tail retracted, and stretched her forearm through the membrane until she was able to give the whiphound a gentle lob into the space beyond. It sailed on like a rod-shaped miniature spacecraft, red eye blinking as it went into active scan and threat detection mode, a summary of its results appearing on Sparver's visor.

The whiphound bounced off the rear door, then came slowly to rest.

'Clear,' Singh said.

'Proceed,' Perec answered.

When Dreyfus entered the interrogation room Devon Garlin and Balthasar Stasov were still facing each other across the lone table, Garlin shaking his head in response to some unheard query from the doctor. Stasov turned to meet Dreyfus, mirroring the other man's gesture.

'It's no good. He just won't admit remembering me.' Stasov's eyes wandered back to the trawl, wheeled back into a corner of the room but still maintaining a threatening presence. 'Do you propose to put him back under that thing?'

'Do you think it would teach us very much, beyond his tolerance for pain?'

'I rather doubt it.'

Dreyfus moved around to Garlin and released his restraints. 'That's why I'm trying a different approach.'

'What now?' Garlin asked. 'Going back to the tried and true methods? A locked room and some time alone with me? I'll spare you the trouble. You could break every bone in my body and I wouldn't be able to give you the answers you want. About your stupid clinic, these deaths, this man . . .'

Dreyfus grabbed Garlin by the collar and with a grunt of effort hauled him to his feet. 'I agree. You aren't responsible. But Caleb is, and I need you to get me close to him.'

'This brother of mine who doesn't actually exist?'

'We'll find out soon enough.' Dreyfus shoved Garlin in the direction of the door, Garlin stumbling on unsteady legs before gaining his balance. He braced a hand against the mirrored partition, turned back with his head lowered and his eyes half shrouded.

'Where are we going?'

'Lethe. There's a party of prefects already there, but I figure Caleb's much more likely to negotiate with us if we bring along a human shield – especially if it's his brother.'

Garlin touched his swollen lip. 'This isn't going to end well for you, Dreyfus.'

'I'd like to join you,' Doctor Stasov ventured, piping up in his high, quavering voice. 'You'll accept that I have a somewhat personal stake in the matter. His family ruined me and built a lie on my reputation. I'd very much like to see my story vindicated.'

'If it's true, you will,' Dreyfus said. 'But I only have room for one passenger in the cutter. Besides, I'd be taking a civilian witness into a questionable situation.'

'And I don't count?' Garlin asked.

'You're a grey area,' Dreyfus said.

The four prefects went through into the chamber. Singh recovered her whiphound. Kober examined the controls on the chamber's far end. 'Vacuum beyond here as well, sir,' he told Sparver. 'But I think it's safe for you to follow us through.'

Sparver pushed through the membrane, much as he had done when going through the suitwall in the first place, except that its grab on him was slighter and the membrane was intelligent enough to know to leave his suit in place. His push carried him through on a slow, bending arc, until he landed and assumed a standing position next to the others.

Perec turned the sharp beak of her visor to him. 'Ready, sir?'

'Go through,' Sparver said.

Kober operated the door. Sparver steeled himself for an inrush of air, but the vacuum reading had been accurate. Beyond the airlock, stretching away to infinity, was an extension of the same red-lit chamber. Sections of it were lighting up in sequence, receding further and further into the distance.

It looked impossibly long, but Sparver knew Lethe was only seven kilometres across at this point, and he doubted the shaft extended much more than half that distance.

'Forward scout mode,' Perec said, flicking out the tail on her own primary whiphound. 'Ascertain the length of this shaft, then hold station at the far end. Gurney: instruct your number one to define a hundred-metre moving secure zone.'

Picking up on Perec's command through the suit channel, the whiphound lunged forward, flicking itself faster and faster with rhythmic pulses of its tail, finding traction even in the near-weightless conditions. Gurney's unit sped away just as quickly initially, but only as far as one hundred metres, before swivelling around and locking its eye onto them.

The prefects advanced, moving along the tunnel in loping, dreamlike strides. Perec and Kober led the squad, Singh and Gurney following behind, Sparver bringing up the rear. Perec's whiphound was still racing ahead, already half a kilometre down the shaft, finding only the same clean-walled corridor with its converging lines of red striplights. A minute passed, then another. Three minutes, then five. Trained to communicate only when necessary, the squad moved in silence. He had to admire their discipline, but Sparver would have appreciated a little mindless small talk to settle his jangling nerves.

Perec's whiphound slowed as it neared the limit of the shaft. It came to a halt, scanning rapidly, feeding pictures through to their visors. The shaft had widened out into a small holding area next to an internal airlock or bulkhead door.

'That's got to be the top of the connecting shaft that leads down to the habitable volume,' Sparver said.

Perec's whiphound held its ground at the head of the shaft, maintaining watch for any hitherto undetected threats. Gurney's whiphound caught up with it ten minutes later, and the prefects were only just behind it. Kober wasted no time in determining that the door was the upper access point to an elevator shaft.

Some of the power indications were active, but Kober could neither call nor confirm the position of the elevator. He spent a couple of minutes trying to coax a response from the control panel, then turned to Perec with a shake of his helmet.

'Get the door open one way or another,' she said. 'We can drop down the shaft if necessary. One of us can carry Prefect Bancal.'

Kober set his primary whiphound to sword mode and cut open the control panel casing. Inside was a gooey, glowing confusion of tangled connections and modules.

'Attempt interface,' he told the whiphound, holding it by the handle while its filament formed a questing tentacle, using the quickmatter mechanisms on the second edge to override or hotwire the panel systems. 'Panel confirms vacuum in shaft,' Kober said, after a few seconds. 'Elevator seems to be at the far end. I think we can open the door, but I can't rule out booby-traps or a false pressure reading.'

'Tell your whiphound to open it in twenty seconds,' Perec said. 'Squad: fall back thirty metres and assume defensive posture.'

Kober issued the command, leaving his whiphound still interfaced with the panel, and scuttled back to join the others. The prefects crouched low against the wall, tucked their heads down and formed cross-shaped defences with their arms. Sparver hunkered down and closed his eyes, not caring to dwell on how little protection his m-suit would give against flying debris or a sudden pressure blast.

He need not have worried. The door opened without incident, not even a breath of air escaping from the shaft.

The squad advanced back to the holding area. Perec approached the dark void beyond the now-open door, steadying herself by one hand against the doorframe as she peered in and down.

'See anything?' Sparver asked.

'Just a vertical shaft, Prefect Bancal.' Perec opened her fist. 'Here, boy.'

Her whiphound sprung into her grip, snapping its filament into itself.

'Drop to the limit of this shaft. If you survive the impact, hold station at maximum threat readiness. We will descend on suit thrusters.'

Perec flung the whiphound into the void, giving it an initial burst of momentum to assist it on its way.

'Good luck,' Sparver heard her whisper.

The whiphound dropped, freely at first and then skidding against the wall. The further it went the more speed it picked up, the walls of the shaft racing by ever faster, a moving plug of darkness hovering just out of range of the whiphound's battery of sensors.

'One kilometre,' Perec announced. 'Still in vacuum.' Then, after what seemed to Sparver to be only a few more seconds: 'Two kilometres. No alteration in the shaft.' Then: 'Three. Must be close to halfway down, still no sign of . . . shit.'

Sparver had seen it too, a sudden bottom to the shaft, rising up unexpectedly soon. The whiphound's feed had gone dark. He frowned to himself, wondering why the whiphound had failed to detect that abrupt end to the shaft, when it should have been scanning well ahead of itself, preparing to use its traction coil to slow down as it neared the bottom. He only had to think about it a fraction longer to realise that there could have been no fault with the whiphound, and what had appeared to be the bottom of the shaft was nothing of the sort.

It was the elevator, coming back up.

'Back off,' he said.

'I . . . yes,' Perec said. 'Immediate fallback.'

'You want me to try shutting the door?' Kober asked.

'No time,' Perec said.

Kober retrieved his whiphound. The prefects scuttled back to the same thirty-metre position where they had waited before, then crouched down and assumed defensive postures. Sparver took shelter behind them, mind racing as he tried to calculate how much time they had. The shaft was still in vacuum, still silent, not even a hint of vibration to give a clue as to the elevator's approach – if indeed it was still racing towards them.

It was almost an anticlimax when the elevator came. They saw it rising through the door: fast but not too fast, obviously decelerating rapidly as it neared the upper end of the shaft. A blur of motion like a ramming piston, a soft thud as the elevator's momentum was absorbed, and then silence and stillness. All they could see of the elevator was its own door, lined up with the open door in the shaft but presently sealed.

'Hold,' Perec warned, as Kober made a move to break formation. 'We still don't know what's behind that door.'

It was sensible advice because when the elevator door did open, it was as if a bright, soundless bomb had gone off. The shaft shook, flakes of debris shaken loose, a cloud of shock-frozen air blasting past the party with almost enough force to tear them off the wall. It had not been a bomb, though, but merely the sudden decompression of the elevator, which must have been filled with air all the time it had been on the way up. Some safety circuit should never have allowed that door to open into vacuum, but Sparver guessed that time – or the damage already done to the outer door – had confused the system.

'Better hope there wasn't anyone in that thing,' Gurney said.

Still no one moved. They were waiting for the cloud to disperse, to get a clear view of the open elevator. Sparver watched intently. As gaps began to open up in the white confusion, so his eyes insisted that there was a form coming into focus, an upright shape like a tall, waiting figure.

He was hoping it was his imagination. The gases would thin out and there would just be the empty elevator, summoned by some automatic protocol once it detected activity at this end of the shaft.

But Perec said: 'Someone's there.'

The grey shape gained form and solidity. It was standing in the elevator, seemingly unmoved by the explosion.

Perec unclipped her second whiphound. 'Forward scout mode,' she said, in little more than a whisper.

Still wreathed in the dispersing traces of air, the figure stepped out of the elevator, placing one very precise and careful footfall after the other, managing a slow and deliberate walk despite the near-weightlessness.

The last few gasps of air pulled away from the form. Sparver stared at it, trying to make sense of the conflicting information reaching his eyes. The figure seemed more animal than human, and yet there was something very wrong with its basic proportions. It was taller than any of the prefects, yet there was nothing above the shoulders.

The headless form lifted an arm. It was carrying something, a dark object with the purposeful lines of a weapon. Slowly it brought the arm to the level.

Perec's whiphound flung itself at the arm and the weapon. It made a noose of its coil and slipped the noose around the arm, swiftly and accurately as a carnival trick. The coil tightened and the arm and the weapon fell away, severed along a clean smoking line.

The figure toppled slowly forward, bouncing softly before coming to a halt.

Singh and Gurney dispatched whiphounds to safeguard the fallen form until it could be inspected at close range. Perec used hand gestures to signal the party to advance. They crept nearer to the body, wary of sudden movements. The severed arm had been holding a rifle-shaped thing. Sparver knelt down and extracted it from the pawlike grip of the hand, prizing furry fingers open to release the weapon.

He recognised it for what it was. A crossbow.

Then he turned his attention to the headless body. Beneath its layering of brown fur was the suggestion of powerful mechanical musculature. Where the head had been – if indeed there had ever been a head – was a ragged collar, and a busy mechanism of bearings and pipes, cut clean at the level of the neck.

Perec turned to him. 'This might sound impertinent, Prefect Bancal. But do you have the faintest fucking idea what this thing is?'

Sparver met her eyes. His expression was all the answer she really needed.

'I think we'd better take the lift,' he said.

Dreyfus cleared Panoply and notched up the acceleration. The cutter was on an expedited burn, eating into the fuel reserves that it would need to make its own way back home. This emergency crossing would get them to Lethe in just under twenty-seven minutes, a trade-off that Dreyfus considered more than satisfactory.

'Captain Pell has undocked and pulled back to just outside the exclusion volume,' Aumonier told him over the link. 'There was an attack from the anti-collision systems, but we don't think it damaged the cruiser too badly. '

'He still isn't answering?'

'Nothing, despite repeated requests. We're agreed that this isn't like Pell?'

'Pell's been duped. My guess is that he's standing by to re-dock if he gets the call from Sparver.'

'Do we think that Caleb's able to hijack our communications that way?'

Dreyfus picked his words carefully, not caring to utter a direct lie to Aumonier if he could help it. 'If the brother's responsible for Wildfire, then I wouldn't put this past him.'

'Damn it all. Didn't we patch all the holes last time?'

'There are always more holes. If there weren't, we'd be out of a job.'

'Sometimes I wouldn't mind being out of a job,' Aumonier said.

Dreyfus heard the quiet strain in her voice and knew exactly how she felt. They were all on the limit, all on the point of breaking. 'Maybe the brother will give us some answers,' he offered forlornly, before signing off.

'There is no brother,' Garlin said, strapped into the position to the right of Dreyfus, exactly where Grobno had been before Dreyfus handed him back to the Ultras. 'Stasov's admitted he has a grudge against the family. Why would you believe a word he says?'

The cutter made a sharp course change, a lumbering multi-hulled cargo hauler looming close to starboard, then swerving past in a blur of navigation lights. Traffic control had done their best to clear the lanes for this rapid crossing, but there were obviously some loose ends. Dreyfus tightened his restraint belt against his paunch, just in case.

'Stasov was treated badly by the Vois, but that doesn't mean we should dismiss his story.'

'I was in that room, Dreyfus. I heard the conversation. It was going on in front of my nose. No one's been frozen that long. The moment Spider-fingers mentioned—'

Dreyfus regarded him. 'What did you call Stasov?'

'Read as much into that as you like.'

'Do you remember something, Julius? The first time you and I met. Properly, I mean. In Stonehollow.'

Garlin shrugged. 'Clearly it left a mark on you.'

'I think it left a mark on both of us. Let me jog your memory a bit, though. You were delivering a lecture – one of your public rallies. I was the man in the crowd, wearing a hood, trying to pass unnoticed. You picked me out with uncanny accuracy, even though you had no reason to suspect that I was present.'

'Oh, yes. I remember now. I think the meeting ended with you face down in the mud, floundering like a beached whale.'

'Good. Then you'll also remember the Amerikano woman.'

'The what?'

'Her statue. The pioneer, the settler. She had her fist digging into the ground, trying to scrape some life from this new world. All very tragic.'

'It was a statue. I needed somewhere to stand, to address my gathering.'

'And you just happened to choose her, of all people. There were other statues in that habitat, Julius. But I think she called to you. You felt an affinity with her – even if you couldn't articulate it.'

'Didn't you hear what Stasov said? That whole mess happened three hundred years ago.'

'There's a connection,' Dreyfus said. 'I'm sure of it now, and deep down so are you. But I don't blame you for not remembering. Stasov said you'd already had at least one round of induced amnesia before he ever started working for the family. I think that was to suppress the memory of whatever it was that linked you to the Amerikano tragedy. But you got another dose, after your mother died. Pushed everything back even further. It's still in there, though, and my money says that Caleb's treatment wasn't anywhere near as effective. It's closer to the surface with him.'

'I'll say one thing, Dreyfus. You may not be making any sense, but at least you've stopped blaming me for Wildfire.'

The cutter took a nosedive through the middle of a ring-shaped habitat, violating several dozen traffic regulations in one swoop. Dreyfus studied his guest, ruminating on his own feelings towards Garlin and the bruised dignity he still remembered from the encounter in Hospice Idlewild.

'You chose to make yourself a person of interest,' Dreyfus said. 'And I had a job to do.'

CHAPTER TWENTY

The elevator door closed, sealing the five of them into a little moving cube of vacuum. The inertial tracker in Sparver's helmet recorded their progress, marking the kilometres as they descended.

'I think I might know what that thing was,' Kober said, almost hesitantly, as if he were wary of making a fool of himself.

'If you have an idea, share it,' Perec snapped.

'I don't know why it didn't have a head. Maybe it did, once. But the rest of it reminded me of something I saw in the history lessons. When they sent people here, those early colonists . . . the ones raised by robots. The psychologists weren't sure whether or not to make the robots look like robots, or people, or something else. I think they tried all the different approaches, in all the colonies they tried to start. But none of them helped much.'

'Kober's right,' Sparver said, memories of his own sharpening into focus. 'They knew the children needed mentors. Guiding figures, to help them with the first phase of development, until the colony had passed through a generation or two and become self-sufficient and stable. That was the plan, anyway. Some of the robots were done up to look like people, and that didn't work too well. Close but not quite right – and even a child can pick up on all the ways that it's wrong. The Ursas were another approach. Forget trying to pass them off as people, go the other way instead. Big, furry teddy bears. Mentors and friends. But they didn't work out any better than the humans, in the end.'

'You think that was an Ursa?' Perec asked.

'After three hundred years, maybe not an Ursa exactly. But something that was meant to remind us of one,' Sparver said.

Perec turned her visor to face him. 'What do you think we're dealing with here, Prefect Bancal?'

'Ghosts,' Sparver said. 'Bad memories. Some seriously bad history. That'd be my wild stab in the dark.'

They had already passed the three-kilometre mark, and soon it was four, then five. They felt glued to the floor now, but that was only in comparison with the near-weightlessness they had experienced before. After the sixth kilometre the elevator began to slow down, preparing for a smooth arrival at the base of the shaft. Their weight peaked, then settled back down to close to a gee.

Perec still had one whiphound. She fiddled with the setting dials, a nervous but understandable act of triple-checking.

'Be ready,' she said.

Sparver felt a barely perceptible halting of the elevator. He eyed the door warily, deciding it was wiser not to place his trust in any of the functions or readouts of the lock mechanism. There could be anything beyond that door, from vacuum to a thousand crushing atmospheres of acid. He wondered which of them would be better off in either scenario: the prefects in their tactical armour, or him in his tissue-thin m-suit. At least it would be *quick* for Sparver, if his worst fears were justified.

'Air exchange,' Singh said. 'I'm reading a rising partial pressure.'

'Confirmed,' Perec said. 'Sniffer says breathable, too. But don't take any chances.'

Sparver's faceplate readout picked up on the same injection of air into the elevator. As the pressure pushed towards one atmosphere, his m-suit sagged around his form like a deflated bag.

'Equalising,' Kober said.

Without fanfare, the elevator door opened, an external door opening a moment later. Sparver blinked against unexpected brightness, disconcerting after the dim lighting of Lethe's corridors and shafts.

The elevator faced the base of a steep-sided pit, with dark walls to either side, and a rectangle of hazy, wavering brightness above. The pit extended a few metres away from the elevator, with a set of plain-looking stairs climbing to the level of the top of the walls.

Perec was the first to step out. She gave an order to her whiphound and sent it slinking up the stairs, until it fed back a view of the terrain surrounding the pit.

Sparver took a moment to process what he was seeing. Nothing at all had prepared him for the procession of shapes and textures and colours streaming across his faceplate as the whiphound panned its eye to take in the full panorama. He had been counting on some kind of artificial volume, it was true, but not even his wildest imaginings would have touched on the spectacle as it now presented itself. It was a jungle: a dense, luscious explosion of life and form, plants and trees throwing back a shimmering palette of too-vivid greens, of leaves and ferns scissoring against a sky of impossible blazing blue, seemingly too deep and distant

341

to ever be contained within the smallness of Lethe. There were flowers, too: shocking pinks and blood crimsons, fiery oranges and rich blues, a superabundance of colours jarring his eyes, each jewel-like swatch jangling against the blue-green as if it hovered on some distinct plane of its own, unconnected to the great mass of the jungle. It was beautiful, in an over-ripe, gaudy sense. But what struck Sparver most forcibly was a powerful impression of wrongness. There was something too vivid and oppressive about this jungle, and all that he knew of Lethe told him that it had no business being here.

He didn't like it.

Still, they had come to investigate.

Perec walked slowly up the stairs, her whiphound circling the edge of the open pit, ready to defend the position. She reached the top, took a step onto the level ground, made a cautious observation of her surroundings, then gestured for the others to climb after her. Kober, Singh and Gurney followed, with Sparver being the last one out of the pit, struggling up the tall steps, which had clearly not been optimised for a pig's stride.

They were in a small clearing, bordered on all sides by the lurid green of the jungle. Curving above them was that too-blue sky, a projection onto the artificial ceiling of this opening inside Lethe. If the ceiling was dome-shaped, then they seemed to have come out nearer the edge than the middle. Under their feet was a carpet of grass, so uniform in colour and height that it could have been manicured. There was even a door-like rectangle of grass and sub-soil hinged back from the pit, ensuring the pit's presence would be much less obvious when sealed.

'It's a biome, obviously,' Perec said, as if someone needed to fill the silence that had followed their emergence from the elevator. 'Energy-intensive, too, keeping all this biomass alive. Now we know why this rock was still using so much power. Is this anything you were expecting, Prefect Bancal?'

'No,' he answered. 'Not headless teddy bears, not jungles. But I'd like to take a look further in, if we can.'

'Sword mode will take care of this vegetation pretty easily,' Kober said. 'Our whiphounds can clear a path ahead of us.'

'No need,' Singh said. 'Looks like someone's already gone to the trouble.'

She was pointing to a notch in the clearing, where a clear, if narrow, trail led into the depths of the jungle, more or less in the direction Sparver had intended to go.

'If that was there when we arrived, I missed it on the sweep,' Perec said.

'I guess it wasn't that obvious,' Gurney said, not sounding in the least bit convinced.

'Singh,' Perec said. 'Order your primary to hold this area while we move into the overgrowth. If we need to get out of this place in a hurry, I don't want to waste time searching for that elevator entrance.' She called back her own whiphound. 'Forward scout mode. Ten-metre secure zone, following the line of that trail. Clear overgrowth as you go. Proceed.'

Perec's whiphound nodded emphatically and headed out of the clearing. The trail was densely canopied and the whiphound soon passed out of sight, its presence betrayed only by a rapid, machinelike threshing as it used its second edge to widen the trail. The whiphound's moving point of view appeared on their visors, as it forged its way down a narrow corridor of darkening, thickening green.

The party set off after it, moving in single file with Perec in the lead and Sparver at the rear. They still had seven whiphounds to provide immediate cover, Kober donating his secondary unit to Perec, all four operatives using their whiphounds in sword mode to scythe away any lingering obstructions. They kept a respectful distance between each other, keeping out of range of the swing of the whiphounds' stiffened cutting filaments.

Soon the canopy had closed over them almost completely, forming a dappled ceiling, and the trail's meandering path quickly snatched the clearing from view.

As the cutter made its final approach to Lethe, Dreyfus reflected on what he knew of Aurora's capabilities and intentions.

He could guess what had happened with Captain Pell and the prefects aboard the *Democratic Circus*, although it was not a theory that he had the slightest intention of voicing in public. Aurora must have intervened, overriding the cruiser's communication link with Panoply and substituting her own orders for those of Jane Aumonier. Where the Supreme Prefect desired a cautious, deliberate approach, Aurora sought only the quickest route to provocation. In Caleb she saw either a threat to herself or at the very least a human puzzle that intrigued her, something which demanded her immediate and thorough interest.

She had given Pell the instruction to return to Lethe, and through no fault of his own Pell had assumed the change of intentions was valid. Sparver, too, would have had no cause to second-guess the supposed word of Lady Jane.

Dreyfus already knew Aurora could push her presence into Panoply's secret layers, infiltrating virtual spaces and communications channels, and now he had given her the means to reach the closed archives of the Search Turbines. All this was dangerous enough, yet he was certain that manipulating information was not the limit of her capabilities. If she wished, Dreyfus felt sure, she could have turned this cutter around and sent it scuttling back to Panoply. She had not played her hand, though, and that led Dreyfus to conclude that whatever now happened would be satisfactory to Aurora. The initial act of provocation had been achieved; the truth regarding Caleb would now come to light one way or another.

She was present, he believed – some part of her, at least. Watching and listening, even if she had other eyes and ears elsewhere. He almost felt he owed her an acknowledgement. But they knew each other well enough by now. She would know that he knew, and that was enough.

'Something amusing you, Dreyfus?' Garlin asked.

'Just thinking about an old acquaintance. The trouble with you being puppeted by Caleb is that you can't really help who else you come to the attention of. Ever felt like a fly in a spider's web?'

'No. Have you?'

'Once or twice.' Dreyfus tapped the console and brought up an enlargement of Lethe, now close enough for visual acquisition. 'There it is, Julius. Ring any bells? If Stasov's right, you spent half your childhood inside that rock, convinced you were still living in Chasm City. I bet this isn't quite the way you imagined your glorious homecoming. Your mother died here, I think. Before her shuttle broke up on re-entry to Yellowstone, she was already dead and gone. Are you starting to remember anything of how it happened?'

'You're crazy, Dreyfus.'

'But not so crazy that I can't tell when a man's starting to question his deepest assumptions. You do remember Stasov, whether you want to admit it or not. And that means there's a chance the rest of it's true as well.'

Garlin's jaw moved, as if he meant to offer some riposte. But nothing came.

The console chimed with an incoming transmission from the *Democratic Circus*.

'Dreyfus. How are you doing, Captain Pell?'

'A little surprised to see you arrive unannounced, Prefect. Have you been in contact with Prefect Bancal and the others?'

'No . . . not exactly. And I don't suppose you've had any word from inside Lethe?'

'They went dark soon after we undocked. About twenty minutes ago we picked up a small seismic event, and if we've localised it correctly it was near the top of the elevator shaft. Am I missing something here, Prefect?'

'If you are, Captain Pell, you're not the only one. I'm taking the cutter in to the docking port. Give me covering fire if I run into the surface defences, will you?'

'Are you sure you don't want to dock with us first?'

'No time. Once I'm docked, return to Panoply. Disregard any contravening orders you receive between now and then. You'll be debriefed upon arrival.'

'Why would I disregard . . .'

'Just do it, Pell.'

The cutter veered hard for Lethe.

Marlon Voi regarded Julius with a look composed of equal parts admiration and venom – not a little impressed by the thing he had brought into the world, and not a little horrified by it as well, it seemed to Julius.

'Let me tell you what I already figured out for myself, while I still have the chance,' Julius said, with a sort of chilly bonhomie. 'Caleb and I were never your sons. You and Mother . . .' His voice caught as his thoughts dwelled on the image of her, dead on the ground, brought low by his own hand. 'You weren't our real parents. We were raised by you, and you went to a lot of trouble to make us feel like your natural heirs, but we were never your flesh and blood. That was all a lie.'

They were walking behind Lurcher, as the robot trudged back to the house. The robot was carrying the body of Aliya Voi, lolling in its arms just as if she had fallen asleep. Marlon and Julius were carrying the equally limp form of Caleb, who was alive but unconscious. Julius had permitted the robot to administer an additional sedative to his brother, taking no chances with Caleb causing further trouble.

'You're wrong,' Father said. 'It's not how you think it was. You have our genes. You were both Vois. Didn't you see it in your faces, when you compared them with our own, or the portraits in the house?'

'Faces can be made to look any way you like,' Julius said.

'There wasn't any need to. You are our sons.'

'We had dreams, Father. We were part of something that happened far too long ago for us to be your sons.'

Father nearly stumbled under his share of Caleb's burden. 'You were never meant to remember any of that.'

'Any of what, exactly?'

'It's best left as is. The less you recollect, the happier you'll be.'

'I've just shot and killed my own mother, *Marlon*.' He said his father's name deliberately, certain of the hurt it would cause. 'Remind me why I'm meant to feel happy about anything?'

'You don't know how much worse it could be.' Father – Marlon – paused, needing to draw breath before they continued. It was a long, winding route back to the Shell House and he was not accustomed to exercise. 'Was it really a trick, Julius?'

'Yes. Caleb made me see a lion. He placed the figment in my head. That's what I thought I was shooting.'

Marlon seemed to accept the plausibility of this explanation. Perhaps he had seen enough of Caleb's spitefulness and talent for manipulation to form his own judgement. 'Then Caleb made a deliberate choice to have Aliya murdered?'

'He was afraid she'd revoke our powers, with or without your agreement. She was thinking of it, wasn't she?'

'She saw something in your brother that concerned her, yes.'

'And me – was I a concern?'

'She thought you had a wiser head on your shoulders. Or were kinder, at least.'

'I think she was a little wrong about both of us. She couldn't have guessed Caleb would go that far. Even I didn't realise.'

'You got your retribution, from the looks of it. What have you left of his brain, Julius?'

'Oh, enough. He'll be fine, when he comes round. Eventually.' Julius reached out to give Marlon an encouraging shove. 'C'mon. The sooner we're back at the Shell House, the sooner I can explain how things are going to be from now on.'

Marlon's eyes registered fear. 'What exactly do you have in mind?'

'Oh, nothing too serious as far as you're concerned. I'll be leaving, but once I've set myself up in the outside world I still want access to the family money, which means there can't be any scandals surrounding the Voi estate.'

'A murder isn't serious enough for you?'

'We'll have to make it look like something other than a murder, won't we?' Julius said this as if he were explaining something to a child, which was not greatly at odds with the way he now felt about Marlon. 'You and I, we'll rub heads and think of a way to explain her death. Make it look like an accident. A great tragedy. It'll put an awful toll on you, of course, so you'll withdraw from public life – even more than you already have. But you'll still be here, and so will Caleb. I'll leave the two of you to stew in your own guilt.'

'You can't go anywhere,' Marlon said. 'The world isn't ready for you. You don't even exist . . . legally, I mean.'

'Oh, I figured that out already. I'm a non-entity, a non-citizen.' Julius spared a hand to tap the side of his head. 'But you've instilled a great gift in me, Marlon. I can choose to become whatever and whoever I want. I can alter any packet of data I wish, any record. I can make a past for myself – a name and a history that feels as real as anyone else's. Admit it – you were going to have to lie about us eventually, weren't you?'

'Not this way. Not now.'

'It's sooner than I'd have liked as well,' Julius said. 'But it's not my fault that Caleb brought this on us.'

'You can't just leave,' Marlon said. 'You don't know what's out there. What's *really* out there. You're not prepared.'

'Then you'll show me,' Julius replied.

They brought the bodies to the Shell House. Aliya was placed in one room, while Caleb's unconscious form was taken to the one where Julius had found the sleeping Doctor Stasov. Julius told Lurcher to monitor Caleb and sedate him if he woke up.

Marlon tried to give an overriding order to the robot, but Julius had reached inside Lurcher and given himself command precedence. Marlon persisted long enough to establish that he had no authority over the robot, at least not while Julius was present.

Some fleeting, furtive notion played across Marlon's face.

Julius felt the tickle as Marlon tried to reach into his skull, attempting to issue the revocation command.

'No,' he said gently, pushing his father's intrusion aside with more tenderness than he felt. 'That won't work. I can see how the blocking action works, and what I need to do to circumvent it. It's actually pretty easy. I wish I'd seen it sooner, then I could have told Caleb not to worry about either of you being able to revoke our powers.'

Marlon tried again. Julius rebuffed him with a little more force.

'Now what?' Marlon asked, drained of hope, his options exhausted.

'Nothing bad.' Julius tried a reassuring smile. 'You're just going to stay here and keep doing what you do. I know it'll be lonely, but you'll adjust. Make of Caleb what you will – he's of no interest to me now.'

'But Aliya . . .'

'Her death will have to be explained, yes. I've an idea, but it's a little tricky, and you'll need to cooperate on your end of the story. But you'll have a great incentive to do so, so that shouldn't be a problem.'

'They'll see she was murdered.'

'Then there can't be much of a body left for anyone to pick over.' Julius brightened as he felt his plan gaining connective tissue. 'She's been going into space a lot lately, since you can't be bothered to leave the Shell House. That's true, isn't it?'

Marlon's look was distrustful. 'What of it?'

'We'll use that to our advantage. Put her body into the private shuttle, send it into orbit, then have it malfunction on the way back. Burn up, crash, leave just enough genetic material to satisfy the curious. No suspicion would be attached to you – far from it. You'd be the tragic widower, the latest in a line of Vois to be burdened by a terrible twist of fate.'

'Why wouldn't they suspect me?'

'Because you wouldn't have the means to make an accident like that happen, even if you wanted to.' Julius shrugged. 'It's easy for me, though.'

'How can you be so cold about this?'

'I'm just reverting to type, Marlon – springing back to the monster you've always known me to be. What was it Doctor Stasov said, when you were arguing with Mother . . . Aliya? You were making monsters out of monsters?'

'You don't know what you were.' But a single shudder of ran through Marlon, as he found some desperate composure. 'You'll help me dispose of the body, like you said.'

'Good.'

'But not the way you think.'

He took Julius to the edge of the dome, to the spot where Lurcher had been repairing the panels.

They stood together, father and son, looking out at the lights and towers of Chasm City.

'You think it's yours for the taking,' Marlon said eventually. 'Close enough to touch. A dream of a city, waiting to bend itself to your will. All those millions of lives, hardly knowing the force that's heading their way. The power you've imagined. The things you could do with that power.'

'What of it?'

'Do you see that panel that's a little cleaner than the rest?' Marlon nodded to make his point. 'See if you can remove it.'

'Don't be silly. Caleb and I tried forcing every panel on the perimeter when we were younger. The more you told us we weren't old enough to go into Chasm City, the more we wanted to.'

'You weren't as strong then. Anyway, there's a knack to it. Press the panel against its frame, then apply a little clockwise rotational force. The seal should release.'

'If it was that easy . . .'

'Do it,' Marlon said.

Something in that command compelled Julius to obey, as if permitting Marlon one last order for old times' sake. He moved to the panel, braced himself – glancing back in case there was some trick about to be sprung on him – and settled his palms on the cold, clean glass of the panel. He did as Marlon had instructed, and after sufficient resistance to have deterred a younger version of himself, he felt the glass click and unlock from its seal.

Carefully Julius extracted the panel and set it down on the ground, resting against the bottom edge of the dome.

A chilly draught touched his face. He raised his eyes to the gap in the dome, expecting to see Chasm City's lights with more clarity and brightness than before, now there was no glass between him and the city.

There was only darkness.

His senses robbed of distant reference points, Sparver had to keep reminding himself that he was inside a cold lump of tumbling rock, not on the surface of some verdant, abundantly forested planet. Every footstep was taking him along the arc of a slowly curving floor, but with the oppressive sensory overload of the jungle it was impossible to tell he was walking on anything but a level surface.

'I saw something ahead on the feed,' Perec announced, when they were two-thirds of a kilometre in from the clearing. 'Just for a second, when there was a gap in the cover. Looked like a big structure, a kilometre or so further on. Maybe less. Hard to judge how big or how far away it was. Feels like this path is taking us there, whatever it is.'

Sparver had also seen something but the glimpse had been too brief to offer anything substantial. Whatever it was they would get there soon enough, he felt certain.

It took less than a minute for the party to reach the point where the whiphound had gained that momentary glimpse of the structure, but the jungle seemed to have closed that particular sight-line. Perec crouched down to approximate the whiphound's doglike viewpoint, then used her own unit to hack away some more of the foliage, all to no avail. From his vantage point behind her Sparver noticed an odd subliminal flicker on the whiphound's second edge, where it encountered the greenery.

'Everything all right, Dalia?'

'Just some resistance, Prefect Bancal.' But she turned around to face Kober. 'Did you lock in the effector settings on this unit?'

'There's nothing wrong with my whiphound . . .' Kober said, trailing off when he noticed – in common with the offers – the abrupt termination of the visual feed from Perec's forward scout unit.

'That's not normal,' Gurney said.

Sparver had begun to notice the flickering effect on his own whiphound. A spangle of blue and pink flashes emanated from the cutting edge whenever it came into contact with any part of the jungle. The effort of swinging the blade was becoming harder, as if the cutting edge were dulling, meeting resistance.

A deep apprehension settled in his gut.

'Close up whiphounds,' he snapped. 'Nobody cut or touch anything. This isn't a jungle.'

'What the hell is it?' Perec asked.

'Quickmatter. Somehow. Certainly whatever the whiphounds touched, and maybe everything we can see. We're deep in the middle of it.'

'That's . . .' But Perec must have caught herself before she offered reflex contradiction. 'This jungle goes on for kilometres. If it's all quickmatter . . . we've never seen or trained for anything like this sort of concentration.'

'Quickmatter can't hurt us,' Kober said. 'There are safeties. We can conjure it out of the way . . .'

Kober used his free hand to make a conjuring gesture, palm to the jungle, fingers outspread, pushing back against air. The jungle should have detected his desire and at least made a show of partial retreat, but there was no response.

'It's not obeying,' Perec said.

'It won't,' Sparver said. 'Not for us, maybe not even for someone with a head full of implants. Someone else is controlling it. The best we can hope for is that we don't provoke it.'

They snapped their filaments back into their handles, clutching the whiphounds like truncheons, and advanced carefully along the path, all too conscious of the blades and fronds that brushed against their suits. Soon they came to what was left of Perec's whiphound. It was on the ground, filament flicking limply, sparks dancing from the blade to the handle. Perec made to reach for it.

'No,' Sparver said.

She jerked back her hand in time. A network of fine green cilia had already begun to wrap itself around the handle. Where the jungle floor touched it the whiphound was losing form, its edges turning furry. It was in the process of being dismantled, its parts absorbed into the self-replicating mass of the jungle.

'We'd better get some distance from it,' Sparver said. 'Gurney, Singh. Get back to the clearing and see if you can ride that elevator back up to the entry shaft. Instruct Panoply that we need an immediate enforcement action, with quickmatter specialisation.'

'I . . . yes, sir,' Singh said. 'We'll see if we can make it back.'

Gurney and Singh set off back the way they had come, walking at first then breaking into a jog just before their black suits passed out of sight. Sparver watched them go with profound unease, uncertain if he had improved their chances or just made them worse.

'Let's keep moving,' he said resignedly, while Perec's whiphound sparked and fizzed in its grassy crib. 'This path was cleared for us for a reason.'

'I don't like it,' Perec said.

'Me neither. But I'm not turning back just yet, not while we're still dealing with Wildfire.'

They quickened their pace. Their whiphounds might have had their filaments retracted, but that did not mean they were totally useless. Perec was taking the lead, sweeping her whiphound back and forth like a wand or divining stick, relying on the scanning and threat-detection systems to offer some advance warning of trouble. Sparver followed with his back to Kober, unnerved – but not entirely surprised – to see that the walls of the trail seemed to press together once they had passed, leaving barely any trace of the path they had followed.

Singh and Gurney were still moving, at least. Their feeds were still playing, and Perec kept checking back with them for verbal updates.

'It's not resisting us just yet,' Singh reported.

'Good,' Perec said. 'Maintain your pace and stay calm.'

The world suddenly turned white, and after a soundless instant a shockwave hit Sparver just as if he had walked into an unyielding door. After-images fogged his eyes. Through pained slits he watched the whiteness die away to a sullen, green-filtered glow. Overhead, where the gaps in the canopy still allowed glimpses of blue, a soot-black cloud billowed and rose and dissipated. The prefects paused for a moment then resumed their advance, not needing to dwell on the obvious facts of the whiphound malfunction.

'Gurney. Singh. Were you clear?' Perec asked.

'Clear,' Singh said. 'Inertial fix says we're within one hundred metres of the start point.'

'Good. If your luck's in, that elevator's still waiting at this end of the shaft.'

A red outline showed on Sparver's faceplate, pulsing for his attention. It defined a low, cryptic form, a blob of matter moving somewhere ahead of them, hidden from his eyes by layers of intervening foliage.

'Tracking it,' Perec said, tension in her voice. 'Permission to deploy second edge.'

'Keep it sheathed,' Sparver said. 'We want to stay on the right side of this jungle.'

'Damn it, Bancal,' she hissed. 'There's *something* moving out there.'

Sparver decided to ignore the breach of etiquette. 'Easy, Field. If your whiphound detects an approaching threat, it will still go fully autonomous. Its reflexes are a thousand times faster than your own, so start trusting them.'

'I think I saw it,' Kober said breathlessly. 'Something black, behind the ferns. Just for a moment.'

Sparver was still directing most of his attention to the rear of the trio.

'What did it look like?'

'Not sure, sir. Big, low. I think I saw eyes. Some sort of animal.'

'Keep moving,' he said, as much for his own benefit as the others'.

The whiphounds were still targeting the moving form, but the quickmatter was obviously confusing their acquisition and range-finding faculties, the shape remaining amorphous and poorly separated from the confusion of surrounding forms. There was no surprise to be had in that, Sparver thought. He thought it highly unlikely it was made up of flesh and blood.

'I see a second trace,' Perec said. 'Something else moving, on the other side of the trail. They're coming closer. What the hell are those things?'

'Cats,' Kober said.

'I'd really feel better with a sword in my hand,' Perec said.

'Go ahead,' Sparver relented, deciding that a psychological boost was what counted now. 'One-metre extrusion, and keep that edge away from any part of the jungle.' Sparver unclipped his second whiphound and deployed its traction filament. 'Protective cordon only, no second edge until I give the order. Proceed.'

The whiphound nodded and began to loop around the trio, whisking through the foliage but making no effort to clear away any part of it. Sparver then deployed his primary whiphound in sword mode, almost ashamed at how much better he felt when he had that time-honoured weapon in his grasp.

They moved on, the black shapes prowling close by but not yet letting themselves be seen. At last, through a thinning in the canopy, Sparver caught the white apex of the structure at the middle of the dome and realised they could not be far from it now, maybe only a few hundred metres. Whatever the nature of the building, its curving, spiralling architecture was more organic than geometric.

The path kinked. Ahead, emerging quite abruptly, was an opening, a smaller version of the earlier clearing, where at least two trails crossed each other. Sparver had the sense that the opening had not existed until they were very close to it, the quickmatter foliage reorganising itself like a clever stage set, falling into place just in advance of the actors. That was the least of his concerns, though.

A huge black cat blocked their way. Its stance was assertive, four powerful paws planted on the ground, its long body a study in predator biomechanics. Its tail curled high behind it, its head and neck lowered with belligerent intent, two preternaturally yellow eyes gleaming.

The cat was an absence with eyes, a moving inkblot with sentience. Slowly the mouth widened, white teeth gleaming into visibility.

The cat took a forward step.

Sparver's whiphound gathered itself into a bundle and flung itself at the cat, extruding its filament to the fullest extent as it spun through the air.

Sparver only had time to observe, not to react.

His whiphound tried to wrap itself around the cat. Instead, the filament slipped all the way through, even as the cat remained whole. The whiphound redoubled its efforts, confused but determined, gamely convinced it could still disable this identified threat. Still its coils fell through the cat as if it were made of smoke.

Now a second cat emerged into the clearing, eyes and teeth flaring from the perfect void of its body.

The first cat had wearied of the whiphound's efforts. With an insouciant paw-flick it sent the whiphound tumbling into the jungle, whereupon there was an immediate flicker of pink and blue sparks.

Sparver pushed to the front of the party. He still had his primary whiphound. He knew that the cutting edge would achieve nothing against the cats. He pulled in the filament and levelled the handle at the closest cat.

'Mark target. Grenade mode, minimum yield, contact fuse.'

He lobbed the whiphound, then sprung around and flung himself to the ground. Perec and Kober followed his lead, and then a white pulse bleached the world, accompanied by a shock wave and a burst of heat that Sparver felt all the way through his m-suit.

Kober was already giving a similar order to his own whiphound. 'Mark target. Grenade mode . . .'

'Don't waste your time,' Perec said.

Sparver stumbled to his feet and turned to assess the damage. The whiphound had excavated a small crater in the floor of the clearing. But the first cat was reconstituting itself, tributaries of black flowing in from all directions, pouring out of the ground as if it bled some dark, living ichor. The other cat had not been hurt at all.

Now the second quickened its pace.

They had two whiphounds left.

'Protective cordon,' Sparver said. 'Both units. That's all we can hope for.

They can't stop those cats but maybe they can keep them from reaching us for a few minutes.'

'And after that?' Perec asked.

The whiphounds formed their cordon, a moving corral around the party. The trio advanced into the blasted clearing. The cats, the first now fully reconstituted, closed in on the cordon from either side, prowling around it like a pair of orbiting moons.

A voice blared into his skull, breathless and anxious. 'This is Singh. We're back at the starting point. But the elevator's gone.'

'Then summon it,' Perec said with admirable calm, little in her answer betraying their present circumstances.

'I have. But I can't tell if it's responding or not. It's kilometres to the other end of that shaft. We've got another problem. I think something's been tracking us. We're picking up shapes . . . things . . . closing in on the clearing.'

'Here's some advice,' Perec answered. 'Don't engage. Find the best cover you can and get behind a defensive cordon. Repeat, *do not* engage.'

'I . . . yes. Understood. We're at the pit now. There's something else, too. We found two things in the pit that weren't there when we left. Giving you visual now, Prefect Perec. Please advise.'

'Thank you, Singh. I see what you're seeing.'

Sparver saw it as well, projected onto his faceplate. The image was shaky, as Singh fought to control his nerves. Lying in the pit side by side, perfectly formed, as neat and solid as if they had been there all the time, was a pair of crossbows.

'Don't touch anything you don't have to,' Perec said. 'You'll be all right, Singh, as soon as that elevator arrives.'

The cats continued circling the party, occasionally testing the whiphounds with a lunge or a feint. Sparver had to admit that his knowledge of actual cats was not exhaustive. But something in the way these forms moved and behaved convinced him that some fundamental, feline algorithm was governing their actions.

'Look,' Kober said. 'Ahead on the trail. Three of them, just like the ones in the pit.'

Kober was right. Three crossbows lay waiting, one for each of them, only a few metres beyond the front of the moving cordon.

Something flicked from the jungle, a blur of green, and one of the two whiphounds vanished.

One of the cats saw its moment and flung itself at Kober, bringing him down instantly. The other cat joined its mate and the two of them hauled Kober's flailing, scrabbling form into the jungle, a curtain of green opening and then closing behind them.

Sparver saw his own moment, too. He sprang forward and snatched up two of the crossbows, even as the third seemed to be melting back into the ground. He tossed one of the weapons to Perec, who caught it one-handedly. Even as he did this, the final whiphound was snatched away into the greenery.

'It's a game,' he said, struck by a sudden, lurching intuition. 'The jungle's setting the rules, not us. We can hunt or be hunted. But this is all we get to use.'

He examined the crossbow. It was a simple, if elegant, thing. Lodged in the groove of its barrel was a single arrowed projectile, finned and barbed like a miniature spaceship.

Off in the distance Kober was screaming.

'We've got to help him,' Perec said, staring down at her own crossbow, her hand shaking.

'He's gone,' Sparver said, surprising himself with the firmness of his response. 'Understand that. He's beyond any help you or I are capable of giving.' He raised his own crossbow, sighting along the groove. 'Our duty now is not to die, if at all possible. We have a mission, an enforcement action. So I suppose we'd better make these things count.'

'This isn't how I thought it would play out.'

'Me neither.' He started walking, trusting the trail to take him nearer to the structure he had glimpsed earlier. 'But it's a better than zero chance, and if those are the only odds we get, we'd better make the most of them. I'm willing to bet we only get one shot with these things. Wait until there's no chance of missing.'

It was a relief of sorts when Kober fell silent, but only a small one, because that silence surely meant the cats would soon move on from the temporary distraction he had provided.

Sparver and Perec continued their advance, the trail opening up ahead of them, thickening and closing behind. Sparver was struck by an unwelcome mental image, that they were two pieces of food being squeezed along a digestive tract. It was not a position he much enjoyed finding himself in. But he was under no illusions that the jungle would not punish any attempt to ignore or negate the game.

'Whatever happens to us,' Perec said, twisting around to cover their rear, 'this is only going to end one way for whoever's behind this. Panoply will tear this place apart, quickmatter or not. Even if the Supreme Prefect has to petition for the use of special weapons. They'll give it to her, this time – all the way to nukes.' Perec was breathing hard, and

Sparver guessed that talking was her preferred psychological defence mechanism when under intense stress. 'No one wants to think about a motherlode of hostile nanotechnology drifting through the Glitter Band like a rogue cancer. They'll use whatever it takes to turn this place to dead ashes.'

Sparver twitched his crossbow to the left and right, seeing cats where there were just black shadows.

'Your point being?'

'This feels like some sort of suicidal endgame. Like we've been lured into a house someone's preparing to burn to the ground.'

'That's a cheering thought, Dalia.'

But it was one he shared, whether or not he cared to admit it. That image of the digestive tract flashed back to him. They had been shepherded to this point long before they reached the jungle, he knew. Perhaps from the moment the flood brought Thalia and him to Elysium Heights, if not sooner. Coaxed and prodded when they thought they were making independent deductive leaps, so that their actions were always destined to bring them to this place, the arena of this terminal game. And with a shiver of insight – one whose steps he could not have easily diagrammed, even to his own contentment – Sparver intuited that this process had begun not with Wildfire, not with the crisis of the last four hundred days, but years or decades earlier. Some great slow mechanism had been set in patient motion, and this was the culmination of it.

'There's an opening,' Perec said, excited and fearful in the same breath. 'It's the heart of the chamber. We'll be safer there.'

'You think?'

'Better than this. We'll have a chance of spotting the cats before they close in. And maybe there's some rock, some inert matter, that we can get to. We just need a bridgehead, something we can defend until Panoply arrive.'

Ahead, the path widened out, edges of foliage framing a large open area consisting of a concentric pattern of formal gardens, encircling the tall building whose spiral, organically derived architecture he had already glimpsed. There were windows set at haphazard intervals into the ascending, coiling levels, and doors at the base, facing onto a slightly elevated terrace.

'It's the Shell House,' Sparver said. 'I recognise it from the Garlin case files. But it shouldn't be here. He was born and raised in Chasm City.'

'Could it be quickmatter?'

Sparver wanted to offer some reassurance, some consoling hint that they might find safety in the structure. But Perec deserved better than that. 'Whatever it is, I don't trust it. Though it seems to be waiting for us, and it would be rude to turn down an invitation.'

'Perhaps the cats have given up on us for now.'

'That would be nice,' he said, clutching his crossbow tight as they broke out of the jungle, into the central area.

There was no sign of company, an observation that did nothing to lessen his nerves. They crept into the open together, back to back and circling slowly as they moved. They were moving along a dirt-lined path, hemmed by rock gardens that had the same too-vivid coloration as the foliage in the jungle, the plants and flowers almost migraine-bright.

Perec jerked suddenly, her elbow jabbing into his back. 'I thought . . .' She caught her breath. 'Just a shadow, was all. I'm sorry.'

'Don't apologise. It's all right to be twitchy.'

They walked and circled, gradually narrowing the distance to the Shell House. 'Can I say something, sir?'

'You say what you like, Dalia.'

He sensed her hesitation before replying. 'I'm glad it was you they sent us, sir.'

'Glad it was me, or glad it was a hyperpig?'

'Both, sir. You have a reputation, and . . . well, if there was anyone I'd sooner be in this mess with, I can't think of who they are.'

'Mm.' Sparver mulled this, not entirely certain of how he was meant to take it. 'And this reputation of mine?'

'You tend to come out of things, sir. In one piece.'

'It helps being small,' Sparver said. 'We get overlooked. Also, we're good at squeezing out of places.'

'I'm sure there's more to it than that.'

'You'd be—' But he stopped, his heart racing. He had seen something, some liquid pooling of shadow and light on the periphery of the open area, near the point where they had emerged from the jungle. He raised the crossbow, aimed it at the spot, and was an instant away from firing when he decided the pattern was illusory, just his brain making a cat out of chaos. He breathed out, made to lower the crossbow.

Perec fired. He felt the recoil, her back to his.

Slowly he turned, wanting – and not wanting – to see a cat, because that would mean that she had not wasted her bolt. By way of a bonus, too, it would be good if the cat were dead, or dying.

But there was nothing.

'I thought . . .' Perec started. 'I was sure. I saw it. It was there, coming out of the green . . .'

'I believe you,' Sparver said.

Perec lowered her crossbow. 'I shouldn't have fired. I've wasted the bolt.'

'It's not your fault. Whatever you saw, it's what this place wanted you to see.' Sparver took a step away from her. 'Dalia, I'm going to ask you to accept an order. You'll take this.' He made to pass her his own crossbow, with the bolt still loaded. 'It's worth more to you than it is to me.'

'Prefect Bancal . . .'

'Take it, Dalia. When this place really turns against us, this m-suit of mine isn't going to make much difference. But your armour might buy you a little time.'

'Like it did with Kober?'

'Better a second or two than nothing at all. Have the crossbow.' Sparver reached out to take her empty weapon and hefted it. 'I've still got a club. You'd be surprised what I can do with a club.'

An order had been given, so she accepted it, nodding once in acknowledgement at the transaction that had taken place.

'Thank you, sir. I won't make the same mistake twice.'

'You see those doors?' Sparver said, nodding at the base of the Shell House. 'That's our objective. I can't promise it's going to be any safer in there than out here. But I'd still sooner take that chance.'

They were moving again, Perec taking the lead this time, sweeping her crossbow around, Sparver feeling the nervous energy coming off her, only ever a twitch away from firing. They left the rock gardens behind, setting out across an open area encircling the building, where all the paths converged. Perhaps the building was a forlorn hope, he told himself – just as likely to be made of quickmatter as the rest of their environment. Perhaps its very walls would bleed more cats, or something worse. But where there was a possibility of shelter, of establishing some bridgehead, he could not ignore it. Besides, one of the objectives of an enforcement action was the securing of evidence. If there was evidence in the Shell House, he was duty bound to record it – even if none of his observations ever made it back to Panoply.

They were nearing the raised terrace when the cats came back.

Perec saw them first, pooling out of the distant margin of the jungle, black ink-blots coalescing into animal forms, moving with the low-shouldered gait of confident predators in clear sight of their prey. Two cats, then three. Three cats for one bolt. Sparver almost laughed. There was no hope of reaching the Shell House now.

'You should run, sir,' Perec said, as the cats gathered speed, approaching along one of the converging paths. 'You'll be faster in that m-suit. I'll hold them back as best I can.'

'No,' he answered, doubting very much that he would be faster. 'We don't run. Not now. We hold this line, as best we're able.'

'Sir . . .'

'It's all right, Dalia. The game was loaded against us. We shouldn't feel too bad about it.'

He was impressed with the way Perec held her nerve, waiting until she had a clear shot at the nearest of the cats, taking down one of them when it was only a dozen bounds away, the cat splashing down into a flattened black puddle, the other two moving through it with gathering strides. By now both of their crossbows were useless except as clubs, but they raised them anyway, even as the cats seemed to compress in on themselves before launching into the air. One of them took Perec, the other Sparver. At the first clawing impact his crossbow was wrenched from his grip, sent spinning away. The cat hammered him to the ground. Perec groaned, and a smear of red washed across Sparver's vision.

Someone's blood. It could have been his, but he wasn't sure. That was one of the odd ironies of his existence. When you got down to corpuscles, humans and hyperpigs weren't so unalike.

CHAPTER TWENTY-ONE

Dreyfus detected the shift in his weight which heralded the elevator's imminent arrival at the base of the shaft. He turned to Garlin, managing a laconic smile as he met the other man's gaze through the visors of their m-suits. 'Any second now, one of us is going to have the great pleasure of proving the other one wrong. I hope you're ready for it, Julius.'

'Oh, I'm ready. I've never been more ready.'

'Nice show of strength. But I know a chink of doubt when I see one.'

The elevator arrived with a soft bump, the airlock starting to sequence almost immediately. Dreyfus touched a reassuring hand against the two whiphounds he carried, preparing himself for whatever lay just beyond.

The inner and outer doors opened.

A prefect, in full tactical armour, was waiting on the other side of the lock, a fist raised as if they had been hammering against the door until the moment it opened. The prefect almost fell into the elevator. Dreyfus caught a stencilled name, Singh, and some dim association brought a face to mind, one of the intake of '23 or '24, or maybe a year or two earlier. A good kid, he thought absently, one of the more promising candidates for rapid promotion . . .

Dreyfus grabbed Singh before she stumbled.

'Singh. It's Dreyfus. What the hell's happening? Where is the rest of your squad?'

'Close it, sir. Get the elevator going back up. They're still out there.'

Dreyfus took Singh's beak-visored helmet between his hands. 'Singh. Listen to me.' He snarled out her name. 'Singh! Where are the others?'

'Gone, sir. It got Gurney. Took him. I don't know about the rest. Comms went bad after the cat . . .'

'The cat.' Dreyfus frowned, wondering if he might have misheard. 'What do you mean, cat?'

'We've got to get back up the shaft, call in Panoply . . .'

'We *are* Panoply, Singh. You and me. The first and last line. Now slow down and tell me what's happened here. Devi, isn't it?'

'Deepa, sir. Devi was in the stream above me. Deepa Singh.'

'Yes . . . I remember. I taught you situational processing.'

Garlin leaned in. 'Whether she wants to take the elevator back up or not, Dreyfus, it isn't happening. The controls have just frozen. Looks like we're stuck here.'

'Did you bring weapons, sir?' Singh asked.

'Nothing out of the ordinary, besides dual whiphounds. Ought we have?'

'It's wrong here, sir.' Singh twisted back to look over shoulder, as if she expected something to come at them. 'It looks like a jungle. But it's not. It's a huge mass of quickmatter. The cats were part of it. We couldn't conjure it, couldn't make it safe. Our whiphounds started to malfunction, and then Prefect Perec . . . she sent Gurney and me back for help, sir. To call in heavy enforcement. We were trying to get back up the shaft, to reach Pell . . . but the elevator was gone. And then the cats came again . . . all we had was these.' She raised the object that Dreyfus had barely noticed until then: a crossbow.

Dreyfus noted that the crossbow had already discharged.

'What happened?'

'I shot one of the cats. When the dart hit, the cat stopped. Died, I suppose. But Gurney missed and there was still another cat. It took Gurney into the jungle. There wasn't anything I could do. I was just hoping the elevator would get here in time . . .'

'Let me see the crossbow,' Garlin said.

'We have to move, sir,' Singh said to Dreyfus, offering the weapon to the other man. 'It's still out there. Others, too. Prefect Perec said they were having trouble. She'd seen the cats. She told us not to engage. I hope they're all right.'

Garlin caressed a hand along the smooth, seamless lines of the crossbow. 'Is this is a trick, Dreyfus?'

'Why would it be?'

'I know what this is.' Behind his visor, Garlin's face tightened at the arrival of some unwelcome recollection. 'I think I made one like it once. I remember shaping the quickmatter, getting it to form the design I had in mind.'

He kept staring at the crossbow, lost in some rapture of amazement and horror.

'You were here,' Dreyfus said softly, feeling a strange and distant sympathy for Garlin. 'This place. It's where you learned everything that made you what you were.'

'Something happened,' Garlin said, lowering the crossbow but still holding it by its stock. 'Something bad.' Anger flared in his eyes. 'What the hell have you done to me?'

'Shown you a door.' Dreyfus turned back to Singh. 'The cat that you killed.'

'There's a pit outside, sir. Stairs leading up, then a clearing. That's where I shot the cat, where it fell. If it's still there . . .'

'If the dart kills cats, then we need that dart,' Dreyfus said.

'It's still just one bolt, sir. I think it was luck that I got that cat at all. Gurney's got a much a better sidearm rating than me, and . . . I mean, Gurney was . . .'

'Singh,' Dreyfus said sharply, sensing that she was on the brink of falling apart. 'Deepa. Listen to me. Remember what I taught you. Your situational processing class.'

He heard Singh take a deep breath. 'You said there was no situation so bad that we were ever justified in giving up, sir.'

'Correct.' Dreyfus spoke slowly, calmly. 'We have suits and air, and the entire resources of Panoply ready to swoop in on Lethe any moment now. You've proven that this environment has rules.' He gave her a sharp pat on the shoulder. 'Now let's see if that cat's still where you left it.'

'And me?' Garlin asked.

Dreyfus took the crossbow from him and passed it back to Singh. 'I'd stick with her.'

Outside the elevator was the sheer-walled pit that she had described, with a set of blocky stairs climbing to the surface at the other end of it. Singh went up first, pausing as she approached the top, cautiously raising her head over the rim, then scrambling up onto the level ground with the crossbow still in hand. 'I can see the body, sir. It's still there.'

'Any sign of the other one?'

Singh looked around. 'I think we're all right for the moment. But we're going to have to get close to the edge of the clearing, and it could be hiding.'

'Then we'll be sharp about it,' Dreyfus said.

He followed Singh up the stairs, taking only the briefest of moments to assess his surroundings. Blue sky above, with a barely detectable trace of domed curvature. Dense green foliage hemming an open area, the leaves, ferns and vines almost glowing with an inner luminosity. It was unreal, a dream made manifest.

'It wasn't like this when we got here,' Singh said.

Dreyfus settled his gaze onto the puddle of black that was his objective. 'I'll retrieve the dart. Do you remember where it went in?'

'Just behind the shoulder, on the left side.'

'Good.' He nodded at Garlin, who was standing with his hands on his hips, looking around with a dazed look on his face. 'Stay with Prefect Singh.'

Dreyfus deployed the first of his two whiphounds in a moving cordon and jogged to the cat, crouching low as he approached, ready to make an immediate retreat. He could only see a few centimetres into that thick green curtain, and yet that was enough to convince him of its full and belligerent potential, a machine that now had him in his gears. He forced his attention to the corpse, a black form like a cat-shaped hole punched into some other reality. He had assumed that its details would become more pronounced as he neared it, but even now his eyes seemed to slide off it, finding no purchase. It had no depth, no texture, no gradations of light and shade.

He reached out, his gloved fingers seeming to stretch into a bottomless void before they contacted the hard tail of the dart. If the cat and the crossbow were made of quickmatter then in all likelihood so was the dart. But it felt solid and metallic in his fingers, and tugged loose with only a pop of resistance.

He closed his fist around it and jogged back to the others, stooping from breathlessness when he arrived, the whiphound scooting to his side.

Sparver heard the voice before he placed its origin. He was lying on the ground, playing dead after coming round from unconsciousness, certain that this subterfuge remained the only survival option open to him, however slight its chances of success. He had assumed it was only a matter of time before the cats came back for him, finishing off their brutal business. He was weaponless now, exhausted and shocked. The only mystery was why they had left him alive in the first place. Dalia Perec was silent, but he could still hear her moans playing through his head.

Yet the voice was insistent. 'You can get up, pig-man. I see you for what you are. Something ridiculous, even if you weren't lying in the dirt like a discarded toy. But you're not one of them. You carry the burden of crimes committed against your kind, but you were not – as far as I am aware – the direct perpetrator of crimes against others.' A kind, solicitous tone entered the voice. 'You may stand. If you and I have business – and that may be the case – the nature of it has yet to be determined.'

Footsteps padded softly on grass. A pair of shoes came into view, belonging to legs that rose up and beyond Sparver's immediate field of view.

'Prefect,' the voice said, lower now. 'Let's put aside the pretence, shall we? It's not very dignified, lying like that. Not a very fitting posture for someone who has come this far, against such odds. You deserve better

363

than to lie there in the dirt like a dead thing.' The figure stepped closer, a shadow fell across the ground, and Sparver felt a hand close around the scruff of his neck, grasping him by the m-suit. 'Here. Let me help you to your feet.'

Sparver was yanked from the ground in one smooth movement, the speaker letting out only a tiny grunt of effort as he bore Sparver's weight. 'Now, pig-man. Stand. At least we can make an effort to look each other in the eye, can't we?'

Blood still smeared the m-suit visor. Now he was standing, it began to run off the self-cleaning surface. Through this dissipating pink film, Sparver stared at the man who had hauled him off the ground.

He was familiar and yet not so. He had the face of Devon Garlin, but there was a maturity to it that was absent from the face of the public figure. The countenance was slightly broader and heavier, somewhat more blemished and lined, markedly more characterful, as if it had lived more and seen more than its bland public counterpart. The eyes were wearier, sunk more deeply in their sockets, the skin around them more elaborately wrinkled, the eyelids heavier and more sagging. There was no scar beneath the right eye. Above the eyes the brow had more lines to it, and the forehead was more prominent, the hair wirier and starting further up the scalp. Sparver might not have been the best at telling humans apart, but even with his limitations he felt that this was unquestionably the face of the same man, but with decades more life added to it, and little evidence of rejuvenative procedures being used to undo the effects of ageing.

Beneath the head, a thick, muscular neck, a barrel-chested torso, strong arms and shoulders, the sturdy, top-heavy physique barely concealed beneath a plain black outfit of trousers and tunic, devoid of frills or ornamentation. And yet unquestionably the face and body of the same man he had helped detain in Fuxin-Nymburk.

'How are you here, Devon?' Sparver asked.

Puzzlement pushed a notch into the man's forehead. 'Why do you call me that?'

'Because I've seen you before. Everyone has. You're Julius Devon Garlin Voi.'

'And yet by your tone you seem not to be wholly certain of that assertion.'

'I took you to Panoply. You've been there ever since.'

The man bit down on his lower lip, ruminating on this point. 'Then it would seem unlikely that I am here as well, would it not?'

'You're older. Bulkier. But I've seen your face on a thousand broadcasts.'

'And your point is?' The man still had his hand on Sparver's neck, but he released it now. Then, with a detached, practical manner, as of one cleaning the face of a clock, or brushing dust from a portrait, he began to unpeel the front of Sparver's visor. The m-suit material was tearing and shrivelling at the touch of his fingers, breaking away in smoky threads. 'There, there,' the man said. 'You don't need this encumberment, not here. You can breathe easily without it, and at least we can look each other squarely in the eye, can't we?'

'How are you doing that?' Sparver asked, as the man dabbed away more and more of the m-suit, flicking its gluey traces off the tips of his fingers like someone punching through a cobweb.

'You established the nature of the jungle and the cats, didn't you? It's all quickmatter, just like this suit of yours, and there's nothing I can't do with quickmatter. I am just willing it to surrender its integrity, and so it does.' The man smiled: it was the smile Sparver had come to despise like a repeated lash against old, raw nerve endings. 'But don't fear, pig-man. I haven't allowed you to come all this way just to kill you now.'

Sparver forced himself to take in Perec's body, what he could see of it, her tactical armour melted and deformed where the quickmatter had attacked it. 'Then why did they have to die?'

'I only needed a single witness. You're as good as any. Better, as I have said, in that you are more blameless than many. Are you blameless, pig-man? What's your title, exactly?'

'Prefect Bancal. And you are under Panoply observance.'

'Yes – good. I admire your rectitude, your devotion to the calling, against all the visible odds. But your friends are dead, Prefect, and you are powerless. Turn around, will you?'

When Sparver did not turn around, the man took him by the shoulders and forced him to obey.

He studied the pale pearl-white gleam of the Shell House, its spiralling, organically inspired contours.

'Do you recognise it, Prefect Bancal?'

'I don't know. How many guesses do I get?'

The man punched Sparver in the small of his back. The force of the punch sent Sparver sprawling forward, snout down in the dirt, feeling as if a battering ram had just been driven into the base of his spine. The man's shadow fell over him again, then he felt fingers close around the scruff of his neck once more. But there was no m-suit to muffle the hold now, and the pain of fingers digging into flesh made Sparver let out a small shocked grunt, even as he landed back on his feet.

'Ground rules,' the man said. 'You are here at my sufferance, Prefect, and my forbearance is not without its limits. There is nothing so fragile as the tolerance of a man who knows with complete conviction that he is going to die.'

'Do you?' Sparver asked, wheezing out the words.

'Well, of course. They won't let me live, will they? Not now, when there is so little to be gained by *not* allowing me to die. They will decide that any operatives still present in Lethe are regrettably expendable – understandable, given the lack of contact – and order Lethe's total destruction. We both know they have the means. The remaining Wildfire cases will die, as Panoply surely knows, but they will console themselves that nothing could be done to save those people anyway.'

'You're wrong. We have a plan to save them. It's already working.'

'How little you know,' the man said, almost fondly, as if he might pat Sparver on the head at any moment. 'The means to preserve those people lies with me, not Panoply. Every day, every hour, by force of will, I choose to permit them to live. I am in their heads, whispering the spell that stops them from dying. If I cease to whisper that spell – because I choose not to, or because I am dead – then they will die. It is as simple as that.'

'I don't see what you'd gain from being dead.'

'You misunderstand my intentions. I have already achieved all that I desired. The Wildfire emergency has sown terror and confusion, and it is not yet finished. No one, even you, can really be sure who is next. Does it really end with the names on the list? I'll let you in on a little secret, shall I? I only ever touched those two thousand citizens. No one else need fear Wildfire, when it finally burns through that list of names. There will be no more deaths, at least not as a direct consequence of the clinic. I'll have had my justice. But it won't end there, not for Panoply, not for the Glitter Band. Public confidence in your organisation couldn't be lower, Prefect. But it's only going to get worse, when the people see how ineffective you were in the face of this emergency. The breakaway movement will hasten. There will be misjudgements . . . over-reactions on both sides. Regrettable acts. Provocation and counter-provocation. Wiser minds will attempt to slow the fragmentation, even turn it back. But that wheel, once started turning, will not be easy to stop. The Glitter Band will begin to destroy itself, riven by centrifugal forces of naked greed and craven self-interest.'

'I'm glad you've thought this through.'

This drew wry amusement from the man, rather than another punch to the spine. 'Oh, I have. Thoroughly. But unlike my brother – the man you *think* you know, the man whose face reminded you of my own – unlike him, I'm under no illusions that there is an upside to this chaos. Caleb, you see, for all his faults – and there are many – Caleb still has an idealistic streak. Mistaken, foolhardy, but sincerely held. He thinks he can make the world a better place, and I have helped him along in that conviction. Opened doors for him, you might say. Given him a little helping hand, without his knowledge.'

'Who is Caleb?'

'You know him, Prefect. Weren't you the one who detained him?'

'I detained Julius Devon Garlin Voi,' Sparver said.

'No,' the man answered. 'That was Caleb. I ought to know. I am Julius Devon Garlin Voi. I am and always have been.'

'Load it,' Dreyfus said.

Prefect Singh primed the crossbow, latched it and slid the dart back into its groove, folding a small retaining clip down over it.

'Did you really make this?' she asked Garlin.

'Yes.' He nodded, something between shame and pride in his features. 'I could make another one now, if we had time. It's just quickmatter. I was always pretty good at conjuring it. I wasn't the best, though . . .'

'Caleb was,' Dreyfus said, drawing a reproachful glance from Garlin. Yet no contradiction, for now.

'Who are you, sir?' Singh asked.

'He's Devon Garlin,' Dreyfus answered, guessing that she had already worked out most of the truth for herself. 'Julius Devon Garlin Voi. Presently a witness in the Wildfire emergency. Julius was raised here, Deepa, along with his brother Caleb. It's an exact copy of the Voi residence in Chasm City. Julius doesn't remember too much of what happened. But it's starting to become clearer. Isn't it?'

'I don't remember Caleb,' Garlin said – but without the flat denial of earlier. 'But I do know this place. And there was always someone else here. I didn't play those games on my own.' He paused, swallowed. 'There was a game that involved hunting. I . . . one of us . . . made animals. We chased them down for sport. But it wasn't like that cat. They weren't solid, they weren't real. They were just figments.'

'Consensual hallucinations,' Dreyfus said. 'Real enough to the eye, but incapable of harming you back. Something obviously changed, though.'

'That's what I wanted to do,' Garlin said wonderingly. 'Make them realler. I told him . . . Caleb . . . what I could do with quickmatter, if I had half the chance. I knew I could make a place like this, make a better kind of game. But this place isn't anything to do with me, Dreyfus. You have to believe it.'

Dreyfus looked at him, gave a slow but considered nod. 'I do. For once,

I'll take you at your word. This is hard for you, I know. But we have to see it through.'

'You really think he's here?'

'I think he's been here for a very long time, Julius.' Dreyfus turned to face Singh. 'You say there hasn't been any contact with the other party since the trouble started. Do you think you can retrace their steps?'

Singh pointed to an area of the clearing, near the jungle wall. 'There was a path into the jungle, but it came and went.'

Dreyfus directed a question at the waiting whiphound. 'Can you retrace Prefect Singh's movements based on her tracker?'

The whiphound nodded, projecting a drunken scrawl onto his faceplate. There was a scribble of dense movement around their present location, then a meandering, looping trail which went out and back again. The general thrust of the course was towards the middle of the dome, but Singh had still had some way to go when she turned back.

'Get us to the point where the party separated,' Dreyfus said. 'Straightest possible route. Forward scout mode, five-metre secure zone. Proceed.'

The whiphound moved off, heading to the spot in the jungle wall that Singh had indicated. Dreyfus followed, but kept a wary distance, holding his hand up to urge Singh and Garlin to exercise the same caution, not that either of them were exactly straining to dive into the jungle.

'Dreyfus . . .' Garlin began, sounding very much like a man about to unburden himself of a confession.

'Later,' Dreyfus said.

The whiphound met the wall, whisking its filament in a fan-shaped blur, like a rattlesnake reversing with its tail upraised. Brilliant flecks of green began to fly away from the cutting edge. The whiphound started to excavate a low, stoop-ceilinged tunnel into the jungle mass. Dreyfus watched, saying nothing, trusting in nothing. He had no expectation of success. But he could not very well lecture Singh on the demands of field service if he himself did not explore all possible opportunities, however doubtful they appeared.

'Dreyfus. Listen to me. There's something near us. I can tell.'

'How?'

'I don't know. A prickly feeling that we're being watched. But more definite than that. Look, you've been trying to convince everyone I have secret powers until now. Don't be the one to doubt me when I tell you I can sense something.'

'I know they're still out there,' Singh said. 'Is it working, Prefect Dreyfus?'

368

'Too soon to be sure,' he said.

The whiphound had burrowed five or six metres into the jungle. It was still moving, and the tunnel walls – cut back neatly, like ornamental hedges – were not yet closing in after it. But Dreyfus knew there was nothing special about his whiphound, compared to the units the others had been carrying.

Now pink and blue sparks lit the green tunnel.

'It's encountering resistance. It won't be safe for us to follow.' Dreyfus reached out, opening his hand in a clear retrieval gesture. 'Come back,' he stated, just in case the whiphound needed persuading.

The whiphound abandoned its cutting and began to retreat along the tunnel. It was slower than it should have been, as if some damage had already been done to its core systems. With a certain numb resignation Dreyfus watched as a vine extended itself from the wall and snagged the whiphound. The vine coiled around it. Then the whiphound was gone, snatched into the green mass, a flash and a flicker showing through the foliage.

'We think one of the other whiphounds blew up,' Singh said. 'I don't know if Prefect Bancal and the others got away in time. Perhaps we should get back down in the pit, in case this one explodes.'

'That's the last place we want to be,' Dreyfus said. 'We still need to find a way out of this clearing.' He unclipped his second whiphound and set it on a cordon patrol, lapping around the party but refraining from straying too close to the clearing's edge. Then he raised his voice to a shout. 'Caleb! Can you hear me? I'm certain you know we're here. There's no reason for you not to.'

He lowered his voice before it turned hoarse, his breath fogging the m-suit visor until it cleared itself.

'Or for me to shout through this suit, I suppose,' he added, more softly. 'If you're there at all, you'll be aware of every word we've said.'

'You sound like a mad man,' Garlin said. 'Screaming at the trees.'

'I'm hoping to persuade your brother to grant us an audience.'

'You don't even know if he's real, let alone that he'll want to speak to us.'

'To us, maybe not,' Dreyfus admitted. 'But to you? Why wouldn't he jump at the chance of a brotherly reunion? Although I suppose that rather depends on what led to the two of you going your separate ways, and you with no memory of him.'

'Dreyfus,' Singh said sharply.

He turned, picking up the warning in her voice. A low black form was taking shape near the fallen cat. It seemed to puddle out of the green,

369

coalescing out of convergent threads of liquid blackness, clotting together into a single animal whole.

The whiphound detected its presence and deflected its cordon patrol to approach the cat.

'Wait until it's nearer,' Dreyfus said quietly, as Singh made to raise the crossbow. 'I trust your aim. But the bolt will have more power the nearer it is.'

'It was just luck, the first time.'

'I doubt it very much, Deepa. You knew what to do then and you know what to do now. But make the shot count. It's all we have.'

The cat was now fully whole, the last of the black strands separating from the jungle and vanishing into the animal's voidlike silhouette. It prowled to the fallen cat, sniffing around it with a brittle, easily distracted curiosity. It touched a paw to the blackness, two voids connected. Then it withdrew. If it detected some kinship in the murdered creature, the effect was slight and soon forgotten.

The cat locked its attention onto Dreyfus, Singh and Garlin. Two eyes, the white teeth. It walked closer, one footfall then two, with a slow but gaining intent, until its steps became strides, the strides elongating, the cat seeming to flatten itself into a perfect moving darkness, following an invisible parabola. The whiphound intercepted it, the cat pawing it aside with an effortless disregard, the whiphound sparking and flashing as it fell to the ground, writhing like a poisoned snake.

Then the cat was running, and Singh levelled the crossbow.

'Wait . . .' Dreyfus mouthed.

But Singh knew better, for she had done this once before. The crossbow snapped and the dart launched itself into the cat. It was fast: very fast. Dreyfus barely had time to track it, before it sank into the cat's chest, just below the neck.

It was a good shot. The cat dropped with a sudden, conclusive urgency, as if cables had yanked it to the ground. He should have trusted Singh to know what she was doing.

'I'll get the dart,' Dreyfus said, fixing his eyes on the spot where it had gone in.

'No,' Singh said.

There was another cat, clotting into solidity at the clearing's edge. In that instant Dreyfus knew with total certainty there would never be time to retrieve the dart.

The cat attacked, duplicating the slow but rising tempo of the other, but this time with nothing to stop it. No whiphound, no dart, no armour that would make the slightest difference against a weapon made of predatory quickmatter.

Garlin raised a hand, palm flattened and upraised. Through his m-suit Dreyfus saw a tremble and a curl to his lip, a sneer of cold command. Garlin's arm stiffened. The cat increased its run, arcing and flexing like a black banner behind a kite. And then stopped, not out of its own volition, but because it had run into an invisible surface, the cat pouring its momentum against that impasse, spreading in concentric waves, losing form and coherence.

Something like astonishment dropped Garlin's jaw. He held the stance, the cat like some fast liquid stream that had hit glass. The black remains splashed and curdled but did not reform.

Garlin maintained his stiff-armed posture until there seemed no possibility of the cat reconstituting itself. Then he angled his arm down, flexing and re-flexing his fingers as if he did not quite understand what he had done, or what might yet lie within his capabilities.

'I . . . remembered,' he said, with a sort of astonished reverence. 'I knew what to do. I just . . . wished it to stop.'

Dreyfus took his first breath in at least twenty seconds. 'You used to play the same games, Julius. If Caleb can speak to quickmatter, then so can you.'

Garlin was still working his fingers, curling and uncurling them in a strange and restless fascination, as if some electric power now lay within his grasp, and he could not quite bring himself to stop enjoying the novel, tingling thrill of it. He let out a small quiet gasp.

'Caleb will have sensed you, I think,' Dreyfus said. 'If he didn't already know you were present. But you have the edge, for now. See if you can do something about that jungle, will you, before any more cats come back?'

Garlin turned and raised his hand at the now impenetrable wall where the whiphound had tried to excavate a corridor. His eyes narrowed with concentration, his jaw set with determination and a dangerous, self-admiring charisma.

The jungle puckered in, resisted – like an elastic surface, rebounding after a punch – and then formed a corridor into itself.

Dreyfus looked at Garlin, glad that they had been spared the cat, but equally certain that something was now loose over which none of them, most especially Devon Garlin, had any sort of sovereignty.

'Let's go,' Dreyfus said.

371

CHAPTER TWENTY-TWO

The man who insisted that he be thought of as Julius Devon Garlin Voi placed a comradely hand on Sparver's back. 'They're here, my little friend from Panoply. Three of them, one that I know as well as my own shadow. They've defeated the cats, by various means. I could send more – create an overpowering force of them – but that would be churlish, after all the trouble they've gone to.' He squeezed Sparver's shoulder, a little too forcefully for the gesture to feel anything but bullying. 'We'll see how strong he really is.' He made a sweeping, theatrical gesture in the direction of the spiralling property. 'Let's take a stroll to the Shell House, shall we?'

'And if I said no?'

'I could pull you apart like straw, make you squeal with the best of them. Admit it: you do have some curiosity. You must be asking yourself *why* I chose those particular Wildfire cases, out of all the hundred million citizens?'

'If there's a reason, I'm sure it makes perfect sense to you.'

Something twitched in the cheek of the man's broad but familiar face. 'A bad thing was done, Prefect – a secret, clandestine crime. It came to a culmination with the birth of my brother and I, but we were not the start of it.'

They crossed the level, manicured ground before the Shell House, then went up onto the paved terrace fronting the main entrance. Sparver had debated his options for escape or resistance and concluded they were non-existent, given the man's demonstrable control over every aspect of his environment.

'If you know about a crime, you should have reported it through the official channels,' Sparver said.

The man, walking alongside him now, favoured him with a pitying smile. 'It would have been damaging for the Voi family, and we couldn't accept that.'

'Isn't that what you're hoping for now?'

'Yes, but it's later now – much later.' The man gave a soft, mocking laugh. 'No; it was my justice or none at all.'

They went in through the main doors, into a cool-shaded lobby, with black and white floor tiles, decorated plasterwork and an impressive staircase at one end.

'It might help if I knew what sort of crime we were talking about.'

'There was a . . . let's call it a gambling syndicate. A group of citizens dedicated to the art of the wager, staking ever higher bets on increasingly unlikely or speculative outcomes. Their craving was an addiction, an appetite that could be dulled but never satiated.'

Sparver thought of the linking connection between the Wildfire cases, the propensity for risk, but rather than interject decided it was wiser to let his host keep talking.

'Their desires demanded an endless supply of new forms of competitive diversion. At first, these could be met through legal means – placing wagers on games and challenges that would not have troubled any of the law enforcement bodies. But in the long run that was insufficient.' They had gone through an arched doorway into a connecting room now, and the man paused at one of the ornamented panels in the wall. It had a pastel backing with scrolling decoration around the borders. He touched a hand to it and the panel slid aside, an operation that struck Sparver as surprisingly cumbersome and mechanical.

Beyond was a dark, sloping passage, descending into the basement levels of the house.

'Go on, Prefect,' the man said, giving him an encouraging shove. 'I insist you bear witness, if nothing else. It's that or cease to be of use to me.'

They walked down the sloping passage. It went down some way, then reversed direction and continued descending, carrying on until they were obviously deep within the bedrock under the domed enclosure.

'There was a figure within the consortium,' the man went on, his tone of address still affable enough. 'A man who shared the acute desires of his fellows for novelty and risk, but who was also in a position to provide them . . . at least up to a point. He became the consortium's facilitator. It was he who proposed the final wager – the darkest game of them all. Shall I tell you this man's name?'

They had come to a heavy, utilitarian door at the base of the sloping corridor. 'Wild guess,' Sparver said. 'Marlon Voi?'

'My father. Our father, I should say. Marlon had the dual benefits of prestige and long habits of secrecy. He came here – to this little rock. He owned it already, so that wasn't a problem, but he still needed all his resourcefulness to lay the ground for the final wager.' The man unlocked the heavy door. A draught of cold, stale air hit Sparver, and a crack of dim, golden light pushed through as the door opened.

'And this wager was . . .?'

'The settling of an age-old question,' the man said, ushering Sparver through into the chamber beyond. 'Are you intimately acquainted with the early history of our settlement, Prefect?'

'I hear it didn't end well.'

Corridors and rooms radiated away from the chamber beyond the door. The man closed the door behind them, and at once it became impossible to tell it was there at all, leaving only a row of grey panels along one wall. Sparver took in his surroundings, conscious that he seemed to have stepped back a few hundred years compared to the elegant furnishings of the Shell House. These corridors and rooms were made of angular, prefabricated components, with grilled vents, caged ceiling lights and snaking lines of cables and pipes stapled to the walls. Now and then there was a window, set within an armoured frame. The environment hummed with the throb of generators and air-circulators. It gave off a steely, antiseptic stench.

'You would certainly not call it a shining success,' the man said, steering Sparver to one of the windows.

There was some sort of shutter on the other side of the glass, but the man worked a control and the metal protection whisked aside with a solid clunk. For once, the window was set at a height that easily suited Sparver. Beyond was an alien landscape, stretching impossibly far into the distance.

'Do you recognise it?'

'Someone sent me a postcard once. It's Yellowstone.'

The man seemed pleased by this observation. 'Enough to reinforce the desired impression, which was that the children were present on the surface of that world, in a settlement made by robots. It worked well enough, at least for the first few test generations.'

'I don't understand.'

The man worked the control and sealed the window shutter again. 'In a short while I'll ask you to excuse me, Prefect, while I go and greet Caleb and his guests. But we're not quite done down here. There's a small favour I'm going to ask of you in a moment – you might almost say it relates to a private wager of my own.' A sudden eager interest showed itself in his face. 'Tell me – have you grasped the point of this, of Marlon's last game?'

'You mentioned generations.'

'I did, and for good reason. Boys and girls would be . . . created, born, and then immediately placed in this simulation. They would know nothing but these walls, no companionship but themselves, no guidance beyond that offered by the robots – the Ursas. The parameters would vary from run to run, the outcome monitored, and those that wagered on a particular result would be rewarded, or penalised.' They walked away from the window, through a connecting bulkhead – heavy as an airlock, and painted with black and yellow stripes – into another part of the complex. 'Therapies were applied to make the boys and girls reach maturity more rapidly. A spread of wagers covered all eventualities. Fortunes were banked – egos nailed to the mast of one outcome over another.'

They were walking through what Sparver decided must be some sort of infirmary, lined as it was with couches, beds and antique-looking items of surgical equipment.

'And the generations – what happened to these boys and girls?'

'They were painlessly euthanised at the end of each run, and a new batch prepared.'

Sparver swallowed his distaste. 'But you were one of them. How did you get out?'

'The problems had been building for some while. Until at last there was a . . .' The man paused, his throat moving, tension bunching the muscles around his mouth. 'A massacre. A psychotic episode, the other children butchered. Just two survivors out of the whole run. Caleb and myself, with knives in our hands, standing amid the blood-spattered bodies of our fellows. Even for the refined tastes of the consortium, that was just a little *too* much.' The man allowed himself an ironic smile. 'It was the end of the wager, the end of the whole enterprise. Everyone bailed, desperate to unsoil their hands of this regrettable episode. Pacts of secrecy, threats of dark recrimination should a word of this escape to the wider world. An agreement that the members of the consortium would seek voluntary amnesiac therapy, to blot out any knowledge of their involvement. It worked, for the most part – they forgot their part in it all. There was just one, lingering snag.'

'Somehow, you and your brother didn't die.'

The man gave an appreciative nod. 'Marlon grew a late conscience – he wanted to atone for his part in the spectacle. What better way than to redeem the two boys? So he took us, and with the reluctant consent of Aliya, who had never been more than an unwilling bystander in the wager, it was agreed that we would be raised as their own sons. Which, in a sense, we already were. Marlon and Aliya had contributed genetic information to the project – as had the other participants. We were true-blooded Vois – just not born of our mother's womb.'

'But you knew what you were.'

'Not after we'd been put through a round of the same sort of amnesiac therapy. We were given a second phase of conditioning, reinforced with a second lie. That we had been born in the Shell House, that we were the natural heirs of the old lineage. And for a little while, neither of us ever questioned that story. Not until the bad dreams started haunting our nights . . .'

At the far end of the infirmary the man touched a control and another door opened. He beckoned for Sparver to step through into the narrow, red-lit chamber beyond. Sparver did so without resistance, even as he took in the room's sole occupant, and by a series of mental leaps deduced who that person must be.

'Marlon,' Sparver said.

'You're not slow, Prefect – I'll give you that. And I'll credit you for not stating the obvious, which is that Marlon Voi is supposed to be dead.'

'It doesn't look much like living to me.'

'I doubt that he'd disagree with you, in those rare moments when he entertains a lucid thought.'

Marlon Voi was a husk, a shrivelled grey form propped up on an angled bed, his sightless eyes fixed on the ceiling. A grey blanket covered all but his head and shoulders, with wires and nutrient lines feeding into him from the banks of archaic medical devices positioned around the bed. Other than a door at the other end of the chamber there was nothing in the room not related to the immediate business of life-support. Screens flickered with pulse profiles and neural graphs. Monitors chirped and beeped in a low, lulling chorus. In one machine, centrifuge wheels spun, while in another bellows moved up and down in a slow, huffing rhythm. A transparent mask fitted over the mouth and nose of the skull-like head cased within a cushioned frame. The half-collapsed, leathery tube of his neck seemed incapable of ever supporting the weight of that head.

'It's inhuman.'

'Quite a statement, coming from a hyperpig.'

The man moved to the bedside and adjusted some of the settings on the monitors. Next to this monitor was a fold-out tray holding a number of sharp surgical instruments, laid out on a green cloth.

'You know what I meant, Garlin.' Sparver was debating his chances of reaching one of those instruments and doing something useful with it. 'Julius, Caleb, whoever you are. Whatever you think he did, you aren't the one who gets to decide his punishment.'

The man looked surprised. 'I thought that was exactly what I'd been doing all these years. Still, would you agree that he's suffered enough, all things considered?'

Seeing his moment, Sparver made a lunge for the tray. But the man was faster. He grabbed Sparver's arm and twisted it sharply, sending a crunching pain through his shoulder.

'No, not that easily. But I don't blame you for trying.' The man released the pressure on his arm, while leaving Sparver in no doubt that his host would always be faster and stronger. 'I mentioned that private wager of my own. May I elaborate?'

'I'm all ears. I'm told they're hard to miss.'

'When Marlon designed this place, he took precautions. He arranged that the habitable parts of Lethe could be destroyed very easily, and very quickly, by triggering a generator overload. That way, if anyone got too close, the evidence could be eliminated in one stroke.'

'And now?'

'I have arranged for the generators to overload. In thirty minutes, there will be a small but not insignificant fusion event. It will cause quite a lot of damage to Lethe. Marlon will die, and so will I and anyone else unfortunate enough to still be inside this rock. So – my friend – will you, if you are still present.'

'Unless you're planning on letting me go, I guess that's a foregone conclusion.'

'True, but you have neglected one detail. You have learned of Marlon's crimes now, and that makes you a witness. There would have been no point my bringing you here unless I intended that you should convey this testimony beyond Lethe. My word would have meant nothing, but yours, the word of a prefect?'

'Hate to break it to you, Julius, but I doubt that thirty minutes would give me time to get halfway to that elevator, even if it was ready to take me to the docking point.'

'No, you are right about that. But there's another way out of here – another of Marlon's little precautions.' He nodded to the chamber's end. 'Do you see that door? It leads to an escape device. A single-person lifepod, ready to be ejected from Lethe with a centrifugal kick.'

Sparver thought of the readouts he had seen from the cruiser.

'We scanned your rock. If there was an escape tunnel, we'd have seen it.'

'You scanned for density variations. The tunnel is sealed with fine-grained rubble – indistinguishable from the surrounding rock. When the capsule is ready to depart, a pressure seal is blown at the far end. The rubble spills out, and the lifepod follows a few moments later.'

'Good,' Sparver said. 'Any objections if I get into it right now? I mean, if you're planning on dying, and he's going at the same time . . .'

'I'm afraid it's not quite that simple. You're right that Marlon's essential fate is sealed. But here's an interesting ethical dilemma – my private wager, if you like. Under the present arrangements, that door won't open until Marlon is dead. It's linked to the life-support systems.'

'The point of which is . . .?'

'You'll have to kill him to save yourself. Oh, he'll die anyway – that's plain. But it's not *quite* the same thing, is it? You'd be killing a man many minutes before his allotted moment. If it was years, or even months, we'd have no hesitation in calling it murder. But taking minutes off a life – where does that put you?'

'In the shit, most likely.'

'You have a delicate turn of phrase, I'll give you that. Still, it's not just your own life at stake. Get out now – soon – and you might be able to do something. Effect some course of action, however futile it's likely to prove. But you'll have considered that already. Factored it into your moral calculus.'

'You've obviously mistaken me for a deep thinker. Is it possible you've got the wrong pig?'

The man attended to one of the life-support devices, triggering a subtle but definite shift in the pattern of monitoring noises, like a change from a minor to a major key in a melody.

'I'm restoring him to consciousness now, Sparver. There wouldn't be any point in you killing him if he were not capable of understanding his fate. I can't promise you the most enlightening of conversations – he's too far gone for that – but you'd be the one doing most of the talking, in any case.'

'What about you?'

'Pressing business awaits. I have to go and attend to Caleb, give my brother the welcome he deserves.' The man turned from the figure that he claimed was his father. 'Kill him as and when you see fit. I've left you ample means to do so. They say that pigs lack the capacity for truly creative thought, but I'm sure you'll give the lie to that.'

'You might have overestimated this pig,' Sparver said.

'Then this is your chance to rise to the occasion.' The man began to step out of the red-lit chamber. 'But I wouldn't take too long about it.'

At last they broke through the final layer of the jungle and the Shell House stood within view. Dreyfus took a moment to compare it with his memories of the crumbling ruin inside Chasm City, certain that the two structures were identical in all significant respects, but unable to shake the impression that this version was by far the larger of the pair. Perhaps it was the cleanliness of the spiralling architecture, burnished to a hard lustre under the blazing blue of the dome, that made it appear grander, more substantial – more fitting of the family name to which it belonged.

Garlin paused with his hands on his knees, mentally and physically drained by the effort of resisting the jungle. Dreyfus did not doubt that the task had taken its toll. Equally, he had watched Garlin grow in confidence and fluency as his buried skills reasserted themselves. This was more than just the supple, off-hand faculty with quickmatter that any wealthy son might have had drummed into him since birth, like an aptitude for duelling or cruel put-downs. It went much deeper than that. Garlin was re-learning a virtuoso talent, one that would have been impressive enough even if it had concerned itself with the ordinary, willing quickmatter of the Glitter Band and Chasm City. But this quickmatter was supposedly slaved to the will of Garlin's brother alone.

And yet he had learned to shape it – to twist its narrow loyalty from one sibling to the other.

And he had been getting better at it, Dreyfus knew.

'I suppose . . .' Garlin said, pausing between breaths, sweat prickling his brow through the m-suit visor. 'I suppose if ever there was a time to admit that Stasov was right . . .'

'I don't blame you for resisting the truth,' Dreyfus said. 'You were under the influence of multiple amnesiac treatments. But I think we can both agree that there must have been something in Doctor Stasov's account.'

Garlin straightened up. 'My brother's nearby, Dreyfus. I can feel him crawling around in my head.'

Singh, who was standing next to Garlin, offered an arm while he regained his strength. She had lifted up the visor on her tactical armour, deciding – reasonably, it seemed to Dreyfus – that the breathability or otherwise of the air was the least of her worries. It was the first time he'd had a good look at her face, and he chastised himself for misremembering her name from the induction classes. She looked small in that helmet, far too young to be put through this.

'Thank you,' Garlin murmured, with what to Dreyfus seemed like genuine gratitude and surprise at her kindness.

'Sir, it's Prefect Perec,' Singh said, nodding as she drew his attention to a body on the ground. There was a tremble in her voice. 'I can see part of her name, and that's definitely not Kober. Do you think Prefect Bancal made it this far, sir? He only had an m-suit.'

'Doesn't look like that armour helped any of you,' Dreyfus observed.

'He's here,' Garlin said, as a well-built man stepped out of the main entrance of the Shell House, walking casually across the raised terrace, dusting one palm against the other as if he had recently finished some manual labour. The man wore a simple black outfit of trousers and tunic, with the tunic low slashed from the collar, emphasising a powerful chest. His forearms were bare, the tunic sleeves rolled to the elbow. His muscles flexed as he worked his palms together.

'Caleb,' Dreyfus said, recognising the family connection, even though this man looked much older than Garlin, more like a father than a brother.

The man spread his hands and raised his right by way of greeting. 'You've got it wrong, Prefect,' he said, a wry, knowing smile crinkling the skin at the corners of his eyes. 'Or did my brother not remember which of us is which?'

'He's Julius Devon Garlin Voi,' Dreyfus said, but with a steadily draining conviction, thinking of the instances when his witness had indeed seemed confused or indecisive about his identity. 'That makes you Caleb, if Caleb isn't an invention of Doctor Stasov's.'

The man stepped down from the terrace, striding towards the party. 'Caleb's real enough, Dreyfus.' His smile intensified. 'Yes, I'm aware of you – I've been aware of you for a great while. Shall I clarify a few things?'

'Clarify what you like,' Dreyfus said. 'As of this moment you are under Panoply observance.'

The man touched his lip, frowning. 'And the meaning of that is . . . what, exactly?'

'You'll come back with me to Panoply, where we'll talk about the remaining Wildfire cases, and what you're going to do to keep those people alive.'

The man made a show of belated understanding, like someone getting the punchline to a not particularly good joke. 'Oh, I *see*. With you. In your unarmed state, after most of your force has already been depleted.' The man winked. 'Between you and me, Dreyfus, you're not really in a position to make demands.'

The man came to a halt, standing ten metres from the trio. Garlin watched him with a surprising stillness, saying nothing for the moment. With her visor still lifted up, her eyes wide, Singh looked like a startled baby bird glimpsing the open sky for the first time, in all its limitless splendour and terror.

'I suppose there's a point to these deaths?' Dreyfus asked.

'It's here,' the man said, nodding and smiling. 'It's happening. Destruction and chaos. That's all I ever wanted.'

'There's more to it than that. You selected those Wildfire cases. Lured them to your clinic . . . that *was* yours, wasn't it?'

The man started to answer, then made a quick flicking gesture with his hand. 'Do you mind, Dreyfus, if we dispense with these needless barriers to effective communication?'

Dreyfus did not have time to answer. His m-suit peeled away around him, leaving him wearing only the ordinary uniform of his profession. Next to him, Garlin's m-suit suffered the same ruthless obliteration, blowing off him like sea-foam.

'There, much better,' the man declared. 'My brother has a swollen sense of his own competence, you see. Just because he bettered the cats, and persuaded my jungle to dance to his fingers, does not make him the stronger of us. Although once he liked to think he was.' There came the quick flash of a smile, but now it was loaded with venom. 'Tell him, Caleb. Did the crossbow ring any bells?'

'They were . . . my idea,' Garlin said. 'The crossbows, the animals, the hunting games. He didn't want to go along with me.'

'He?' the older man quizzed.

'Julius,' Garlin said, almost coughing the name, as if it took an effort of will to force it out of his lips. 'You. Julius. We were the same age but you were smaller, more timid, more interested in books and stories.'

'Tell them about the story I used to go on about, Caleb. The one you didn't like me mentioning.'

Garlin – the man Dreyfus was now having to adjust to thinking of as Caleb Voi – turned to him with a look of almost desperate hopelessness in his eyes, the last, lingering traces of swagger and disdain sucked out of him by this meeting with his brother, who claimed the name Julius Voi.

'We'd been born in the Amerikano era,' Caleb said. 'In one of their settlements, tended and raised by robots. Until it went wrong, and we murdered the other children.'

'He's both right and wrong, Dreyfus,' Julius said, fingering the slashed collar of his tunic. 'We shared those dreams, shared those memories. They were real, it turned out. But we were born less than sixty years ago and put into a simulation of the Amerikano colony, so that our father – and his friends – might place wagers on the outcome.'

Caleb – the man Dreyfus had brought from Panoply – shook his head. 'He's lying, Dreyfus. I'd know, wouldn't I?'

'If such a thing happened,' Dreyfus said, 'it would explain both your disturbed memories and your genetic connection to Marlon and Aliya Voi.'

'You see,' Julius said, applauding silently. 'Dreyfus sees it instantly.

381

Bravo, Prefect. I like a man who isn't afraid the embrace the truth, however unpalatable.'

'Let's get back to the clinic,' Dreyfus answered.

'You're right – that was mine. I set up Elysium Heights using seed money from the Voi estate, as you realised.' Julius's eyes twinkled in vain amusement at his own ingenuity. 'I also wanted you to find it, Dreyfus, knowing the poor light it would place my brother in. That's why the chain of ownership was cloudy, but not too cloudy, and why you were given a little helping hand with that flood.'

The flood that had nearly killed Sparver and Thalia, Dreyfus thought, as well as leaving an innocent witness dead. But he fought to keep his voice level, his demeanour detached, as if he were asking routine questions in the interview suite.

'And the people on the clinical list?'

'Former members of a consortium. A covert, highly elite gambling ring, with close ties to our father. Not all active participants, but all aware of it, all fully cognisant of the darker aspects of that particular enterprise. They were the ones who wagered on my brother and I, you see, and on the other children. We were there to fend off their boredom.'

Dreyfus shook his head. 'I looked into the backgrounds of the Wildfire victims. There were no prior associations beyond chance encounters, and certainly no membership of gambling syndicates.'

Julius looked pained, like a music tutor affronted by a sudden sour note. 'That's because it was *secret*, Dreyfus. When the wager came to an end, such was the danger of disclosure that each and every member of the syndicate submitted to voluntary amnesia.'

'And the clinic?'

'A *lure*, you slow, stupid man. My means of getting back into their heads. I knew their names, because I was a Voi, and they had all come to Lethe. They were ripe for it – desperate for someone to put an end to their darker desires. And they came, all of them. In ones, naturally, never once guessing what connected them to the other patients.'

'You're a monster,' Singh said.

'But a patient one. Surely you'll allow me that one virtue?'

'Is it all true?' Caleb said. 'Are you really responsible for these deaths?'

'Crocodile tears,' Julius said scornfully. 'Hoping they'll buy you some late sympathy from Dreyfus? That's all it is, Caleb. I know you far too well to think anything else, brother. I know exactly how manipulative you can be.' Then to Dreyfus. 'Did you wonder about the significance of the crossbow, by any chance?'

'Should I have done?'

'Ask Caleb what happened to our mother, Prefect. Then you'll understand.'

Sparver watched for a clear sign of animation in the eyes of Marlon Voi. Not sight – he doubted very much that those eyes were capable of seeing anything – but an involuntary attention, a twitching that had not been there a moment before.

Sparver loosened the breathing mask a little, holding it by one hand while his other held one of the surgical knives that had been provided for him. His shoulder ached where the man had wrenched it, but he still had functionality in both arms.

'Marlon Voi,' he said softly. 'Can you hear me, Marlon? I'm Prefect Bancal. You're in Lethe. I guess you know that.'

Marlon made a long, low sucking sound – a sound less like human breathing than the gurgling of ancient plumbing, rattling and wet from decades of neglect.

He shaped a word. Sparver leaned in closer, loosening the mask by a further degree.

'Kill . . .' the word was. Followed, after another laboured inhalation, by '. . . me.'

The deed would not have been difficult. Sparver could have killed the man directly, or he could have cut some of the connections between Marlon and the life-support equipment. Either way, he doubted it would need more than a few minutes to arrive at the same terminal conclusion.

'He wants me to,' Sparver said. 'Your son. Says he's Julius, and that you deserve everything he's done to you. I don't know about that, exactly. Was it true, Marlon? Was there a syndicate, a sick game played out across generations of children?'

He made the words again. This time there was more conviction to them – sounding less like a plea than an order, delivered in the full and certain expectation that it would be obeyed.

'Kill me.'

'Old habits, Marlon. That's what it sounds like to me. Not asking, but telling. As if that's all the rest of us exist for. Doing what you demand of us.'

'Julius . . . right. Kill me.' Marlon Voi clawed another meagre ration of air into the fetid reservoirs of his lungs. 'I deserve it. Did a terrible thing. But understand.'

The last word had been almost too faint to hear. 'What?'

'Aliya . . . never wanted this.'

'She's dead and gone, Marlon. Past all justice. Just as we all thought you were. She *is* gone, isn't she?'

'Julius . . . killed.' He paused, long enough that, for a moment at least, Sparver wondered if he had in fact died between utterances, sparing him this ethical quandary. 'Her.'

'I believe you,' Sparver said.

'Then kill me. Now.'

Sparver looked at the door. He had been presented with an extremely simple choice, and the means of facilitating it lay in his hand, sharp and clean as a spacecraft exhaust. It was a long shot, but if he took the escape capsule he might be able to get word to Panoply, warning them of the imminent explosion. Even if he failed, he would certainly save his own life. But in doing so he would have to kill a living witness.

There ought to have been no hesitation. Marlon Voi was going to die anyway – and the time left to him was a lot less than thirty minutes.

The blade weighed heavily in Sparver's grip. He moved closer to the man, slipping the mask back into place, muffling it with his other hand, so that he did not have to hear Marlon's distress as he did what needed to be done.

And he began to cut.

'Aliya Voi died here,' Dreyfus stated. 'The shuttle accident was a ruse to conceal the circumstances and location of her death. Was it murder?'

'Of a sort,' Julius said. 'Ask Caleb. Ask him who fired the fatal shot – assuming he even remembers.'

'You killed her,' Caleb said, surprised and certain in the same moment, as if a very clear memory had just presented itself.

'Did I, brother?'

'Yes. You shot her with the crossbow. I can see it now. The look on your face . . .' He shook his head, aghast. 'I don't want to remember, but I do. It's this place, bringing it all back again. She felt we'd come too far, too fast. There was something in us that she didn't trust . . .'

'Something in *you*,' Julius corrected.

'Perhaps. But you were the one who shot her. If she revoked my privileges, she'd have revoked yours as well. You were afraid of that, so you killed her before she had a chance. After that, Father didn't have a chance. He was too horrified to think clearly.' Caleb drew a breath, squaring his shoulders. 'There was something bad in both of us, Julius. Nothing can excuse the things they did to us. But you've gone too far. Stop this now. Let the other people live.'

'It's too late, Caleb,' he said, more in regret than anger. 'Were you not listening just now? I steered Dreyfus to the clinic. Once that was done, it was only a matter of time before he fumbled his way to Lethe. I always knew this day, this hour would come. And I'm ready to die rather than leave.'

'Dreyfus won't touch you.'

Julius glared at his brother. 'Then why did he come?'

'To reason with you,' Dreyfus said. 'To find out what had driven you to this point. To confirm your brother's innocence, in so far as the Wildfire cases go. To see if there was any persuasion I could bring to bear, without incurring the use of force.' He offered his hands, empty of any threat. 'I'd still like you to come with us. We have an emergency action in progress, to safeguard the remaining victims. We can get the implants out of their heads, given time. But you need to help us. The Wildfire incidences have been steepening, and that's surely been your doing – turning the screw on us. But act now, act swiftly, and if we see a levelling off in the death curve, I'll note that you cooperated.'

'And would that earn me a pardon?'

'I can't ignore the murders that have already happened – the Wildfire cases, or the deaths incidental to this investigation. But we'll look into the syndicate's wager. You were victims of a crime before any of this began, and that has to count in your favour. A demonstrable show of remorse now, a pledge to assist . . .'

'You misunderstand me, Dreyfus,' Julius said. 'I don't want your leniency. I don't want anything from you. You can leave or remain, the choice is yours. But my work is done.'

'He knows something,' Caleb said. 'I can feel it seeping out of him. It doesn't matter to him what happens now. He doesn't even care if you try to kill him or not.' His eyes narrowed with a dawning comprehension. 'He's *expecting* to die. This is all just . . .'

Julius made a swatting gesture, as if a fly had just troubled him. Caleb groaned and dropped to his knees, clutching at the sides of his head in obvious agony.

'I've had enough of him again,' Julius said, addressing his audience with an abashed, confiding look. 'Funny how it goes, with family. You don't see them for years and years and you think it will be different – all the old irritations set aside. But he's the same old Caleb he always was. Thinks he's the master of me, the one with all the ideas.'

Caleb rolled onto his side, whimpering.

'Stop,' Dreyfus said, moving to kneel down next to Caleb. 'He doesn't deserve this.'

'Doesn't he?' Julius was holding his arm outstretched, his fingers

385

cradled around an invisible mass, squeezing it gently, almost as if were reaching into Caleb's skull and applying some unspeakable pressure to his brain. 'He was coy about the exact circumstances of Mother's death. Told you some of the facts, but not all of them. He was right about one thing. It was my hand on that crossbow, my finger on the trigger. I put that dart into her. I killed her. But I didn't mean to.'

'It was an accident?' Dreyfus asked, while Caleb drooled and groaned, thrashing along the length of his body. He placed a hand on him, trying to find a way to offer comfort.

'No – not an accident at all. He reached into my head, just as I'm reaching into his now. He altered my visual field. Made me see a cat, instead of our mother. Made me take aim, as if we were still playing one of his hunting games. Made me drop the cat. I was pleased, for a second or two. I was always trying to impress him. Then we went over to see the body, and I saw what I had done. I killed her. But it was his idea, his intention.'

'I'm sorry,' Dreyfus said, looking up from the writhing form. 'But this won't make it any better. Let him go.'

'Stop it,' Singh said, pleadingly. 'Whatever he did, it doesn't excuse . . .'

A rumble ran through the ground.

Julius, distracted for an instant, turned back to the Shell House. Something between surprise and admiration played across his features. 'Did you feel that, Dreyfus? It was the escape capsule, departing Lethe.'

'I don't know what you mean,' Dreyfus said.

'Your man . . . your pig. I presented him with a choice – a simple one. I'm more than a little surprised he took the path he did, though. If I'm being honest with myself, I was convinced he'd hold on to his principles to the end. Even if it meant dying, and surrendering any means of contacting your organisation. That vibration we just felt was the escape shaft blowing out, allowing the capsule to fall away from Lethe. It could only have happened if your colleague was prepared to commit murder to save his own skin.'

'Sparver wouldn't have done that,' Dreyfus said.

'Why not?'

'Because he's not a piece of self-interested dirt. Because he's my friend. Because he's a prefect.'

'Oh, don't be too sure. People will do all sorts of things in extremis. And I really did stress to him that it was only a small murder, in the great scheme of things.'

Behind Julius, a figure emerged into daylight from the Shell House. It was Sparver, his hands lathered in blood all the way to the elbows. Dreyfus watched, glad that his colleague was alive, but that gladness tempered by thoughts of exactly what had transpired below.

Casually, Sparver allowed some small glinting thing to drop from his hand.

'You got me wrong,' he said, calling to the brother who had his back to the house. 'You needn't have troubled yourself, Julius. You see, it wasn't a question of whether or not to murder your father. That was secondary. To me, it was all about evidential preservation.'

Julius bent round, distracted by this unexpected development, shaking his head as if he meant to teach Sparver a lesson in manners.

'What?'

'I killed him, just like you wanted me to. But only so I could stuff his body into that capsule. It's out there now, and it's my guess it won't be more than a few minutes before someone from Panoply reaches it, cracks it open and realises what's inside.'

'You put Marlon in that thing?' Dreyfus asked.

'Yes,' Sparver answered. 'He'd been kept alive in the basement. I had to kill him to get him out of here, but I did so in the reasonable expectation of emergency intervention.'

Dreyfus nodded. 'Good work.'

'One other thing,' Sparver said. 'There's a fusion reactor set to blow. We don't have too long.'

'Did you get word to Panoply?'

Sparver glanced down at his hands again, as if only just noticing the degree to which they were bloodied. 'I did my best, boss. Scratched out a message. Trouble is, I only had one thing to scratch it on.'

'No!' Julius raged.

Then an odd, grimacing look took hold on his face. He twisted back to address Dreyfus and Singh, his mouth twitching but no sounds emerging.

Now it was his turn to buckle at the knees, sinking to the ground, his eyes bulging obscenely large and white in their sockets.

Caleb had stopped writhing. He had seen his opportunity and snatched it. Now he pressed himself up by an elbow, and with the other hand reached out in a beseeching gesture that reminded Dreyfus of the outstretched hand of Adam, in a painting he had once seen. Julius toppled back, squirming under the mounting neural assault from his brother. Caleb, regaining confidence and authority, propped himself up on his knees and then rose shakily to his feet.

'Don't kill him,' Dreyfus urged. 'We need him to keep those people alive.'

Caleb adopted a wide stance, loosening his shoulders and neck like a man preparing for a brawl. He was still reaching out, still inflicting some dreadful punishment on Julius. Then, with his other hand – carelessly, as if it cost him no effort at all – he gestured at the upper levels of the Shell House. Instantly the quickmatter lost coherence, sluicing away in white cataracts. Caleb steered his hand, the play of his fingers like a virtuoso, conjuring more and more of the upper layers to collapse away. The house was melting. No, Dreyfus corrected himself: that wasn't it, exactly. It was more as if the house were a form made from liquid, caught in a snapshot, and now time had been allowed to advance. But selectively, only where Caleb gestured.

Perhaps the show of skill was a little too cocksure, for all of a sudden Julius seemed to shake loose of Caleb's attack. He stumbled to his feet, one hand at his throat, the other shaping a conjuring gesture in the direction of Caleb. Caleb staggered back, his aim awry and causing him to conjure a black smear in the sky.

Julius regained some of his composure. He opened his fists, and some of the white detritus of the Shell House veered from its cataracting course and flowed into his hands. He gathered and balled it like dough. The quickmatter shaped itself into jagged, lightning-like forms, and Julius hurled them at his brother. Caleb rolled aside in time to avoid the first of the strikes, but not the second. It caught him in the thigh, and he let out a scream composed as much of anguish as it was pain. Glancing away from Julius, he shaped a conjuring gesture and turned the impaling form to black smoke. It curdled away from his leg, but left a coin-sized wound behind.

Enraged, Caleb swept a hand across a swathe of the jungle, where it pressed nearest to the Shell House. The organic forms withered under the force of the gesture, turning black and then shrinking and shrivelling. With these dramatic conjurations of quickmatter came an electric tingle in the air, as well as a warm, unsettled wind, as air molecules were caught up in the crash and flow of matter. Dreyfus glanced at Sparver, questions piling up in his head.

'How long do we have?'

'Less than thirty minutes.' Sparver reconsidered. 'A lot less. Twelve, fifteen if we're lucky.'

Beneath their feet, the ground was shaking. Some process of self-sustaining collapse had now taken hold within the architecture of the Shell House, for the building was continuing to dismantle itself regardless of Caleb's direct instructions. Something similar was at play in the jungle, too. It was dying back – reverting to the condition of primal, unshaped quickmatter. Dreyfus watched, mesmerised, as a patch of jungle opened up long enough to permit him a view of two black cats, melting like candles.

'It's no good,' Dreyfus said. 'The elevator went dead after we arrived.'

'I might be able to get back up the shaft on power assist, sir,' Singh said.

'I'm sorry, Deepa. There just isn't time.'

The disappointment he read in her expression cut him to the marrow.

'That's not what you said before, sir, about never giving up. You said we never get to decide when it's too late. But those were just words, weren't they, to get me moving? You didn't really mean them.'

'I meant them,' Dreyfus said softly. 'But I also know when we've lost.'

'No,' said a voice, speaking for the first time since the brothers had commenced their struggle. 'It's not over yet, Dreyfus. I can hold him.'

It was Caleb, standing again now, glancing down at the wound in his thigh then dismissing it as if it were no more consequential than a graze, walking with a limping gait towards Julius, who was also standing but had something like fear showing in his eyes as he took a step backwards, closer to the last, diminishing traces of the Shell House.

'You can't beat me,' Julius shouted, a strangled quality to his voice. 'Once, maybe. But not since then. I learned too well from you, brother.'

Overhead, where it had been wounded, the sky rained curtains of black mist. Slowly that black rot was eating away the blue, turning the brightness of day to an oppressive dusk.

'I know what you are,' Caleb said, reaching out again with both hands, a gesture that might almost have been one of embrace, except that the brothers were still six or seven metres apart. 'It wasn't enough for you, was it? You lived and breathed quickmatter. You could do wonders with it, judging by this place. But you couldn't resist the final step. It's in you. I can sense it.'

'No,' Julius said.

But something unsettling was happening to Julius. He was blurring at the edges, a fine smoke coming off him, breezing away on the shifting winds. The ground shook under Dreyfus, nearly throwing him off his feet, and every instinct in his body screamed for him to run, to find some illusion of shelter, no matter how pointless it might prove.

'Boss,' Sparver said, pointing at something beyond Dreyfus's line of sight.

The brothers stumbled near each other. It was as if each were walking into a gale, being pushed apart, yet both determined to overpower that opposing force, seeking some final connection. Julius was growing more tenuous: he was losing body mass, a much thinner and frailer human core beginning to show through as successive layers of quickmatter peeled off him, forming a buzzy, indeterminate cloud above the siblings. The battle was not yet done. Caleb was continuing his dismantling attack on Julius, yet some of the liberated quickmatter was being drawn to Caleb now, clotting itself onto his body, and he twisted and pawed at it, convincing Dreyfus that Julius was not yet done.

'Prefect Dreyfus!' said Singh, and at last he snapped his gaze from the confrontation, realising what Sparver had been trying to tell him, and what Singh had now noticed for herself. The ground was shaking for a reason, and if some part of that was due to the battle between the brothers, it was not the sole explanation.

Machines were breaking through into the chamber.

There were three points of emergence that Dreyfus could see, scattered around the border of the Shell House. Sharp, scissoring mandibles were pushing through the last layers of rock and soil which formed the bedrock of the chamber, accompanied by the hum and flash of energy tools, until at last the machines were able to shrug their low, sleek, multi-limbed bodies out of the ground, flopping onto the sides of the newly excavated holes. More machines followed the first trio, at least a dozen of the quick, beetle-like forms for each point of entry. Dreyfus tried to feel relieved at this sudden intervention, but he couldn't suppress the prickle of disquiet he felt at the emergence of the machines. Unless he was mistaken, he recognised them.

They were weevils. Military-grade assault robots, equipped with the means to cut through the fabric of a habitat, gaining entry to the soft, vulnerable core within. There, weevils could work all sorts of havoc. And they had, not too long ago. Dreyfus knew far too much about weevils, and he had not counted on seeing them again.

Yet here they were. Not running wild, though, but turning inert once the chamber had been breached. And there was something else worth noting, too. On the side of each weevil, glowing in silver, was the raised gauntlet of Panoply.

'What are they?' Singh asked.

'Someone's bad idea,' Dreyfus answered, drawing no judgements for the moment.

Then something else came out of the nearest excavated shaft. It flung itself into the air, landed deftly and settled on its traction coil, the red eye of its head sweeping the chamber.

Then another.

Then another.

Whiphounds were bursting out of the ground like the fruit of some strange new harvest. They were obviously under a variety of orders. Some held station, some formed into cordons, some went scouting off at high speed. Still more came.

Then a head popped out of the nearest hole. It wore the black tactical armour of a Panoply enforcement squad. The figure scrambled onto the level ground, then reached down to assist a second member of the squad. Then a third. A similar process was happening at the other entry points, prefects emerging in growing numbers, some of them carrying whiphounds, some with heavier armaments.

The ground was still shaking, but not as badly as before. The sky had stopped curtaining, and the jungle had withered back to a final, unchanging core of dormant quickmatter. The air was quieter. Distracted as he had been by the arrival of the weevils, Dreyfus realised he had taken his eyes off the brothers.

But now there was only one. A figure lay on the ground, surrounded by a lingering haze of dark particles, a nimbus of still-active quickmatter.

The first prefect who had emerged strode up to Dreyfus, raising the visor of their tactical armour as they walked. Dreyfus lifted his hand, intending to issue a warning that he could not guarantee the safety of the environment. Then he realised how much weight that would have carried, given that he was standing there in only his normal uniform.

Besides, the prefect was Thalia.

'We had no choice, sir,' she was saying, as if he had already fired a volley of questions at her. 'When Pell resumed contact, we knew we had no confidence in the situation here. The Supreme Prefect took the decision to escalate to an immediate enforcement action.' She looked around, squinting into the dying light of the chamber. 'Did you manage to apprehend . . .'

'I don't know,' Dreyfus said, returning his gaze to the lone figure. Was it Caleb, or was it Julius? He had no immediate way of telling. And as he watched, so that busy, buzzing nimbus seemed to plunge itself from the solitary form, the body arcing off the ground, then slowly relaxing. 'I don't know,' he repeated, unsure quite what he had just witnessed, except that it was an ending of sorts.

Then a sort of focus found its way back into his eyes. 'Thalia, we have a problem. Sparver says this whole place could go up at any minute.'

'I know, sir. We got his . . . message just as we were closing in.'

'He did what needed to be done. Tell the enforcement squad to make an immediate retreat back the way they've come. You've got ships docked at the other ends of these shafts, haven't you?'

'Yes, sir. Corvettes and a couple of cruisers, fixed on with grapples, and the *Democratic Circus* isn't too far away, if we need to pick anyone up. We capped the shafts with portable airlocks, just in case you weren't wearing suits when we broke through. Sir, exactly why is this place going to go up?'

'The fusion generator. There isn't time to explain, I'm afraid. Everyone has to leave now.'

'What about the others, sir?'

'They're all dead, Thalia. Kober, Perec, Gurney. And I'm not even sure about Devon Garlin. Do you see that person on the ground? I want him taken into protective custody. But you're to instruct the squad to treat the body as a possible quickmatter hazard.' Dreyfus looked around. 'This whole place is dangerous, Thalia. It seems dormant for now, but it's not good to be here a second longer than necessary.'

'I'll arrange an immediate evacuation, sir.'

'Good. See that Sparver leaves with the first wave, will you? He's been through the mill.'

'He looks like it, sir. I'll make sure he doesn't put up a struggle.'

Despite everything Dreyfus found the energy to smile. 'You will, I don't doubt it.'

'You should leave as well, sir.'

'I will – just as soon you've taken care of the witness.'

Thalia passed on his orders and the arrangements were soon in place. Dreyfus paced nervously, every second feeling like an hour, but it could not have been five minutes before the enforcement squad had an inert-matter evidence cocoon around the unmoving form, and in short order they were lowering the cocoon back down the shaft, Thalia barking instructions with precision and confidence, leaving nothing to chance. After that, the enforcement squad, their whiphounds and weevils began to manage a staged withdrawal, falling back in waves.

'There's a lot to talk about,' Sparver confided.

'You can save it for later,' Dreyfus said, unable to stop himself from adding: 'If there is a later.'

The squad had rigged up an emergency suitwall, like an upright glass sheet fixed in a portable frame. Dreyfus and Sparver stepped through it, gaining fresh m-suits. It was a necessary precaution, in case something went wrong with the airlock seals between here and the grappled ships.

Thalia came back over. 'Heavy technical have a thermal reading on the fusion generator, sir. Someone's rigged something, and it's definitely getting hot, but they don't think it's quite ready to go critical.'

'That's hardly a reassurance,' Dreyfus said.

'There's evidence here, isn't there, sir? To do with Wildfire, and I'm guessing the clinic as well?'

Dreyfus could not deny it. 'Enough to put a very different slant on those victims, if half of what we've been told is true. Never mind rewriting the history of one of our most trusted families.'

'It can't be lost, sir,' Thalia said. 'That's paramount, isn't it? A few of the heavy technicals think they can get in and stabilise that core, before it runs away. We've got the equipment, we've mapped an access route, and there's still just enough time.'

'What do you mean, we?'

'I'm volunteering sir. Insisting, in fact. Evidential safeguarding, sir. You drummed that into us from day one. There isn't time to argue, anyway. We're going in. There should be a shaft under the remains of that house, if the weevils can clear it for us quickly enough.'

'There is a shaft,' Sparver said, his hands and arms were bloodless now that he had been cleansed by the suitwall, but Sparver was still eyeing them with a certain lingering distaste. 'I saw it. Went all the way down it, too. You're right about the evidence, Thal. It can't be lost when this place goes up.'

'Good,' Thalia agreed. 'Pipe your instructions through to me as soon as you're on the cruiser.'

'Better still, why don't I come with you?'

She looked at him, Dreyfus reading a mixture of gratitude and wariness in her expression. 'You don't have to, Sparver.'

'I'd kick myself if I didn't. One thing's clear, though. Boss man knows too much for him to stay here any longer. I'd get down that rabbit hole, sir.'

'We've got work to do,' Thalia said, planting an arm on his shoulders, ready to steer him back to the remains of the Shell House. 'C'mon, Field Bancal. Let's go and make Lady Jane proud of us.'

Dreyfus watched them head away. She would be proud, he knew, regardless of the outcome of this particular piece of last-gasp heroism. But long before Jane Aumonier would have cause to hear about their actions, Dreyfus had already witnessed them.

All things told, he was not displeased.

Then someone patted him on the arm and nodded to the hole in the ground. It was time to go.

CHAPTER TWENTY-THREE

The air in the tactical room had been one of extreme weariness for so long that Dreyfus had difficulty remembering how it had been before the onset of the Wildfire crisis. Probably not too different, he decided phlegmatically. They had always felt as if they had the weight of all the worlds on their shoulders, even when – in cruel, capriciousness hindsight – they had actually been enjoying one of those rare intervals of routine operations between emergencies.

But there was something different today, he noted. The analysts and seniors were just as worn out as they had been at the very height of the emergency. But now they could see the end to it all. A glimmer of hope – a thread to cling to. It was giving them all a sustaining spark, a last drop of fuel to get them through the night.

Tomorrow, or the day after tomorrow, or the day after that, they might be able to sleep again.

Some of them, at least.

'There is still a great deal of uncertainty in the forecasts,' Aumonier told those present, her voice low with exhaustion. 'But one thing seems clear. From the moment Tom witnessed the consolidation of Julius and Caleb . . . whatever the actual nature of that event . . . there has been a suspension in the Wildfire deaths. We've seen no new cases, either in the general populace, or among the citizens already moved into our care. Of course, we've learned from our earlier errors. We're holding all the citizens within full reach of abstraction, so there's no risk of the signals being blocked. And the witness—' Something tightened in the already drawn lines of her face. 'We've taken the same precautions. Except we don't know whether we're dealing with a living person or not. The body looks alive, it's breathing, there's a heartbeat, but it's unresponsive to external stimuli and Doctor Demikhov dare not go near it with any of his customary devices. We can't guess what's going on inside the head, and I'm strongly minded not to poke it.'

'You're right not to,' Dreyfus said, cradling a cup of lukewarm tea. 'I don't know if that's Julius or Caleb, or both. But somewhere in there, someone is keeping those Wildfire cases from triggering. It's buying us the time we need, to get the survivors into emergency surgery.'

'A sudden blooming of remorse?' asked Baudry, doing nothing to mask her customary scepticism.

'I don't know,' Dreyfus said, puncturing her mood by not giving the flip answer she must have been expecting. 'There might be altruism in it, but I'll leave that to the specialists to work out. It could also be that there's a desire to punish the survivors by means other than a painful death.'

'With justice, you mean?' Clearmountain asked.

Dreyfus nodded. 'Thanks to the efforts of the Heavy Technical Squad – and Ng, and Bancal – we have the evidence we'd have lost if Lethe had been destroyed. It'll take a while to comb through that little goldmine. But I'm confident we can recover the identities of those involved with Marlon Voi's syndicate.'

'And you think it'll match the patient list extracted from Elysium Heights?' asked Ingvar Tench.

'I'd be surprised if it didn't,' Dreyfus said. He paused and reached below the table, coming up with the apple he had brought with him from the refectory.

He pushed aside the unwanted tea and took a bite from the apple, to the visible disgust of the seniors facing him.

Jane Aumonier, though, just smiled.

The grey mist of early morning lay like a shroud over Necropolis, the city of the dead. Dreyfus walked slowly, his hands behind his back, silent save for the soft crunch of his shoes on the gravel pathway. The air reaching his lungs was the air in the immersion room, but had the illusion been better he liked to imagine he would have savoured the cool, still taste of this place. It was not a bad place for contemplation, as he was beginning to discover. Perhaps he ought to spend more time here, when he needed to clear his mind of the clutter and distractions of Panoply. Even his personal quarters could be too confining, when he needed real space for reflection. But then again, he thought, it might not be the healthiest of habits to develop, spending time with the dead.

The woman he had arranged to meet was ahead, waiting on one of the benches next to the path, her composure relaxed, hands crossed in her lap, her gaze seemingly fixed on the rippled grey waters of the lake, and the faint upsweep of land beyond that was half lost in the fog.

'Cassandra,' Dreyfus said gently, alerting her to his arrival.

She turned to him with a surprising expression of warmth in her face, as if they were starting to fall into the role of distant friends. 'Good morning, Prefect,' she said, making to rise from the bench. 'It's been a little while, hasn't it? I was starting to think you'd forgotten about all us poor dead souls here.'

'I wasn't likely to forget,' Dreyfus said as he approached, motioning for her to remain seated. What he had to say to her would not take terribly long, and in so far as it mattered at all, he felt the news would be better delivered to her sitting down. He had tended to form an instinct about such things.

'They don't allow us much in the way of news from the outside world,' Cassandra Leng said, turning her elfin face to regard him as he eased his bulk onto the seat, just close enough for easy conversation. 'But word seeps in, especially when we get a new guest. You can't do much about the information the new beta-levels bring with them, can you?'

'Not much,' Dreyfus admitted, looking at his shoes.

'So how is our little emergency? I presume it had you running around so much, you couldn't spare much time for us ghosts?'

'We had a breakthrough,' Dreyfus said. 'A significant one. It's early days, but we're not really expecting any more Wildfire cases.'

'That's good,' she said, but with a questioning tone, undoubtedly picking up on his less than ebullient demeanour. 'Isn't it? I mean, good for those people who might have died, less good for those of us who already have. But we've talked about the condition of being dead often enough. I shouldn't blame you for things that already happened, if you've really made a breakthrough.'

Dreyfus fiddled with his fingers. 'I'll tell you something about the Wildfire cases who haven't yet died. Pre-cases, I suppose we should call them. They've been identified from a master list, and we're busy rushing them through emergency surgery, to remove any possibility of their implants going wrong. It's still a logistical challenge. There are many hundreds of them, and at no point can we risk any of them being out of range of abstraction services.'

'The rumours said the complete opposite – that you were trying to get people away from abstraction.'

Dreyfus nodded heavily, the fabric of his collar digging into his neck like a noose. 'We got it wrong – got it completely the wrong way around. That cost lives. But eventually we understood the nature of the emergency, and how to proceed. Now we're quietly confident that we can process those citizens, and free them from any risk of Wildfire.'

'They'll be very grateful,' Leng said.

'For a little while,' Dreyfus said. 'Until we issue the arrest orders. It's a complicated charge, and it's not quite clear where it fits into our jurisdictional envelope. But we're liaising with Chasm City as well, so between our two agencies we'll make sure we find the right legal framework for prosecution.'

Her face pinched, as if she had bitten into something sour. 'I don't understand. You're *arresting* those people? On what basis?'

'Historical involvement in an illegal syndicate. All the names on our list have been tied to a clandestine organisation, with links to Marlon Voi. That's why it's complicated. But we're pretty confident we can prove the connection. After that . . . well, there's a range of penalties to be considered. Again, it's an unusual case, so there aren't any obvious precedents. Exactly what statute covers the raising of successive generations of children in an illegal experiment in retrospective social engineering, with each batch of children being doomed to euthanisation when they've served their purpose?' He looked at her with a sharp, quizzical intensity. 'It's a tough one, wouldn't you agree?'

Something of her usual coolness now returned. 'Why are you asking me, Dreyfus?'

'Because I have another headache,' he said. 'I know what to do with the living cases. Process and arrest. But then there are the ones like you. The already dead. Who are just as culpable.'

She shook her head, making to push herself up from the bench. But Dreyfus reached over and held her where she was seated, not without a certain force. 'It's coming, Cassandra. Justice. Whether you remember the crime or not, there will be an accounting for it. I just thought you'd like to know that. So you can prepare yourself for what may or may not happen. And spread the word among the others.'

'You . . .' She regarded him, some fading hope still lingering in her eyes. 'I liked you, Dreyfus. I confided in you. Felt that I'd found a friend. Someone who began to understand.'

'So did I.'

'And now?'

'I've got a job to do.'

Her coolness sharpened. 'Bastard. I thought you'd come to talk to me, like an old—'

'Policeman,' Dreyfus said, rising from the chair.

He could have returned to the immersion room immediately, but the encounter with Cassandra Leng had rattled his nerves and Dreyfus needed time to settle them. He did not like being cruel, but there were occasions when it was demanded of him; when, on balance, a small portion of cruelty now offset a greater one later on.

Walking along the path, mist on either side, glad to be alone with his thoughts, he became aware of a slow clapping.

Then she was next to him, walking alongside. For once she had discarded the prop of her throne.

'That was very good, Dreyfus. Very nicely handled. They will be a headache, won't they? How do you punish the already dead? Turn them off?'

'It's not for me to make the law,' Dreyfus said, irritated by her arrival, but knowing nothing he said or did would persuade her to take her leave. 'It's not even a Panoply matter, I imagine. It was a serious crime, but it didn't have any direct bearing on polling or Glitter Band security.'

Aurora looked astonished. 'How can you say that, when it led to so much trouble?'

'The law concerns itself with first-order effects,' Dreyfus answered.

She skipped along, picking up the hem of her dress. 'So stoic. So noble-minded. I don't suppose a word of gratitude's out of the question, is it? You wouldn't have had that list if it wasn't for me.'

'You obtained the passwords from me under false pretences.'

'I did what needed to be done. No harm came of it, did it?'

'You used the same trick to send Sparver into Lethe, against Aumonier's direct orders. That cost the lives of three prefects.'

She shrugged. 'Then recruit some new ones.'

'You know what, Aurora?' Dreyfus said sharply. 'Just when I'm in danger of thinking there might be a trace of humanity in there, you go and remind me of what you really are. A cold-blooded monster, interested in one thing only.'

'Dresses. Puppies. And ice cream. Mm. Is there more?'

'Did you extract the intelligence you needed on the Clockmaker?' He chose not to wait for her reply. 'If so, just get the hell out of the Search Turbines before you leave too many fingerprints.'

'Scared someone will ask questions about how I breached Panoply's innermost secrets?'

'Not really. You're always telling us you're a superior intellect. I'll just shrug and say you got around our best defences. Do you honestly think they won't believe me?'

She pondered this, finger to her lips. 'Then again, we'll always have it between us, won't we? It will be our *thing*, won't it? A shadow hanging over us. One of us, anyway. I can't say it's likely to be a problem for me, but you, on the other hand . . .'

'You need me,' Dreyfus said. 'You won't admit it, but I'm useful to you. So you'd be very unwise to do anything that might damage my standing in Panoply.' He walked on, the fog curling around them thicker than it had been before, making it hard to see the way ahead. 'That doesn't mean I'm in any hurry to do business again, Aurora, just in case you got the wrong idea.'

'And there was I looking forward to catching up on all the news, from the horse's very own mouth. Do you have any plans for the survivor?'

'You'll need to be a little more specific than that.'

'The son. Caleb or Julius, or both, whichever name you've decided is the best fit.'

'We're sticking with Devon Garlin for now,' Dreyfus said. 'It's the name under which the brothers came to our attention, and you can't argue that there's a certain circularity in going back to it. Not that Devon has much to say on the matter.'

'Yes,' she said delicately. 'I hear there had been . . . damage. But there's obviously enough of an intellect still alive in there to understand what needs to be done with regard to the Wildfire cases.'

For once Dreyfus felt no need to disagree with her. 'More than an intellect. I think there's a mind, a conscience, left inside Devon Garlin. But whether that mind owes more to Julius or Caleb, I can't say.'

'And did you get to the bottom of the confusion, in the end? The man we thought was Julius was Caleb, and vice versa?'

'I doubt we'll ever have a definitive account,' Dreyfus answered. 'Some evidence really does get lost for good. But Doctor Stasov thought that Julius was always the favoured son. He offered me a theory, and it's as good as any other.'

'Pray tell.'

'Caleb set up Julius to murder Aliya Voi. Julius shot his mother, thinking it was just part of the sporting games they liked to play. Until then, Caleb was the stronger brother – the one most adept at quickmatter and abstraction manipulation. And the one most feared by Aliya.'

They walked on into the thickening mist.

'Continue.'

'I think it pushed Julius over an edge. He turned on Caleb – really turned on him. I think Julius almost killed Caleb. Then he fled – left the Shell House, disappeared into obscurity, using his skills to move without suspicion. Caleb stayed behind in the Shell House, with only Marlon to look after him. But Marlon had always been more fond of the other boy. I think that's when Marlon administered Caleb with a second round of amnesia treatment – blotting out the memory that he'd ever had a sibling, and acting as if Caleb was really Julius. In that pliant state, Caleb accepted it. He started thinking of himself as Julius. Later, he left the Shell House and took on another name: Devon Garlin. But he always believed he was Julius.'

'Until you brought him home,' Aurora said. 'I agree with you, Dreyfus. As a theory, it's as good as any other. This Doctor Stasov interests me quite a bit. Perhaps I'll find a way to drop in on him one day, see what he has to say.'

'I'll warn him to expect you.'

'Oh, don't do that. I do so like surprises.'

Dreyfus stopped. 'Then you'll love this.'

Aurora stopped as well, taking heed of the thing Dreyfus had already noticed. It had emerged from the mist, blocking their path ahead. It was a simple affair, a plain stone plinth about as high as Dreyfus's chest, and had the circumstances been different, Dreyfus would have stepped around it with barely a glance, presuming it a part of the ordinary architecture of Necropolis.

But the plinth did not belong here, and there was nothing ordinary about it at all.

'If this is your doing . . .' Aurora said, her voice reduced to a warning sibilance.

'It isn't.'

They walked up to the plinth. It was not the plinth that most troubled Aurora, but the small shining thing set upon it. It had a square case, resting on four little lion's feet. She stood transfixed, her eyes level with the clock face. Behind bevelled glass panels spun a ticking complexity of gears and wheels.

'I swear, if this—' she began.

'It wasn't here before,' Dreyfus answered, a prickle of cold tracing its way down his back. 'I promise you that. It's a symbol, a message. And I don't think it's meant for me.'

She reached out as if to take the clock from the plinth, to examine its beautiful form. But at the last instant she scowled and gave a fierce hiss, swiping her hand, knocking the clock to the ground, where it shattered into a thousand tiny pieces of glass and brass.

They greeted him in the long-hemmed black vestments of their order, with wimples over their heads and metal snowflakes chained around their necks. Dreyfus recognised the young man well enough from his last visit, giving Sebastien a nod before acknowledging Sister Catherine.

'Normally,' she said, leaning heavily on her stick, 'this is the point where you apologise for not visiting us lately, and I gently chastise you about the fact that it's been much longer than you think. Months when you think weeks, years when you think it only a matter of months.' But now her long, grave face found some rare humour. 'I'd be wrong, though, wouldn't I? It really hasn't been more than weeks. What brings you back so swiftly, Tom?'

'Do I need a reason to visit, Sister Catherine?'

'No, and I'd rather this was the norm, instead of the exception.' Offering a guarded smile, she nonetheless beckoned him forward. 'Come, anyway. You're always welcome. We've forgiven you for that bit of unpleasantness last time.'

'That's good of you,' Dreyfus said.

'I have some news about Valery, too. I think you'll be pleased.'

Dreyfus had learned not to raise his hopes. 'I'm always keen to hear about progress.'

'There has been real advancement, Tom. I sensed it before your last visit, but I didn't want to jump to hasty conclusions. But I think she is making a concerted effort to find her way back to us. There *is* language inside her. I'm more convinced of that than ever. It just needs time, and persuasion, to achieve its full flowering.'

'Whatever it takes,' Dreyfus said. 'I'm truly grateful, Sister, for all your efforts.'

'It's not much to ask of us, Tom.'

Dreyfus chose his words carefully. 'Then I'm going to have to beg your indulgence with another favour.'

Sister Catherine studied him with a guarded interest, conceding nothing. 'Really?'

'The bulk of your cases come through the incoming ships,' Dreyfus said. 'The passengers who don't respond well to reefersleep. That's true, isn't it?'

'You know us well by now.'

'But there are also other cases that come your way. Like Valery. It wasn't reefersleep that damaged her mind, but you've still taken her in, still given her kindness and support, and helped her find the path back.'

'We'd be remiss if we didn't extend our welcome to all needful cases, Tom.'

Dreyfus looked back the way they had come, judging that they had given him enough time to prepare the ground. Here they came, walking slowly: Sparver on one side of their guest, Thalia on the other. Each supported an arm, guiding the man as if he were blind.

'Now I understand why you came in a bigger ship than usual,' Sister

401

Catherine said, with just the tiniest shading of displeasure, as if he should have been more forthright from the outset.

'These are my friends,' Dreyfus said, indicating the two prefects. 'Sparver Bancal and Thalia Ng. The man they're helping is . . . well, I imagine I don't need to tell you who he is.'

'I recognise him,' she said, in a low and level voice. 'But he seems different to the man who came here. There's damage, obviously, or they wouldn't need to help him like that. But he's older.' Now her face turned to his with questioning severity. 'Is it really him? No place for anything but the truth, Tom, when you petition our mercy.'

'It's Devon Garlin,' Dreyfus said. 'But there's another part to him that you didn't see before. If and when he starts to regain powers of communication, he may think of himself as two different men. Which would be the more dominant, I can't say. Or say for certain that there's any chance for him to become more than he is now.' He glanced down, ashamed in some small way that he had gone to even the small deception of not mentioning this to her earlier. But it had seemed prudent to keep the arrangement as low-key as possible. 'I just thought, if anyone could show him kindness, it would be the Hospice.'

'And this fabled kindness of ours,' Sister Catherine said, her patience very clearly near its limit. 'Is he deserving of it?'

'Part of him is,' Dreyfus answered.

She leaned even more heavily on the stick, shaking her head, some keen but weighty process of judgement occupying her thoughts. 'I have always taken you as a man of your word, Tom. Please don't give me cause to change that opinion.' She gave a quick, birdlike nod. 'We'll take him in. How could we refuse?' Then, to Sparver and Thalia: 'Will you bring him the rest of the way, prefects? It's quite a long walk, but you'd be made welcome at the other end of it.'

'No,' Thalia said, eyeing Sparver, as if the two of them had already settled on their decision. 'We'll just go back to the ship, if that's all right.'

'I'll take him the rest of the way,' Dreyfus said, reaching out his hand, allowing Thalia to guide the other man's arm, until Devon Garlin's fingers touched his own.

'Good morning, Julius,' Marlon Voi said to his son, standing next to his bed with the robot immediately behind him. 'You look rested. Stronger and healthier by the day.'

There had been a fog of impressions as he surfaced to consciousness, but other than some faint, fading after-images, that confusion was lifting, banished by the light of day flooding into his bedroom.

'I dreamed of Mother again,' he said.

'That's to be understood.' His father's look was sympathetic, but not without the shadow of some subtle strain, borne longer than was fair. 'It's good that you keep a memory of her. She was kind to you and only wanted the best for you in your life beyond the Shell House.' He reached down and settled a hand on his son's shoulder. 'Be strong, Julius. She knew that you loved her.'

He thought of the account he had been given of Aliya's demise, of the tragic malfunction of her spacecraft as it returned to Yellowstone, burning up in the atmosphere like a gold-bannered comet, dripping sparks of itself across half the world, like an anointment.

'I never got the chance to say goodbye. I mean, not properly.'

'Nor did I,' his father said. 'And we'll carry that regret for the rest of our lives, Julius. A sadness lodged inside ourselves, that only we truly understand. But we mustn't be beholden to it. Your mother would have wanted us to carry on, to honour her memory, but not be shaped by it. It's enough to remember her, and know that she was a good woman.'

He nodded, accepting this on the surface, but very far from internalising it. He felt sure that they had had this conversation, or some permutation of it, on several previous occasions. His father at his bedside, smiling benignly, Lurcher the robot there with him, the room swept by cleansing shafts of light. A new start to each day.

'Join me for breakfast,' Father said.

He washed and dressed, pausing only to touch the fading scar under his right eye, an area of pale roughness that he would doubtless have fixed when he moved into the world, but which in some curious, occult fashion seemed only to make the rest of his face seem more balanced, more handsomely proportioned.

Perhaps he would think about keeping it.

Downstairs in the Shell House they breakfasted and spoke largely of inconsequentialities. The son devoured news from the outside world, from Chasm City, Yellowstone, and the ten thousand artificial worlds of the Glitter Band. He would soon be a part of that domain and he desired to move confidently in it, ahead of all the latest gossip and fashions. But his father seemed to be closing in on himself, his interest in wider affairs dwindling. He rarely left the Shell House, content to oversee his diminishing fortune from within the dome.

On the other hand, he did not deter the boy from his enquiries.

'We hardly ever speak of the contingency these days,' he ventured, studying his father for hints as to his private feelings on that matter. 'But it's still expected of me, isn't it?'

His father feigned innocent interest.

'The contingency, Julius?'

'It was something I was meant to know about. A kind of . . . family secret.' He leaned in, added quickly: 'But a good one. Not something bad. More like a duty, an obligation, that we carried. To help the world when it needed helping. To make a vote go one way, if it needed to.'

His father's face clouded. 'Even if we had the means, Julius, such an intervention would be deeply unethical.'

'We do have the means. I remember you showing us.'

'You've mistaken one thing for something else, Julius. Perhaps we spoke about the good work of Sandra Voi, and how the Voi kernel underpinned all that we hold most dear. Perhaps I even showed you how it would feel to be a part of the outside world, when at last you move in those circles. To be immersed in abstraction, for every instant of your life.' He gave a sweet, tolerant smile. 'But there was no more to it than that. We're just a family, taking our turn to fade into history. There was never any contingency.'

He nodded, looking down at his breakfast, certain nonetheless that he remembered things differently.

'Perhaps it was just a dream.'

'Perhaps it was,' Father said agreeably, reaching to pour himself some more grapefruit juice.

'But there's something else.'

'Go on.'

'I know it sounds silly, but when I was younger . . . was there ever another boy who used to come and visit us?'

Father looked amused. 'Another boy? I think I'd remember. No; you were schooled on your own, Julius. You were sensitive and seemed content with your own company. Your mother and I were both of the view that you had all that you needed for your development, and you never expressed any view to the contrary. You had Lurcher, you had free run of the house and the gardens . . . a kingdom for one boy.' He reached over and squeezed his son's hand. 'What more could you have wanted?'

'I don't know,' he said. 'I just keep remembering . . .'

Father twisted around in his chair and called beyond the breakfast room. 'Lurcher, would you come here for a moment?'

'Good morning, Julius,' Father said to his son, standing next to his bed with Lurcher immediately behind him. 'You look rested. Stronger and healthier by the day.'

There had been a fog as he surfaced to consciousness, but other than

404

some faint after-images that confusion was lifting, purged by the light of day.

'I dreamed of her again,' he said, and smiled, because the memory was pleasing.

One day the son found the white tree again.

It was in a part of the grounds where Lurcher had been busy re-landscaping, tearing up old pathways, planting and transplanting over them, forging new routes through old growth. While Lurcher was elsewhere some buried impulse had driven him to explore, hacking through the wildening greenery until at last he reached a sort of secret clearing, a curtain of new growth hemming in the barren ground around a dead, white tree whose shape and presence induced in him a powerful sense of recognition.

Confronted by the tree he stopped and stared for a long minute, transfixed by a sudden upwelling of forbidden memory. The tree's roots, where they showed above ground, were a mazy, muscular tangle, like the limbs of some indolent sea monster. Between the roots were gaps and crawl-ways, allowing entry into the cool interior of the tree's hollowed-out trunk.

He advanced, resting a hand on the tree, the touch unloading an additional cargo of recollection. Of long afternoons spent avoiding lessons, of daydreams and the private games he had shared with another, quieter boy. He could see the two of them with perfect clarity, perched high in the tree's upper levels, lords of their own creation. Trading stories, inventing games, plotting the future.

Pocketing the knife he had used to fight through the densest vegetation, he crouched low at the roots, inspecting the gaps between them. He pushed a hand through some of the narrower points, feeling the space open up beyond, but if he had ever been able to squeeze through those constrictions he was too old now, with most of the height and broadness he would carry into adulthood.

But there was still a gap that he could just about squeeze through. He struggled in, grunting with the effort, nearly jamming himself tight once or twice. Once he was through the worst of it, though, it was an easy wriggle into the main part of the trunk, hollow for the most part but still divided into a number of ascending chambers, each of which he had to contort himself into before proceeding to the next.

At the top, six or seven metres from his starting point, the trunk flared into a kind of bowl, dead arms radiating out in all directions. He was unconcerned about squeezing back down through the trunk: he could easily climb down the outside, if he chose, and then jump the last few metres. But for now he was content to settle onto the natural seat formed by a wooden ledge inside the tree, feeling himself slot into the position like the last piece of a puzzle. He had been here before. He was certain of it, and his bones and muscles remembered, even if his conscious mind held no clear trace of the prior occasions.

He thought of the other boy again. They were both sitting on the same ledge, but he was bigger, looking down on his slighter companion as he explained the terms of some new game he had just devised. The other boy was reluctant, needing persuasion.

Now he noticed something.

His fingers had picked up on it before his eyes did. A rough but deliberate pattern of scratches, on the inside of the trunk. Exactly at the level where a boy might carve something, on a boring afternoon.

He shifted to move his own shadow out of the way, squinting and frowning as he made out the intent of the marks.

I AM JULIUS
I AM CALEB
I AM JULIUS
I AM CALEB

He reached into his pocket for the knife, flicking out its ever-sharp blade, the blade that would cut any material but living tissue, and began to gouge out an addition to this series of inscriptions.

I AM JULIUS
I AM JULIUS
I AM JULIUS

He stopped, frowning deeper. There was an itch in his fingers. They wanted him to do something. There was another itch in his brain, faint but nagging.

He scratched again.

I AM CALEB
I AM CALEB
I AM CALEB

Deeper and deeper, gouging the dead wood with increasing pressure, increasing fury. Each stroke, each whisker of wood flaking away, each new letter, only enflaming him further. Until the action became animalistic, a purposeless wounding.

I AM CALEB
I AM . . .
I AM . . .
I . . .
I . . .

Until he fumbled the knife, dropping it down the chambered labyrinth of the trunk, hearing the hollow reports as it clattered from level to level.

He had been breathing hard, working himself into a frenzy. Almost shocked at himself, he slowed his inhalations until a fragile, tingling calm had returned. He was sweating, his hand shaking.

Whatever the tree represented, whatever the significance of the messages it contained, he did not wish to be inside it any longer. Bracing with both arms, still trembling, he hauled himself out of the hollow top of the trunk. He balanced his feet on the thickest parts of two of the main branches, then began to descend, the dead wood creaking under the shifting load. He was nearly ready to drop to the ground when he heard something.

He looked around, just in time to see Lurcher emerging into the clearing, the robot's arms laden with gardening equipment. For an instant their eyes met: his own against the robot's solitary, unblinking pupil. Then he chanced a drop the rest of the way, landing clumsily but avoiding twisting his ankles in the roots.

He was confounded. He had broken no rule by visiting this tree, violated no directive, stated or implied. But still he felt ashamed that the robot had caught him here. Ashamed and obscurely certain that Lurcher read something in his face, some mute incriminating testimony that made explicit what he had experienced only a few minutes earlier.

'I . . .' he began. Then trailed off, thinking of the knife he had dropped. The knife, he decided, could stay where it was.

Late that evening, high in the Shell House, just before drowsiness snatched him to unconsciousness, he stirred from his bed and moved to the window. Fingers of light played through the shutters, shades of orange and russet, accompanied by a distant crackling and hissing that rose and fell in random, tide-like waves.

Cautiously, struck by some faint sense of impropriety, he opened the shutters on the glassless window and took in a breath. The evening air

407

flooded his lungs, sooty with combustion products. He coughed, a sudden human sound that seemed louder than it had any right to be. Then stifled any further coughing with his hand.

Across the grounds, far from the Shell House – but still within the family dome, rather than beyond it, in the greater expanse of Chasm City – something was on fire.